7 Scorpions:
REBELLION

Mike Saxton

Eloquent Books

Eloquent Books
An imprint of Strategic Book Group
P.O. Box 333
Durham CT 06422
www.StrategicBookGroup.com

ISBN: 978-1-60911-286-8

Printed in the United States of America

Book Design: Rolando F. Santos

This book is dedicated to my wife, my mother, Mike Wolter, Shawn McQuillan, and Milton Jackson. Without all of you, this wouldn't have been possible. Thank you all from the bottom of my heart.

Prologue

For years, people talked about various ways that the world would end - plague, floods, sunbursts, nuclear war, the Wrath of God, amongst others. The truth is, the world didn't end; it changed. Like the many significant changes in the world, this change was painful and wrought with strife. It began on May 7th, a day that began like any other day. People around the world went about their typical routines. Soon they found out that this day was different, and it started with a fierce video feed which came through every television, internet connected computer, and cellular phone. The feed showed the dark, shadowy figure of the last person to ever address the entire world through the modern communication system.

"Attention citizens around the world. It is time to take a break from the activity of your daily life and look around you. Do you see the mindless cattle that you have become? Slaves to your technology. Slaves to your governments or your warlords. Slaves to your limited knowledge of the world. You are poison to the planet as well as each other. Humanity has become a cancer, one that has raged out of control. It is time to mark this day on the calendar, the 7th of May, as the beginning of a new age. As God did with the flood, it's time to purge this world of the corruption and begin anew. Remember me, for I am the Zodiac, I am hatred incarnate, and I will watch this world burn in the cleansing fires of the apocalypse, and be reborn in my image!"

There was silence for a moment as the video feed ceased. The hustle and bustle of life came to a stop. The stillness was then broken by an event that would come to be called the Flash Storm. First came a quick light, then massive explosions simultaneously lit off in every major city across the world. The intense heat, flames, and wind scorched and destroyed structures, cars, and people themselves. No one saw it coming. There was no warning. There was no terrorist chatter. There was no one to respond. In mere minutes, the entire world was thrown into chaos. Capital cities were gone. Governments were virtually wiped out.

In the days that followed, amongst the chaos and the rioting, the Dark Ones, also known as Seekers, blazed through the ruins of society. The brutal soldiers of darkness were completely covered in a black, mesh armor and wore helmets with blank faceplates. They were emotionless and relentless in their pursuits. On their shoulders were extraordinarily bright lights. They would come in the dark, their very presence striking uncontrollable fear in the remaining population. Their menacing lights were all that could be seen. They did not reason. They did not feel pain. They did not hold back. They did not stop. They began the worldwide genocide of humanity.

On September 6th, what most people came to call the day of the fall, Zodiac declared himself the Lord and Master of the North American continent. The remnants of the government and military had fallen. There were no more world communications. There was no resistance, no organization. Across the planet, mass hysteria gripped the survivors. Conflicts broke out. The Middle East was annihilated with the very nuclear arsenals that were meant as a deterrent.

It truly seemed that the worst parts of the religious texts had come to pass. The country that, love it or hate it, was always looked to for leadership had fallen. But then something happened. Out of the shadows, a glimmer of hope appeared in an unusual place. A man who had been in self-imposed exile for over a year came out of hiding...

Chapter 1

Hartford, Connecticut, had its fair share of street violence in its past. The former home of the state capital was anything but paradise. Then the Flash Storm came. The tall office buildings began to topple. The Charter Oak Bridge collapsed into rubble. The capital building crumbled into debris. The governor's mansion lay in ashes. It made gang violence look like a schoolyard kickball game. After the dust began to settle, a group of Connecticut residents got together to rebel against Zodiac's forces and a group of them set up shop in the ruins of the former capital. Somehow, some way, the Seekers discovered where they were, and attacked in force, soon after sunset.

The screams of the rebels could be heard for quite a distance as the Dark Ones descended on their ranks. There was no hesitation. If a rebel was in the sights of a Seeker, they were as good as dead. It was said that one could literally feel Zodiac's Grand Army draining the morale from the battlefield. One man was the exception, an outsider. He stood on the ruble of one of the fallen bridges and took aim with his rifle. He squeezed the trigger and sent a shot soaring, straight through the head of a Seeker. Immediately he hopped down from his vantage point to find a new one before other Seekers honed in on his location.

The strange man was a loner. He hadn't felt that he was part of the world in quite a long time. He was not tall for a man, five feet ten inches. He had a stature though that was unbending. His long hair was tied back in a ponytail. He normally wore some type of black leather pants, biker boots, fingerless leather gloves, and a black, short sleeve leather jacket which was always open to display the saying on his shirt, "Live Free or Die." It was that phrase that led people to believe he may have come from New Hampshire, but no one knew. He could have adopted the former state's quote because it was especially applicable to the times at hand. The most distinctive feature of this stranger was the markings on and around his right eye. On the eyelid was a tattoo of a "7." Surrounding the eye was a fierce looking scorpion tattoo, the body just below the eye and the tail wrapping around the socket.

The stranger had been referred to as "the man in black" by many or as the scorpion man, but his true name was Vincent Black. It wasn't his name that was important though, it was what he stood for. Many said that he could not be killed, that they had witnessed him being shot and immediately rising unscathed by the wound. Others conjectured that he was stronger than ten men and had the dexterity of a cat. Still others reported that he sensed trouble before it happened. There were even extreme stories of him firing lightning bolts from his hands, summoning massive storms, and even turning his own body to solid metal.

Vincent had his occasional chuckle at some of the rumors he had heard about himself. In a time where chaos reigned, people were looking for a prophet. It was true that Vincent was not like most other people. He thought it was funny that reports varied from being a bit extraordinary to a real live Superman.

Standing behind a large concrete boulder, Vincent knew there was trouble on the other side. Two Seekers had seen where he had gone and decided to follow. He strapped his rifle to his back and pulled two 9mm Beretta pistols from their holsters on his hips. He had them loaded with armor piercing rounds prior to his arrival in the ruins of Hartford. Now was a matter of perfect timing. He did not want them to see him coming. The reports about his danger sense were accurate. Vincent possessed a type of sixth sense; he could pick up immediate danger to himself and from where it was coming. This was an extremely useful talent in the post Flash Storm world.

Vincent waited until the exact right moment, when the tingling in the back of his head stopped. He could see that the bright beams of light coming from the Seekers' shoulder lights were no longer pointed in his immediate direction. Another accurate report was his speed and dexterity; he moved like a cat. He charged his way around the large section of bridge with his guns pointed outward. Before either Seeker could even acknowledge him, he put a bullet through their heads, dropping them to the ground. He felt the tingle again. It was coming from his right. He immediately spotted a third Seeker that was attempting to tackle him, and allowed the Grand Army soldier to grab his right arm. At that moment, he threw his enemy as if he was a rag doll, head first into another large section of bridge. He heard the sound of the dark warrior's neck breaking from the intense impact.

Knowing it would be dangerous to remain in one spot for more than a few moments, he went on the move again, holstering his pistols and climbing sections of collapsed bridge like a primate in the rain forest. He had a nagging feeling that there was a satellite watching this site, so from the higher ground he immediately drew his rifle again and used the scope to look around. The Seekers were making their way toward him, even disengaging rebels to do so. The rebels had no idea that he was there, nor did they have any idea why the Dark Ones were losing interest in them. Vincent quickly assessed the situation and saw several places where he could still remain above ground level. With an impressive jump, he took two well placed shots putting a bullet through the chest of one Seeker and the throat of another, dropping them. While still holding his rifle and with minimal effort, he made a twenty foot leap to the top of another large chunk of bridge. Soaring through the air, he twisted to avoid enemy fire. The Seekers did not fire out of emotion. Each shot was calculated and any normal man would have been cut down by the barrage. Vincent had enough time to take out two more Seekers before making the leap to a section of collapsed office building.

Just like the Dark Ones, each shot he took was calculated. He was one man with a limited amount of ammunition. He did not wish to run out, not that he was defenseless. He was sure that the Seekers were regular humans, not some kind of enhanced super soldiers. They moved like regular humans, which worked well to his advantage. Utilizing his rifle sight again, he took aim on two more of his dark enemies. The first one received a shot to the chest. Before Vincent could make the second shot, the section of concrete that his foot was on began to crumble, so his shot only hit the target in the leg. There were no screams of pain. Vincent regained his footing and jumped to another section of collapsed building. It was fortunate that there was so much debris; the Seekers had to remain on foot or bring in air support, which they lacked. The ruins also provided many great hiding spots.

Vincent took aim once again, he still had plenty of rounds in this magazine and he wasn't even remotely tired. In actuality, he was just getting warmed up. This time though, he noticed that there were three Seekers pinning a group of rebels. He fired his first shot, shattering the spinal column of one of the Dark Ones. The other two mechanically still fired on the rebels, one of them received a gaping hole in the chest and dropped to the ground. Vincent fired his second shot, splattering the brains of the second Seeker on some debris. His third shot rang out and penetrated the jugular of the third one, causing blood to spray everywhere. A tingle in the back of his head told him to jump, which he did, right before a grenade made its way to where he had been. He quickly arrived at the spot where the rebel group was. There were three left. One appeared to be in his late forties or early fifties. He was clean shaven, which was unusual post Flash Storm. He had a full head of gray hair, a chiseled face, and looked as though he may have played football or been involved in some heavy type of work at one point. Next to him was a young girl, probably pre-teen. She had a scar on her right cheek that appeared to have originated from a deep cut. The last standing rebel was roughly Vincent's height, and was rail thin. He had a mustache that was purposeful; the rest of his face hadn't seen a razor in a few days. His hair was spiked and Vincent wasn't sure if it was from lack of hygiene or intentional.

"You, you're that scorpion guy. The man in black," the older gentleman point blankly stated.

Vincent looked him directly in the eyes, "Yeah, that's me. Name's Vincent. Guess the Seekers found out Hartford's inhabited again." He got a tingle in the back of his head and immediately turned and fired his rifle, sending a bullet through the heart of a Seeker. He then spun back around.

"How...how the hell did you know he was coming," asked the tall, skinny rebel.

"Not sure. I just get a tingle in the back of my head, it kind of points me in the direction and I react. You guys have a withdrawal plan?" asked Vincent.

"Withdrawal? Ha. That's funny. This is where we withdrew to. Every time we got into it with the Seekers, we got demolished. Our people, they're tough. They've been through a lot over the past few months, but these Seekers. They just seem to suck the morale and courage right outta people. Doesn't seem to affect you though," the older rebel stated.

"Yeah, great to be immune. Listen, we've got to get you all out of here. Any way to call to the others," Vincent inquired.

"Been using these short band radios, but we haven't gotten any responses," answered the older man.

Vincent looked around. His danger sense wasn't creeping up on him at the moment. "We've got to get into the sewers. We can move around down there, where the satellites won't see us."

"SATs? I thought those were gone," said the skinny man.

"No, Zodiac controls them now. All of 'em. Great huh? He cut off world communication to all of us, and had a readymade system for his own use. I think I saw an exposed sewer cover over this way," Vincent responded.

"What about everybody else?" asked the young one.

"They're dead or captured by now, the amount of firing has dropped significantly and I can see the shoulder lights from those cretins," the skinny man pointed out.

"Well Vincent, I have a thousand questions but I guess they can wait. If you can get us out of here, I'll be eternally grateful," the old man stated.

"Then follow me, I never liked Hartford much anyway," Vincent replied.

They made their way to the exposed sewer cover. Vincent reached down and lifted the cover as if it was made of aluminum foil. "You made that look easy," the skinny man said.

"Just get the hell in there," Vincent snapped. The three rebels wasted no time in descending into the tunnels. Vincent followed but before he descended, he tossed a grenade to the base of a section of collapsed rubble. He quickly dropped into the sewer, recovering the hole. A moment later, a loud boom rang out and the four could hear debris falling. The tunnels actually shook.

"What did you do that for?" asked the older man.

"If they're watching us from SATs, they'll know where to go. I don't want to make it easy on them. I just hope we're not trapped down here," Vincent answered.

"That's um...that's great. We might be stuck? Wow, this turned out to be a really great day," the skinny man said.

"We're alive, aren't we? Let's take one thing at a time. Where are we headed?" asked the older man.

"Dunno. Out of here sounds good to me, how about you?" Vincent asked in return.

The older man and the skinny man looked at each other. The older one spoke up, "You don't have a plan?"

"Nope. Do you? I wasn't expecting to run into you. I just wanted to get out of there before they raze the place with the Apocalypse Dozer," responded Vincent as he began walking, the others immediately followed.

"What's an Apocalypse Dozer?" inquired the skinny man.

"It looks like an oversized wheat reaper but it tears up buildings and trees instead of wheat," the older man said. "I've never seen it but do you think they'd seriously send it here."

"Yup," Vincent answered.

"Why?" asked the skinny man.

"So they can make sure that they get me," Vincent replied.

"You? What's so special about you?" the skinny man had a puzzled look on his face. "I mean other than the fact that you're obviously some kind of super soldier or something."

"Don't know. They seem hell bent on finding me though," Vincent responded.

"So why did you come to Hartford anyway?" asked the older man.

"I was actually just passing by when I saw that the place was under siege. I'm always looking for a good reason to waste some Grand Army goons," Vincent answered.

The young one was noticing the horrid stench of death in the sewers. They obviously hadn't been flushed out since the Flash Storm happened. She also noticed that there were cracks and weak spots, most likely caused by the collapse of the tall buildings above. "I don't like it down here."

"No one does squirt," responded the skinny man. "So Vincent, I guess we've been rude and haven't introduced ourselves to the man who saved our lives. I'm Josh Tyler. This guy here is Chris Talbot. The talkative one over here is Andromeda Page."

Vincent didn't respond.

"Hey, did you hear me?" Josh was clearly annoyed.

"Shhh," Vincent responded, putting the index finger of his right hand to his lip, his eyes looking up. "You hear that?"

"Hear what," asked Josh.

Suddenly, there was a rumbling. It felt as if the earth itself was shaking. "What the hell is that, an earthquake?" asked Talbot.

"If only we were that lucky. It's the Apocalypse Dozer," Vincent stated. "We need to hurry."

He immediately started into a jog, the other three following along. The rumble was getting closer. Loud crashes began echoing through the tunnels. Andromeda, Talbot, and Josh were all struggling to keep up with Vincent who was moving at a snail's pace in his opinion. "Hey man, what's the story with this Apocalypse Dozer?" Josh asked.

"Let's just say it's something you don't want to wait around for," answered Vincent. "I know it's tough, but keep moving."

They hurried through the tunnels until they noticed Vincent slowing down. Talbot spoke up, "Why are we stopping?"

"They don't know where we are. Hear that? The rumbling is getting further away," Vincent said.

"Man, you have some good hearing, or maybe mine just sucks now that I've gotten older," Talbot stated.

"I have good hearing, not extraordinary, but good," Vincent responded.

"Yeah, well, you do everything else extraordinary, just what the hell are you?" asked Josh.

"Long story, I'm what happens when the government screws with things that it shouldn't," answered Vincent.

Josh let out a sigh, "Dammit, look up ahead."

"Blocked, it must have collapsed, we've gotta turn around," Talbot stated.

"No, we go back, we're gonna be crushed by that oversized garbage disposal," Vincent pointed out as he kept walking.

"Maybe we can meet up with the others," Josh said as they approached the collapsed tunnel.

"If there was anyone left alive after the Seekers raided, they're dead now. We aren't going back," Vincent told them.

Talbot, Andromeda, and Josh just looked at each other. After a moment, Talbot spoke up, "What the hell is that supposed to mean? You haven't given us any answers!"

"Look guys, let's get out of here alive, then I'll answer your questions as best I can," Vincent tried to ease up on them realizing that the whole world being turned upside down happened only a few months ago.

"That's all well and good but we still have to get through this tunnel and there are some large chunks of concrete here," Josh pointed out.

Vincent didn't say a word. He simply walked over to the first large chunk of rubble, reached and found a good grip with both of his hands, then hoisted the chunk out of the way as if it was a pebble. He continued to move the debris until he cleared a path. The whole time, his three companions just stared at him. "Instead of gawking, you should follow me through this path; it's open on the other side. Looks like the sewer didn't completely collapse."

Vincent began making his way through the small opening. Unable to say anything out of total awe, Andromeda, Talbot, and Josh followed him. They once again broke out into a jog for a couple of minutes, until they reached a ladder leading to the surface. "Up here, the dozer is still pretty far out and the Seekers should be with it," Vincent stated as he headed up the ladder.

Josh raised his eyebrows, "What do we do once we get up there?"

"I've got a pretty sweet ride waiting for us. Can't believe I actually left this thing unattended in Hartford. A few months ago, there's no way in hell I would have done that." Vincent cracked a smile and moved the sewer cover, then hurried the rest of the way to the surface.

"He's crazy," Josh said to Andromeda, who did not respond, but headed up the ladder behind Vincent. Talbot simply put his hand on Josh's shoulder for a moment then joined them. Josh followed. When he got all the way to the top, he saw Talbot and Andromeda staring in the direction behind him. He turned to look and the sight he witnessed was such that he could not even comment.

"Th…that's gotta be the Apocalypse Dozer?" Talbot managed

to say. "I could have gone the rest of my life without seeing it."

"Yeah, I think that's the general consensus of anyone who's actually seen it and lived to tell about it," Vincent stated.

The four looked to see something that was a perversion of an old wheat reaper. It was massive, either black or navy blue, had spotlights on it, but no obvious place for a pilot. It was difficult to judge the size from where they were, but it towered over everything; its chopping mechanism in the front was almost as big as the rest of it. They watched as it continued to roll though Hartford, grinding up everything that remained in its path. It appeared unstoppable. Though it was quite a distance away, they could see that there were various weaponry systems on it, including chain guns and missile launchers.

"Come on, before a SAT gets overhead and figures out we're here. They're probably grinding everything up hoping to exterminate any rebels that might be hiding," Vincent pointed out.

"Okay, but how...is that your car?" Josh's jaw almost dropped.

"Yup. Nice, isn't it," said Vincent, pointing to the black Mustang GT convertible. "Get in, I'll speed us out of here."

Josh and Andromeda got into the back seat, and Talbot rode shotgun. Vincent got into the driver's seat. The convertible top was up; after all, October nights in New England usually didn't lend themselves to being convertible or motorcycle friendly. Vincent immediately started the car and hit the gas to get out of what was left of the once capital city of Connecticut.

"Where are we going?" asked Josh.

"Away from here," responded Vincent. "Why? Do you know a good place where we can lay low?"

"Lay low? Man, we gotta join up with the rebellion," Josh exclaimed.

"What rebellion kid? Everyone who stands up to the Seekers gets captured or killed," Talbot pointed out. "We just need to focus on staying alive."

"Man after my own heart," Vincent stated.

"So what's your story Vincent? I mean, if we're just driving, maybe you can give us some more details on these things that you seem to know so much about. And hell, while you're at it, reveal that 'S' on your chest," Josh inquired.

"Josh, shut the hell up," Talbot scolded.

"Nah, don't worry about it Talbot. What do you want to know?" asked Vincent.

"What's up with those tattoos on your eye? The scorpion and the number 7 on your eyelid?" Josh eagerly asked.

"They're the result of the government playing around with things they shouldn't," Vincent responded.

Josh shifted in his seat, "I thought *you* were the result of the government playing with things they shouldn't."

Vincent shot him a look through the rear view mirror, "I am. Look, I got 'selected' for a little experiment. Me and six others. The first six were failures. I wasn't."

Josh's right leg began to shake, "What happened to them?"

Vincent looked in his rear view mirror to see the eager Josh awaiting his answer. "They died."

"Oh...sorry. I guess I should've figured that one out for myself. What the hell was it?" Josh continued his inquiry but was cut off by Vincent holding up his hand.

"Do me a favor. Near your feet is a grenade launcher. Hand it to me," Vincent calmly requested.

"That's what this thing is? What do you need it for?" asked Josh.

"Just do it, now," Vincent said with a calmness that was almost frightening.

"Okay, okay, here ya go, geeze," Josh handed Vincent the weapon just in time to see something pop up from the trees on the side of the highway. It appeared to be some type of sleek helicopter but it had no blades on it and made no discernible noise over the sound of the Mustang's motor. It could have easily been mistaken for some type of UFO. "Jesus, what the hell is that!?"

Vincent didn't answer. He immediately swerved as a hail of gunfire rang out and struck the spot where they would have been if he hadn't pulled an evasive maneuver. He then quickly swerved in the other direction and successfully dodged another hail of gunfire. "Hang on," Vincent warned.

"How the hell are you doing that? It's like you know where they're gonna shoot before they do," Josh cried out.

"That's because I do," Vincent calmly stated. He slammed on the brakes and spun the sports car around. Quickly pushing a button while the wheels weren't moving, the convertible top began to retract. The helicopter-like vehicle passed overhead but quickly looped and turned around to face them.

"Oh shit, oh shit, oh shit," Josh babbled.

"Talbot, take the wheel," Vincent directed as he stood up, one foot on the center console and one on the back seat. He was facing the rear of the vehicle. Talbot quickly obeyed, moved to the driver's seat and pealed out. The tires let out a loud squeal and a cloud of smoke, but Vincent never lost his balance.

The strange looking aircraft was approaching quickly. With the grenade launcher in hand, he pointed it upward, in the direction of the helicopter. "Are you crazy? You'll never hit something like that with a grenade launcher," Talbot warned.

"Oh ye of little faith," Vincent answered. "Josh, point your pistol at them when they begin to get close and start unloading."

"WH...WHAT!?" was all Josh could respond with.

"Listen up, if you want to live, you'll point your damn pistol at that thing and start firing!" Vincent yelled. Andromeda was crouching on the floor to keep the bitter wind from freezing her to death.

"I can't hit that! I'm just a regular guy, I'm not cut out for this fighting shit," Josh panicked.

"Josh, that's the Seekers sucking away your morale. It's an illusion. Tune it out of your head," Vincent said. He looked at the poor young man who only a few months prior was probably a big time nerd who spent most of his time in his room or basement where everyone went with their computer issues.

Josh let out a few loud, forced deep breaths then popped up and yelled at the top of his lungs, "Aaaahhhh! Die you Seeker bastards!" He started firing on the helicopter-like pursuer. Interestingly enough, the bullets were hitting it though they were just bouncing off the bulletproof exterior. The diversion was all Vincent needed. The hail of gunfire caused the pilots to come in closer to the car before firing. They didn't get the chance; Vincent pointed the grenade launcher and fired. The explosion rocked the front of the vehicle. It remained intact but the pilot lost control and it went down on the middle of the highway. It bounced and rolled for several hundred feet before grinding to a halt.

Vincent dropped down into the passenger seat and said, "Go

back to the wreckage. I want to check something out."

"Alright," Talbot responded and turned the car around. After a few moments, they were directly next to the wreckage. When the car stopped, Talbot re-engaged the convertible top and turned on the heat, as driving fast with the top down in October made him feel as if his bone marrow had frozen. Vincent got out and hurried over to the wreckage, which had flames and smoke pouring out of it, but no explosion. Josh couldn't control his curiosity and got out behind him.

"Hey, what are you doing?" asked Josh.

"I'm curious about something," responded Vincent.

"Isn't this going to explode?" Josh was being cautious as he stood behind Vincent and peered around.

"Don't know. Maybe. The good news is I'll sense it before it does. Besides, there's only a little bit of fire, nothing to worry about," Vincent stated. He climbed onto the wreckage which was on its side. He grabbed onto the hatch and with a huff, he tore the door off.

"Holy shit man, you're like the Hulk or something," Josh exclaimed as he stood there gawking.

Vincent didn't turn around, he just answered, "Hardly, the Hulk is green and pissed off all the damn time." Looking inside, he saw the subject of his curiosity. There were two Seekers inside; one was impaled by a piece of the wreckage and most likely dead. The other was unconscious but still alive. He unclipped the safety belt, pulled the enigmatic soldier of Zodiac from the wreckage and slung it over his shoulder.

"Are you shitting me? You just nabbed a Seeker," Josh almost fell over from the concept of this.

With the Seeker slung over his shoulder, he jumped off of the wreckage and landed in front of the fidgety rebel. "Yeah, that's the idea. I have some rope in the trunk, do me a favor and grab it so I can tie up this bastard."

Josh hurried back to the car. "What the hell are you guys doing? We've gotta get out of here…Did Vincent just nab a Seeker?" Talbot was wild.

"Yeah. He's gonna tie him up and take him with us," Josh responded as he fiddled around with the stuff in the trunk. He didn't pay much attention to all of the things inside, but noticed that there were some weapons and rations.

Waiving his hands in the air Talbot said, "Why the hell would he do that?"

"When he gets over here, you can ask him," Josh answered as he found the rope, grabbed it, then shut the trunk. Vincent had set the Seeker down on the road a few feet away at this point and Josh brought the rope over to him.

"What do you hope to accomplish with this?" inquired a confused Josh.

"Know thy enemy," was the only response Vincent gave. He looked over the fallen soldier. Not a square inch of skin showed. The face plate of the helmet was plain. It appeared to have one-way transparency and completely hid the face of whomever or whatever was below it. He tied up the soldier and brought him to the car, throwing him in the back seat, busting one of the shoulder lights that wasn't broken from the crash. "Josh, keep an eye on our guest. I don't believe the fear aura functions if the Seeker is unconscious."

Josh and Vincent got in and Talbot said, "Alright, we need a destination. Of course, we're pointed right back at Hartford."

"Hey, we could join up with the rebels at Southern," Josh suggested.

"Hartford is destroyed, we'd have to take back roads to get to I-91 and hope that nothing else gets in our way," Talbot pointed out.

"Wait, Southern? As in Southern Connecticut State University? They're on a college campus?" Vincent asked seeming agitated.

"That's what I heard. Not a bad idea huh? Set up those dorms as barracks," Josh said with a smile on his face.

"Stupid. So damn stupid. We need to get there before that dozer does," Vincent warned.

"Why do you say that?" asked Josh.

"First, Southern is above ground, which means the SATs can spot the collective activity. Second, that dozer just turned and is heading in that direction. It'll flatten all of New Haven and turn anyone there into hamburger. We've gotta get them out of there!" Vincent exclaimed.

"How about we dump the Seeker," Talbot vigorously suggested.

"No, I want to know what makes these guys tick. I've got some suspicions. In the meantime, let's get to New Haven before that giant shopping center does," Vincent stated.

Chapter 2

The location was Peterson Air Force Base, Colorado. It used to be the home of the NORAD U.S. Northern Command. It was now under the control of the self-proclaimed Lord and Master of North America. The room was dark, except for the glow of the various monitors and the LEDs on the control panels. Standing alone, hands behind his back and watching the views carefully was the one known only as the Zodiac. He wore a flexible mesh armor that was similar to the Seekers but far more menacing. The shoulders, elbows, and knees had spikes protruding from them. The helmet, as with the Seekers, had a one way transparent face plate with no markings. The remainder of the helmet however, appeared as a type of dragon head, with the mouth wide open containing the front face plate. From the back of his neck draped a long, black cape.

Zodiac stood silently, watching the footage. Appearing before him were various accounts of the activity of the mysterious "man in black", who managed to not only elude the Seekers, but actually cause damage. The various recordings that were set on looping playback in front of him were not very revealing. Not a single frame of video displayed the man's face. Zodiac was deep in thought when he heard the door to the room open.

"Lord Zodiac," said the voice.

"Come in," Zodiac responded. "So you have finally found a witness."

"Yes, and as per your orders, I came to inform you immediately, but, you already knew, didn't you?" the voice asked.

"You are my second in command General Callous. I do not need to read your mind. Your surface thoughts though, those were strong when you entered and they jumped into my psyche as if they were their own entity. Come, I wish for you to be present when I interrogate the prisoner," Zodiac said as he spun around, the cape waving in the air.

"Yes sir," General Callous bowed. The general's mesh armor was far more like a Seeker than Zodiac's. The biggest differences were the horns on the helmet and the various markings on the chest plate. Unlike the Seekers, Callous did not wear a face plate. "I must ask though, what is so special about this man?"

"I am hoping this interrogation answers that question," Zodiac responded as they exited the room. There was no one in the hallway. No staff bustling with reports. Nothing. The two continued walking toward the interrogation room.

"But I see you must think he is important in some way," Callous replied.

"If he is who I think he is, then yes, he is extremely important. The man that I am thinking of has his roots on the East Coast of the former United States. He spent time away, and I am curious if he truly has come home," Zodiac was talking cryptically.

Callous looked at his leader to whom he was undyingly loyal. "Is that why you wanted Hartford leveled?" asked the General, who was attempting not to try the patience of the supreme.

"Yes. When you informed me of rebel activity, I thought best to be thorough. When is the footage of the assault coming in?" asked Zodiac.

"It should be here momentarily. By the time you are done with the prisoner, it should be on your view screens," Callous told him.

"Excellent. I knew I let you keep your free will for a reason," Zodiac replied as they entered the interrogation room.

It was a generic room with a table and the prisoner cuffed to a chair. There were no windows, save the one way panel. Zodiac did not wish to hide from this man, who was already hyperventilating at the sight of the brutal dictator. "I assume by your reaction and the extreme stink of fear that no introduction is necessary," Zodiac stated.

"You...you're the Zodiac," gasped the prisoner, a man who

16

looked to be in his early forties although just being in Zodiac's presence would probably age him from the sheer terror he felt.

"Yes, and I have heard that you have seen the man in black in person. The one with the scorpion tattoo on his eye," Zodiac said. He then reached his hand and grabbed the top of the man's head. "I don't wish to waste my time getting you to tell me what I want to know. I prefer to tear it from your very soul!"

The blood curdling scream that came from the prisoner would have unleashed a terror in others that would hardly be rivaled by any other sound. Zodiac, who was not known to play games with people, was on a mission. He had no time to waste. Over the previous few months, in the ensuing chaos of the Flash Storm, he had mobilized his Seekers to finish off key military installations, usurp the use of the Satellites orbiting the planet, and most of all, to continue the purge of humanity.

Zodiac's head was filled with the mental imprints of his victim. He sorted through everything; he specifically wanted this man's recent memories. After a few moments, he saw an image, a man who stood a little less than six feet tall. This "witness" apparently did not get a good look at him because he had no clear memory of the face, just the scorpion tattoo. "RRRRRRRRRAAAAAAAAAAAAAAAAA!" Zodiac growled. The witness was convulsing, blood began coming from his nose, ears, and eyes.

"Lord Zodiac," said Callous, "what did you see?"

"I...SAW...NOTHING! This maggot is useless!" Zodiac yelled, still holding his hand on the man's head. The victim kept convulsing until his eyes became bloodshot and his body went limp. The savage dictator pushed the head down and stormed out. Callous followed.

"He did not see anything?" Callous inquired.

"No, he didn't. Not anything that's useful anyway. Anyone can put a damn scorpion tattoo by their eye; I want to know this man's identity! I need that footage from Hartford," Zodiac snarled as he made his way back to his control room, the general in tow. They both entered the room.

"The field commander says you'll be pleasantly surprised," Callous stated as he loaded up the video feed.

"I had better be or I'll turn him into a Seeker," Zodiac threatened.

The video began playing. It was a satellite feed from the attack on Hartford. Zodiac watched as a man dressed in black was hopping from rubble chunk to rubble chunk, taking out Seekers with his rifle at each stop with quick and brutal accuracy. The man in black then dropped down onto one of the piles and took a few moments. He dropped another Seeker then slid down to ground level. Surprisingly, there was a clear enough opening to watch the action. He took out two Seekers with his pistols. He noticed a third, hidden Seeker tried to get the jump on the man, but when grabbed, he simply flung the soldier head first into a chunk of ruin. It was at the moment he threw the Seeker that he had looked up momentarily. It was enough. Zodiac didn't say anything. He paused the video feed and slowed it backward. "So…it is you," the dictator said softly.

Callous could almost sense a smile from his master, "You know him Lord Zodiac?"

The dictator did not take his eyes off of the screen. It was indisputable. Not only did he have the scorpion tattoo, he had a "7" tattooed on the eyelid of the same eye. "Yes General, I do know him. His name is Vincent Black, and he's not to be underestimated as it seems our forces have been doing."

"I do not mean to question you my lord, but where do you know him from?" inquired Callous.

Zodiac still didn't turn from the monitor. "But you are questioning me."

"Apologies my liege." Callous quickly grew silent so as not to invoke the wrath of his master.

"It's quite alright, you should know something about the man whose capture I am sending you to oversee," Zodiac said, and Callous could swear that the dictator was still smiling underneath that helmet of his.

"You…you're sending me? For one man? My lord, please, there are commanders who would be well suited for this task," Callous almost sounded like he was begging.

"General Callous, I merely want your presence and direct involvement in the operation. Despite the fact that your armor is built to enhance your physical attributes, you are still no match for Vincent Black in a one-on-one confrontation. No, I need you to make sure that the commanders understand the importance of finding and capturing this man," Zodiac explained.

Callous was still confused, "He shows no fear of the Seekers."

Zodiac nodded, "That is because he is immune to their fear aura. As I said before, do not underestimate him. In the same respect, do not overestimate the Seekers' ability to confront him. He is more powerful than a hundred of them."

"What is he?" Callous could not hide his concern.

"He is what happens when the government messes with things that they shouldn't, and they certainly shouldn't have attempted to create a one man army if they couldn't control him," Zodiac gave a cryptic answer.

"But, you know him? How…?" Callous was going to question Zodiac further but then he remembered who he was talking to.

"Hmm hmm hmm, you hesitate to ask? That's probably a good thing. I will tell you this; I have known Vincent Black for my entire life. I know him and his entire history. What makes him the most dangerous is that he knows mine, as well; he just doesn't know that he knows it yet. I do not wish for him to discover it," Zodiac explained.

"Then why do I not just kill him and end the threat?" asked Callous.

"I have use for him, I wish to take advantage of that opportunity before simply deciding to dispose of a possible asset," Zodiac stated.

"Would he join us?" Callous wondered out loud.

"One never knows until one tries. We have come this far, toppling every government on the planet. The pockets of resistance that are left have fallen before us with little difficulty. I don't believe that we have limits," Zodiac boasted.

"Very well Lord Zodiac. If I have to I will flatten the entire East Coast to find Vincent Black," Callous promised.

"General, you may flatten the entire East Coast anyway," Zodiac stated.

"Of course my lord. I will return with Vincent Black," Callous assured.

Chapter 3

"Think we ditched the spies in the sky?" asked Josh while they sped down the road.

Vincent looked at him briefly, "If we hadn't, we'd have more Seekers up our asses."

"Alright, then we can continue our Q & A," Josh quickly replied.

Andromeda had yet to speak a word during the entire trip but finally asked, "Are you a good guy?"

"Drom, what kind of question is that!?" barked Talbot.

"It's alright. Depends on your definition of a good guy," answered Vincent.

"Are you a super hero?" Andromeda asked with her young, innocent sounding voice.

"There's no such thing. They're just people trying to make things right. In this case, get us out of here alive and get this group of rebels out of harm's way before they get themselves killed," Vincent assured.

"Well, you have super powers. That makes you super. You're trying to make things right, so that's a hero. So put them together and you're a super hero," Andromeda declared.

"Kid has a point," Josh stated.

Vincent ignored Josh, "Listen, I'm no hero. I just figure we should get these people out of the way of the Apocalypse Dozer and figure out what makes the Seekers tick."

"What makes you tick though?" asked Josh, his right leg shaking again.

"Oh here we go," Talbot rolled his eyes.

Vincent had a half smirk on his face, "If you want me to say it out loud I will. I'm part of a super soldier project from before the Flash Storm."

"How were you chosen? Were you in the army or special forces or something?" Josh looked at him intensely.

"No. I never had military training. I applied to the air force a while back, but they wouldn't take me because my eyesight wasn't correctable to 20/20, which is kind of ironic since it's 20/5 now," Vincent had a slight chuckle. "No, it wasn't a question of body at that point; it was a question of mind. It was a question of will. I guess I kind of caught their attention when I sucked up a dose of radiation that should have killed me, and was still ticking a year after it happened."

Josh wasn't sure how to respond, but settled for asking, "How did you manage that?"

"Honestly? I decided that I had some things I needed to do before I left this world. Then these guys got their hands on me and decided that there were a lot of things I needed to do before I left this world. They built me up to be the perfect soldier physically. The combat skills I had to learn the old fashioned way, but I have to say it's easier to do that when you're stronger and faster than normal humans," Vincent explained.

"Alright, forget this shit. We know you're tough but here's what we don't know. How the hell do you know so much about Zodiac and his cronies?" Talbot asked, still watching the road and dodging various piles of debris and other obstacles that had come into place since the Flash Storm.

"I was just outside of Los Angeles when the Flash Storm happened, far enough away to survive, close enough to see what happened. I've crossed this entire country, always keeping on the move. I've watched whole towns of people rounded up by Zodiac's Seekers. Anyone who resists is killed. Zodiac doesn't threaten. He doesn't intimidate. He has an endgame in mind and he isn't negotiating. I saw that dozer plow through a town, cutting down every house, building, tree, and person in its path," Vincent explained. "I decided to come back to the East Coast to find a few people."

"Did you find them?" Josh looked intent again, his leg still shaking.

Vincent shut his eyes for a moment, the "7" tattooed on his right eyelid showed perfectly at that point. He then opened them and turned to look at Josh, "I found marked graves. I didn't bother digging them up to verify. They died not that far from here. That's why I was in the area in the first place."

Josh's face sunk, "I'm sorry man, I didn't know."

"Do you have a place to go at all?" asked Talbot.

"I go wherever the road takes me. I have no friends or family left that I know of. The world has gone to hell and there doesn't seem to be a safe haven anywhere. If it's not Seekers, its warring factions fighting for whatever scraps they can find," Vincent stated.

"Hey, if it helps, we have no idea where we're going either, I mean after New Haven that is," Talbot acknowledged.

"Guys, I think this Seeker is waking up," Josh began pressing against the side of the car as he realized that there was no place to go. The Seeker began to stir. Talbot pulled the car over.

"Why did you use a turn signal? It's not like the cops are going to come and get you and that flashing light just draws attention," Vincent pointed out.

"Sorry, force of habit. Not used to living in hell yet. Although I think a GT motor pulls in more attention," Talbot responded.

"Touché," Vincent said.

Within moments after Talbot had stopped the car, the kidnapped Seeker let out a loud, piercing screech. It was an inhuman noise that gave everyone a chill, straight to their bones. That was of course except for Vincent, who looked at the prisoner for a moment with curiosity then said, "Shut the hell up." He balled his hand into a fist and knocked the Seeker unconscious again.

"What the hell was that!?" cried Josh, still holding his ears. Andromeda had her legs curled up and was holding them, burying her face behind her knees.

"Some type of built in response in case they're captured probably. A failsafe," Vincent answered.

"It was like the wail of the banshee. I felt more of a chill than when we were driving with the top down," Talbot admitted.

Vincent opened the door and got out. He folded the passenger seat down and said, "Come on, let's get that thing out here."

"We dumping it?" asked Josh.

"No, I want to see what's under that helmet," Vincent told him.

Talbot got out of the driver's side; Josh rushed out as fast as he could. Andromeda did not hurry but she climbed out while keeping an eye on the Seeker. After everyone was out, Vincent reached in and grabbed the prisoner with one hand and dragged it out. He laid the soldier on the side of the road. "Sure you wanna do this Vincent?" asked Talbot. "That scream. Who knows what could be underneath?"

"I've been suspicious of something for a little while. I have to know. You're all welcome to turn your heads if you want but I'm gonna look," Vincent stated. Andromeda buried her face in Talbot's abdomen. Chris Talbot did not look away as much as he wanted to. Nor did Josh. It was like being in the living room with a crummy TV show on, they wanted to look away but they could not. Vincent reached down and found the latches to detach the helmet. Putting both hands on the expressionless article, he removed it.

"I think it would have been easier to deal with if that was a monster," Talbot said. It wasn't a monster. It wasn't some banshee. It was human. A man. Probably in his early twenties. He had blonde hair that was slightly long and wavy.

"What the hell? They're human? They always seemed so mechanical," Josh stated.

Vincent was looking over the face of his adversary and then he noticed something. "Look, by the eye sockets."

"Red marks, looks like...oh my God, this guy was lobotomized," Talbot stated. "But how the hell could they function as soldiers?"

"I have no idea Talbot. Let's get out of here, there are lights in the distance and that's never a good thing," Vincent stated. He picked up the Seeker and put him back in the car. Without saying anything, Andromeda and Josh got in the back seat with the unconscious Seeker. Talbot got into the passenger side and Vincent took over driving.

"Why are we keeping this thing with us?" asked Josh.

"We're bringing it down to Southern. I think it'll help for people to see that the Seekers are human. Besides, after we get them to clear out, I want to open this guy's skull up and see if we can figure out how Zodiac controls them," Vincent answered.

Josh wrinkled his face a bit before responding, "Wait. You're gonna dissect this guy?"

"Yeah, that's exactly what I'm gonna do. Why? Are you gonna call the feds on me? This could answer a lot of questions that I've had floating around in my head for a while. It may also give us a better understanding of how they operate so we can fight them," Vincent argued.

"Let's just get there and get everyone out. We can worry about human rights shit later. We seem to be making good time," Talbot interjected.

"Yeah, well, it's nice when there's no traffic. We'll get on I-91 soon and be well on our way. Might as well enjoy having the roads now before they crumble," Vincent said.

"Vincent," Andromeda spoke up.

"Yeah," Vincent responded.

"Are we gonna make it?" she asked.

"Of course we are. I've been dodging the Seekers for a while. I know how to stay off the grid," Vincent assured her.

"No. I mean people. Are we going to be extinct?" there was a single tear that ran down the young girl's face, which Vincent noticed when he looked in the mirror.

"That's not gonna happen Andromeda," Vincent answered.

"Promise?" she asked with her eyes glued to the rear view mirror where she could see Vincent's face and the ever menacing scorpion tattoo.

Vincent hesitated for a moment before answering, realizing the weight of what he was about to say. He had been content to just play the avoidance game with the Seekers. He asked himself why, after only knowing these people for a couple of hours, did he suddenly feel as if he should be doing more? Then he looked into the mirror where he knew Andromeda could see his eyes and said, "I swear on the friends and family I just saw buried, humanity is not going to go extinct."

"Thank you Vincent," Andromeda said as she leaned back in the seat and shut her eyes. It was like the fear of the unknown had disappeared the moment Vincent made his promise. She truly believed that he was a superhero. Things were silent for a few minutes, until the young girl fell asleep. Josh had winked off only moments before.

"Did you mean that Vincent? Did you mean what you said to Drom?" asked Talbot.

"I never make promises that I can't keep," responded Vincent.

Talbot looked over at him, "I took you for the guy that keeps moving, a drifter."

"We're all drifters in our own way. Look, I don't know what we're gonna do and I don't know how we're gonna do it but we sure as hell aren't going to lay down and die. There's been enough death over the last few months," Vincent stated.

"I sure hope you're right," Talbot encouraged.

Vincent kept his eyes on the road but said, "Do you know of any other rebel cells? I know there are people all over the place who are attempting to fight back, but is there anything that even resembles some type of organization?"

"Yeah. There's New Haven, based at Southern which you know about. There's also Danbury and Bridgeport on the West side of the state," Talbot informed him.

"What about Groton, at the sub base?" asked Vincent.

"Groton was taken over; it's a Seeker base now. I heard something is going down in the New London area, but I have no idea what," Talbot answered.

"So basically, there's nothing to speak of in the Southeastern region of the state," Vincent summarized.

"Yeah. I know from Hartford we sent some scouts to various areas. Something big was under way out there but they couldn't tell much and no one else has made it back since," Talbot responded. "Are you planning something?"

"I'm just trying to get my bearings around here. So I assume no one else knows that the Hartford group was wiped out," Vincent guessed.

"We use short and long range radio. We told the others when we were attacked. Unfortunately, the entire group was wiped out, except for us, before we could tell them about the dozer. No one around here has ever seen one of those things. Despite the rumors, I'll bet most people doubt that something like that could even exist. I still can't believe that monster exists," Talbot explained,

25

grabbing onto the handle when Vincent dodged a large chunk of debris that appeared to be a piece of a small airplane.

"Misinformation and lack of information are going to be our two worst enemies. Not to mention that even if all of what remains of this state is talking, it's just one small group. At this rate, Zodiac will use the old divide and conquer technique, which won't be hard since the divide is already there," Vincent stated.

Talbot looked over at the man in black, "Vincent, I hope you know what the hell you're doing because I have a feeling that you might be our only hope."

Chapter 4

D anbury, Connecticut. Prior to the Flash Storm, it was the seventh largest city in the state. Adjoining New York, commuters were able to live in Connecticut and work across the border. But that was before. Though there had been no flash bomb placed in Danbury, many of the residents had perished in New York City during the Flash Storm. In the days after, the dreaded Seekers marched on the area. Those that weren't dead were taken. They never had a chance.

Danbury had never been so quiet. In the post Flash Storm world, noise just attracted trouble. The rebels who had taken refuge in the city did not wish to attract trouble. They had no plan. The enemy was practically invisible. No one knew who or what to go after. Fear was at an all time high. The big broadcast before the Flash Storm didn't last long enough for anyone to trace, not that it would have done any good. All that was going through this group's head was the need to survive. They needed hope.

The City of Danbury used to have a few decent golf courses. Those had become overgrown with vines and weeds over the summer and one would be lucky to even find the hole, never mind hit a ball toward it. The golf course by the highway was no exception. The rebels had posted three people to take watch at this location. It was a good vantage point, if the enemy was using the roads. Routes I-84, 202, and 6 were all viewable. The lookouts would have plenty of time to get word to the rest of the group.

In theory it was a great idea, but Alexis Hera was none too thrilled with the arrangements. She had celebrated her 22nd birthday on the day of the Flash Storm. She had long; slightly curly blonde hair, blue eyes, and a figure that would make even the most loyal man fill his head with sinful contemplations. Her attire wasn't helping to divert the eyes of her teammates either. She was wearing form fitting motorcycle leathers and boots. She had a pistol holstered on her right hip and a nightstick on her left hip. She probably would have been a model if things had been different with the world. Everyone had said she was crazy for riding a motorcycle in the beginning of October but she wanted to be able to get out of dodge quick, and the clunky pickup truck that Derek and Ron came in made her feel less safe than something with two wheels and no walls. The truck had a machinegun mounted in the back with a belt feed of 5.65 mm rounds. She was still not sure where they got it. Assault weapons were banned long before the 28th Amendment was passed repealing the 2nd Amendment right to bear arms.

Alexis, who went by the nickname Lexi, sat on the roof of the country club with her binoculars. She scanned around diligently, looking for possible Seeker activity. Derek and Ron were on the ground smoking cigarettes and talking about God knows what. The snickering and "maleness" reminded her of high school. Lexi did not like high school and she certainly didn't like being reminded of it either.

"Hey, you guys want to keep it down? You won't find it funny if the Seekers come and shoot your balls off," Lexi snarled.

Ron and Derek looked at each other and cackled like a couple of children getting away with something. Ron was the first to comment, "Wow, you're even hotter when you talk like that Lexi."

"Yeah, why don't you just relax?" Derek sarcastically suggested.

"The Seekers hit Hartford, and we haven't heard from them since, so no, I won't relax and neither should you two idiots," Lexi snapped.

"There's nothing here the Seekers would want. Besides, with those lights they have, we'd see them coming a mile away, without any need for a lookout," Derek pointed out. His buck teeth, red hair, and freckled face became highly accented when he spoke.

Lexi just rolled her eyes, "The funny thing about lights is they

28

have 'off' switches."

"Hot *and* a comedian, isn't she Derek," Ron said snidely.

"Oh my God! She's so gonna slap you," Derek responded as he reached up and flicked Ron on his large ears. Both men would have loved an opportunity just for physical contact with her, even if it was only to get pummeled.

Both obnoxious men looked up, waiting for a response or for her to come down and start throwing fists but she didn't. She was staring intently through the binoculars. "Hey, we were just kidding, no need to blow us off Lexi," Ron assured. There was still no response.

"C'mon, don't be like that!" Derek begged.

"Shit! We've got incoming!" Lexi shouted. She grabbed her radio and repeated the same message to whoever was listening. She then made her way to the edge of the roof, fortunately only one story high, and slid off, hit the ground, rolled, and stood up immediately.

Derek and Ron were both just looking at each other then looked at Lexi and said at the same time, "What!?"

"Clean the wax out of your ears and get in that truck. The Seekers are on their way!" Lexi snapped as she hurried over to her motorcycle. It was a black sport bike with a 1200 cc motor and very little weight so it made quite the effective getaway vehicle.

Derek and Ron hurried to the truck which was next to Lexi's bike. Derek got into the driver's seat and Ron jumped into the back of the truck and armed the machinegun. Lexi started up the bike at the same time that Derek started the truck. He turned on the radio to listen to the chatter.

"We've got incoming over here too!" one voice cried out.

"Holy shit, there's hundreds of 'em! Oh God, get us out of here!" another voice came.

"They're gonna hit us from all sides!" yet another voice rang out.

Derek, Ron, and Lexi could see the bright lights approaching. They were coming from air and land and there were a lot of them. The sound of explosions and gunfire began to fill what had been a silent night. "C'mon guys, let's get these Seeker bastards!" Lexi yelled.

"Are you crazy? They'll kill us. We've got to get out of here!"

Ron screamed over the sound of the motors.

"Stop being a coward, grow a set, and let's fight back," Lexi snarled. She hit the throttle and headed for route I-84. She knew that it would be the fastest way to get to the Danbury Mall where many of the non-combatants were. The truck followed as she got onto the highway. She slowed a bit to allow Ron and Derek to catch up but then noticed the lights of one of the odd-looking bladeless helicopters in the not too far distance.

Derek had the window between the cab and the bed of the pickup open. He saw the lights in the rear view mirror. "Shit Derek, they're coming! Oh God, they're coming! There's no escape!" Derek heard Ron panicking.

"Shoot at them moron!" Derek yelled at him.

Ron moved the machinegun and opened fire on the bladeless helicopter. He had never fired a heavy machinegun before. Actually, prior to the Flash Storm, he had never even held a pistol, let alone handled heavy artillery. His inexperience, coupled with the overwhelming fear that filled him as the distance between the truck and the Seekers closed, made his shots highly inaccurate. Almost all of the bullets passed by the strange aircraft and flew harmlessly into the night. He did not know how many but at least a couple of the rounds struck but did not seem to be slowing the vehicle down.

"Derek! They're not going down! I shot at 'em and they're not going down!" Ron was panicking again, almost to the point of tears. The Seekers opened fire with a chain gun. The rapid fire began tearing up the highway behind the truck. Closer and closer they came until they started striking the bed of the beat up vehicle, punching massive holes through it. The line of fire approached fast and a round ripped through Ron's abdomen, tearing him in half. He was still alive when the top half of his body landed on the road, spilling his organs from underneath. Another round struck Derek's head, bursting it as if it was a melon. Their vehicle had been torn apart by the fury of the high velocity rounds.

Lexi saw that the Seekers made quick work of her companions. She quickly averted her eyes from her rear view mirror. Ron and Derek had been irritating, but they did not deserve to die like that. She saw the turn for the mall coming and she took it.

The Seekers were still too far away to be accurate, which was fortunate, because they began to fire. Chunks of the exit bridge that she was on were blown off; she would not be going back the way she came. Now on route 7, she hit the throttle again while it was still straight to gain some ground, then she laid off to take the severe bend and get to the road where the mall was.

The ramp was only about half of a mile long, but it felt like it took forever. She was horrified when she got off the exit to see that the Seekers had already begun to lay siege to the mall. From the air and land they were pressing the rebels. She could see that most of the rounds that were being fired off by her comrades were either missing their targets or harmlessly bouncing off the super hard mesh armor of the savage dark warriors. The massive parking lot in front of her was a slaughterhouse. Rebel after rebel were gunned down by the ruthless barrage from their mysterious enemies. The thought of continuing to watch was unbearable.

Lexi's father had been the ridicule of the town. He was what many referred to as a "gun-bunny". He even made his own ammunition, not trusting the "government-controlled retailers" to provide the quality ammunition he was looking for. He had been laughed at for his ways. When the federal gun ban was passed, their house was ransacked by law enforcement. Dad, being the smart, if not suspicious man that he was, had hidden the weapons in a lead-lined underground cache. He did not survive the coming of the Seekers but Lexi did, and she escaped with some of the armor piercing rounds her father had made. The last clip for the pistol that her father had given her was loaded and ready to go. She claimed she could shoot a whisker off of a cat from fifty feet away. Now was the time to find out.

Lexi knew she had one chance to get a drop on the Seekers. While the heavy artillery was focused on the building, she headed straight across the road, through the intersection, and into the parking lot. Pulling her pistol she fired while in motion. The first round struck a Seeker in the back of the head, penetrating the helmet, and dropping the dark soldier to the ground. Her next round penetrated the neck of the Seeker standing next to the one that she had dropped, inflicting another fatality to enemy forces. Two more rounds penetrated the chest plate of another Seeker who had two thirteen year old boys in its sights. The enemy soldiers

31

began to return fire. As robotic as they seemed, she was a small target on a fast moving motorcycle and the shots went wild.

Lexi continued to move around the lot, firing her gun when she could and attempting to draw fire. Unfortunately, several of the rebels weren't armed with guns, and even the ones that were had been quite ineffective. They were being slaughtered. Despite her vast skill with firearms and a motorcycle, she alone was not enough to defeat the armada that had invaded. As more and more rebels fell, two of the bladeless helicopters approached on either side. Her gun was out of ammunition. She looked up and saw the chain guns pointing at her and knew that this was it. She dropped her gun to the ground and put her hands on her head. She wasn't sure if that would work figuring that they most likely would blow her apart anyway, but they didn't. They just held their positions.

Lexi noticed that most of the fighting had stopped. What remained of the rebels holed up in the mall had been captured and were being paraded into the parking lot. She had no idea what was going on outside of her line of sight. She heard a few explosions come from within the building, brief spats of gunfire, screams, then nothing. She could only assume that the last of the rebels that were holed up inside were being killed.

A third bladeless helicopter arrived and landed near her. The contraption barely made any noise and she wondered how it managed to fly in the first place as it had no apparent propulsion systems. A side door opened and an individual stepped out. He was tall, well over six feet, compared to her height of five and a half feet. The man did not appear to be a Seeker. Despite similarities in armor, there were different markings and he did not wear a helmet. He did have two of the Dark Ones with him however.

The tall, armored man walked over to Lexi, with a stride of confidence and victory. As he got close, he bent over and picked up her gun. "You did all of this damage with this little thing? You are quite the specimen aren't you? I am Commander Mullen, and you are?" he asked.

"Not impressed. If you're going to kill me then just get it over with you Seeker bastard!" Lexi snapped.

Mullen laughed, "Resilient to the end I see. I am no Seeker, but I do command them. They are quite obedient. It's interesting that they do not strike the fear in you that they do all of the others.

Very fascinating."

"So you're just a traitor then, slaughtering innocent people," she growled.

"So near-sighted. I am a traitor to nothing. Lord Zodiac has a vision of a world without chaos. A world without conflict. He sees a world where the planet is healed and war is a thing of the past," Mullen informed her. "And there is no such thing as an innocent person."

"And we all start singing Kumbaya and hug trees. That really doesn't sound like someone who's responsible for the deaths of millions," Lexi resisted.

"More like billions really, but those are details. How about you tell me how you are immune to the fear aura of the Seekers," Mullen asked.

"How about you tell these two to stop pointing their guns at me or I'll shove one of them up your ass," she threatened.

"Wow, it's too bad we have to dissect you to find the answers that we're looking for," Mullen retorted. He then motioned to the two Seekers standing by him, "Take her. Keep her separate from the others. We'll sort the rounded up rebels into combatants and non-combatants."

"Why?" asked Lexi.

"Why would you care?" inquired Mullen.

"Humor one who is about to be a science experiment," Lexi stated, still not showing any sign of fear.

Mullen did not bother to hide his sadistic smile, "Very well, I will entertain your whim, if not for my own amusement. The non-combatants will be put to work, the combatants will become Seekers…As for you…well…you will be cut open and analyzed for whatever trick you have that allows you to resist fear so well. If we can spare you, then you will have the honor of joining Lord Zodiac's Grand Army as a Seeker also."

"Go to hell, I won't join you!" Lexi spit at him.

"My dear, you won't have a choice, when we remove your frontal lobes and reprogram your brain, you will be unquestioningly loyal," Mullen laughed.

Most others would never have had the gall to do what she was about to do. Natural fear and self preservation instincts would take over and force the person to go along with the enemy and hope for a chance to escape. Alexis Hera did not have such instincts however. Hidden in the sleeve of her jacket was another pistol. It was small but up close, with armor piercing rounds, it was enough. Flicking a hidden mechanism, the weapon slid out into her hand. She immediately fired on one of the Seekers with the gun pointed at her and put a hole in its blank, menacing face-plate. Before the other one could react, she dropped into a roll and went between the extremely tall Mullen's legs. She stood up on the other side and fired again, putting a hole in the other Seeker's head. Mullen spun around just in time to see the look on Lexi's face as she put a bullet in his, dropping the Seeker commander. She grabbed her other gun from his newly fallen corpse and hopped onto her motorcycle.

The other Seekers must have been disrupted by the death of their commander as they hesitated in initiating a counter-attack. That hesitation bought her enough time to start the bike and take off. The Seekers began to fire on her but their shots went wild. Two of the bladeless helicopters pursued.

Lexi knew she could not go to Hartford; the rebels there were gone. The next logical choice was New Haven. She had been a resident of Connecticut for her entire life so she knew multiple ways to get to the same place. She decided that she would stay off I-84, with it being a main highway. Route 25 to 15 would get her to where she needed to go and without the traffic that once plagued the main roads in this region of the state. She hoped that she could dodge the Seekers that she noticed following her.

For several years, new motorcycles had no longer been equipped with an off switch for the lights. It was considered a safety feature and at the time it was. In this new world order however, it was a liability. Fortunately, a month prior, foresight had caused Lexi to rewire her bike so that she could shut the lights off to avoid aerial detection. Flipping her after-market switch, she pulled off the main road and into the wilderness. She pulled over and waited for a few moments. The Seeker aircraft were circling overhead shining their lights into the area. When they could not find her, they continued on to look for her. It was at that point that she backtracked to pick up route 25 again and continued on her way.

When Lexi was sure that things were clear, she flipped the

lights back on and continued to ride. Despite the protective coverings, she was starting to get cold and was concerned that her reflexes might not save her if she could not see an obstacle far enough ahead. With a comfortable view in front, she began to think about what Commander Mullen had told her. He had talked about lobotomizing rebels and creating slaves and Seekers out of them. But what were the slaves for? How does one program the human brain? She hoped that the rebels in New Haven could shed some light on what she had discovered. She figured that they may need to capture a Seeker alive.

Despite having had five months to get used to the new conditions, it was still surreal that the roads were no longer bustling with cars. Matter of fact, she was probably the only one left crazy enough to even be on the road. Everyone knew that the Seekers primarily struck at night, which was the most advantageous to them.

As Lexi sped down the deserted roadway, she tried to focus on her task and not think about the slaughter that she just witnessed. She tried not to think about the fact that they stood no chance against Zodiac's advancing forces. There was no army coming to help. There was no one to call. They were on their own against the vast and murderous forces of the mysterious dictator. All she could do was to keep on surviving. Her attempt to keep her mind from wandering failed miserably, and a single tear ran down her cheek, under her helmet.

Chapter 5

Air Force One used to have the distinguished function of transporting the President of the United States to various areas of the world. It was heavily armored and had more backup systems than anyone could have ever imagined. It even had an escape pod for the president with a tracking device in the event of a worst case scenario. It was a magnificent plane, and Zodiac decided to have a second one built. The first was for him, the second was for General Callous. The dictator knew that truly loyal and qualified individuals were extremely difficult to come by and despite his paranoia of independent thought, he needed some people to keep their free will. Despite his immense power, he could not be everywhere at once and all supervisory personnel needed to have their minds to direct the Seekers and the slaves.

The General sat in the "war room" on his craft while it was in flight toward what only a few months prior had been the state of Connecticut. He had two individuals with him. One was a lackey who had not been lobotomized, the other a Commander. There were no longer the large number of ranks that there had been in the military. Zodiac thought it was facetious and a waste. He had one general to lead in North America, where he had his greatest level of control. He allowed Callous to appoint a handful of lackeys to assist him. Finally, no unit of Seekers could go anywhere without a Commander at least in contact, and no slaves could work on a project without a Commander that was reachable as they could not think for themselves, only follow orders. For every Commander there was at least one "backup" Commander in case something happened to the primary.

On the view screen, the image of a man wearing Commander Armor appeared. He was a middle-aged man, probably in his mid to late 40's. He had a full head of gray hair but that was probably the only sign of age that his body showed. He was in peak condition. "General Callous, sir," the man said.

"Commander Triton, what happened to Commander Mullen?" asked Callous.

"He's dead sir, killed by one of the stinking rebels," responded Triton.

"Vincent Black was there?" Callous was curious.

"No, sir. He was killed by another rebel," Triton became a bit hesitant.

"And how, pray tell, was this allowed to happen!? No officer has been killed by anyone except for Black or by Lord Zodiac himself since this conflict began. Do we have another altered human on our case?" Callous was obviously annoyed more than he was concerned.

"I don't think so sir. She..."

Callous slammed his fist on the table and caused it to snap. "She? SHE!? Some girl killed a Commander in the Grand Army? Either Mullen was an idiot, or the rest of you are defective," Callous snapped.

"No, sir. She's obviously highly skilled but even more so, she seems unaffected by the fear aura of the Seekers. The only casualties that we suffered were from her," Triton reported.

Callous went from irritated to visibly intrigued. "So, Mullen underestimated her. The fool deserved what he got and probably suffered a much better fate than if Lord Zodiac had dealt with him. What about the rest of the rebels?"

Mullen kept a straight face. "Those that survived have been contained. We are sorting them now."

"Excellent, the more slaves we have working on the project, the faster it will reach completion," Callous announced. "So all of the rebels have been drawn out in the Danbury area?"

"Yes sir. The airport had some additional rabble hidden there, but we flushed them out easily. The Seekers are combing the rest of the city now. Once it's clear, as per orders, we will move on to the rebel cell at Bridgeport. We have another squad, the one from

Hartford, heading to New Haven," Triton said proudly.

"Do you have any identity on the woman who managed to cause the damage?" asked Callous.

Triton shook his head, "Not yet, the rebels aren't talking."

"Then kill them one by one, in front of the rest, until they answer!" Callous barked.

Triton nodded, "Yes sir."

"And Commander Triton? Call me back as soon as you have the answer I am confident that you are going to get." Callous gazed at him, his point having been made abundantly clear.

"You will be hearing from me soon," Triton said giving every indication that he understood completely. The communication then ended.

Commander Triton stepped out of the bladeless helicopter after his conversation with General Callous and walked over to a group of rebels that the Seekers were holding at gunpoint, their shoulder lights were practically blinding the already frightened people. The rebels were kneeling on the ground with their hands behind their heads, looking down at the ground. This particular group numbered at least one hundred, and there were many more groups all over the parking lot. He approached a young man, actually more a kid than anything else. The boy couldn't have been more than 15 or 16 years old. He had a shaved head and olive colored skin. If there were still schools, he may have very well been on a football team. "Who was the woman on that motorcycle? What's her name?"

The young man didn't respond. The commanders knew that Zodiac didn't care for playing around with the "prey". He always said that it was a waste of time. So Triton responded to the silence in the way that the dictator would have if he had been there; he grabbed the young man's head and twisted it, so that all around him could hear the crack of his neck as his now lifeless body dropped to the ground.

"Why are you doing this you monsters!?" a woman, probably in her thirties, stood up and screamed. Triton didn't even acknowledge. As if knowing what he was thinking, the closest Seeker raised his rifle and fired a single shot through the woman's forehead, spraying blood and pieces of her brain on the people behind her. The lifeless corpse fell to the asphalt with a thump.

"I want to know who that woman on the motorcycle is!" Triton yelled over the frightened cries. "Start answering or I will count to three and then start killing you one by one until I have my answer!"

"We don't know who she is," a man, probably also in thirties yelled out.

"That's not an answer," Triton said as he pulled out a pistol and shot one of the rebels in the head. The bullet passed through in a downward angle, also passing through the chest and heart of the rebel behind, continuing on to hit the leg of a third rebel, who yelped in pain and fear.

"Man, none of us know who she is!" the same man yelled.

"None of you know? Okay, then you're all useless," he said. He didn't even need to give his order verbally. He waved his hand and the Seekers began firing on the group. Blood and flesh flew and splattered as rebel after rebel fell under the barrage of gunfire. Triton laughed a hideous, almost demonic laugh as he heard the cries and pleas of each person get snuffed out. Internal organs spilled and limbs flew off as the brutal attack did more than kill this group; it mutilated them.

"Stop! Oh please no! Oh my God," Triton mockingly cried out until all one hundred were on the ground. "Make sure they're all dead; shoot them until they turn to juice if you have to."

The savage commander walked several feet to the next group. "You all just saw that. It's the penalty for lack of cooperation. I want to know who that woman on the motorcycle was or the Seekers will slaughter you too. And just for the record, I hope you don't answer because that was a hell of a lot of fun."

"Alexis Hera. Her name is Alexis Hera," a voice came from the crowd.

Triton stopped, put his hand to his ear and said, "Repeat that, and stand up so I can see you."

A woman, most likely in her early forties stood up. She had streaks of gray through her brunette hair and her face was beginning to show some wrinkles. "Her name is Alexis Hera. She's lived in Danbury for years."

"Well now, the rest of you can thank her, she just saved your lives. Come over here and you two, next to her, you come too for your reward," Triton summoned.

The woman began to make her way over, still holding her hands on the back of her head. The two individuals next to her were both men in their early twenties. They looked at each other without standing up, a bit confused.

"Yes, you two, I don't have all damn night, get up and come over here." Triton made a hand gesture.

The two men obliged and within moments were standing next to the woman who revealed Lexi to the demented commander. "Wh...wh...what is our reward?" one of the men asked.

Triton opened up with a large grin and answered, "You get to entertain me." He pointed his gun at one of the young men and fired a round through his throat, causing him to fall to the ground writhing and bleeding. He quickly pointed it to the other man and fired a shot through his open mouth, before he could scream. The bullet tore out the back of his throat and killed him instantly. The bleeding man watched as the body of his fellow rebel dropped.

"Why? Why? Why? WHY!?" the woman kept repeating.

"Because I can. Because you are all a blight on this planet. A disease. You especially are the lowliest of the low, betraying one of your comrades to save your own skin. You deserve to die like the animals that you are," Triton said as he struck her on the side of her head with his pistol, causing her skull to cave in. Moments after her body dropped, the first man breathed his last.

"Take the rest of them and load them on the trucks. We should be able to recycle these pathetic insects into something more useful," Triton waved his hand around and the Seekers obeyed without a word and without emotion. Triton returned to the aircraft to report to Callous.

"General Callous, I have wonderful news," the voice of Commander Triton sounded through the speaker. Callous had the broken table removed from the room.

"Stop sounding like a fairy and get to the point," Callous responded.

Triton was visibly uncomfortable, "Um...yeah...um...the name of that girl is Alexis Hera. Apparently, she's a Danbury native."

"Good. Now get the rest of those rebels to processing so we can put them to actual use," Callous ordered and he cut off the communication. He already heard the clicking of buttons on a keyboard. It was the commander that was with him.

"Quick search should pull up any records we have on her," the commander stated. A few moments later, images flooded the screen where Triton's image once was. "Now this is interesting. She is a young lady; her birthday was on the day of the Flash Storm. How ironic. Father was military…hmmm…there are gaps in service, most notably for the two years prior to Lord Zodiac's ascension."

Callous was intent on the screen, "What of her medical history?"

"Right here," responded the commander.

The general's pupils dilated as he read the reports, "Now that IS interesting. She apparently had been diagnosed with a brain tumor at age 13. They originally believed that it was terminal but they later discovered that they could use an experimental procedure to remove it. The intrusion wasn't without side effects though; there was damage to her amygdala. This woman is unable to feel fear of any kind."

"General, this could be dangerous if the rebels find out," pointed out the lackey.

"The rebels are nothing more than bands of scared and fearful fools. They will learn nothing. I do feel that we should make it a priority to find her though. Vincent Black may be public enemy number one, but she is public enemy number two. Have her image broadcast to all field commanders and Seekers. I want her ALIVE, make sure that is crystal clear," Callous ordered.

"Yes sir," both said at once.

"Now leave me," Callous directed. Both men obliged without a word or hesitation. Once they were gone and the door closed, the general initiated another communication. Within moments, the featureless faceplate of Zodiac's helmet appeared on the view screen.

"What do you have to report General Callous?" Zodiac asked.

"The rebels in Danbury have fallen, but we have a small problem," Callous informed him.

Zodiac did not respond immediately, but Callous felt as if someone was inside of his head. "You don't truly believe that this is a small problem, I can feel that from here," the dictator chided.

"It may be nothing, but one of the rebels was able to fight back, without fear. I looked into it further and it turns out that she had brain damage to her amygdala, the section of the brain that controls fear responses amongst other things," Callous lectured.

"I know what the amygdala is. So the fear auras of the Seekers had no affect on her," Zodiac was thinking out loud.

"None. She doesn't seem to be affected by fear at all. She was able to kill several Seekers as well as Commander Mullen before escaping," Callous confirmed.

"What is her name?" inquired Zodiac.

"Alexis Hera," replied Callous. "I ran her through special ops databases as well as any black ops I could find and there were no matches. It seems as if she is just really good with a gun and not afraid of anybody or anything."

Zodiac appeared agitated despite having his face hidden, "Did you run her through Project Scorpion?"

"Well...no. What little information we have is not even remotely complete and I thought there was only one survivor," Callous defended.

"IDIOT! Always check all angles, especially when it comes to the former American government. Those fools were the greatest liars and hypocrites ever to exist in this world!" Zodiac barked.

Callous felt a chill run down his spine and he obediently replied, "Yes Lord Zodiac."

"And you were right to order her to be taken in alive. Damage to that section of the brain was not something that I anticipated would become a problem, but I do not wish for Vincent Black to learn of this," Zodiac stated. Callous was not sure he would ever get used to his leader's knowledge of his surface thoughts.

"As you command," Callous said with a full acknowledgment of his master's status.

Chapter 6

"Are you kidding me? Did any of these people think before they acted!?" Vincent shouted in an angry voice as he looked ahead through the windshield at what was once the bustling campus of Southern Connecticut State University. The campus was intact, but there were modifications that had been made. A massive fence with barbed wire had been erected around the grounds. This group managed to dig up some weaponry because there were several individuals set up on roof tops as snipers holding rifles with scopes. Unfortunately, they were not very well hidden and one in particular was wearing a neon green t-shirt that may as well been a neon sign flashing the words "Shoot Me, I'm a Sniper." In addition, somehow, they had managed to rig power to certain areas; one could see artificial lights from quite the distance.

Josh was stunned at the outburst, "What's the problem, I thought you'd be impressed?"

"Okay, it's bad enough these idiots decided to set up shop above ground where the SATs can see them, but they light the way too? There're no damn power stations anymore; this place looks like a giant Christmas tree! Nice job with the snipers too, I could see them from a mile away. They'll be the first to die when the Seekers come," Vincent ranted.

Talbot looked over at him and said, "Yeah, I guess it *is* a little foolish."

"Do people really have no idea what they're facing? Is there really no one around with military or police training, or just some good online video game experience?" asked Vincent.

"Most of the off duty military were killed or went missing after the Seekers first came. We have a few. They're the ones who set this up," Josh informed. "As for gamers, well, no one listens to us."

"How do we get in there?" Vincent inquired with a seriousness in his face that virtually made his scorpion tattoo jump off and start stinging.

"Go around here, there're gates. They'll let us in over there," Talbot pointed. Vincent pulled up to the gates and a young man, probably not even 18 yet was standing guard with an AR-15 pointed to the Mustang.

"Who are you and what's your business?" the young man said, attempting to sound tough. He wasn't able to pull it off very well.

"I'm here to save your asses from yourselves and your idiotic setup," Vincent barked as he looked at the unsure teenager.

"Oh…well…um…wait a minute…You're the man in black. The scorpion guy," he said after he noticed Vincent's conspicuous and famous tattoo.

Vincent clapped his hands slowly, "Yeah, that's me, now open the damn gate."

"Wait, is that a Seeker?" the kid asked while pointing.

"Yeah, now let's move it, there's no time to screw around!" Vincent barked. The young man motioned and two more individuals opened the gates. He drove in and pulled into one of the parking spaces.

Josh gave Vincent a cold stare, "You didn't have to be so hard on him."

Vincent turned and looked at him with a look of disgust, "We don't have time for touchy, feely shit. People are being wiped out every day and this place has a big red bull's eye on it. The Seekers are probably already done looking for us and on their way here." After a few moments he continued, "And I have to say, this is the first time I've seen so many empty parking spaces on a college campus."

Josh couldn't even respond. He knew Vincent was right. The rebels in New Haven were in danger. They didn't know about the Apocalypse Dozer, or the extent of the capability of the Seekers. It would be a slaughter worse than Hartford. They all got out of the car, Andromeda still remaining silent. Vincent reached in and grabbed the still unconscious Seeker and threw him over his shoulder. There were several people around, some carrying weapons, some not. Most of them looked and smelled as if they hadn't bathed in weeks. The ones in eye shot were staring at the group and eying Vincent, whose existence many believed was just a story. They saw him with what appeared to be a Seeker over his shoulder and they were in awe.

"Who's in charge here?" Vincent yelled out, not feeling the need to go looking around.

"I am," he heard from behind him. When he turned around he saw a sight he did not expect. The person who answered was a young man, probably in his early twenties. He stood about 6 feet tall and looked to weigh about 190 lbs. He was well toned and his stance indicated that he had served in the military. Standing next to him was a brunette woman with red highlights. She was about 5' 8". She was quite attractive and by all appearances was in her third trimester of pregnancy.

"And you are?" asked Vincent.

"I'm John Decker. This is my wife Evelyn," John introduced.

"People just call me Eve or Evey," Evelyn added.

Vincent stared at John, "Good, you have an evacuation plan?"

"Of course we do," John answered.

Vincent looked at him with an intensity that once again almost made his scorpion tattoo appear to come alive, "Then you need to implement it. Now!"

"What the hell are you talking about!?" John took a step backward.

"You are looking at the only survivors from the attack on Hartford. Have you heard anything from the other cells?" inquired Vincent.

Eve gripped her husband's arm, "We haven't heard anything from Danbury, they missed their last check but they're usually behind anyway."

"They're most likely dead, and you'll be too if you don't get everyone out of here!" Vincent warned.

"We're well fortified and much better armed than Hartford.

We can't keep running from the Seekers. We need to stand up to them," John put his foot down.

"You'll get crunched up by the Apocalypse Dozer if you stay," Josh interjected.

John had a look of skepticism, "What the hell is that?" A group of onlookers were gathering. "Is that a Seeker over your shoulder?"

"Yeah. And to answer your other question, the Apocalypse Dozer is a giant monstrosity that'll come through here and rip down everything, and kill anyone in its path," Vincent stated.

Eve put her hand on her pregnant belly and said, "John…"

"I'll handle this Eve. Listen, what's your name Mr. Man-In-Black?" asked John in a sarcastic voice.

"Vincent," he answered.

"Vincent, you come storming in here with outrageous claims of some giant machine that's going to wipe us all out and you have a Seeker over your shoulder. You understand that I can't just order an evacuation on this," John said, standing his ground.

Vincent laid the Seeker on the ground, which turned everyone's attention away from the quarreling men. He then moved almost too fast for the human eye to see, rushing up to John Decker, grabbing him by the neck with one hand and grabbing his sidearm with the other. The movement ended with Vincent standing in front of the rebel commander, pointing his own gun at his head. "We don't have time to deal with this shit. Order an evacuation and stop being an idiot. You have four witnesses here and your arrogance is going to get all of these people, including your pregnant wife killed."

"How did…"

"I would have to be an idiot not to figure it out," Vincent cut her off.

Several rebels took note of the confrontation and drew their guns. They were uneasy but held fast. "Listen, I don't know how the hell you moved that fast but you aren't going to threaten me into ordering an evacuation. How do I know you don't work for that insane dictator Zodiac?" John asked. "You especially seem to know a lot about him and his dark army."

"We have no time Vincent, if they don't want to evacuate, we should just get the hell out of here," Talbot urged. It was then that they heard the sound of a motorcycle. Vincent flipped the safety of the gun on and handed it back to John. He looked behind him and saw someone dressed in tight fitting, black motorcycle leathers riding a sports bike.

"Damn rice burners," Vincent commented.

Everyone then turned and watched the stranger get off of the bike. The visitor was definitely a woman, the form fitting clothes revealed that. She removed her helmet, revealing the face of a highly attractive blonde. "Am I interrupting something?"

"No, nothing at all. And who the hell are you?" asked John, wondering when his camp became so popular.

"My name is Alexis Hera, I was stationed in Danbury. We were attacked by a swarm of Seekers, I think I'm the only one who escaped, everyone else was either being taken prisoner or being murdered," she explained.

"Looks like you should re-think your earlier statement about evacuation commander," Talbot advised.

"Look Decker, Zodiac has control of the satellites. Any above ground rebel buildup will be found. This place, as impressive as it is, just painted a target on you and everyone else here," Vincent stated.

John looked at Eve, who merely nodded her head. Finally, he picked up his radio and said, "Evacuate. This is a code red. Everyone get out of here, now."

Lexi walked over to the downed Seeker while this conversation took place. "You captured a Seeker?"

"Yeah, and we noticed that he's lobotomized," Josh felt he needed to speak.

"Holy shit!" Lexi exclaimed in a low voice while looking over the dark warrior. He didn't look so tough in his current condition. She suddenly stopped and looked up.

Josh caught the quick change of expression, "What is it?"

"That noise, it sounds like a thunderstorm, but the night sky is completely clear," Lexi stated.

Vincent looked over. His face sank. He felt the tingle in the back of his head even before he saw the lights and the movement, as well as the massive silhouette of what he knew to be...

"Shit. It's the Apocalypse Dozer and the Seekers. They're here, LET'S MOVE OUT!" Vincent yelled.

"What the hell is an Apocalypse Dozer?" Lexi asked, seemingly unconcerned.

Josh just grabbed her arm and pulled, "No time for that now, let's get the hell out of here!"

The scene was utter chaos. No matter how well planned something is, the human factor always enters. In this case, it was a human factor driven by shear, primal fear. It was the fear of being exterminated. They weren't ready for what was coming, what they saw closing in on them. The rebels were scattering, running in circles. People forgot where they were assigned to go, they fought with each other. Vincent looked in front of him and saw a rebel who was not paying attention run into Eve, knocking her to the ground. He immediately rushed to the pregnant woman's side and hoisted her up as if she weighed a few ounces, even with the Seeker once again slung over his shoulder. "Where the hell is your escape vehicle?" Vincent yelled to John.

"Follow me," John responded. Vincent obliged. Talbot, Andromeda, and Josh all followed out of instinct. When Lexi turned to her bike, she saw that it had already been nabbed by someone who took off with it.

"Hey, that's my bike dammit!" she yelled. It fell on deaf ears. She then turned and hurried to catch up with Vincent's group. The rumbling was getting closer. It was easier to make out what the sound really was. It was whole buildings being crushed by the enormous Apocalypse Dozer. It plowed through, its massive spinning blades grinding up any structure in its path.

The numerous lights of the Seekers were getting brighter and brighter. The sound of gunfire could be heard in the distance as miscellaneous people still scattered about New Haven were being gunned down. Those in the path of the massive machine of death and destruction were shredded to tiny pieces. The panic at the former university was getting worse. Not a single bus had departed yet.

John was hurrying, followed by his wife, Vincent's group, and the new arrival, Alexis. A few stragglers had joined up. They were running toward a parking garage. "Up ahead, in there, that's where the buses are," John said. They all heard the next sound, the sound of "fzzzt". In a flash, a series of missiles streaked through the sky and struck the parking garage. Not built to withstand a

48

bombardment of Hellfire missiles, it began to collapse.

"Everyone back!" Vincent yelled. The group turned and hurried in the opposite direction. Andromeda finally made a sound, it was a scream. Between the rumble of the collapsing parking garage and the rumble of Zodiac's forces moving in, the noise was virtually unbearable. Coupled by the night with the extremely bright lights and the chaotic screams of the frightened rebels, it was like a nightmare made reality.

"Oh God, that was our way out! Oh God!" Eve panicked.

"That's where all of the buses were huh?" asked Talbot. The group had stopped for a moment.

John threw his arms in the air, "Yeah, that's it. We're screwed."

Vincent walked over to him and looked him in the eyes, "We don't give up. EVER. This campus is big, what about shuttle buses. That would be big enough for us."

"Shit…of course, we even loaded those with supplies, just in case. C'mon, we need to hurry," John demanded as his heart was racing. They hurried as fast as they could.

The bladeless helicopters were over campus now, with Seekers descending into the crowd. Gunfire was erupting as the rebels were so consumed with fear, they could not fight back with any effectiveness. It was a slaughter. The dark soldiers began entering buildings to capture non-combatants hiding out within. Anyone who resisted was shot on the spot. Interestingly enough, most were so filled with fear, they gave up almost immediately.

The building that the group was approaching had a sign in front that was labeled "Department of Public Safety and Campus Police". Parked outside were three shuttle buses. "Up ahead, the one on the far left," John stated. They all headed directly for it. Explosions could be heard all over the place as more Hellfire missiles were striking targets. The rumbling of the Apocalypse Dozer was getting louder and louder.

Everyone got on board the shuttle. Talbot looked at John and said, "Go, be with your wife. I see the keys are in the ignition, I'll drive. I know the roads in this state like the back of my hand and I'll get us far from that giant monster."

John simply nodded and went all of the way into the back with Eve. Andromeda, Josh, and the three stragglers followed.

Vincent stayed up in front and unloaded the captured Seeker onto the seat next to him. Lexi sat in the front too, across the aisle. Talbot closed the door and turned the engine on. He quickly put it in reverse, backed up, and then slammed it into drive so they could head out.

"You okay there Talbot?" Vincent checked.

"Scared out of my mind, but I know it's just the Seekers' bad vibes," Talbot stated as he headed to the edge of campus. He crashed through a section of fence and managed to make it onto the road. As they pulled away, Vincent stood next to Talbot. He then turned around and looked directly at John.

"Hey Decker, are we being followed?" asked Vincent.

"No, those bastards are hovering on the campus, they probably didn't even notice us," John answered.

Vincent turned back around and looked at Talbot, "If there are any tunnels or anything we can park in, let's do it. We need to make sure we stay off SAT imaging...At least we have a full tank of gas."

"Thankfully," Talbot said, his heart rate was slowing back down a bit.

Lexi got up and went over to Vincent's seat, next to the Seeker. She looked him up and down. She poked at his cheeks with no response. She then opened his mouth, also with no response. Then she opened his left eye and saw that the pupil was dilated and the eye was moving rapidly until suddenly it stopped and focused on her. The other eye immediately opened and once again the dark soldier unleashed a gut wrenching screech. Everyone in the van began to scream and cover their ears, except for Lexi and Vincent. Lexi simply said, "Shut the hell up," and punched him, knocking him out.

"Wow Vince, there's a girl after your own heart," Josh yelled out.

Vincent walked over to Lexi and said," That was impressive."

"Yeah, well, these bastards have killed enough people," Lexi responded.

"Alexis, right?" asked Vincent.

Lexi nodded, "Yeah, but people just call me Lexi. And you're Vincent, proof that the famous Man in Black IS real."

"Not famous, just trying to survive. So, you weren't scared?" inquired Vincent.

Lexi looked up at him," I can't get scared."

"Nice talent," Vincent was also making eye contact.

"You don't seem scared either," Lexi pointed out.

"I'm concerned, but I have no use for fear. It was the extreme fear caused by these Seekers that made that scene a massive panic," Vincent replied.

John whispered something to his wife. After she responded with unintelligible whispering, he walked over to join Lexi and Vincent. "What are we going to do with this Seeker?"

"We're going to see what makes it tick," Vincent stated, then turned to Talbot and asked, "Where are we headed?"

"New York. I figure we cross over and head upstate where the population is minimal and the Seekers are less likely to find an interest in us. At least that way we can regroup, maybe come up with a plan or something," Talbot answered.

"We have enough gas?" Vincent inquired, his facial expressions made it obvious that his thoughts were racing a mile a minute.

"I sure as hell hope so," Talbot stated.

Vincent tapped on the pole by the driver's seat, "Alright, let's do it."

Josh gave Vincent a look, "So, you're in charge now."

"You got a better idea, I'm all ears," Vincent responded.

John went silent. Lexi then spoke up, "Listen, I escaped from the attack on Danbury, but I learned some things from their commander right before I put a bullet in him."

"You killed a commander?" Vincent could not hide that he was impressed with the woman.

"Yeah, the asshole underestimated me," Lexi cracked a half smile.

"I'll make sure that I don't," Vincent assured.

"What's a commander, are they lobotomized too?" Talbot interjected.

Lexi shook her head, "No, this guy spoke to me. He was actually kind of a nut job."

"They're not lobotomized. They seem to have their free will," Vincent informed them.

51

"Alright, I just have to ask for a favor. Since this is going to be a long ride, can we lay all of our cards out on the table so we know what we're dealing with?" John asked.

Andromeda got up and moved over next to Eve. She sat down, pulled her knees up and put her head down. "Hey, we're getting out. We'll be safe now," Eve tried to assure the girl. Andromeda did not respond. Eve reached a hand out and put it on the young girl's shoulder, who responded by leaning over and putting her head on the soon-to-be-mother's shoulder. Tears began to stream down her face. Josh stared out the window. The three newcomers, who had not introduced themselves, sat quietly, lost in thought.

"Well, you're the leader, you go first," Lexi pointed to Vincent.

"You sure you all want me to be the leader?" Vincent asked.

"Hey, you're the superhuman one, I think that makes you the boss," Talbot replied, still watching the road. He was running the fog lights only in an effort to keep as low key as possible.

"Superhuman? What the hell is he talking about?" Lexi was looking at Vincent when she said it.

"Sure Talbot, broadcast that. You know there's more to me than just that," Vincent became defensive.

"Superhuman how?" John piped up.

"I know that. I'm just saying, if we had to put it to a vote or go about determining leadership the old fashioned way, no one here could hope to beat you," Talbot clarified.

"Now you make me sound like Zodiac. I'm just trying to keep us alive," Vincent stated.

Lexi made a whirling motion with her index finger, "Um, can we go back to the whole superhuman thing?"

"Want it or not, I think you've got it now," Talbot said.

"HEY, WHAT THE HELL IS THIS SUPERHUMAN TALK!?" Lexi shouted. Everyone stared at her for a moment.

"I'm what happens when the government plays around with things that they shouldn't," Vincent enlightened.

"Well what do you do, other than being strong as an ox?" asked John.

"He's strong as hell and has the dexterity of a cat. Sees danger coming before it happens too," Talbot interjected.

"I heal fast too," Vincent threw in.

"How fast?" Lexi was intrigued.

Vincent reached down to his boot and pulled out a knife with his right hand. He then held up his left arm for everyone to see. "This fast," he said as he thrust the blade through his forearm. He let out a small grunt from the pain.

John's heart skipped a beat. "What the hell, are you, crazy!? Why did you do that? You just screwed up your arm!" he barked. Lexi did not respond, she just continued to watch.

"Watch carefully," Vincent answered as he removed the weapon. Those up close watched as the bleeding stopped almost instantly. They were able to see the flesh grow and close layer by layer as the muscle tissue reformed, then the skin closed up over it, and then small hairs grew out of the spot where the wound had been. This all happened in a few moments, leaving no scarring.

"That's...unreal," Lexi finally commented.

"There, I've put my cards on the table," Vincent pointed out.

John reached out to Vincent's left arm and ran his fingers over the spot where he had stabbed himself and said, "How did this happen? Who did this to you?"

"I told you, some idiots decided to play with forces that they should have left alone. I'll give you my life story later," Vincent stated.

"But if we could duplicate what was done to you..."

"...you can't duplicate what was done to me. Don't even try it. Don't even think it. I said it and I meant it, this isn't a path that ever should have even been looked at, never mind walked," Vincent cut him off.

"But..."

"...No. This isn't something that you need to...TALBOT, HIT THE BREAKS!" Vincent suddenly yelled.

Talbot slammed on the breaks and the shuttle bus squealed to a halt. As he took a moment to observe outside, he saw an obstacle a short distance ahead in the form of a flipped over Volkswagen bug, next to two smashed up sedans that were unrecognizable. "What the hell? That's great. The damn road's blocked," he complained.

"An accident?" Lexi asked.

Vincent shook his head, "No, it's a damn road block. I think it may be some kind of trap."

"That whole danger sense thing?" John questioned.

"I refer to it as a sixth sense. I want everyone to keep their heads down," Vincent directed as he squatted down. Talbot turned off the internal lights. Everyone did as they were told.

"Seekers," John suggested.

"No, they wouldn't hide like this. They'd be blasting those lights in our faces to blind us and then they'd either be taking us as slaves or killing us," Lexi pointed out.

"Highway bandits. The lowest of scum. We're in a fight to survive and our own people are robbing us," Talbot said with disgust. "Ever deal with these bastards Vincent?"

The group leader sighed and rolled his eyes. "More often than I'd like to think about. Unfortunately, desperate people don't necessarily do the most logical or reasonable things. Talbot, open the door, I'm going out there. Anyone have any type of night vision goggles or anything?"

"Vince, don't go out there," Talbot warned.

"I'm coming with you, no need for you to go out there alone, healing power or not," Lexi insisted.

"Shit, nothing. We don't have night vision anything," Josh complained.

"Lexi, I'll be fine, just keep your gun ready to give me some cover if needed," Vincent instructed her.

Lexi shook her head. "I can provide better cover out there. I'm not afraid."

"Yeah, you mentioned you can't get scared. You'll have to put *your* cards on the table after we're moving again," Vincent requested. "C'mon then. The rest of you, stay in here and stay down."

Talbot opened the door. Vincent and Lexi hurried outside.

Chapter 7

Commander Jade stood on the observation deck of the BFT-5000, called the Apocalypse Dozer by the rebels, observing her handy work. Utilizing the immense doomsday vehicle and her armada of Seekers, she laid waste to almost all of what had been New Haven, Connecticut. The surviving rebels were now in her control. Flipping on the view screen, it was time to report her progress to General Callous.

"Callous here," the General said from Air Force One.

"This is Commander Jade. The assault on New Haven is complete, no casualties," Jade reported.

"Excellent. I do hope you left some of the rebel scum alive. We need more slaves for construction," Callous cackled.

"Of course, General. As we speak the prisoners are being prepared for transport to the conversion facility. The fools never stood a chance," Jade actually snickered a bit.

General Callous was quiet for a moment, and then asked, "What of the two targets of interest? This Alexis Hera and Vincent Black?"

"I am reviewing the video footage of the battle. I will report to you anything I find," Jade acknowledged.

"See that you do. I will be landing at Bradley Airport in a couple of hours to oversee the remaining phases of the construction personally. Lord Zodiac has requested that we make this a top priority," Callous informed her.

"It will be magnificent. Everything that we have worked toward is coming true, just as Lord Zodiac promised. I find that the anticipation is sending chills down my spine," Jade responded.

Callous had an amused chuckle, "I am sure Lord Zodiac has noticed your diligence to be superior to that of the other commanders. I believe that you can expect to be rewarded. The New World Order is coming to pass. He is concerned about these two individuals though, and they need to be dealt with."

"And they will be, General. Everything is falling into place. Once Bridgeport falls, the rebel cells in the Connecticut territory will be no more. Nothing will stop the supply lines for the project," Jade assured.

"As we speak, Commander Triton is mopping up the Bridgeport cell. I will need you to take the BFT-5000 there and to Danbury and flatten those miserable cities. Any of those cockroach rebels that remain in hiding can be ground up for worm food," Callous ordered.

Jade was surprised to hear of the change in command, "Triton? What happened to Mullen?"

"He was a fool who left himself vulnerable and paid the price. His stupidity can be a lesson to all commanders. The Seekers will obey your every order, so utilize their obedience and shield yourself," Callous was clearly annoyed.

"Yes general, lesson learned. I will take the Apocalypse...I mean...the BFT-5000 as you ordered once we have finished flattening New Haven," Jade promised.

"Hmmm...yes, Apocalypse Dozer. That is the nickname that those insects gave the BFT-5000. Sounds like something some idiot came up with in a dream...although it does sound quite menacing. Continue to review the footage and report back to me anything that you find that could be useful in tracking down Hera and Black," Callous directed.

"Of course, General," Jade replied. Callous then terminated the communication.

Looking at the view screens, Jade reviewed the footage taken by various Seeker units and the BFT-5000 during the attack. She scanned carefully. The chaos that erupted in the attack made her job significantly easier in conquering the doomed rebel base, but it made the job of combing through the footage much more difficult. Setting everything in slow motion, she watched the cowards scatter like cockroaches in the light. She was disgusted that at one time she felt intimidated by people like this. They were weak and sickening individuals who deserved their fate as far as she was concerned. She may have actually felt a bit of pity for them if she didn't hate them so much.

It took concentration for Jade to avoid being lost in the pleasure of watching the slaughter and destruction of those that she despised so much. She followed the footage of the assault aircraft unleashing hellfire missiles on the various structures that used to compose the Southern Connecticut State University campus. A scene that caught her attention was a group that was making its way toward the parking garage, where intelligence gathered indicated that their getaway vehicles were stored. It was then that she saw it. Both Vincent Black and Alexis Hera were amongst a small group making their way toward the structure when it was destroyed. Footage of them was shaky from there on out, but she was able to put together that they were making their way to another area of the campus. Unfortunately for her, they fell off of surveillance at that point.

Jade slammed her fist down, annoyed that they were so close. Could they have been killed in the attack? Ground up by the massive BFT-5000? No. These two were different from the others. She would need confirmation before she would report that they had been killed. Considering their orders were to keep them both alive however, she wondered what would be done to her if her forces caused their deaths. She could not worry about what ifs until she knew the two fugitives' fates.

It was at this moment that two Seekers silently entered the room with a prisoner. They threw the lowly, middle-aged man who had a hunched neck, short white hair with gray streaks, and peach fuzz all over his face, onto the floor. This man had probably been almost 6 feet tall at one time but now he was only about 5' 8" due to the malformation of his neck and back. He wasn't a normal prisoner though, he was the snitch that had given the Grand Army the information they needed to hit the base hard and fast and without casualties. They had promised this man a place in the New World Order as a reward. It was an interesting concept, since the only thing that Jade saw was a slimy worm that betrayed his people.

Jade walked over to the pathetic man and looked down at

him. He was quivering on his knees, unable to make eye contact with her. "So, you're the one who gave up the escape plan and the locations of your supplies," Jade said in a firm voice.

"Y…yes. I helped you, pl…please," the man stuttered.

Jade put her hand up to her ear and shouted, "PLEASE WHAT!?"

At the sudden increase of her volume, the man actually urinated in his pants. Tears started running down his cheeks as he shook. "Pl…pl…please d…do…don't k…k…kill m…m…me," the man could barely speak he was shaking so hard.

"You're disgusting. You remind me of people I used to know, selfish creatures that were out for their own gain even at the cost of the lives and hopes and dreams of others. You're a bully and a backstabber," Jade chided.

"I…I…I…"

"SPEAK UP, I CAN'T HEAR YOU WORM," Jade shouted. The man almost had a heart attack.

"I didn't…b…bully a…anyone," the man managed to utter.

Jade just shook her head, "No, you're even worse. You pretended to be their friend while you sold them out. You're like the people I went to school with. You're like pretty much every damn person I knew. We had this arrangement for the past two weeks so tell me, during all of that time did you hide out, pretend to be sick, or did you eat with them? Did you play cards with them? Did you take guard duty? DID YOU CONTINUE TO PRETEND YOU WERE WITH THEM WHEN INSTEAD YOU WERE GOING TO LEAD THEM TO THE SLAUGHTER!?"

"Th…they were dead…a…anyway. I…I had to d…do wh…wh…what I c…could to sur…sur…survive," the loathsome man still had tears streaming down his face, the urine in his pants began to release a stench. The Seekers were unaffected but it made Jade wrench her nose.

"Nice excuse. I doubt it makes you sleep better at night. You make me sick. I despise being sick. I despise all of you sniveling wretches. I HATE YOU ALL!" Jade yelled. All the man could muster was a scream before the angry commander's foot went clear across his face, sending him to the floor. Blood went flying from his now broken nose and split lip. She then immediately started kicking him in his abdomen and head while she continued to yell, "I HATE YOU! I HATE YOU! I HATE YOU!"

The Seekers stood by, emotionless and expressionless and simply observed. They no longer had the capacity to feel repulsed or pity. The traitor was dead well before Jade finally stopped. The enhancements given to her by wearing her commander armor made her a bit stronger than she was without it. She was breathing heavily. This episode was more draining emotionally than physically. She looked down for a moment at the bloody mess that used to be a person. He may have even been a decent person before the Flash Storm. But those days were no more. The world was irrevocably changed and this traitorous heathen was a perfect example of that.

"Get this waste of water and amino acids out of my sight," Jade ordered, waving her hand to the Seekers. They obeyed without question. Jade liked having them around. They never questioned her. They followed their orders precisely, as if they were robots. Once they cleared out of the room, Jade grabbed the com.

"Attention control, we are to finish flattening this worthless city then move on to Bridgeport and Danbury. All hail Lord Zodiac."

Chapter 8

Vincent and Lexi stood back to back, about twenty feet behind the shuttle bus. On either side were three men, six in total, who all looked like they were in a biker gang. They were all drunk and smelled of both a football locker room and a brewery simultaneously. One of them, who appeared to be about 100 pounds overweight and had a beard down to his chest, almost like a Santa Claus from hell, stepped forward. He was facing Vincent, standing about five feet away. He had not drawn his gun, but the others had various sub-machineguns and shotguns.

"That's a nice set of wheels you've got. I don't think any of you need it," the fat man said.

"Not really a fair assessment since you don't even know us," Vincent responded calmly.

Lexi whispered to Vincent, "These drunken thugs don't scare me."

"Nothing seems to," Vincent whispered back.

"Well, life isn't fair, that should've become *real* obvious on May 7th. Now, kindly have all of those on board step off, leave all of your stuff and have fun dodging the Seekers," the gruff man said in a voice that indicated he'd had too many cigars over his lifetime.

"I have a better idea. I'll forgive this little incursion because you're obviously drunk and I'll let you walk away, minus your weapons and ammunition," Vincent replied.

The whole group began to laugh, letting out little coughs from years of smoke inhalation. "You're a gutsy one, aren't you," cackled the big man. "You're not gonna find yourself so funny when we splatter you and your girlfriend's brains all over the damn road!" All of the men pointed their guns, and the fat man pulled out a double barrel shotgun.

"Hey Lexi, I'm not up to anything dishonorable with you," Vincent warned.

Lexi had a confused look, "What the hell...huh?"

Lexi was cut off as Vincent had a tingle in the back of his head. Moving in a blur, he swept the young, fearless girl off her feet and into his arms. Then he leaped into the air just at the moment the thugs fired. Being the foolish drunks that they were, their bullets went at each other. Three of them were killed instantly; one from a shotgun blast to the chest, two from rounds hitting their heads. Two fell to the ground injured. Surprisingly, only the fat man remained standing, unscathed. Vincent landed on the other side of him and put Lexi back down.

The heavy man did not even turn around. His heart rate shot through the roof, far more than if he had been confronting a Seeker. *Click!* The next sound he heard was the cocking of Vincent and Lexi's pistols. "Picked the wrong bus to hijack asshole," Vincent snapped.

"So what now," the thug asked. "You gonna let me go?"

Lexi and Vincent looked at each other then looked back at the fat man. "I think I'd rather know where it is you hang your coat chunky," Lexi taunted.

"Go to hell bitch, I ain't showin' you shit!" He was attempting to put on a brave front, even though he had his hands in the air and hadn't turned around yet.

"Turn around prick," Vincent ordered.

The street bandit turned around and gazed at the two of them. "What the hell are you?" he asked.

"I'm what happens when the government plays around with things that they shouldn't," Vincent answered.

"What is that, like your calling card?" Lexi whispered.

"Yeah," Vincent responded to her then turned his attention back to his prisoner. "So, were you just going to kill the whole bunch of us?"

"No, just wanted some supplies. These are tough times," the large, frightened man uttered, unable to make eye contact.

"People like you disgust me. We're in a war for our very survival and you're pushing people around that you perceive as weaker than you are. Tell me why I should allow you to live. Tell me why I shouldn't just end you and minimize the risk to good people," Vincent threatened.

"YOU CAN'T FIGHT THE SEEKERS! THEY DON'T EVER STOP! THEY DRIVE YOU MAD WITH FEAR JUST BY BEING NEAR THEM! I DID WHAT I HAD TO DO TO STAY OUT OF THEIR PATH," the panicky bandit yelled.

"Why don't you keep your voice down fat man before you bring the Seekers here," Lexi suggested.

He began to slowly reach for his sidearm, "Let them come. Maybe they'll take you all out..."

Bang! Bang!

Lexi and Vincent both fired a round each into the chest of the bandit, dropping his corpse to the road. "So, what about the other two who lived?" asked Lexi.

"Leave them here to die like the vermin they are. We don't live in a world where we can be touchy feely. We bring them along, they'll betray us the first chance they get," Vincent replied.

"Fair enough," Lexi agreed.

"Y...you can't just leave us here," one of the men protested.

"To quote an old campaign slogan, 'Yes We Can'," Vincent said as he walked by the injured man. "You prey on other people; you're as bad as Zodiac and his Seekers, so you can share their fate."

Lexi spit on the man as she walked by. "So, what about the barrier," she asked.

"I'll get them," Vincent informed her as he walked over to the Volkswagen first. He noticed that the others had inconspicuously picked their heads up and were watching him carefully. On a calm day, Vincent was able to press three tons, so picking up this little bucket of bolts was not an issue. He grabbed the strong point on the bumper where a tow truck would normally latch on to. He lifted the front wheels off of the ground, then got underneath and braced his other hand on the frame. He then lifted the car over his head and threw it into the trees on the side of the road. Several small animals squealed in protest, but none dared show their faces.

"Holy shit! So, uh, this whole government playing around with things stuff, can we talk about it? I knew some jocks on the sauce when I was in high school but it was nothing like this," Lexi was impressed.

"I'll tell you when we get back on the bus. It ain't roids," Vincent responded.

As Lexi and Vincent began to walk toward the shuttle, they noticed that John was standing and pointing a gun at Talbot's head. Talbot was shouting protests but they couldn't make out what he was saying. A moment later, they figured it out. He didn't want to leave the two of them there, but John was ordering him to. Talbot shifted the vehicle into drive and headed for the opening that was left when Vincent tossed the VW aside.

"That son of a bitch," Lexi said softly as she pulled her gun and took aim.

Vincent put his hand on the gun and said, "No, you might hit Talbot. Decker is not leadership material; he's acting out of fear."

"Yeah, except he's gonna leave us here with nothing," Lexi pointed out.

"We don't have 'nothing'. I doubt these thugs walk around looking for prey. There's got to be a camp or something around here," Vincent said as the shuttle headed down the road and off into the distance.

"And I'm sure they're gonna be so damn hospitable after we just killed their buddies and left them for dead," Lexi sarcastically complained.

"If you have another idea, let's hear it. Otherwise, there's a good possibility that they were it. They obviously had no idea what they were doing, otherwise they wouldn't have split three on either side of us," Vincent observed.

Lexi holstered her gun and said, "Fine. We'll do it your way."

They walked over to observe the two thugs. Both had been mortally wounded and had bled out in the previous couple of minutes. Neither would be of any use now. Vincent snorted, "Great, they're both dead. Let's head into the woods and see if we can find a trail. I'm sure these drunken idiots didn't have any idea how to cover their tracks," Vincent suggested.

As the shuttle bus continued to head further and further away from Lexi and Vincent, Eve finally spoke up, "John, you've lost it."

"No Eve, everyone else here's lost it," he grunted as he continued to hold his Beretta to Talbot's head. "You'll thank me later, I'm protecting us all."

"You just made us dump the only two people we know of who can stand up to the Seekers. You're an idiot," Josh moaned.

"Shut up you skinny little computer nerd. I served in Iraq and Afghanistan. I know how to assess a military situation. Am I the only one who saw this Vincent pick up a car and throw it like it was a tin can? He's a freak, and so is that woman who seems to fear nothing," John ranted. He was sweating bullets even though the heat was on low.

"You have no idea what you just did Decker. You've probably doomed us all," Talbot said in a deep tone.

John wiped the sweat from his face with his free hand, shook his head, took in a deep breath and said, "No, I've saved us. They're probably working for Zodiac. Did you know he's psychic? I'll bet you didn't. Yeah, so he's got some crazy ability and now we see that these two do also? DO THE DAMN MATH!"

"John, calm down. Lexi doesn't have any special powers, she just isn't afraid of things." Eve spoke in a calm voice but she was clearly nervous. "Just put the gun down and let's go back and get them."

"WE'RE NOT GOING BACK EVE. Do you understand that? Do all of you understand that? I'm in charge, I have the combat experience. The best thing we could have done is get rid of those two and we did," John shouted. His face was quite pale as he wiped more sweat from his brow.

"You're not looking so good there Decker. How about you sit down and relax a bit," Talbot suggested.

John pressed his gun into the back of Talbot's head and shouted, "DON'T TELL ME TO RELAX. I have the responsibility of your lives on my back so just shut your mouth!"

"You have no responsibility to us. You're kidnapping us. There's no other way to put it," Josh declared.

Without even looking, John calmly said, "I already told you to shut up, so if you don't, I'll be more than happy to silence you." Josh did not challenge the statement. Despite his annoyance, he was not a soldier like Decker was.

"John, please, stop doing this. What's gotten into you?" Eve pleaded.

"Eve, don't you turn against me too. I'm doing this for you and the baby," John replied.

"I have no idea what you're doing or why you're doing it, but you're obviously sick. This isn't like you," Eve stated.

"Listen to your wife man, put the gun down," Talbot demanded.

"Another word out of you and I'll empty the contents of your skull onto the dashboard. You just wanna go back and pick up those two Zodiac collaborators. Well I won't let you." John was having difficulty maintaining his focus and his hands began to shake.

"Listen to yourself. Vincent and Lexi tried to help us. I don't know why Vincent can do the things he does and I don't know why Lexi isn't afraid of anything but I don't care. It's not like you to abandon one of your own," Eve pointed out.

"DAMMIT EVE, SHUT YOUR MOUTH..."

Screeeeeeeeeeeeeeeeeeeeeeeeeeeeeeeeeeeeeeee!

The Seeker had awakened. In the turmoil, they had forgotten all about their unconscious prisoner, who was not restrained. The dark soldier stood up. John turned and tried to aim his Beretta, but the Seeker was too quick with an uppercut that knocked the former New Haven cell leader to the floor. He picked up the gun and turned, opening fire. The first rounds penetrated the chest of one of the rebels from New Haven, dropping him to the floor. The bullets went straight through and out the back of the shuttle, putting small bullet holes in the rear exit door. Andromeda tucked herself between her seat and the floor just in time to avoid a round that penetrated the seat in front of her. Josh pulled the pregnant Eve Decker down and put himself on top of her in an attempt to protect her. The remaining two rebels from New Haven attempted to work up enough courage to charge the dark warrior, but their own hesitation made them easy targets and they were both riddled with the remaining bullets in the clip.

Screeeeeeeeeeeeeeeeeeeeeeeeeeeeeeeeeeeeeeeeeee!

The Seeker let out his massive screech again as he realized he was out of bullets. Talbot took a deep breath and pushed the overwhelming fear into the back of his head. He then slammed on the breaks. The unbraced Seeker fell to the floor near John, who immediately kicked the dark soldier in the head and knocked him out once again.

Everyone was silent for a few moments, looking around at each other, except for Andromeda, who was still hiding between her seat and the one in front of her. Josh moved away from Eve who sat back up. The shuttle was stopped. Talbot was still looking out the windshield when he broke the silence and said calmly, "I think you'll understand what I mean when I say that you are relieved of your command, John Decker."

Eve rushed over to her husband. "John," she said as she shook him. He was unresponsive, his eyes were open but they were staring off into space.

"What the hell is wrong with him?" asked Josh.

"I...I don't know. John, c'mon baby, please respond to me," Eve begged.

Talbot left his seat and went to John and Eve. He knelt down and put his hand on John's forehead. "This man was drugged. I think it's ecstasy. That would explain his paranoia. Eve, does your husband do drugs?"

"N...no! How the hell do you know these symptoms?" asked Eve.

"My idiot brother and his two idiot sons all used to do E together. I'm quite familiar. I'm just curious as to how he got it in this environment," Talbot stated.

"My husband isn't a junkie. He liked his whiskey a bit but nothing like this. He wouldn't do it, especially with the baby coming," Eve pleaded.

"I believe you. He's a first timer. John, listen to me." Talbot gave him some light slaps to the face.

"I killed them. It's my fault. I'm a murderer," John began rambling.

"Shit, he's high as a kite," Talbot sighed.

"I'm sorry, I'm so sorry. I killed them. It's my fault. I'm sorry," John continued to ramble.

Eve was watching her husband with a deep concern, "What do we do?"

"We go back and get Vincent and Lexi," Talbot declared. "And for God's sake will someone tie up and put a muzzle on that damn Seeker!"

Josh leaned back, put his hands behind his head and said, "They're gonna be pissed."

"Okay, so I'll admit that following the trail of drunken street bandits was a pretty good idea," Lexi admitted. She and Vincent had arrived at the "camp" of the bandits that had jumped them. There were no guards or anything resembling a watch. They were standing in a clearing several hundred feet into the woods. The trail they had followed might as well have been paved; the brush had been flattened with constant use.

Looking over the "camp", it was made up of numerous vehicles large enough to accommodate people for sleeping. There were three full sized vans, one of which was parked permanently as it had no wheels. There were what appeared to be four of the fold-down sleeper trailers, although they looked to be older, at least 20 years. Only one of them looked like it could be moved anywhere; the other three had either no wheels or were heavily damaged. There were various other, smaller vehicles; a Bronco, two pickup trucks, and four motorcycles. There was also a larger, fifth wheel trailer. The fifth wheel stood out, not only due to its size, but the fact that the door's normal locking mechanism was missing, and was replaced with a bar and a padlock on the outside.

Both Lexi and Vincent drew their guns and began approaching the site. The only sounds they could hear were various woodland animals. They looked in the vehicles one at a time, and found they were all unlocked. There was nobody. Vincent was distracted for a moment as they walked by the motorcycles, two of which were Harleys. Lexi elbowed him, "Hey, they're not going anywhere."

"Sorry, I'm back," Vincent replied.

They began to approach the fifth wheel. It was large, probably 25 feet long. As they got closer, they realized that the windows had black out tints on them. "Black outs on the windows, a bar and padlock on the door, what the hell do they have in there?" asked Lexi.

Vincent looked at her with a half smile, "Let's find out. Cover me; this is gonna make some noise."

Vincent put his gun away and walked over to the door. He paused for a moment...no tingle. He reached his hands for the bar and grabbed hold, then stopped at the muffled sound from within. "You hear that," Vincent whispered.

"Hear what?" inquired Lexi, cocking her head a bit.

"Some kind of muffled sound," he responded as he gave the door a puzzled look. "Shit, I think someone's in there."

"Well, bust it open and we'll find out," Lexi demanded.

Vincent obliged giving the bar a good, firm tug. A tug from Vincent however, can be quite destructive and the bar, along with the locking mechanism quickly tore off the side of the trailer with minimal effort. He tossed it aside and drew his gun so fast that Lexi barely noticed him move. He stepped back and pulled the door open, then motioned for his unlikely partner to follow.

Both stepped inside, Vincent facing left and Lexi facing right. They were not expecting what they saw. There were numerous scented candles set up all over the place. Spread out everywhere were various pornographic magazines. There were also tubs of assorted lubricants on what was supposed to be functioning as a kitchen table. Vincent could see straight into what had been the master bedroom of the trailer. The bed was missing. Since the door was not the full width of the room, he could not quite make out what was in there. The entire place was lit by a few glow sticks. New ones, still in the packaging, were spread about the place.

"I can see to the end of the trailer this way. Other than being really kind of creepy, there's nothing much," Lexi stated.

"I thought you couldn't get creeped out," Vincent smirked.

"Funny. I don't feel fear, but things can still creep me out," Lexi clarified.

Both Lexi and Vincent began slowly walking down the hallway toward the bedroom. As they got closer, they did not like what it was appearing to be. When they were near enough and looked in, their stomachs were turned. They saw two men, tied up on the floor, both wearing nothing but underwear. There were various restraints around the room. It looked like a scene from an underground pornographic movie. "I can deal with Seekers. I can deal with Zodiac. This is just unreal," Lexi said as she holstered her gun. The two men looked up at them, breathing heavily.

"Mmpf. MMPF," were about as close to words as the two gagged men could get out.

Vincent also put away his gun and pulled a knife from his boot. He squatted down and cut the restraints from the two men. Both of them immediately backed into a corner, shaking violently but saying nothing. "Hey, we're gonna get you out of here," Vincent promised. The two continued to cower from him; they were looking directly at his face.

"Vince, they're looking at your tattoo," Lexi pointed out.

"C'mon guys, it's just ink, it doesn't sting," Vincent began, but then he noticed a marking on the left arm of one of the men. It was a matching scorpion tattoo. "Wait a minute, what the hell is that?"

"Y...y...you," the man on the left was shaking as if he had hypothermia.

"Why do you have that tattoo? I know why I have it, but why the hell do you!?" asked Vincent.

"Night Viper, you're him," the man on the right declared.

Vincent stopped for a moment. "Where did you hear that name? What do you know?" Vincent inquired, anger filling his voice.

"Vincent, what's Night Viper?" Lexi was confused.

"Kind of a codename that I haven't gone by in quite a while," Vincent answered then turned back to the two men. "You bastards were at Project Scorpion, weren't you? WEREN'T YOU!?"

"Y...yes...we were." The man on the right seemed to be doing the speaking.

"Then you can both stay here and rot in hell," Vincent growled and walked out of the room.

"Vince, wait up," Lexi shouted as she followed him out of the room and subsequently out of the trailer. "Vince, c'mon wait up."

Vincent stopped, turned around and looked at her. His eyes were filled with anger. "What!?"

"What the hell was that back there? We both know what was going on. Those guys have been raped who knows how many times by these animals. We can't just leave them," she stated.

"Of course we can. There isn't enough time in their miserable lives to rape them enough to make up for what they've done, what everyone at Project Scorpion did," Vincent turned, bowed his head, and clenched his fists.

"What is it Vincent, what did these people do that was so bad?" Lexi asked with genuine concern.

"They made me what I am. They made me their puppet, one of their damn super soldiers. They had no right to do what they did to any of us," Vincent said in a low, guttural voice. "Those bastards have the right to fear me. They helped create me."

Lexi had a look of concern on her face, "Are they like scientists…or something."

Vincent shook his head, "No, they were probably guards or something. Odd that they would be out here. The compound for Project Scorpion was quite a bit further north."

Lexi slowly approached, "Look, whatever they did to you, we can't just leave them here. Maybe they can help us. Where is this compound?"

"I don't remember exactly where. I was pretty disoriented when I got out of there. It's underground though, so it would be a good place for us to head to, at least to figure things out," Vincent admitted.

Lexi shook her head, "Hopefully Zodiac didn't beat us to it."

"I have my doubts that he even knows where it is. This whole thing was off the books, no record of it ever existed. There's no way the administration would ever want to be tied to a place like that. The clandestine shit that went on there would have cost them all their careers. If Zodiac is using the old records to find the locations of compounds to take over, he'll never find this one," Vincent informed her.

Lexi looked back at the fifth wheel trailer. There had been no movement of any kind that she could tell. "Look, we only have six dead thugs and this setup can sleep more than that. We should just figure out right now if we're going to grab these guys or not."

Vincent still was not looking at her. He looked up at the sky. The stars were out and there was a half moon. Out in the middle of the woods, with the star and moonlit sky, one could easily forget the death and destruction that had been running rampant throughout the world for the past five months. "Let's get 'em, they might be useful."

Lexi nodded her head. She had not known Vincent Black for very long but she suddenly felt as if she had known him for years. She realized that there was far more depth to this man than she had originally thought. She stepped up to the trailer and peered inside. "Get dressed and come on out you two."

"Is he going to kill us?" one of them called out.

"Not unless he has to come in there to get you," Lexi answered. She heard scrambling inside and she stepped back from the doorway. Vincent was still staring at the sky and not looking at them but she had the feeling that he was completely aware of what was going on. It did not take long for the two men to find ragged clothes and come outside.

Vincent continued to have his back turned to the two former Project Scorpion employees, "We're going to the compound that housed Project Scorpion. You're bringing us there."

The two men looked at each other. "The compound was shut down. It might not even be there anymore."

"It's still there, and we're going to it," Vincent argued.

"Even if it is still there, it's probably sealed. There's no way to get in. Why would you want to go there anyway?" asked one of the men.

"It was the place of my re-birth. It was a place where innocent people died. We might be able to make it do some good for once. Besides, do you have a better idea? Maybe the place you were re-assigned," Vincent said slyly.

"The Seekers destroyed our new location. We tried to set up another…"

The first man was elbowed by the second man, who said, "It was invaded and most of the people were killed or taken hostage. We escaped, only to get jumped by these sadistic bastards and kidnapped."

Vincent quickly spun around. Grabbing Lexi, he pulled her to the ground just moments before gunfire rang out. The more talkative man took several rounds to the abdomen and chest. The quieter one managed to dive to the ground. Several rounds of enemy fired passed through the space that he had been in only a moment before.

"Woo hoo! Get 'em Donny," one of the thugs yelled. It appeared as if Lexi was correct in her assessment. The six men they

71

had killed in the road did not comprise all of the bandits.

Vincent and Lexi drew their guns and scattered. More gunfire rang out, but it was clumsy. They didn't seem to be very good at hitting moving targets. Vincent, moving almost too fast for the human eye to make out, pointed his gun in mid-run and fired a well placed shot through the throat of "Donny", dropping him to the ground.

"Oh shit! Donny! Dammit how did that boy move so fast?" a street bandit called out and then started firing wildly in their direction. Lexi did a military crawl to behind the fifth wheel. Even if she *could* feel fear, she wouldn't now. These guys were so drunk that it was rendering them virtually ineffective.

Vincent jumped onto the roof of the fifth wheel. The sight of him doing that dazzled the drunken street bandits for a moment, which would cost them. Taking careful but quick aim with his pistol, Vincent put a bullet between the eyes of two of them. Feeling that telltale tingle in the back of his head, the third one managed to get him in his sights. His response was to jump onto the roof of the Bronco, then roll down and land on his feet on the other side.

"What the hell are you boy?" the bandit yelled.

Lexi used this opportunity to come up behind the bandit. He may have been drunk, but he was still fast. The thug whipped around and in a moment, they had their guns pointed at each other.

"Drop it," Lexi warned.

"You got spunk girl. Maybe we should settle this like they did in the old west. Let's draw," the bandit suggested.

Lexi quickly dropped to the ground. Before her adversary knew what had happened, her gun was pointed up while his was still pointing to where she had been standing only a moment ago. "Let's not," she responded, and then pulled the trigger, sending a round through the bottom of his chin and up through his brain, dropping him.

"Nice move," Vincent complimented as he approached her and held out his hand. Lexi grabbed hold and allowed the super soldier to pull her to her feet.

"Thanks. Not so bad yourself," she returned the compliment with a smile. "What about our 'friends'?"

"The talkative one got wasted. The other one managed to crawl underneath that pickup truck," Vincent answered. He called out to the traumatized man, "Hey, it's clear, you can come out."

He slowly crawled out, stood up, and brushed himself off. "It still amazes me," the man stated.

"What?" replied Vincent.

"I saw you. You moved like lightning. You jumped on top of that trailer from a standstill. They did a hell of a job on you," the man said in awe.

"How about you tell me your name?" Vincent demanded.

"Anthony. Anthony Salerno. Most people just called me Crisco or the Crisco Kid," he complied.

Lexi made a disgusted look with her face. "Please don't tell me that name has the connotation I think it does."

Crisco immediately became defensive, knowing that Lexi's mind was in the gutter. "Nothing nasty. I just use Crisco for pretty much all the cooking I do and a bunch of other stuff. You know it makes good hair grease?"

"Well 'Crisco', you probably know more about what they did to me than I do. I sure as hell couldn't do all of this before your goons grabbed me," Vincent gave him the look of death.

Crisco put his hands up in front of him and shook his head. "I…I don't know how much control you think I had, but I was just security. They didn't tell me too much. I heard some things while I was there. I…I could come with you and help you."

Vincent shook his head. "Or betray us."

Lexi grabbed his arm and whispered in his ear, "Vince, he might be able to help. How much do you remember about that complex?" Vincent didn't respond. "That's what I thought. C'mon, he's just some lackey, he probably had no idea."

"Very well," Vincent said in a low grunt. "I saw a bunch of useful supplies. We should load up that Bronco since it's covered. It'll be good in the snow too since we're going up north."

"D…does that mean I'm coming with you," Crisco said with a new glimmer of hope in his eyes.

"Yeah. You able to sit down?" asked Vincent.

"Vince, what kind of question is that!?" Lexi snapped.

"A serious one. I want to know how much space we're going to have in the back. If he can't sit down, he needs to lay down, less

73

room for supplies. Not trying to make light of what happened to you but this is a quest for survival and I want to grab as much stuff as possible," Vincent covered himself. Part of him just wanted to insult Crisco. He was projecting his frustrations on the man.

"Yeah. I can sit. You get used to pretty much anything including being violated," Crisco said in a far too chipper voice.

"This is a disturbing conversation," Lexi pointed out.

"Hey, what's that noise," Crisco asked. It was the sound of a motor and the sound of sticks snapping and foliage tearing. They saw what looked like head lights coming down the same path that Lexi and Vincent had not too long before.

"Any tingle?" asked Lexi.

Vincent had a half smile. "None. I think our comrades just changed their minds."

Crisco squinted from the oncoming lights. "Who?"

The shuttle they had taken from Southern Connecticut State University emerged from the trail. It came to a complete stop several feet away. The side door opened and seconds later, Chris Talbot stepped out. "I'm sorry about that episode back there. It's been dealt with. Looks like you guys came across the bandits' set up."

"Yeah. Now what the hell happened earlier?" Lexi had her hands on her well formed hips.

Talbot put his hand on his forehead. "Apparently Decker had a dose of ecstasy. It made him paranoid and he completely flipped out. Then that Seeker woke up yet again and killed those other three stragglers we had from Southern before he could be subdued."

"What about the others?" Vincent was concerned.

Talbot perked up a bit. "Josh is still his sarcastic self. Andromeda is fine but is still probably balled up between two seats. Decker's wife is worried as hell. Who's this guy?"

"Call him Crisco. He was held captive by these street thugs, and he's a lucky find. He's gonna lead us to a spot where we can lay low and figure out what we're gonna do," Vincent answered. "There're some supplies in a few of these trailers. I say we load up for the trip. I'll take this Bronco for some extra cargo room."

Josh emerged from the shuttle. "Vincent! Lexi! Awesome! Can we get the hell out of here?"

Vincent shook his head. "Not yet kid. We've got a stash to raid."

"What about that Seeker Vince. We can't keep dragging him around, he's a liability," Talbot pointed out.

Vincent looked around. "Anyone here have any medical training?"

"I used to be a field medic," Crisco piped up.

Vincent pointed with his fingers and said, "Good. You and Josh are going to open up that Seeker's skull and check his frontal lobe."

Josh had a puzzled look. "Huh?"

"I ain't no brain surgeon. It'll kill him," Crisco said.

"That's fine. He's been lobotomized. I assume you know what that is," Vincent stated.

Crisco nodded. "Yeah, I know what that is. Why would Zodiac lobotomize the Seekers? Wouldn't that make it so that they couldn't fight?"

"That's what I want to know. I want to know what makes these things tick. Obviously they are, or were at one time, human. We need to know what Zodiac did to them," Vincent was adamant.

Crisco paused for a moment. He wasn't expecting this. "I just don't feel right about doing an operation like that on a live patient. It just seems cruel."

Vincent rolled his eyes. "Then kill him. He most certainly will kill you if he gets the opportunity. Wake up soldier - there is no more Geneva Convention. There is no more Council on Human Rights. There is no more United Nations because there're no more nations to be united. Just open up that thing's skull and find out what the hell is in there!"

Josh grabbed onto Crisco's shoulder, "C'mon, he's the boss, let's just do it."

Vincent looked at Talbot. "We'll have Eve look after her husband and Andromeda. The three of us are going to raid this place and load this shuttle and Bronco with everything that we can fit. I saw some gas cans too, so we'll fill up. By the way, grab some of that booze."

Lexi stared at Vincent, "Not that I have a problem with getting drunk but aren't there more important things to be getting?"

"I can't get drunk ever since they pumped up my immune

system. Alcohol can be a good bartering tool. Besides, it may relax Crisco a bit," Vincent pointed out.

It occurred to Vincent during the following moments that none of these people really had any reason to obey his orders, other than possibly being frightened of him. They just seemed to do it. Not only that, they looked to him for direction. Twenty-four hours earlier he hadn't even known any of them and already they were obediently doing as they were told, even though some did not particularly like their assigned tasks.

There had been no time for introductions, so Josh just relayed Vincent's directive to Eve and Andromeda and by default, John. No one even responded. Eve had just nodded. He and Crisco then grabbed the Seeker and carried him outside of the shuttle bus. "Josh, I need a field medic kit to do this. It'll have a bone saw in it," Crisco stated as they laid the unconscious dark warrior on the ground.

Josh squirmed a bit, "I think we've got one on the shuttle."

"Really?" Crisco was surprised.

"Yeah, it was supposed to be an emergency escape vehicle for the rebel base in New Haven. I heard mention that they had all sorts of things stowed in the luggage compartment. I'll go check," Josh responded as he rushed off.

Crisco looked at the Seeker. "I'm sorry to do this, but you'll be better off. You have no mind of your own and that's not right. I need to ask you a favor. I need you to reveal Zodiac's secrets in regard to you guys. Please, don't die in vain."

After a few moments, Josh came back lugging a sack full of supplies. It had a red cross on it. "I hope this is what you wanted."

Crisco opened it and began pulling out instruments and tools. "Yup. First things first." He flicked a hypodermic needle. "I'm going to O.D. this guy on anesthetic. Might as well be humane…if he was lobotomized he is as much a victim as the people he killed if not more."

"He killed three people that I never got a chance to know. We should draw this out!" Josh snarled.

"It wouldn't do any good, he probably doesn't really feel pain," Crisco replied as he injected the anesthetic into the vein of the Seeker. "Besides, I've seen torture. I wouldn't want to inflict

76

that on anyone."

Josh squatted down to watch, "Fair enough."

Crisco felt for a pulse. "He's dead. Time to go in. Hand me the scalpel?"

Josh grabbed it. He was a techie but he knew what a scalpel looked like. He obeyed. Crisco took it and made an incision on the skin around the forehead. He then peeled it back. "Geeze, it always looked better in the video games."

"That's because it's not real in those. Hand me the bone saw," Crisco replied.

Josh had never seen one but he figured out what it looked like. It was the only thing in the bag that one could identify as a saw. "Here. It's not gonna cut through his whole head, is it?"

"No. I'm just trying to save time. We don't need to make sure that his head can be reconstructed," Crisco informed him as he took the saw and began to cut away at the skull. In moments, he was able to reveal the brain. He gasped at what he saw.

"SHIT! What the hell is that!?" Josh called out.

"I have no idea. It seems to be attached to his brain though. It looks man made. I need the scalpel again, and the tweezers," Crisco requested as he continued to stare at the small device inside of the head of the now dead Seeker. It looked like a spider. The "body" was an inch long capsule. The "legs" were small protrusions that entered into the brain. Crisco cut the device out of the body.

Having heard the commotion, Vincent, Lexi, and Talbot all rushed over with their guns drawn. They stopped when they saw that their comrades were still alone and they put their guns away. "What happened?" asked Lexi.

Crisco held up the small, spider-like device, "This. I've seen some crazy shit before, but nothing like this."

Vincent looked at it for a moment. "The compound that we're heading to...I assume there's still some kind of lab in which we could try to analyze this?"

Crisco nodded and replied, "There *were* labs in there, but I don't know what kind of condition they're in now. Besides, are any of us scientists or at least computer engineers?"

"I'm a computer guy," Josh piped up.

"We'll have to figure it out. That must be *some* unit to control the Seekers, but I want to know how it works," Vincent stated, staring at the odd device.

They heard quick, light footsteps. Lexi turned around to see Andromeda running to them with a small device in her hands. "Andromeda, what's that?" Talbot asked.

She handed it to Vincent who looked at it intently. "It's a transmitter. Where did you find this?"

"A dead rebel on the bus," Andromeda finally spoke.

Josh had a sudden look of panic, "What the hell!?"

"We've gotta get out of here; those Grand Army goons are probably on their way. Josh, you and Crisco put that body in one of the trailers. Talbot, you and Lexi see if you can get the bodies of the other four bandits and toss them in too," Vincent directed.

"What are you gonna do?" Lexi asked intently.

"I'm gonna grab that pickup truck, load it with those six bodies from the road and bring them back here. If the Seekers are coming, they can find this camp and blow it sky high. With any luck, they'll think we're dead - at least for a little while so we can get as far from here as possible. Hopefully they don't have a SAT overhead watching us now," Vincent answered.

Everyone immediately went to their tasks. Vincent jumped into a working pickup truck. The keys were in the ignition and it actually started right up. There was only a quarter of a tank of gas, but it was more than enough to perform its function. After he sped off, Crisco said to Josh, "so how long have you known him?"

Josh smiled, "Like 8 hours."

"And you trust him?" asked Crisco. They slumped the body of the Seeker down in one of the trailers.

"He saved my life. Same with Andromeda and Talbot. We owe him. The night we've had, we should have all been dead and we would've been if Vincent hadn't shown up," Josh responded.

"He ever mention the name 'Night Viper'?" asked Crisco as they exited the trailer to go retrieve a bandit body.

"Never once. Comic book character or something? Sure sounds like it," Josh replied as they approached another body. Lexi and Talbot were loading a body into one of the trailers as they were speaking.

"No, I was just checking," Crisco stated and then went silent.

Josh shot him a brief look of suspicion, but they continued about their tasks. It wasn't long before Vincent came back with the pickup truck and the six bodies from the road.

"Alright, we drop the rest of these bodies inside the trailers then we leave the bodies of the three rebels outside. If they decide to inspect the site, I want them to see rebel bodies," Vincent declared.

Josh asked, "And what if they do a close up inspection?"

"They'll figure out this is a hoax and continue to come after us. Either way, it slows them down while we make our way north," Vincent explained.

After everyone did their morbid duty of placing the bodies as strategically as possible, they left the transmitter inside the fifth wheel. Vincent, Lexi, and Crisco got into the Bronco, everyone else returned to the shuttle. Within moments, they were back on the road and on their way to upstate New York.

Chapter 9

Commander Jade stood in the command center of the BFT-5000, also known as the dreaded Apocalypse Dozer. She could see the last few people scattering in a desperate attempt to avoid the massive behemoth of destruction, but to no avail. There was barely anything recognizable left after she passed over them. As the last neighborhood of what had once been Bridgeport, Connecticut was flattened, she felt a tingle down her spine. As far as she was concerned, every person that wasn't a part of Zodiac's Grand Army was her enemy and she was destroying them. They had virtually no opposition in their rampage. She decided to report her progress to General Callous.

It took only a moment to get through to the General and his face appeared on her view screen. "Commander Jade, what have you to report?"

"Bridgeport is destroyed. We're heading to Danbury soon," Jade answered.

Callous let out a little chuckle. "Excellent. I will be landing at Bradley in a few moments."

"General, far be it from me to question Lord Zodiac, but destroying these cities is also destroying the main routes through Connecticut. How are we going to get supplies to the site?" Jade asked.

"We will be constructing a bypass road. In the meantime, crews will mine the ruins and remove the metals. Recycling is key after all," Callous answered. "Now, what of those rebels that escaped? Lord Zodiac anxiously awaits the capture of Vincent

Black and Alexis Hera."

"One of the rebels that escaped with them is an agent of mine. He was carrying a transmitter. I have sent a squad of Seekers to follow them and wait for them to set up camp. They need to be caught with their guard down," Jade reported.

"I should remind you that sunrise is coming soon; the advantage of night serves us well," Callous said.

Jade nodded, "Of course. They will not be at large for much longer."

"Excellent…General Callous out," he said and his image disappeared from the screen.

Jade stood in silent contemplation for a moment. She was missing something. She didn't understand how they were going to mine metal out of ruins. She continued to wonder what Zodiac's interest was in Vincent Black. She knew he was different. Something made him more than human. Suddenly she snapped back to the present as she realized that her Seeker squad was nearing the location of the rebels.

"Couldn't get the damn satellite over the site in time," she mumbled out loud. Then she pushed a comlink button and spoke into it, "Attention ASD-14, come in." ASD stood for Airborne Search and Destroy.

"Roger," responded a monotone voice.

"I was unable to task a Satellite to your location so I will be relying on your video feed," Jade stated.

"Video feed on, Commander," the monotone voice responded again.

The image came up on her view screen. She saw as the lead Firehawk (one of the bladeless helicopters) was approaching what appeared to be some kind of camp. It was a jumble of various trailers and vehicles. It was the location of the transmission. "Are there any signs of activity?"

"No command, it appears quiet," the response came.

"Raze it," Jade ordered. She sat back and watched the show.

Upon receiving the orders, the Seekers immediately engaged. The lead Firehawk sent hellfire missiles at the motorcycles and pickup trucks. They struck and exploded with ferocity, sending the flaming husks of vehicles into the air. The supporting Firehawk opened fire with its chain guns, riddling the trailers with bullet holes. The lead commenced firing with its chain guns on the fifth wheel trailer. After a few moments, the side doors to both bladeless helicopters opened, and four Seekers from each descended on ropes to the ground. They readied their weapons and spread out.

The group of Seekers searched the entire site. Each Seeker was equipped with a video feed on their helmets which was relayed back to Commander Jade. She could run the faces of any bodies they found through facial recognition software. Several of the bodies were riddled with holes from the chain guns; others were burned in the explosions. As near as they could tell, all of the bodies were male.

Two Seekers entered the fifth wheel trailer for a closer look. They never felt fear when they saw the home-rigged explosives, nor did they feel fear at the realization that they had triggered a trap. The explosion that ensued killed both instantly, their armor unable to absorb the immense blast. The massive explosion sent shrapnel and debris everywhere. Three other Seekers were killed in the blast and the brutal barrage of shrapnel. One of the Fire-hawks caught a portion of the explosion. It rocked and swayed in the air but the emotionless pilot was able to bring it back under control. The other hawk descended and picked up the three surviving Seekers.

In the lead helicopter, the pilot opened up comm. again, "Command, this is ASD-14."

"I saw it pilot, we've been had. Rejoin us. They've fallen off of the radar. I'm sure they'll resurface," an angry voice responded.

"Roger," the pilot responded with the lack of feeling expected from the dark warriors.

Commander Jade was not in the mood to contact General Callous at the moment, so she opened up the video feeds from the Seekers that were at the camp site. She began running the faces through facial recognition. Almost all of them were former members of a biker gang that used to cause trouble in the Northeast. She also saw three familiar faces. One was her informant. The other two she recognized as rebels that had tagged along when Vincent and the others escaped from New Haven.

"Why would they leave these three? Only one of them was an agent of mine. Unless they were already dead to begin with," Jade was thinking out loud. "Wait a minute!"

She flipped to the video feed from the attack on Southern Connecticut State University. She scrolled through the footage until she got to the section that she wanted. Zooming in on Vincent, she was beginning to put the pieces together. He had been carrying a Seeker. The soldier must have been unconscious. Maybe he awoke and killed those three rebels.

"This is not good at all," Jade continued to think out loud. "Vincent Black caught a Seeker. Not good at all." She knew she was going to have to report the possibility of one of their soldiers falling into enemy hands but she was not yet ready. It was time to start searching through the various government databases that they had commandeered. She wanted to know who or what Vincent Black was.

In the time before the Flash Storm, Bradley International Airport served as the major Airport in Connecticut. Though it had "International" in its title, its service overseas had been limited through most of its history. When one would book a ticket it would be labeled as Hartford, when in reality the airport was actually situated about twenty minutes north of Hartford in Windsor Locks.

The runways were empty, although several 747 and 767 aircraft were sitting dormant at their hubs, as they had since May. It was actually a peaceful scene until suddenly, the sound of jet engines erupted from the sky for the first time in 5 months over the airport. From the dark skies above, an unusual aircraft came in for a landing. It was what used to be Air Force One, now carrying a very important figure for the Grand Army of Zodiac.

As the massive aircraft's brakes and flaps grinded it to a halt, General Callous became anxious. He wanted to get to the construction site as quickly as possible. He knew that Commanders Jade and Triton were sending more slaves for processing and conversion, far more than he had expected. On the one hand he was pleased. More workers meant faster construction. On the other hand he was concerned. The slaves were flesh and blood and needed to be fed. He needed to divert more supplies to the site, and he needed to get them there quicker than before. This would disrupt his plans, but one thing Callous was good at was being flexible and making last minute adjustments as needed. His other purpose in coming to the East Coast was also a source of anxiety. Vincent Black and Alexis Hera had thus far evaded capture. The general was anxiously awaiting a call saying that the two had been found, a call that did not seem to be forthcoming.

The former government aircraft taxied to a halt at the spot where it would be greeted by Seekers in military Hummers. Hummers were one of the few breeds of United States Military hardware that Zodiac continued to use. Most of the aircraft, tanks, and other heavily armored vehicles had been destroyed in the Flash Storm or the subsequent Seeker raids. The dictator had preferred to push the top secret, experimental hardware into production for use by his Grand Army. These were things that the world had not seen and he wanted to not only strike fear into anyone who would resist, but he also wanted his weapons to be a mystery to his enemies.

Before Callous could disembark, he was alerted to an incoming transmission. On the view screen appeared a familiar blank face plate. "Lord Zodiac, it is an honor to hear from you."

"Spare the formalities, General. I am curious to know if your commanders managed to find Vincent Black and Alexis Hera," Zodiac got right to the point.

Callous shook his head, slightly nervous, and reported, "Black and his band of rebels escaped but Commander Jade is pursuing them."

"Commander Jade," Zodiac sounded intrigued. "Yes, that's good. She is the perfect person for the job."

General Callous was taken aback by Zodiac's assessment, but he quickly regained his composure, hoping his leader would not pick up on his discomfort. "The good news is that they have captured more vermin to convert than we had originally anticipated. Once more supplies are directed here, construction will speed up exponentially. We already have power running at the site."

"Good. I expect the ziggurat to be fully operational within the allotted time frame. In the meantime, have we accounted for all nuclear weapons?" asked Zodiac.

"Yes sir. The commanders have been diligent in their pursuit of the nukes. We know that there were eleven unaccounted for by the U.S. government, but records show that they are either irretrievable or not a threat," Callous answered.

"Good. Report to me when you arrive at the construction site," Zodiac ordered.

"Yes my lord." Callous bowed as Zodiac's image disappeared from the screen. His mind wandered a bit as he exited the plane to the greeting of several Seekers, who were not going to be engaging him in conversation. He knew that Vincent Black was different, but in the grand scheme of everything they had going on with establishing their foothold of power, why was this one man so important? Super soldier or not, he was still one man. Alexis Hera, as far as he knew, wasn't even a super soldier! Callous let the thought pass from his mind; he had too many other things to concentrate on. He knew that Jade was one of the most competent commanders they had...if anyone would find the two targets, it was her.

Chapter 10

The road was as empty as it had been for the past five months except for two vehicles. A university shuttle bus following a 1995 Ford Bronco. They were headed north, into upstate New York where they hoped that their new ally would lead them to a place where they could lay low and regroup. It was the place that their leader, Vincent Black, was altered into a super soldier by the U.S. government. Within the Bronco, the silence was broken at last.

"So, uh, seems like we lost 'em," Crisco said nervously, trying to end the silence as best he could. He was uncomfortable enough as it was around the man he knew as the Night Viper.

"Yeah, well, hopefully they just laid the site to waste and didn't care about taking any of us alive. If they wanted us, they would've sent a group of Seekers in and figured out that the whole site was a ruse," Vincent replied without taking his eyes from the road.

"So um, yeah. Well as long as we lost 'em." Crisco was having a hell of a time trying to keep the conversation going.

"Lexi, you mentioned not feeling fear. Is that a metaphor for being a daredevil or do you really not feel fear?" asked Vincent.

Lexi was looking out the side window at the scenery. Sunrise was coming within a couple of hours and she realized that she was getting tired. "I don't feel fear. I can't feel fear."

"Really? How did that happen?" Crisco called out from the back seat.

Lexi did not take her eyes away from the window. "Cancer. It gave me a gift and a curse."

Crisco had a confused look on his face. "I thought cancer just killed people or people killed it."

"I had a brain tumor, near the amygdala, a walnut sized portion of the brain that controls fear and some other things. They were able to get rid of it, but I had brain damage and haven't felt fear since. I was 13," Lexi explained.

"Ouch. You lived though, that's good, right?" Crisco tried to be cheery.

"Yeah, I got to survive to see the Apocalypse and to fight a nightmarish bunch of dark soldiers who are virtually unbeatable. Yeah, I'm fortunate," Lexi snapped.

"Cancer...yeah, my gift and curse too," Vincent added.

At that, Lexi popped out of her daze and looked over at the man she barely knew but trusted with her life. "You had cancer too? How?"

Vincent kept his eyes on the road. "Long story."

Lexi put her hand on his shoulder, "We have time Vince. C'mon, if we're going to try to survive together, we might as well know a few things about each other. Besides, Crisco back there seems to know a few things about you...Night Viper."

Vincent sighed. He realized he wasn't going to be able to skirt around the questions forever. "So be it. Let's just say that life was a little tough for me growing up."

"That gave you cancer?" Crisco interjected.

"Shut up and let me answer your damn question!" Vincent growled. Lexi snickered. Crisco shut his mouth. "Basically, there was a radiation leak and two nuclear technicians were trapped with it. I decided to play hero and get them out and was exposed to a massive dose of radiation. It should have killed me but something made me hold on. I kept myself alive through sheer force of will, even as my cells began to go haywire. It was then that I decided that if I was going to die, I was going to take down as many of the scumbags that were killing society as I could."

"Holy Shit, you're that vigilante that was in the L.A. area. I remember now...yeah, they gave you the name Night Viper," Lexi perked up.

Vincent nodded. "Yeah, I went with it. I was so damn naïve. It wasn't a comic book, it was real life. I tried to do as much as I could and I ended up on the radar for Project Scorpion. They kidnapped me when I was in a weakened state and brought me across the damn country to upstate New York. I couldn't find out as much as I wanted, but apparently I was their seventh attempt at whatever it was they were trying to do. That's where the number seven on my eyelid came from."

Lexi looked at Vincent intently, "What about the scorpion?"

"When I escaped from there, and I barely remember it I was so disoriented, I saw that symbol. I had this done to remind me of what our government was willing to do to innocent people. It's kind of a memorial to the six people I never met who died perfecting a procedure which would save my life," Vincent explained. "So Crisco, how much of this did you already know."

Crisco held up his hands and shook his head in the fashion he tended to do, "I already told you what I knew. I was security, nothing more. Everything was on a need to know basis and they decided that I didn't need to know."

Lexi reached to her sidearm and pulled it out. She held it on its side with both of her hands. "Crisco, does the last name Hera sound familiar?"

Vincent glanced over and saw her pistol up close. It had an engraving on the handle of a scorpion, identical to the tattoo on his eye. "Lexi, where did you get that?"

Crisco looked over Lexi's shoulder at her sidearm, "Oh shit. That's impossible. That's just too much of a coincidence."

Vincent glanced at Crisco in the mirror and said, "Start talking before I regret taking you along."

"Captain Hera. Captain James Hera. That's his gun; it was his pride and joy. Other than that picture of some little kid he used to cart around," Crisco answered. "Why?"

Lexi turned in her seat to face Crisco, "My full name is Alexis Hera. Jim Hera was my father. He gave me this gun before he died."

Crisco clutched his head, "Geeze, you were that little kid? I thought that was his grandkid in the picture or something."

"Small world ain't it?" Vincent added.

Lexi faced Vincent and said, "This was the assignment he couldn't tell me about. He had been sent away for months at a time. We didn't know where and we didn't know why. We couldn't contact him or anything. When he came back, he was different.

What happened there?"

Vincent shook his head. "Look, I was disoriented but the bits that I remember, I didn't leave there peacefully. I...I killed people on the way out. They tried to stop me."

"Underline tried," Crisco slipped.

"Shut up Crisco!" Lexi snarled.

"I don't even know the extent of what was done there. I just know that they changed me. They used me as their damn pin cushion," Vincent continued.

"They saved your life," Lexi reminded him.

Vincent sighed, "Yeah, it never occurred to them to check to see if I wanted to be saved."

"Well this conversation is turning really upbeat" said Crisco, once again throwing in his two cents worth.

"You *don't* want me to deck you Crisco. I might take your head clean off," Vincent warned.

Crisco ran his thumb and index finger over his lips in a zipping motion and said, "Point taken."

"Look, I'm not a depression case. After the whole incident with the radiation I went out to L.A. Subsequently I escaped Project Scorpion and went away for awhile. I was heading back to L.A. when the Flash Storm hit. It took some time before I realized the true extent of what had been done to me and what had changed. Something weird too...my fingerprints changed," Vincent explained.

Lexi had a puzzled look on her face, "That's weird. Did you ever do a DNA comparison?"

"No, I wasn't really sure where I'd find a reliable one. Besides, I was concerned for those that were closest to me. I figured the best way to protect them was to be as far from them as possible, which was actually part of my reason for going out there the first time. I had been in a self-imposed exile for over a year before finally deciding to come back out again," Vincent revealed as he dodged a pot hole in the road. "Then low and behold, I tried to protect everyone and they ended up dying anyway when the Seekers came. Go figure. Everywhere I go there's just death and destruction."

Lexi's puzzled look changed to concern, "Vince, whatever happened can't be undone now; we just have to go on from here."

"What we have to do is survive," Vincent replied.

"My father used to have a great quote. 'All that is needed for the triumph of evil is for good people to do nothing.' He said it all the time," Lexi stated.

Vincent gave her a glance, "Edmond Burke. Good saying. Wasn't it actually 'good men'?"

Lexi snickered, "Yeah, my father was pretty progressive for a hardened military man. Listen, what happened to you, what the government did to you was horrible. You went through an ordeal that I can't imagine, probably no one can. Here's my observation though...you have been helping complete strangers and they've gravitated to you. In a matter of hours you've gained a following that looks to you as the leader. Like it or not, you have a responsibility to them. Maybe it's time to take what those bastards did to you and use it to invoke a change."

"Like a rebellion?" Vincent asked.

"How long can we all run? Zodiac is sending his Seekers out everywhere. We now know what he does with the prisoners he takes. He lobotomizes them and puts those spider-looking things inside their heads. It's got to be some kind of control mechanism. It's only a matter of time before we're killed or worse, turned into one of those mindless zombie soldiers. I, for one, would rather die fighting that mass murderer," Lexi declared.

Silence followed Lexi's comment. There was honest and deep contemplation from all of them. Finally, Vincent broke the silence, "I can't promise anything. There's so much that we don't know. With world communication down we don't even know who's out there. We're going to need people, firepower, and a huge damn miracle like no one has ever seen."

Lexi actually had a smile come to her face. "Does that mean you're sticking with us?"

"Like you said, doing nothing will insure Zodiac's ultimate victory and our ultimate demise. I'm looking forward to tearing that bastard's mask off with my bare hands. Yes, I'll stand by you. First things first though. We need to get to that base and see what we have to work with. You got the two-way there?" Vincent held out his hand for the two-way radio. Talbot had the other one. They were only good for about a mile, which was more than enough since they were only about fifty feet away from the shuttle.

Crisco handed it to Vincent and said, "Here ya go boss man!"

Vincent took it and gave Crisco a twisted look. He pressed the button and said, "Talbot, come in. Talbot."

"This is Talbot, over," a voice came over the radio.

Vincent pressed the button again, hesitated for a moment, and then said, "I need to talk to Josh."

"Coming right up," Talbot obliged.

A moment later, Josh's voice came over the radio. "What do you need Vincent?"

"I have a question for you. I heard you mention something about being a techie. What's your area of expertise?" asked Vincent.

A buzz came from the radio then Josh's voice again. "I worked in information security. Kind of a funny thing, I was arrested for hacking, then employed as an anti-hacker."

"Actually, that kind of thing was fairly common. When we get to our destination, I'm gonna need you, so I hope the past five months haven't caused you to forget what you know," Vincent responded.

"It's like riding a bicycle. What do you need me to do?" Josh's voice was filled with excitement.

Vincent felt a surge of pride like he hadn't felt in a while. "I'll tell you more when we get there. Just start jostling your brain to shake the cobwebs out of the IT stuff. Vincent out."

Lexi continued to look at Vincent, "So, we're really gonna do this. It sounds like you're formulating a plan."

Vincent gave her another quick glance. "Yeah. Like it or not, we don't have a choice. I've got some ideas brewing, but I need a complete picture of the resources we have at our disposal before going any further."

"Looks like the Night Viper is back," Crisco stated, and then flinched.

Vincent noticed the flinch in the mirror. "Why the hell are you flinching?"

"I don't want you to punch my head off," Crisco cowered.

Lexi and Vincent started laughing hysterically. "I'm not gonna punch you. Look, I'm sorry we got off on the wrong foot. I know you had nothing to do with what was done to me and in your defense, I probably killed people who may have been your friends."

"Nah. I didn't like any of them and I couldn't wait to get out of there. Never expected to end up captured by street bandits though," Crisco replied with an uneasy look on his face. He was happy that neither Vincent nor Lexi noticed it.

"Fair enough," Vincent stated.

"Are we there yet?" Josh asked impatiently.

"I have no idea where we're going. I'm following Vincent. I have to say though, it's a lot easier to follow someone when there aren't a bunch of idiot drivers on the road," Talbot responded.

Josh's right leg was nervously shaking. It was an idiosyncrasy with him. When he was worked up about something, that leg wouldn't stay still. His left leg was significantly more relaxed. "Vincent has some idea for me when we get to this compound and I just want to know what it is. I haven't sat in front of a working computer since the Flash Storm."

Talbot rolled his eyes, "Here we go."

Josh put his hands on the seat in front of him and leaned forward. He was sitting two seats back from the driver's seat, and Talbot could see him perfectly in the rear view mirror. "Were you the one who got excited in school when the teacher called on him?"

Josh leaned back and said, "Depends on the class. I took this law class in High School as an elective because I thought it might be interesting. The teacher was really hot. Of course, one day her husband came in and his biceps were bigger than my whole body so that shot the whole 'hot for teacher' fantasy to shit."

"Somehow I think your fantasy was gone far before the husband showed up," Talbot cackled.

"Hey, Vincent thinks I can help him, so I'm not worthless," Josh said defensively.

"I never said you were worthless. I just don't think you had a shot with that teacher," Talbot clarified.

"You guys really look up to Vincent. Didn't you just meet him?" Eve spoke up. She was sitting in the back row and had John lying next to her with his head on her lap, though there wasn't much space for it with her very pregnant belly. She had one hand on the haven for her unborn child, and the other on the head of her husband. He was asleep, but he didn't snore. Actually, he barely made a sound. If one didn't see his chest expanding and contracting, one might have thought he was actually dead.

Josh turned his head to look at her, "Look, I've said it before and I'll say it again. He saved both our lives from a whole mess of Seekers."

"I know, I know. And I also know John was way out of line with that whole episode but don't you guys wonder about him? I mean, he picked up that car and threw it like it was a tricycle. Olympic weight lifters can't do that," Eve pointed out.

Andromeda actually spoke up, "He's a super hero. Of course he can throw a car. He threw a giant lump of concrete when we first met him. I, for one, am glad that we have a super hero on our side."

Eve tipped her head back a moment then adjusted herself ever so slightly to make sure that she didn't wake her husband up. She had been having trouble staying comfortable since she hit the third trimester of her pregnancy. "But that's just it. This is real life. For something like that to happen to Vincent, it's just…I don't know. Is he former military or something?"

Talbot looked at Eve in his rear view mirror. "Not that we know of, but who cares? I don't care if he was a convict as long as he's on our side."

Josh nodded in agreement, then turned back to face Eve. "I'm just glad that he's been leading us. I sure don't want that job. And no offense, but your husband's leadership ability leaves something to be desired."

"MY HUSBAND IS A GOOD MAN!" Eve shouted.

John stirred and sat up. Eve leaned back, sighed, put her hand on her head and continued to hold her pregnant belly with the other one. "Eve, he's right."

"John, how can you say that? You weren't yourself! You were drugged! Probably by that person who was carrying the transmitter," Eve said defensively.

John just shook his head. "No Eve, that's not it. It's my fault that all those people died in New Haven. I was stupid, pigheaded, and stubborn. I thought that by being one of the few military trained people left, I knew what would be best and I was wrong."

"There's no way you could have known that was going to happen. Strange people that we didn't even know showed up and demanded an evacuation and you questioned it? That's not your fault…anyone would have done the same thing," Eve argued. While Josh was watching this unfold, and Talbot was tossing the occasional glance in the mirror, Andromeda was curled into a ball and turned sideways, watching Eve and John.

John shook his head, "It wasn't my right to risk all those lives. Anyone who didn't die then would have had a far worse fate than just death. They were going to turn them into one of those mindless zombie soldiers if they haven't already. As former military I should have taken into account that Zodiac would have satellite imaging. I saw the Seekers before; I knew we were outgunned and outnumbered. We had mostly non-combatants. My internal desire for glory and heroism just caused more pain and suffering. Vincent is a much more realistic and effective leader than me." He leaned back and looked at the ceiling. Eve could not respond as tears began to run down both of their cheeks.

"Listen, what happened is done. We can't do anything else about that now. We just need to make sure that we survive," Josh stated.

John shook his head, "No. We need to make sure those people didn't die in vain. It sounds like Vincent has a plan. I hope it's a plan to strike back at them. If we keep running, Zodiac will eventually find us. Whatever's going on, Vincent is more than just leading us."

Talbot swerved to avoid a pothole. "You're talking rebellion. There's a problem though - three rebel cells in Connecticut were wiped out in one evening by Zodiac's forces and we can only assume the fourth suffered the same fate."

John reached out with his hand and touched Eve's belly. He felt the kick of his unborn child and finally managed a smile. "Then I really hope Vincent knows what he's doing, not only for our sake, but for the sake of my unborn child and the future of humanity."

Following that statement, everything went silent. Andromeda laid down across the seats on her side of the back row of the shuttle and tried to sleep. Everyone else sat in silent contemplation. The events of the past several hours were a lot to handle mentally, for everyone. The idea of possibly going from being on the defensive to the offensive was almost overwhelming. No one in the shuttle could figure out how they would do it, but they had a new breath of hope. They believed that Vincent Black, formerly known as the Night Viper, would be able to make it happen.

No one knew how long they had been riding in silence, but it made everyone jump when the two-way broadcasted Vincent's voice, "Talbot. Hey Talbot, come in."

He grabbed the radio, "This is Talbot. What's going on Vincent?"

"We're going to pull off up ahead. Lexi and I are going to do a bit of recon on foot to make sure the place is vacant. We need Josh with us, the rest of you should stay back and wait," Vincent answered.

Josh stood up and made his way to the front and held out his hand for the radio. Talbot obliged and the moment he had it in his hand, Josh spoke, "Why me? The only reconnaissance I ever did was in video games. I don't know if Halo 3 qualifies as experience."

"We're going to need your help getting us into the complex; it has a computerized lock," Vincent insisted.

Josh hesitated for a moment then replied, "Alright."

Talbot watched as the Bronco pulled off to the side of the road. He was surprised that the shuttle and Bronco had made it this far without needing more gas. Looking outside, it appeared that the sun was rising. At this time of year, it was a good twelve hours between sunset and sunrise. The attack on Hartford had begun just after sunset. "I can't believe all that's happened in twelve friggin' hours," Talbot thought to himself. "And most of that time has been driving up here to the middle of nowhere." He followed the Bronco to the side of the road then into the woods.

"Where the hell are we? Didn't we pass Lake Placid like a half hour ago?" Josh asked with certain sarcasm in his voice.

"We're in the middle of nowhere, a perfect place for a military installation that's doing things they don't want anyone to know about," John responded. "The good thing is we've got this canopy of trees and dense foliage; it would be hard to spot us up here from space. I hope this place is deserted, it would be perfect for us."

Talbot put the shuttle in park then shut off the engine. He looked ahead and saw Vincent and Lexi get out of the Bronco, "Kid, you know what you're doing with this shit? I mean, once you get there it's a military complex, probably has some crazy lock."

Josh sighed, "When I started working in information security, I was employed for a little while with the Department of Defense. You wouldn't believe the shit I had to sign and the interrogations that I had to go through. The thing is our former President was paranoid. He knew that there had been clandestine things done under the previous administration, many done with the idea of 'plausible deniability'. He didn't like that. He wanted to know that if he ever needed to get in somewhere, he couldn't be locked out, so there's a back door into every military installation in the country."

"You consulted for the DOD and you choose now to tell us? Does Vincent know?" asked John.

"I don't know. I told him I did information security but he seems to know everything. Anyway, the problem is, there couldn't be one way to get into everywhere. God forbid if someone got their hands on that they would have an open door to any installation. No, there's an algorithm and three different keys that you need," Josh explained.

Vincent and Lexi were walking toward the shuttle. Talbot opened the door for them and said, "Keys? Like house keys?"

"No, Mr. Stone-Age. Virtual keys. Fortunately for all of you, I ignored the clause in my contract that said 'forget everything you just did'," Josh smiled.

Vincent and Lexi came on board the shuttle, "Ready to go and work your magic on this place Josh?"

"Sure am," Josh responded as he got up. He checked to make sure that his gun was loaded, although he figured if they ran into trouble he would hide and Lexi and Vincent would kick their asses.

"Vincent, how the hell did you know that brainiac here could crack into a military installation," Talbot asked.

"The name Josh Tyler was all over every underground news source in the country. I know he consulted for the DOD, so I figured he had a better chance than any of us of getting in there. Don't worry Josh, right now you're our most valuable asset. We'll watch after you," Vincent assured.

Josh breathed a sigh of relief, "Thanks for that. So, if we get the all clear, we come back and get the Bronco and the shuttle, then load up."

Vincent shook his head, "No. We're bringing one of the radios. Talbot, we'll give you the all clear, then signal Crisco over in the Bronco and head down there. He knows where it is. In the meantime though, maintain radio silence until we know that this area is secure."

"Got it Vince," Talbot nodded.

"Look, I just want to tell you all that I don't believe in coincidence. We have a former security guard from this compound, a DOD consultant and hacker, all in the same group. We were meant to find this. I don't know what you all believe but I'm sure that we're here for a reason. Above all else, I want you to maintain focus. We *will* survive this ordeal," Vincent stated. He could see the inspiration seeping into the others, even the Deckers. Andromeda slept through the whole thing.

"Alright, let's go and get this over with. The sun's coming up and we should get underground as quickly as possible," Lexi pointed out.

As they were leaving John called out, "Good luck guys...and thanks Vincent. I'm sorry I ever doubted you."

With a nod, Vincent, Lexi, and Josh exited the shuttle. They began to head through the woods. "How far is it?" Josh was looking around the wooded area nervously while picturing scenes from several horror flicks.

"About a half mile through here. We're taking a more direct way, the roads are much longer," Vincent answered as they hustled through the woods.

Josh let out a nervous laugh, "There was a time when I would've been afraid of a hike like that. I guess five months of running for your life has the benefit of getting you in great shape."

"You know, if we had to obey speed limits coming up here, it would have taken us twice as long. There were times when I was looking out the window for cops," Lexi stated.

Josh managed to avoid a branch that was snapping back into

place after Vincent pushed it. "Yeah, well, there was a time when I would've been scared out of my mind attempting to hack a DOD compound."

"Let's keep it down as much as possible, we'll reminisce when we're inside and secure," Vincent reminded.

Josh, Lexi, and Vincent were pleasantly surprised at how quickly they were able to cover the distance to the compound. Though they could not see their destination yet, they could see the electrified and barbwire fence with the warning signs all over it.

"Do Not Enter"

"Warning: Restricted Area"

"Warning: Electrified Fence, risk of death or serious injury"

The fence was probably ten feet tall. Vincent reached down and grabbed a twig, then threw it at the fence. They could hear the crackle of electricity as the twig smoldered. "Shit. That's a buzz kill," Josh mumbled.

"You jumped higher than that while holding onto me Vince. You could just jump us over," Lexi suggested.

Vincent nodded and said, "Exactly what I was thinking."

Josh put up his hands in protest, "Whoa, time the hell out. You're going to jump us over that fence? Are you crazy? One false move and we're toast."

Lexi gave Josh a little poke in the ribs, "C'mon Josh, where's your sense of adventure?"

"I left it in my other pants," he replied sarcastically.

"I'll go first, I've been looking forward to another ride," Lexi smirked. She walked over to Vincent who scooped her up as if she was nothing more than a rag doll. Then he squatted down, and jumped into the air, soaring well over the fence and landing on the other side, putting Lexi back on her feet.

"Keep watch to make sure there's no one around. I'll go get Josh," Vincent said, then turned around and jumped back over the fence. "Your turn."

"Okay, hold on a second. Wait a minute. I mean, I've gotta weigh more than Lexi does," Josh was clearly nervous, which was actually amusing both Vincent and Lexi.

"The guy can pick up a car and throw it, I doubt it matters. Besides, you probably don't weigh that much more than me. Grow a pair and enjoy the ride," Lexi taunted.

Josh's leg was doing its nervous twitch. "Thanks. Thanks for that. I appreciate the confidence booster. Just…just give me a minute here. Gotta get into the mental…whoa!"

Before Josh could finish, Vincent scooped him up and leapt into the air. All Josh could say while they were soaring over the fence was, "OH SHIIIIIIIIIIIIIIIIIIIIIIIIIIIIIIIIIIIIIIIIIIIIIIIT!"

When they landed on the other side, Vincent and Lexi were cackling like drunken hyenas. Josh was not amused. "That wasn't funny guys. Really. Okay fine. Get your damn laugh at my expense. Yeah, great. I feel so violated."

"Oh chill the hell out, you're fine. Now hopefully we're alone out here because we just made a racket. Not very stealthy," Vincent pointed out.

It didn't take long to reach the compound once over the fence. Josh had pictured some large, above ground complex with a huge fence and military vehicles everywhere, but that's not what they saw. The directions they received had brought them to what looked like a utility hub. It was a small building that appeared to be made of cinderblocks and a makeshift roof. There were various metal cabinets that looked like they may have housed electrical panels, both low voltage as well as high voltage.

"Well, this is a plain piece of nothing. Perfect spot for a base. Funny, I don't remember any of this. I vaguely remember being in the middle of the woods though," Vincent revealed, looking around with suspicion.

"Chances are there're several secret exits from this complex; this is the military secret base version of a front door, which I doubt you left through. Judging by how damn strong you are, you probably pummeled the guards and just went in whatever direction you could find," Josh pointed out. He began looking at the various 'utility boxes'.

Lexi looked confused, "Do you know what the hell you're doing? Nothing here is labeled."

Josh didn't look up from what he was doing but responded, "Yup. They may not have traditional labels, but there are telltale signs. Let me see…yes, this one."

Lexi scrunched up her face and in a sarcastic voice said, "Yeah. Of course. Why the hell didn't I see that?"

"Listen. You two are the bruisers. The fearless one and the one who throws people a hundred feet. Me, I'm the damn techie. Everyone has to contribute something. Just make sure no one's around to shoot me while I do this," Josh scolded.

The hacker began to claw and pry at a utility box to open it but he was unsuccessful and mumbled a series of inappropriate expletives. Vincent walked over and ripped the door off as if it was made of paper and said, "Is this better?"

Josh looked up at him and responded, "Show off."

Behind the door was a computer terminal, with power flowing to it. Lexi looked at it intently and asked, "Did they have to punch something in every time they wanted to come in?"

Josh looked at her, "Nah, they just ran a key fob over there." He pointed at a small, indistinct proximity fob reader.

"Oh," Lexi said and then kept quiet.

"Hmmmm...let me see...this isn't very secure," Josh said as his fingers moved at practically light speed over the keyboard.

Vincent was watching closely. "I was always a GUI fan myself."

"Gooey?" asked Lexi. "That could be badly misinterpreted."

"Graphical User Interface. G-U-I," Josh enlightened. "Mind out of the gutter young lady."

"Alright, so I guess it's obvious that I know shit about computers," Lexi admitted then stuck her tongue out at the computer genius.

Josh's fingers were still moving a mile a minute. "Yeah, well, the most advanced and secure systems use a text based interface. This system is Linux based and it's heavily modified but it's pretty easy. I can get into this, but it'll take a few minutes. I would like to take this opportunity to make sure that you guys know to keep any lingering Seekers from shooting my ass."

"None of Zodiac's goons seem to be around. I'm really hoping that I've been correct in my assumption that Zodiac couldn't know about this place," Vincent mumbled as he kept a watchful eye on the trees around them.

"Actually, it's very likely. If they went the route of taking the Oval Office, there's no way they'd have any idea of a place like this. I doubt it would be in any official or even unofficial database. If this is where they made you what you are, then there's no way they could risk this being tied to the administration," Josh explained as his hands furiously punched in C programming code.

"Good. For once, the United States Government's secrets will actually be useful," Vincent stated.

"Dammit! What the hell!? I memorized this, why isn't it working?" Josh shouted in frustration.

Lexi looked at Josh, "What's the matter?"

"Errors. Damn syntax errors," Josh barked.

Lexi's look changed to total confusion again, "What's a sin tax error?"

"Syntax Lexi. It means I didn't type the programming code correctly," Josh had his head in his hands.

Lexi rolled her eyes, "You mean you have to write a damn program for the back door?"

"Yeah, everything needs to be compiled and run. Limits the number of people who're even capable of attempting to get in. This is it, why isn't it working?" Josh was visibly aggravated.

Vincent pointed to the screen. "You forgot a semicolon there."

Josh looked at him, and then looked back at the screen. He added a semicolon and hit a button combination to compile the code and then run it. After a few moments, they heard the door to the small structure unlock. "You know C? You program?"

"In another lifetime Josh. In another lifetime," Vincent nodded. "Now, before we go in, can you get a status on the compound from this terminal?"

"Checking now. I'm in as a root user so I should be able to... ha! Here's your GUI, Vincent. Let's see. Time to pull up the schematics...SHIT! This place is huge! All systems are on standby. This place is deserted, just as we'd hoped," Josh reported.

"Good. Where's a good place to get the shuttle and the Bronco hidden?" inquired Vincent.

Josh saw a small touchpad and began to move the pointer around. After clicking on a series of icons, he managed to bring up more schematics on the compound. "Right here. There's a lift that's meant for vehicles and large freight to be lowered underground. Give me the radio; I'll let Talbot know where to go. There should be a gate over there."

"Alright, let's get them over here and get into this complex.

We need to get some rest and get all of the information we can. We caught a huge break here, I want to milk it for everything we can get out of it," Vincent declared as he handed Josh the radio. "Especially if I have to go back into this place."

"Sure thing boss. Think we'll turn the tide on Zodiac?" asked Josh.

"I sure as hell hope so Josh," Vincent answered.

Chapter 11

Standing on Interstate 95, General Callous, Commander Triton, and Commander Jade watched in awe. They were facing what used to be the New London area of Connecticut. It was now a construction site for the most massive ziggurat ever built, a temple to the power and status of Zodiac. The completed project would have the massive metal temple side to side stretch from Niantic Bay to New London Harbor, then from the edge of route 95 down to the shore of the Long Island Sound. In plain terms, it was to be roughly four miles from West to East and five miles from North to South.

Tens of thousands of mindless slaves were working diligently to clear the land. The area, once a center of tourism and activity for the former State of Connecticut, included parks, beaches, even a country club. Thousands of people called it home. Now all of that was gone. After the BFT-5000 ripped every structure in the area apart, except for the Millstone Nuclear Power Plant, it was up to the lobotomized slaves to remove all of the debris from the area to begin the project.

"So we're replacing the old Millstone power plant with a plasma beam?" asked Jade.

"Yes, it was a technology that was being experimented with in Florida before we took over. We can literally throw anything in there; a 10,000 degree beam will atomize it, releasing massive amounts of energy. The metals will separate out, which we can harness for more raw materials," Callous answered.

Triton, without taking his eyes off the magnificent spectacle, added, "It seems surreal. This is everything that we've been planning. The United States military is gone. We control this entire continent. Soon, we'll control the entire world."

Callous, standing between Triton and Jade, looked back and forth at the two of them. "There is one more issue which must be addressed. That issue has the name of Vincent Black. Lord Zodiac assures me that he is more of a threat than we could ever know."

"General Callous, he's one man, as I've been saying. He would need to build an army, and the remaining people that we haven't made Seekers or slaves are hiding out. They quiver in fear from our soldiers before they can even see them. Even this Alexis Hera who doesn't feel fear won't be enough for him. We have the armies. We have full control over world communications. I'm not casting doubt on Lord Zodiac's wisdom, I just want to know what is so urgent," Jade rambled.

Callous looked directly at her, "It is not my place to question his will, especially when he's gotten us this far. We, who were nothing more than societal rejects are now the strongest and most powerful people in the world. As far as I'm concerned, he's a messiah. All messiahs have an enemy who will stop at nothing to destroy them. We should not underestimate this Vincent Black. He has more going for him than just extraordinary physical attributes."

Triton addressed Callous directly, "What of the other commanders, General?"

"All have been put on alert, but most of them are patrolling, looking for cells of resistance or preparing to ship supplies here for the ziggurat. He has made a specific request though. Commander Jade, Lord Zodiac would like for you to personally oversee pursuit of Vincent Black and those that follow him. Whatever resources you need will be made available," Callous informed her.

Jade was taken back a moment; she was not expecting this. "He could be anywhere. I will need satellites, Search and Destroy teams."

Callous nodded, "Whatever you need will be provided. He is the only real threat that remains to us."

"Then for the sake of the new world order and our position of power, I will find Vincent Black as well as Alexis Hera and bring them before Lord Zodiac," Jade promised. "And I will kill anyone who gets in my way."

"Excellent. I will be remaining here to oversee the construction personally. Triton, you are in charge of security. Anyone who is not one of ours and still has their free will is to be captured or killed, whichever is easier. At this point, we have plenty of slaves and Seekers," Callous ordered. "Now, enough sight-seeing. It's time to solidify our hold on this world. DISMISSED!"

Both Jade and Triton acknowledged. Jade opened the door to the Hummer she had arrived in and entered, immediately pulling away and headed down route 95. Her contemplation began anew as she had a predicament. How was she going to find a small band of misfits? There was only so much satellite imaging could do. This was one time when they could have used the corruption of the former government. A simple bulletin with Vincent Black's and Alexis Hera's faces all over the news would have generated enormous leads. Now there wasn't even broadcast television. Any stragglers that hadn't left Connecticut, been captured, or killed would be in hiding.

It only took a few minutes for her to reach her Firehawk. The Seeker pilot was waiting for her. The sneaky sun had made its way over their heads at that point, and the Seekers were a bit less menacing to look at during daylight hours. She got on board and the dark warrior asked in the normal monotone voice, "Where to Commander?"

"Norwich. I want to go to the Farm," Jade answered.

The Seeker set the door to shut and engaged the engines, "Right away." With that, the sleek vehicle took off. It's destination - what was once the William W. Backus Hospital, now a Farm for the creation of Seekers and construction slaves. Commander Jade sat back in her seat and calmed her nerves while her obedient soldier transported her to her destination.

Chapter 12

"This place is incredible," John observed as he walked around the underground garage. It was mostly empty although there were two military Hummers still sitting there opposite where the Bronco and the shuttle bus were parked. "How is it that this place has power?"

"My first guess is geo-thermal. A lot of these kinds of compounds rely on that as opposed to the power grid or a temporary generator," Josh answered. They had yet to fully explore the complex. Josh had the job of finding the control center which was actually quite easy. From there, he was able to get the main systems turned on.

"Alright, now that we're all here and underground, the support systems were not on and oxygen levels were pretty high, which tells me that no one's been down here while it laid dormant," Vincent stated.

"How do you know that?" Talbot asked.

Vincent confidently answered, "This place is air tight and without the scrubbers running the C-O-2 levels would have built up. Just to be safe though, I'm going to do a sweep of the place. I want you all to start unpacking our supplies and taking inventory. We need to know what we have and how we can use it."

Josh approached intently saying, "I'll come with you. I've got this lovely little government PDA I found in the control area so I downloaded the map of the place."

"Alright, I'm not expecting trouble and you can make sure I don't get lost," Vincent agreed. "The rest of you all set?"

The replies came in a series of nods. Once again, Vincent was amazed that no one was arguing. He gave a directive and everyone obeyed without question. He had been a loner for a long time and wasn't sure he was mentally ready for this. He and Josh headed out one of the doors. Vincent had both of his pistols drawn as they began walking down the hallway.

After a few moments, Josh piped up, "It's quieter than a Pharaoh's tomb down here."

"Yeah. Too quiet," Vincent agreed.

Josh had a look of concern on his face, "Okay, I really wish you didn't say that. You think something's gonna happen down here?"

Vincent shook his head but seemed a bit distant, "Something's already happened down here. The silence is deafening, I can still hear their screams."

"Vincent, what the hell are you talking about? There's nothing here! Are you remembering something?" Josh gave a concerned inquiry.

Vincent brushed it off, "It's nothing. Don't worry about it. Come on; let's get this over with so we can set up shop down here."

They briskly went through area after area, but there were no signs of recent activity. Vincent's vague memories were beginning to pop into focus, but it wasn't until they came toward the end of their tour that things became amazingly vivid. They approached a locked door with a sign that looked as if it had been added more recently than when the place was built.

"Authorized Personnel – Eyes Only"

Josh let out a little laugh, "Shit, I thought this whole place *was* 'Eyes Only'!"

Vincent put his guns back in their holsters, "I thought you set all of the electronic locks to open."

Josh was running his hand over the door, "I did. This one must not be in the full access template on the access control computer. I wonder why. Luckily I made myself a fob to scan on the reader." He ran the small plastic tab over the reader. It let out a beep and a half second later there was the "click" of the door lock.

Vincent stared intently at the door for a moment, and then pushed it open. The door was thicker than the other ones they had come across. Thick and solid steel. "This place…"

They both walked into the dark room; only a few dim blue lights kept it from being pitch black. Though they couldn't see clearly, it was clear that something had happened in the room - it was in shambles. "Wow, looks like a bomb went off in here," Josh commented.

Vincent shook his head, "No Josh. Not a bomb. *Unh!*" Vincent grabbed his head and grunted in pain. He collapsed to one knee on the floor. His head was rushing.

Josh hurried over to his comrade. Despite being concerned he did not get close enough to touch him, as even a light brush from Vincent could break a bone if one wasn't careful. "Vince, you alright man? Hey Vince?"

Vincent could not hear him. At that moment, a portion of his life that had been a disoriented cloud began to fragment back to the forefront of his memory. He was seeing images, hearing things. This was where it happened. This was the room. He remembered being strapped to a table, probes and sensors all over his body. On his head was some type of helmet with several probes and sensors that connected it to a large machine. The machine had a large crystal, surrounded by glass in the middle. He could not see what was on the other side. He heard voices.

"You see, the process is working," came a male voice.

"Yes but will he survive this? He's the seventh one," asked another man.

"He is different, this one. That's why I wanted him. That's why I pursued him. He has lived for almost a full year after sucking in a dose of radiation that should have killed him within hours. Look at him - no sores, no hair loss. Despite the cancer that is ravaging every organ in his body, his outward appearance is that of a healthy young man. No my friend, we will not fail this time. After all, the Night Viper is a survivor," the first voice stated.

The memory blanked out, and then its spot was taken by another. Who knew how much time had gone by? Something exploded. There was fire. People were screaming. That machine, it was in flames. The crystal had burst into shards. Vincent looked over and saw two individuals in lab coats lying on the floor with the shards of crystal protruding from their corpses. What had happened? He had been dying. Now he was more alive than ever.

How could that be?

He looked down and saw that he was fully clothed. Strange, he had always thought the subject of a major experiment would have had their clothes removed. Something felt different though. He looked up and saw two men with M16 Assault Rifles approaching him.

"Get down on the ground - *now*," one of them shouted.

Vincent had no desire to be probed like a guinea pig anymore. The ceiling was high. He had no idea what possessed him to try the maneuver, but he rushed forward and jumped over the two guards. They seemed to move in slow motion. Before they could even turn their heads he was on the other side of them. He struck the first one in the back of the head. There was a loud "snap," then the guard collapsed and Vincent pulled his bloodied hand away. It wasn't his blood. He just caved in the man's skull with his own fist. He grabbed the other one and snapped his neck as if it was a twig and tossed the body aside. How was that possible? He was throwing them around like rag dolls.

The memory went blank as the previous one had. Yet another memory came to fill in the void. He was in the hallway. Alarms were blaring. Lights were flashing. There were immense amounts of noise. He was covered in blood. Was it his blood or someone else's? At least he wasn't in pain. More security approached from up ahead, but he wasn't afraid. He rushed right at them.

"Shit, here he comes," a voice rang out.

"How the hell does he move so fast!? What did they do to him in there?" another voice yelled.

Shut up. All of you. What did you do to me? What am I? He plowed into the first one so hard that the guard would have had a better chance of surviving if he was hit by a car while checking the mail. Without even looking, Vincent grabbed the head of another guard and smashed it into the wall. Holding an M16 rifle with one hand, he opened fire at point blank range on a third one, riddling him with bullets. The person directly in front of him was not a guard, but an older gentleman. He held up a pistol and fired. Three rounds went into Vincent's chest but there was something strange. He spit out some blood and looked down as the bullets were expelled and the wounds closed. He could feel the pain but he could also feel the torn flesh mending. Within seconds, there were no visible scars.

"What are you? What the hell are you!? No, please," the person begged. He had some type of military uniform but Vincent couldn't make out what it was. He stepped forward and grabbed the pistol from the person who had shot him. He took the butt of the pistol and started smashing the man in the head. Even though he was probably dead after the first hit, Vincent was relentless, yelling at the top of his lungs.

The memory faded and suddenly he was back in the here and now, Josh standing a few feet from him with the biggest look of concern he ever could have thought someone would give him. He was on the floor, clutching his head. Slowly, after a few breaths, he stood up and put his hands by his sides.

"Holy shit Vincent, are you alright!?" asked Josh.

Vincent was shaking his head rapidly, as if there were cobwebs inside his brain that he was trying to loosen up. "I don't know. Memory flashes. Here. Now. I remember some of this. This was the room; this is where they changed me. Project Scorpion. They must've sealed it off after I escaped."

Josh stepped a bit closer and looked Vincent in the eyes, "What did you see?"

"I saw death. I saw rage. I saw something completely out of control. I saw me. I'm not sure they intended to change me to the extent they did. They weren't ready for me. Government bastards. Come on, let's get back to the others and give them the all clear," Vincent answered.

"Sure thing, boss," Josh replied, still wearing a concerned look.

"Oh, and how about we not tell them about this little episode," Vincent requested.

Josh nodded his head, "I wouldn't know what to tell them anyway."

"I don't even think I'd know what to tell them," Vincent agreed.

Eve was sitting on a crate full of MREs that they had taken from the street bandit camp. She was rubbing her pregnant belly and watching as everyone continued to unload the supplies and tried to come up with some sense of organization. "I'm not helpless, you know. How about I do something?"

Talbot shot her a quick glance while carrying two 24 packs of bottled water, "We've got it, we're almost done."

"You don't need to be doing anything strenuous. There's been enough stress on you already," John told her.

"I'm fine. We've all been through the same ordeal. We all saw people dying around us. I just want to do something," Eve replied, then let out a big yawn.

Talbot put the water down with the collection of edibles near where Eve was sitting. He looked up at her and said, "What you need is to sleep for like a day. As soon as Vince and Josh clear this place, we'll all be able to rest up."

"You notice he's not even tired?" asked Eve. "Does he even sleep?"

"I've known the man for half a day. I have no idea if he needs to sleep or not," answered Talbot. "Why are you so suspicious of him?"

Eve continued to rub her belly. She didn't look at Talbot when she replied, "I'm not suspicious of him. I'm more intrigued than anything else. Here's a guy who can take on God knows how many Seekers by himself. What has he been doing for the past five months?"

Talbot shrugged his shoulders, "I have no idea, but even with everything he can do, I doubt he can fight an entire war by himself."

"He's been through a lot, probably more than any of us can imagine," Lexi added.

"What did he tell you?" inquired Eve.

"He hasn't had it easy. He had things going on long before the government picked him up and used him as their lab rat. No one deserves that," Lexi responded, looking down at the floor as she relived some of her own memories in her head.

"I've been hearing this code name thrown around, Night Viper," Eve commented.

Lexi and Crisco looked over at her. Crisco remained amazingly silent, but Lexi didn't. "It was some type of code name or nickname. I don't know what its meaning is or anything else about it, but he doesn't really go by that anymore. Look, I'm sure he'll explain to everyone what's gone on but in the meantime, I don't really think that I or anyone else should be speaking for him, especially since he is the leader of this group."

Eve couldn't get comfortable. She was adjusting every few seconds. "And what *is* this group exactly? What is our purpose? What are we going to do? Are we going to fight Zodiac and the Seekers? They wiped out every rebel cell in Connecticut in one night with virtually no issues. How can we stand up to them?"

"Eve, knock it off. You need some rest. Besides, we don't know about Bridgeport yet," John stated.

Eve stood up immediately, visibly irritated. "I WILL NOT KNOCK IT OFF! This baby is going to come soon, and will be born into this Armageddon that's consumed the world. I want to know that he or she is going to have a chance at a real life, not this running around, praying not to be found and killed or worse, lobotomized and turned into one of those things with blank faces and shoulder lights."

Everyone stopped what they were doing. Eve began to cry. John walked over to her and gave her a hug, "This is why I'm following Vincent. If ever there was any chance for our little one to have a real life after the Flash Storm, it's him. I'm sure he has a plan."

"He does," Crisco piped up.

Eve looked up from John's arms and asked the inevitable question, "What is his plan?"

Crisco backed down a few notches, "I don't know. He was formulating something on the way here but he said he would go over it with all of us, as a group."

Talbot grabbed the last of the supplies from the shuttle; he then stood straight up and said in a stern voice, "Alright, we've all been through hell. We're all tired. We all need rest, not just Eve. Let's just stop this conversation and wait for Vincent and Josh to get back. The thing I want to see in this place is a room with a bed or a cot. Hell, I'd settle for just a rug on the floor."

John nodded his head, "Agreed. None of us are in the mind set to be dealing with any of this at the moment."

Andromeda grabbed a bottle of water, opened it, and started guzzling it like a freshman college student chugging his first beer to impress the women at a fraternity party. She drank it so fast that water ran out of the sides of her mouth and down her chin.

Everyone watched her in silence. When she finished it, she put it down and said, "How many times do I have to remind you all that Vincent's a superhero…he'll save us all."

"You seem sure," Crisco pointed out.

Andromeda stood up and sternly replied, "Of course, because that's what superheroes do."

John looked over at her. "Listen, I don't want to be the one to shoot you down, but in the movies and comics, you have people in tight-fitting spandex who can shoot heat rays from their eyes and fly around. Yes, what Vincent can do is impressive but he, like the rest of us, is still vulnerable. This is real life and the reality is that this is far from over."

"Alright, I'll say it one more time, STOP TALKING ABOUT THIS!" Talbot was visibly annoyed. "Talk about anything else but this."

Everyone went silent. All of the supplies were unloaded so everyone stood around, not making eye contact, looking over what they had done. Finally, Crisco broke the silence, "How about them Mets?"

"Oh Lord, I sure hope those two hurry up," Talbot mumbled.

Everyone whipped their heads around at the sound of a door opening. Josh and Vincent had finished their sweep of the complex. Josh was furiously fiddling with his PDA, although it was not a familiar model to anyone in the room. Vincent approached and began to look at what supplies they had on hand. "The place is clear - no big surprise. There's electricity and running water. We found some more weaponry, although not that much, probably stuff that was missed when they abandoned the place. There are some non-perishable food items too, as well as sleeping quarters; looks like a bunch of individual rooms. They're small, but they're private."

"Running water!? THANK GOOOOOOOOOOOOD. I feel disgusting. There any clothes around?" asked Lexi.

Vincent looked over at her, "There might be some things that got left behind, I don't know."

"There're laundry facilities in here," Crisco stated.

Lexi smirked, "So Crisco, does that mean we all walk around naked while our clothes are being washed? Of course, I 'm not afraid to do that."

"Alright, enough is enough. Josh, you mind showing everyone to the sleeping area? We'll give you all the grand tour later. This place is huge and it's ours so relax, we actually caught a break," Vincent announced.

Josh nodded his head, "Yeah, I'll show 'em. Where're you going?"

"I'll catch up. I'm going to check on something. I have a few things to figure out," Vincent answered.

"Fair enough," Josh replied. With that, he led everyone else out of the room and down the hall, leaving Vincent alone. The newly elected group leader began to take a closer look at what they had with them, and then attempted to answer a major curiosity of his. He walked over to the Bronco and popped the hood to look underneath.

Vincent was not a mechanic, but over the past couple of years he had managed to pick up some useful knowledge on car engines. Looking around, he could tell that this one had been modified. He knew that a 1995 Ford Bronco should not have been able to make it the distance that they had traveled without being severely drained of gasoline. He was also sure that the shuttle shouldn't have made it at all without a refill. He walked over to the shuttle and popped the hood. Looking inside, though the motor was different, he saw some of the same modifications.

"Fuel efficiency mods," Vincent said out loud. "Looks like they were modified by people who trained under the same person. Nothing like this would have passed inspection before the Flash Storm, so it was probably done after."

He shut both hoods, immediately went to the control room and sat in front of a terminal. Unfortunately, he was not the hacker that Josh was and had no way of getting into the computers. He looked around for any printed manuals or materials but found nothing. Knowing that he was going to get nowhere with this, he left and headed to the sleeping area where the others were.

The sleeping area looked like a set of residence hall rooms on a college campus, only better equipped. Each had a bed, a dresser, and a closet as you would expect, but there was also a small entertainment center built into one of the walls with a flat panel television and a DVD player (which ironically also played MP3s and would display JPG images in a slideshow format). Each room had a desk with a computer terminal on it as well. Andromeda was afraid to be alone so she roomed with Josh. He simply pulled a mattress in from another room and laid it on the floor. He gave her the bed. Lexi, Talbot, and Crisco each took a room of their own.

To no one's surprise, the Deckers got a room together. As the married couple lay on their bed, Eve began to calm down. "So, it's been a long time since we slept on a twin bed together."

"Yeah, since college I think," John replied.

"And I wasn't pregnant then," Eve added.

John laughed, "Thank God."

Eve gave him a gentle elbow. "Yeah, well, I seem to remember a couple of scares."

John paused for a moment, with his hand on his wife's belly, "Are you scared Eve?"

"What do you mean?" Eve asked.

"I mean, are you scared to bring a baby into this world," John clarified.

Eve paused a moment, then rolled over and looked at her husband, "Yes, I am. We had such a bright outlook on the future when we found out I was pregnant. Then May 7th came and changed all of that. I know the others think I'm just some rambling, hormone ridden pregnant woman but I just want our child to have a good life and I just don't see how that's possible when there's so much death and destruction. I worry about him or her needing to take up arms against a psychotic dictator with things like that Apocalypse Dozer."

"That's why we fight now. Everyone has a weakness, and Zodiac definitely has his," John assured. "C'mon, let's talk about something else, I've had my fill of that monster and his Seeker buddies."

Eve smiled, "What about names? We haven't agreed on names."

"I liked Rufus," John replied.

Eve gave him a gentle swat to his side and laughed, "What happens if it's a girl?"

"We can name a girl Rufus," John answered.

Eve swatted him again, "Come on, I'm serious."

John looked his wife in the eyes, "Let's see after the baby's born. He or she will have a look about them right? I don't want to decide on Mark and then have the baby look like a Jake."

"What exactly does a Mark or a Jake look like?" inquired Eve with great skepticism.

John squinted his face a bit before replying, "Mark O'Brian? Tell me he didn't look like a Mark."

Eve immediately started laughing, and then clutched her side, "Ow. Don't make me laugh so hard. You're right...he does look like a Mark."

"See, I told you," John said triumphantly. "Do you think Mark was in Hartford during the Flash Storm?"

"I don't know. I try not to think about it. That whole group ended up working at insurance companies. My God, things will never be like they were. Our baby won't even have a social security number," Eve began to get worked up.

"Eve, the world was in trouble before. I don't think we should fight to return it to the way it was. I think we should build a new world. A better one," John was quick to come up with a comforting answer.

"John, promise me something," Eve demanded.

John ran his fingers through her hair. "What?"

"Promise me that this new life growing inside me is going to grow up in a free world," Eve requested.

John continued to run his fingers through her hair and had a half smile. "I promise Eve. Whatever it is we have to do, we'll do it." Of course, what was going on in his mind was, "I have no idea how the hell I am going to deliver on that kind of promise."

Eve shut her eyes as she was severely overtired, "Thank you baby."

Despite all the group had been through, everyone was sleeping like a log, except for Vincent. He didn't sleep at all. He wasn't tired. The fact is, his body worked on a 48 hour cycle, not 24 so he was still wide awake. Since he didn't want to awaken anyone, he decided to roam the hallways, but did not return to the strange room where he'd had his memory flashes.

Vincent knew his memory loss and haziness during the time

he was at Project Scorpion and the few days that followed were more due to disorientation than anything else. He still remembered his entire life prior to the events, including his time as the vigilante who the newspapers labeled the Night Viper. He still was not entirely certain of what they had done to him. He only had small pieces of evidence and he didn't know what they indicated. Outside of his "super powers", as Andromeda called them, there were other strange things. His fingerprints had changed. He used to have a birthmark on his leg - a birthmark that was no longer there. It would make sense that they would change any distinguishing marks if they were going to use him as a soldier.

Vincent walked around the complex repeatedly, doing the best he could to get the layout memorized. He did not experience any familiar memories of any other part of the complex. He decided that it was time to return to the one place in this whole underground laboratory that he had gotten any answers…even if they led to more questions.

The former vigilante was surprised to see Josh was standing there when he arrived. "I knew if I waited long enough, you'd show up here."

"How long have you been waiting?" asked Vincent.

"About 35 seconds," Josh smirked. "Can't sleep?"

Vincent shook his head, "My body works on a 48 hour cycle. It's the middle of the day for me. Even when I do sleep, it's not for more than 4 hours anyway. What about you?"

"I'm a techie; we only sleep 4 hours even though we need 8. I was gonna head to the control room, try and get into some things. I figure if I can get us into the complex, my key will probably get us into all of the systems. Maybe we can find out more about that room before you go in there and flail around like an epileptic elephant again," Josh explained.

Vincent found Josh amusing. He walked over to the computer nerd and said, "Alright, let's go. Do you think we'll be able to find anything?"

As they began walking, Josh looked over at Vincent and said, "You know that the internet used to be military only, right?"

"Yeah, even non-techies know that," Vincent answered.

"Well, basically, they didn't just allow civilians to get on their internet. They created another one. The defense net exists outside of the regular internet. Now, with the Flash Storm, there is no internet anymore, but with the satellites still up in the sky, I'd wager that the defense net is still there," Josh explained.

Vincent looked intrigued, "They'd track us though, if we tried to use their bandwidth. Even if you bounced the signal around, any type of extensive use would be traced."

"Normally, yes, but this case is a bit different. These secret locations couldn't risk being discovered but needed access to government databases and information, so they're rigged in a way that allows access to the defense net, but it's untraceable. Well, it probably could be traced except someone would have to know what they're looking for. If Zodiac is the single ruler, he has to have some way to communicate and share information with his Seeker armies and their commanders. We simply disguise the packets to look like standard chatter so any automated sniffers will just pass right over our hack." Josh was getting excited and his walk became much brisker.

"Hey, didn't your teachers tell you not to run in the halls?" Vincent asked sarcastically.

They both hurried into the control room. Josh immediately sat down and his hands began flying over the keyboard. As quick as they were, it still wasn't possible for him to move them as fast as his mind was going. "Come on, come on."

Vincent sat down in another chair and wheeled over next to Josh, "Whoa killer, you're moving faster than I do."

"You familiar with the Linux environment?" Josh asked without looking away from the screen.

Vincent nodded, "Sure. Not an expert but I used to have a Linux box in the old days. The motherboard shorted out though and I had to scrap the thing."

"Ha! Just what I thought," Josh said triumphantly.

"The defense network," Vincent began to feel excitement similar to Josh as the seal for the United States of America popped up on screen.

Josh stood up and cheered, "Woo-hoo! It's still there! Alright, we can dabble around a bit but first, it's time to make sure no one sees us snooping around." He sat back down and began performing a series of mouse clicks and typing blitzes. Vincent had been quite advanced with his knowledge in information technology back in the day, but nothing like this.

"So, how does it look?" Vincent inquired.

Josh had a huge smile, "It looks like everything is pretty much running off the satellites now, since a lot of land lines were destroyed and cut off during the Flash Storm and the subsequent fights with the Seekers. I'm sure the government server farms as well as the private ones are still safe; a lot of those were built inside of mountains and old nuclear bunkers. If Zodiac was smart, and he probably is considering he's pretty much conquered the known world, he's got all of these things active and their platters spinning!"

Vincent watched over Josh's shoulder, "Are you familiar with the layout of the defense net."

Josh's smile died down, "Not so much. I knew how to get into it in theory, but I never really dabbled much with it, other than certain areas. It looks like some of those areas have changed a bit now. I'm gonna need some time to sift through this stuff. There's a lot here."

Vincent patted Josh on the shoulder, "Good job. You may have just given us the edge we need to fight back against those Grand Army pricks. Fiddle around a bit more, but make sure you get some rest. We're all going to the meeting room later this morning. I want to address everyone at once. It's time to come off the defensive."

Chapter 13

"These design plans are FLAWED!" Zodiac yelled. He was standing in his command center at the former NORAD. His rants fell on the unemotional ears of three Seekers that were in the room with him and a loan man who went by the name of Paul McIntyre. Unlike so many of the people surrounding Zodiac, he had not been lobotomized but was not one of the dictator's commanders.

"They're not flawed; I just need to work through a few more things. Do you realize what it is you're building?" Paul tried to put on a brave front.

"Of course I know, you miserable microbe. I also know that I'm through playing games. My slaves have already begun building the foundation of the ziggurat!" Zodiac barked.

Paul stood after having been pushed to the floor. He was holding his head with one hand and holding up his other one signaling stop. "You have to listen to me. No one has ever attempted something of this magnitude. You're talking about a fifteen square mile fortress made mostly of metal. The weight alone could cause it to slide off, into the Long Island Sound!"

"It won't slide off, because you won't let it," Zodiac demanded. "May I remind you that the only reason you still have a mind of your own is because of this project?"

"How could I forget?" Paul mumbled. "All of that schooling just to build this monstrosity."

Zodiac laughed a sadistic laugh, "Monstrosity? This is the utmost beauty. When explorers found the Mayan ruins, they did not

120

call it a monstrosity, yet those ruins were constructs larger than anything they had ever seen. This…creation…is magnificent!"

"Yes, but that leads us to the other problem I wanted to tell you about. The plasma beam won't provide enough power for this thing once it's finished. With all of the weaponry, computer systems, and even the lights, it needs more power. I took the liberty of adding…"

"YOU TOOK WHAT LIBERTIES!? HOW DARE YOU!" the dictator's voice rang out and penetrated the engineer's soul.

Paul cowered, almost falling back over. He stood about six feet tall but he most likely weighed no more than 150 pounds. He was balding down the center of his head. "I just wanted to show you something that might work, but it will add significantly more weight. Just hear me out."

Zodiac calmed a bit and waved his hand around. "Proceed."

"We can load the top and sides of the ziggurat with solar panels," Paul stated.

"And aren't those extremely inefficient?" asked Zodiac.

Paul put his hands up and shook his head, "The ones that were commercially available were extremely inefficient. The vast majority of light that struck them was not absorbed. Here's the thing though. Since you so graciously gave me access to the United States patent office records, I found a piece of technology that had been suppressed, probably by the oil and coal companies."

Zodiac clenched his fists, "No surprise there."

Paul stopped for a moment, attempting to picture what his face looked like and the expression on it, but then decided that he didn't want those thoughts read and continued, "It's a solar panel that's 92% efficient. This would have devastated the oil and coal industries. They weigh a substantial amount but if we can brace them appropriately, the power will be unlimited."

"Well, that *is* good news. Here I thought I would have to suck the knowledge from your brain and figure it out myself," Zodiac cackled.

Paul was taken back a bit, and let out a nervous laugh, "Yeah, well, no need for anything drastic. I'm doing what you said. I like my brain the way it is, don't really need any ice picks shoved through it."

"I trust the delays will be minimal," Zodiac asserted.

"Y…yes, but I still need a bit more time, I have to recheck the calculations and the designs to make sure that the place can support its own weight, and I am still concerned about the shore. Those areas aren't known for the most stable of grounds," Paul warned.

Zodiac paced around, then turned to look at his view screens. "What needs to be done to verify that the ground is solid enough?"

"I…I need to go out there, to the site," Paul replied.

"Done," was Zodiac's immediate response. "You will be leaving in 30 minutes. My Seekers here will bring you to your aircraft. And there is some whiskey on board; I would suggest you have a little. Calm your nerves. I don't wish for you to have a heart attack before your usefulness is over."

"Oh…okay," Paul acknowledged. He began to follow the Seekers out the door.

"Oh, and Paul," Zodiac called out.

Paul's heart skipped a beat, "Yes?"

"Do make sure that you have done everything right and you don't attempt to sabotage me. For one thing, I'll know; for another thing, I doubt your family wants 'ice picks shoved through their brains'," Zodiac threatened.

"Of…of course. I mean, it's crazy enough to design a place like this, it's another thing to attempt to cross a telepath," Paul acknowledged.

"Then have a good flight," Zodiac said as Paul and the Seekers left the room. He walked over to his control panel and pressed a button. The blank faceplate of another Seeker popped up on screen.

"Yes Lord Zodiac," the monotone drone answered.

"Bring in my special appointment," the dictator commanded.

The dark warrior nodded, "Right away, sir." His image disappeared from the view screen.

Moments later, the door opened and two Seekers came in. They dragged a man by his elbows, a man who wore a black bag over his face. The drones tossed him to the floor in front of the savage dictator. "Leave us," he ordered.

The Seekers obeyed. The man was quivering, still unsure of where he was. "Wh…what's going on here?"

Zodiac tore the bag from his head, "You're my special guest, and I am so glad that you survived long enough to make it here."

"You…who are you?" the man asked with a hint of recognition. He was probably in his early 30's but he might not even have been that old.

Zodiac laughed, "So, you recognize my voice, even through the distorter. I can't tell you how long I have waited for this." He reached up and removed his helmet.

"No…it can't be. There's no way," the man said in disbelief.

Zodiac laughed a maniac's laugh, "You didn't think the sins of the past would catch up to you in the present, did you? Well, I go by a different name now. I am the Zodiac, I am hatred incarnate. Now, FEEL THAT HATRED MAGGOT!"

The dictator reached and grabbed the top of the man's head. Using telepathy, he began filling the man's mind with nothing but pain and suffering…his pain and suffering. "A LIFETIME OF PAIN! FEEL IT! KNOW WHAT IT'S LIKE!"

The screams that emerged from Zodiac's victim were the most inhuman sounds ever, as the brutal dictator unleashed an entire lifetime of pain and suffering in one moment. "HOW DOES IT FEEL NOW, YOU COWARD!?"

Zodiac's enjoyment was cut short as the surges through the man's psyche caused him to have a brain hemorrhage. "No…NO YOU DON'T! SEEKERS! GET IN HERE AND REVIVE HIM! GET IN HERE NOW! I'M NOT DONE WITH HIM!"

Zodiac replaced his helmet just as the Seekers came rushing in. They attempted to revive the man, but to no avail. "Sorry Lord Zodiac, he's dead," the monotone voice came from underneath the helmet.

Zodiac waved his fists in the air, "GAAAAAAAAAAAAAA! Weak fool. All of you were weak, do you hear me? ALL OF YOU! Disgusting. I should be pleased though. You and the others serve as a constant reminder of the dedication I feel toward my cause. Seekers, get this meat sack out of here, burn it in the incinerator."

The Seekers complied, un-phased by their master's outburst.

They removed the body and left Zodiac to his private thoughts. He went to his terminal, logged into the defense network, went into his personal settings and found that a query he had created had returned something. Opening the message, he saw exactly what he had expected. Commander Jade was poking around for information on Vincent Black and Alexis Hera. "Excellent," he thought to himself. "She is a diligent one and will serve me well as General one day."

Chapter 14

Vincent walked into the meeting room a few minutes early. Already Josh, Talbot, Andromeda, and Crisco had taken their seats around the oval shaped table. Vincent did not sit down. He gazed around for a moment; the four had their eyes fixed on him. It made him a little uncomfortable. After a few moments, the Deckers came in. Eve was being helped along by her husband. Vincent noticed that her stomach had dropped. He didn't say anything but he knew that the baby was going to be coming soon. He didn't even know when the little one was due, but it must be close.

"Sorry we're late - a little hard to get around these days," Eve commented.

Vincent shook his head, "Don't worry, you're actually early." The entire group had managed to find new clothes. Josh, Talbot, Crisco, and Vincent all were wearing black army fatigues that had the scorpion logo from Project Scorpion. Eve was wearing a man's button down shirt and trousers. It was no surprise; Vincent doubted that there would be any maternity clothes just lying around.

When the door opened, every male set of eyes was fixed on the sight. Lexi was standing there in a long T-Shirt and nothing else visible. Crisco was completely unable to hide his expression and Vincent was unsure of whether the former Project Scorpion guard was going to pass out or drool all over everything. Her hair was still wet; most likely she'd just finished her shower. "What are you all looking at?" asked Lexi. "I'm not going commando

125

and it's kind of warm in here."

"True, very true," Vincent commented. "Just thought it was a little brave to be walking around here like that."

"I'm not brave, I don't feel fear. Besides, if this is going to be home, I'm going to be comfortable and this is what I did when I had a home before." Lexi shrugged as if everyone walked around like that in front of people they hadn't known very long.

Vincent nodded, "Hey, I don't judge. To each his or her own."

Lexi picked the seat closest to Vincent and shot him a smile, "I know, that's why I feel like I can be myself around you."

Vincent wasn't sure how to respond so he didn't. Instead, he addressed the entire group, "Alright everyone, I asked you all here today because we have an interesting opportunity in front of us. This compound is completely off the grid. In light of everything that happened with the Flash Storm, it's very likely that there isn't even a hidden record of this place's existence, which gives us a bit of an edge. Josh was able to get into the defense net undetected, so we can utilize the satellites to a limited capacity as well as search through the old government databases."

Everyone was nodding their head. For the first time in a very long time, there was a glimmer of hope in their eyes, even Lexi's. "That means we can see what they see?" asked Talbot.

Josh spoke up, "Yup, for the most part. I'm not too familiar with the system itself; I never really used it extensively so I'm trying to educate myself. It's pretty straight forward though. It seems that the feds were copying and absorbing state and local government records too, I found links to DMVs all over the country, school records, and other stuff. Looks like they were compiling information on all Americans...Oh, sorry Vincent, didn't mean to steal your thunder."

Vincent held up one hand and smirked, "Don't worry about it. You're the one who discovered this; it's your right to report on it."

Josh felt a new sense of pride. "Thanks boss!"

Talbot spoke up, "Not to be an old fart but does Andromeda need to hear this?"

"I appreciate your concern for her, but she is a part of this group and she will have an equal spot at this table. If she has anything to say or that she needs clarification on, she has the right to speak up as do all of you. I am not Zodiac, and this is not a dictatorship. Every one of you is here of your own free will, are we all clear?" Vincent became very serious.

Everyone nodded and said, "Yes."

Vincent nodded back. "Good. I know a couple of you got the story and others have bits and pieces so I'm just going to summarize. I have a history with this compound. It housed Project Scorpion, of which I was a guest. The 7 tattooed on my eyelid was from them, because I was the 7th experiment, and I was also the last. The scorpion was something I had done to remind myself of what the government was capable of; and as a way to honor the six people I didn't know, but that were needlessly taken from their homes and families to be lab rats in a sick experiment to create the very process that actually saved my life. The things that you've seen me do…all of that was as a result of what happened to me here. The memories I have of this place are hazy at best, probably as a result of whatever they did. Before we go on, I would like to give any of you the opportunity to share anything that you feel needs to be shared here."

Lexi raised her hand, "I guess you should all know that I'm a cancer survivor. Normally this wouldn't have anything to do with what we're here for, but it's why I don't feel fear. I was cured but it damaged a part of my brain. So yes, I have brain damage - snicker all you want, I usually do."

"We're not going to laugh at you Lexi, nor are we going to laugh at anyone else here. There's a reason we were all brought together and there is a reason that we found our way here. For better or for worse, we are the closest thing to extended family any of us has right now," Vincent announced.

Crisco put up his hand, "Hey, um, just so you all know, I think most of you know, but just in case you don't I'll just tell you now so you hear it from me. I was security here at this compound for a period of time. I was here when they experimented on Vincent. I don't know what they did; that lab wasn't a place we were allowed into unless there was an emergency but, well, I just thought all of you should know."

John raised his hand next, "Hey all. I know that you probably don't have a high opinion of me, and what I am going to tell you

127

won't help. Not even Eve knows this. Chris was right, there was E in my system when I went nuts. I wasn't drugged, I took it myself. The death of those three people is on me. I couldn't handle the pressure of leadership or the pressure of watching all of those…" Tears started to run down his face and he got choked up. Eve put her hand on his.

"John, baby," she said in a calm voice.

John regained his composure, "Watching all of those people that I was responsible for just get slaughtered like animals…I couldn't handle it. I still can't. I'm not meant for leadership. I know that now. I hope that you all can give me the opportunity to earn your trust."

"Well, that was a ballsy move. We've all been through hell, and you have a few extra pressures over the rest of us," Lexi said as she pointed to Eve's belly. "You have my trust; I don't think you'll do anything like that again."

Everyone else was silent for the moment. Vincent then spoke up, "Alright then, we need to talk about the next step, and that's how we're going to take the offensive. Right now we have little information, so we need to know more about what we face."

"Then we should start with making sure everyone around this table knows what everyone else knows," Talbot suggested.

Vincent nodded, "My thoughts exactly. Let's start with the Seekers."

Crisco spoke up, "We know that they're people who've been lobotomized and have some type of implant in the front of their brains. The protective covering they wear is some sort of powerful mesh armor that regular bullets can't seem to penetrate and everyone has a fear reaction when they're near them, except for you and Lexi."

"Well, we know why Lexi isn't fazed by them, but what about you Vincent? Why don't they affect you?" asked Talbot.

Vincent rubbed his chin, "To be honest, I have no idea. I can still feel fear, even though I don't scare easily, so it's not the same as Lexi. It might be part of Project Scorpion. If they were attempting to make me into the perfect soldier, they wouldn't want me to fear anything."

"Despite that, you and Lexi may hold the key within you to stop the fear aura that the Seekers have. If we could nullify that, we could gather others to our cause," John suggested.

"Then there's that implant. Anyone ever see anything like that or do anything with it?" asked Josh.

"It might use nanotechnology; we worked with stuff like that at Berkeley. I'm not an expert, but I can try and at least figure out what its functions are. We can probably guess that they're used to replace the frontal lobe and effectively make people obedient machines but there may be more," Eve added.

Josh looked at the Deckers, "You guys went to Berkeley?"

John nodded, "Yeah, surprised?"

"Just a little," Josh responded.

"Anyone got any ideas on that crazy scream the Seekers have," Talbot asked.

"I've faced Seekers, I've killed Seekers, I never heard a banshee scream like the one we heard from that zombie soldier we had prisoner," Lexi commented.

Josh leaned forward in his chair, "It was suggested earlier that maybe they only do that when in captivity, as a defense mechanism against captors. I'm sure Zodiac doesn't want people knowing the secrets of his Seeker conversion process."

John raised his eyebrows, "That actually makes a lot of sense. Many wild animals have growls or shrieks that they only let out when cornered. It would definitely take captors off guard."

"Anything else on the Seekers?" asked Vincent.

Everyone shook their heads. John then spoke up again, "What about Zodiac himself? Other than that worldwide announcement right before everything went to shit, has anyone seen anything on him or about him or heard anything?"

Again, more heads shaking. "I heard he's got some kind of mental mojo," Lexi interjected.

"Yeah, I heard that too. No one knows what he looks like though, he wears that faceless helmet," Crisco added. Despite his contributions to the conversation, Lexi looked at him with suspicion; he definitely had not earned her trust. The others didn't notice, except for Vincent, and Lexi knew that he noticed.

Eve adjusted in her seat, "Are you saying this guy is telepathic? Come on. He's psycho, not psychic. That's crazy stuff."

"Might not be. Vincent has some of this 'mental mojo' too. He senses danger before it happens," Josh commented.

"Hey, this guy came out of nowhere and practically destroyed the entire world. I'm not sure it's far-fetched to believe that he might have some type of telepathic ability," Talbot interjected.

"I don't really want to go on speculation. We need to know the enemy as much as possible. What we don't know, we find out. We're already at a serious disadvantage; I don't want to go rushing into anything and have this entire operation blow up in our faces," Vincent stated.

"All right, then how do we go about finding out more?" Talbot asked.

Lexi bounced in her seat and said, "We know that not everyone in Zodiac's command has been lobotomized. I killed one of their commanders; he didn't even wear a blank face plate! We should nab one of them."

"Are you kidding me? You're talking about a small group of non-military personnel capturing an officer of their army? Where would we even find one of these people?" John was extremely skeptical.

"Josh's hack into the defense network! Maybe we could track one with it," Lexi suggested.

"Then what do we do? They're probably trained to resist professional interrogators, which none of us is anyway. How would we get this guy to talk once we got him?" John was still skeptical.

"They're probably afraid of Vincent. I'll bet he could get a prisoner to talk," Andromeda spoke up. Everyone in the room went silent and looked at her.

Finally, Josh spoke up, "She doesn't talk much but when she does, she makes good sense. Listen, I can start querying the defense network, see what I can turn up."

"Good, while you're at it, see if you can find out about that activity on the shore. I'm really curious," Vincent requested.

"What about the rest of us?" Eve asked.

Talbot leaned forward in his chair, "I want to check over the vehicles, I'm a grease monkey at heart."

Vincent immediately looked over at him, "I saw that both the shuttle and the Bronco had similar modifications done for fuel efficiency."

"Then I'll take a closer look, and I'll scope out the Hummers too," Talbot said. "Drom can come with me and help out."

The girl nodded her head rapidly.

Vincent looked at Eve and John, "You two should take a look at that spider implant and see if you can make any sense of it."

Eve and John both nodded in response.

"Crisco, I want you to check the complex again, both inside and out. Make sure that the place is secured," Vincent directed.

Crisco nodded his head, "So basically, it's like having my old job back."

"Pretty much," Vincent acknowledged. "I'll join Josh in flipping through the defense network. I used to deal with computers."

"I'll help you out," Lexi immediately interjected, shooting a strange look at Crisco.

Vincent noticed the look she had given to the former guard, even if no one else did, but he spoke as if nothing had happened "The more the merrier - we've got tons of data to sift through and no real direction. There's an intercom system in this place, so you'll be able to call the command center where we'll be. Let me know how things are going in your area. Once we have a better picture of things, we'll meet back here and map out our next move. In the meantime, let's get going."

Everyone immediately jumped up, except for Vincent and Lexi. The blonde haired and scantily clad woman had a look on her face as if to say, "I want to talk to you in private." Vincent understood this clearly and stayed in his seat. Josh was the last one headed out the door and when he noticed his two partners were staying behind, he turned around and looked at them.

"We'll be right there Josh," Vincent told him.

Josh just nodded and walked out the door, shutting it behind him. Lexi wheeled the chair she was in a little closer to Vincent, "Thank you for not thinking I'm a freak and accepting me."

Vincent was a little taken back by this. He was normally good at reading people but this seemed to come out of left field. "You're not a freak. Actually, if anyone is a freak, it's me; I'm the damn science experiment."

Lexi let out a nervous chuckle, "You're not a freak. Look at the way people follow you. Even the Deckers, who were scared of you, now seem to be with you one hundred percent. What is it about you?"

"I have no idea; I've never really been a leader. I just know we have to do something." Vincent was trying not to blush at the rush of compliments. "Why would you think that I wouldn't accept you?"

"In a perfect world, you'd think someone who survived cancer would be looked up to. Not me. In school, everyone thought I was a freak. They liked to play around, since I wasn't afraid of anything," Lexi explained as she began to get teary eyed. "They would say things like, 'oh Lexi, if you're not afraid, you should suck off the whole football team.' 'Hey Lexi, try skydiving without a parachute, you have nothing to be afraid of.' They went on and on and on. The angrier I got, the more they did it. My father called some of their parents and threatened them. That just made it worse. He tried, he really did. When I was seventeen I had this boyfriend who I thought cared about me, but he was just interested in my body. He never got his ugly grubs on it though. I figured his ass out."

Vincent reached over and put his hand on her shoulder. With that, Alexis Hera completely let loose. "Even the guys that I was lookout with in Danbury didn't think I knew that they were taking bets on who could get me into bed first. THAT'S ALL THEY CARED ABOUT! I survived cancer to just be ridiculed by everyone." Lexi was doing everything she could to avoid bursting into tears. She couldn't feel fear, but anger and sadness weren't a problem.

"Your last name, you know what it stands for right?" Vincent asked.

Lexi looked up, "Yeah, Hera was a Goddess in Greek mythology."

"Not just any Goddess, she was the wife of Zeus. She was also the Goddess of Marriage and Childbirth. Now think about that for a moment. That's the perpetuation of life. She was life, not just of an individual, but of humanity. I don't believe in coincidences, like I've said before. I can't change what's happened in your past any more than I can change what's happened in mine, but we can make a pact with each other, right here, right now," Vincent comforted.

Lexi looked at Vincent intently. She wondered to herself why she spilled so much of her personal life to someone she just met, although she felt as though she had known him for years, "A pact?"

Vincent nodded, "Yup, a pact. Both of our lives are going to start from this time forward. No more will we let the nightmares of the past control us. I let mine control me for far too long. After I escaped Project Scorpion, I exiled myself. I left behind everyone who ever cared about me. I let the Night Viper die. I had all of this power, and I just hid and felt sorry for myself while the world was turned upside down."

Lexi sat for a moment, wiping her tears away, then stood up and said, "You have a deal Vincent Black...or should I call you Night Viper?"

Vincent stood up also, "Ha. Whichever works for you."

Lexi threw her arms around Vincent and gave him a hug like she had hugged no other. He hesitated for a moment, and then reached his own arms up. Lexi said, "I'm sorry I flipped out so much. I'm sure you probably thought I was a lot stronger emotionally than I really am."

"You are strong Lexi - never underestimate yourself. You have nothing to be sorry about. You're a human being who's been put through hell for awhile, far before the Flash Storm. I also knew from the moment that I met you that you were sensitive on the inside. Most people with that tough exterior are," Vincent said as he used his index finger and ran it down her nose. "Now, I just have one question."

Lexi nodded, "Sure. Anything."

Vincent let out a half smile, "Is there something up with Crisco?"

Lexi looked at the wall then looked back at Vincent, "I don't trust him. I know we're trying to trust each other here...but I don't know. He's hiding something."

"I'm not getting pinged by my danger sense if that's of any consolation," Vincent assured her.

Lexi shook her head, "It's not that...I just don't know what his intentions are and I think he may have had more involvement with you than he's claiming. Just some of the looks and the body language, it seems off. Not to mention any information he may have about my father and what his involvement was."

Vincent scratched the back of his neck, "To be honest, I'm not sure how much I trust him either; but he helped us find this place and it's definitely dormant. When he gets back from his rounds, I'll take extra care to keep an eye on him."

"Thank you Vincent, for trusting me...for everything. How about we join up with Josh before his mind wanders and rumors spread," Lexi suggested.

Vincent nodded and chuckled. "Sure thing, Lexi. And hey, don't hold this stuff inside. Trust me - I did that for far too long. If you need a listening ear..."

Lexi simply smiled and wrapped her arm around Vincent's as they walked out of the room.

Chapter 15

Occum, Connecticut. The town was named after Samson Occom, who was a famous Native American clergyman from Connecticut. It was completely deserted, except for 35 men and women with guns. They stood in the old playground ready to listen to the person they declared their leader, Carl Woods. Before the Flash Storm, they'd had regular lives. None of them were military. The only one who had come close was Carl, who had been a Norwich police officer for 15 years.

Carl looked around at the people who had chosen to follow him. They were hungry. They were tired. They were scared. Most of them had been wearing the same clothes for a month or longer. They were equipped with whatever weaponry could be found. When firearms were made illegal in the United States, there was a backlog at most police departments. They were given instructions to destroy the weapons but they could not keep up with the processing so as a result, many sat in warehouses until they could be dealt with. Carl had known the whereabouts of one of these warehouses and they had raided it. Unfortunately, the weapons were all standard handguns and shotguns, nothing automatic.

Carl raised his hand and the group went silent, intent on what he had to say. "Brothers and sisters, today I come to you with news most grave. I've discovered that the brave men, women, and yes, children who were ready to stand up to this dictatorship in Bridgeport, Danbury, New Haven, and Hartford have been completely wiped out. We are alone. We cannot wait any longer. There is no army coming to save us. We have to save ourselves.

We know that Zodiac's forces have taken over the William Backus Hospital and are using it for their twisted experiments. I say it's time to strike back!"

Commotion began to erupt. Protests rang out.

"We can't fight them."

"If the rebel cells couldn't stand up to them, then how're we going to?"

"We're as good as dead."

"It's only a matter of time before they get us."

"We should run from here as fast as we can."

Carl simply waved his hands around and said, "Please, everyone, quiet down and listen to me. I understand your fears, I really do. It's difficult to believe that a few months ago there were children playing on these grounds. There were cars being driven up and down these streets. People were living their lives. But that is the past. We are in the here and now. If nothing else, those that fell in the cities should serve as a reminder that sitting around waiting for something to happen is akin to sitting around and waiting to die. Well I for one am not willing to just wait to be taken. We need to bring the fight to them."

More commotion erupted.

"How do we do that?"

"We've never faced Seekers."

"This is crazy."

"I want to go home."

"I just want to find my family and leave this place."

Carl once again waived his hands around to quiet people down. "Enough. People, there is no place to go where we can hide forever. We need to take action. We may not be able to bring Zodiac down, but we sure as hell can kick his dark soldiers out of here and reclaim it. Once we're victorious, others will follow. We just need one victory and word of it will travel. We need to bring back the spirit of who we are, not continue to run scared. None of us has ever faced a Seeker, that's true. But beneath that armor they wear is a flesh and blood human being, and they can be defeated."

The commotion began anew.

"They might be robots or something."

"I heard they're genetically engineered clones."

"I heard that they turn you to stone just by looking at them."

Carl just shook his head. These people had no idea. He wanted to try to make a difference, but he had doubts that this group could handle it. "Everyone, please, calm down. Rumors and speculation won't help anything. This world wasn't invaded by aliens; it was torn apart by a dictator. It's happened before in our planet's history and every time, those rulers were overthrown. Hell, it will probably happen again one day but in the meantime, tyrants can only be overthrown by those dedicated to the cause of freedom, and that my friends, is the cause that we are dedicated to."

This time, there was no commotion. People had stopped and were actually listening. Carl looked around quickly, then, realizing that he didn't have to hush everyone, he continued, "Today, we strike a blow for every freedom loving man, woman, and child. Today, we will destroy that hospital and those Seekers with it. Today, we will show Zodiac that he may have destroyed our cities, but he hasn't destroyed us!"

Now the people began cheering.

"Yeah, we don't need to be afraid."

"Screw that lizard-headed bastard!"

"Yeah, let's kick their asses!"

Carl let them rave for a few more moments, and then waved his hands to quiet everyone down again. "Alright then, here's the plan and with 35 of us, it can't fail." Carl began to explain how they were going to go about their attack. Little did they know, miles above their heads, they were not alone.

Standing in the makeshift control room of the former William W. Backus Hospital, Commander Jade watched the view screen where the operator of the terminal sat, following her every command. The operator was not a Seeker but was a lobotomized slave, so she did not object to having someone linger over her shoulder. Prior to conversion, this slave was an office worker in her mid fifties. Her body was too ravaged by age and lack of care for conversion to a Seeker, so instead she was put to work here. Stripped of her free will, she could only carry out orders.

On the screen was a video feed from an old United States Military satellite that Jade had tasked to be a set of eyes to look for Vincent Black and Alexis Hera. It didn't find the fugitives but it did find a band of men and women who appeared to be armed and gathered in a park only a few miles away from the Seeker Farm that was formerly the William W. Backus Hospital. There was no sound in the feed but Jade had learned to read lips when she was a child.

"This group of ragtag fools are actually thinking of attacking this compound. They must be drunk or something. I'm actually insulted that they're cheering as if their feeble attempt to overthrow us is going to lead to anything more than their deaths," Jade chastised out loud. The slave did not respond, but kept working the keyboard and mouse with her blank stare and clumsy reactions.

"Play that section again," Jade ordered.

"Yes commander," the slave replied as she backed the video feed up a bit.

Jade watched the clip again, mouthing the words she believed were being said. She identified the apparent leader and was attempting to read the lips of some of the others. She had her slave back up the video feed again and again while she thoroughly analyzed the conversation. Assembling the bits and pieces, she managed to find that this group lacked a substantial amount of key knowledge. They knew little to nothing about the Seekers. They knew nothing about the command structure. They knew nothing about the BFT-5000, the Firehawks, or anything else. It was just another band of people who had been hiding out and had now decided to come into the open and attempt a brave, yet stupid feat.

Jade began to cackle, "I needed some entertainment. You may cease rewinding the video. I have what I need. So, what do you think slave? Should I merely capture this group or should I kill them?"

"You do as you wish commander," the slave responded.

Jade sighed. The slaves and Seekers weren't very good for opinion confirmation. Since they no longer held opinions, she was on her own with the decision making. Despite that drawback, sometimes it was nice to talk to them, as speaking out loud helped her work things out in her head and she didn't have to worry about the mindless subordinates breaking an oath of silence.

"Well, let's weigh this out. The destruction of the rebel cells has given us far more fodder to convert to Seekers and slaves than we originally expected and planned for, so we don't really need any more at the moment. Hmmmm...decisions," Jade was thinking out loud. Suddenly an idea came to her for a way to get her answer and amuse herself at the same time.

Commander Jade briskly walked toward the elevators. It was good timing since one of them was coming to her floor. When it stopped, she saw two Seekers escorting a man, recently captured and transported from the Danbury battle, to the conversion room. "Seekers, how fit is this man?" asked Jade.

One Seeker replied in their typical monotone voice, "He is not fit to be a Seeker. He shall become a slave."

They had enough slaves already. She wanted to play with this one. "Hold off on that. I want you to bring him back down to the holding area. I will accompany you." With that, she stepped onto the elevator, which was buzzing from sitting on the same floor for too long. The Seekers obeyed without question.

"Wh...what are you going to do to me," asked the prisoner. The man looked to be around 25, but he also looked sickly and pale. The inspector had decided that he was not fit to be a Seeker but that he should be processed as a slave. She would have to talk to the inspector; this man was not fit to do anything.

"I'm not going to do anything to you...yet. I need to come to a decision and I need your help," Jade informed him.

The elevator doors closed behind the Grand Army Commander after she got in. "I'm not going to help you...," the man began.

Jade interrupted by giving him a kick to the abdomen. He coughed and hacked and gasped. When they arrived on their floor, the doors opened. The two Seekers lifted the man by his arms and dragged him out. "You are going to do whatever I say, you disgusting creature. I am superior to you in every way and your continued life is merely at my whim," Jade barked.

This particular floor had at one time included gift shops, and other types of business. It had now been completely converted to a holding area. There were Seeker guards everywhere. The cries and pleading of the prisoners who had no idea what was about to happen to them were all that could be heard. She stopped and listened for a moment. All of these people, powerless. She held the lives of so many in her hands. At any moment, she could decide to end their lives and it would be so. It was amazing to her how the tide could change. At one time her life and her freedom had been held in the hands of others. Now it was her turn.

"Time to listen up," Jade shouted, but the wails and cries were drowning her out. She pulled a .45 automatic and pointed it at the prisoner that she'd had the Seekers carry off the elevator, then fired a round, blowing the back of his head completely off. Chunks of his brain and globs of blood splattered on the floor behind him.

"DO I HAVE YOUR ATTENTION NOW!? ARE YOU READY TO LISTEN OR DO YOU NEED ANOTHER LESSON IN MAN-NERS!?" Jade yelled in a loud and shrill voice. Everyone quieted down, except for the occasional whimper. The commander enjoyed the whimpers; it was a sign that she had the utmost control in the situation so she put up with them. "Good. I have a dilemma that I require some assistance with. It seems that a band of 35 would-be rebels have made the unwise decision of planning an attack on this installation tonight, no doubt to free all of you. Just so that you don't have any glimmer of hope, I know all of their plans and I assure you, they will fail miserably. My question to you is this; do we convert them to Seekers or do I slaughter them like the pathetic animals they are?"

All of the prisoners began to look at each other. No one responded.

"I don't like to wait. You may want to hurry. My trigger finger is getting itchy," Jade warned. She held up her .45 and smirked.

The whimpering increased but no one responded.

"Alright, have it your way," Jade stated as she pointed her pistol at a middle aged couple huddled in the corner closest to her. The man was using his body to shield the woman but to no avail. Jade fired and the bullet ripped through him then ripped through her before it broke apart hitting the wall.

Horrified screams rang out. Instead of recoiling, Jade stood there smiling. The level of fear that she induced, the effect she had on all of these people was intoxicating. She was enjoying herself. She fired again, one at a time until her gun was empty dropping prisoner after prisoner and laughing like a sadistic clown. "DIE YOU MISERABLE BASTARDS! DIE FOR JUST SITTING THERE

AND ALLOWING THIS TO HAPPEN. THAT'S ALL PEOPLE DO IS JUST SIT THERE AND LET THINGS HAPPEN!" She waited several moments until the screams died down to whispers then back to the mere whimpering that it was prior to her tirade of murder.

"You know what? I think I have my answer. Once again I have been shown that no matter what wrongs are inflicted, humanity just watches instead of acts. Thank you all for your help. I want to remind you all that your situation is hopeless. The will of Lord Zodiac prevails and your wills are insignificant and obsolete. I look forward to enslaving you all, mind, body, and soul," Jade bragged as she turned around and walked away.

In the back of the crowd, a lone figure watched. Unlike the others, he was afraid but not nearly to the extent that he was angry. With the other prisoners feeling hopeless and drenched in disparity, they all began huddling into groups in an attempt to comfort each other as much as possible. The loner remained in the shadows and thought to himself, "This is not over. I swear on the lives of those lost that you will pay dearly."

Chapter 16

"Hey guys, check this out!" Lexi said with excitement to Vincent and Josh. They were still in the control room, feverishly sorting through the mounds of data at their fingertips, and doing their best to remain undetected.

Vincent pushed off the console with his feet, causing the wheeled office chair to glide across the floor to where Lexi was sitting. He looked at the screen and saw an image of her driver's license. "Wow, you're probably one of the only people I've ever seen with a good picture on one of those." She blushed.

Josh stood up and walked over to take a look. "That's impressive. I look like a heroin addict in mine. Wow, this is crazy; the federal government was literally downloading everything from state and local agencies. It's like they were creating a massive data warehouse of everything that's been computerized for every person in the country. You mind if I try something Lexi?"

"Sure, go ahead, you know more about this than me," she agreed and stood up. She was still wearing her oversized shirt, but when she stood up the movement revealed that she was indeed wearing a pair of sweat shorts underneath.

Josh's lightning fingers went to action and within mere moments, several screens displayed. Lexi's credit card transactions, cell phone calls, text messages, and a plethora of other information swarmed onto the display. "My God, a lot of this stuff is protected information. The government was violating their own laws by doing this. So much for the Constitution."

Vincent motioned to Lexi to see if she wanted his seat; she

simply smiled and shook her head then leaned in next to him to get a better view of the screen. Vincent leaned forward. "Unfortunately, the Constitution was being ignored more and more every day by the government. They obviously didn't care to get warrants for any of this stuff. Bastards! They turned citizens into science experiments and spied on us…Look at this; they even have your progress reports from high school in here."

Lexi had a look of horror on her face. "They have my whole life. They literally stole everything. Dad was right."

"Right about what?" Josh asked.

"He was suspicious of the government's activity in the year before the Flash Storm. At first, I thought he was just being paranoid but then they worked to repeal the 2nd amendment and disarm the public. The federal government began heavily regulating the states with the argument that there were too many differences and that policies needed to be more universal. My God, he was right about everything." Lexi had a blank look on her face.

This time Vincent stood up and gently guided Lexi to the chair. She slumped into it and it began to roll backwards a few inches. He said to her softly, "That may be why he left Project Scorpion. He may have seen exactly what they were doing."

Lexi looked up at Vincent, "I want to believe he didn't have anything to do with what they did to you and those six other people. I really do. I hope you believe that my father wasn't evil. Anything he did he would have done with the belief that it was for the good of the country."

Vincent nodded. "I can't imagine an evil person could have raised you." He looked over at Josh and asked, "Is there any way to tell when these records were created? They have to be copies. Most of the originals would be on servers that were destroyed or disconnected now that there's only a defense net."

Josh's hands went to work again and almost instantly he came up with the answer, "Yeah, Lexi's profile here was created a little less than a year before the Flash Storm. Why?"

"We need to query this thing. The private sector information - I want to know when they began collecting it," Vincent stated.

"What's that gonna prove?" Josh asked.

"I want to see if timelines match up. A year before the Flash Storm, there was a lot of strange activity within the government.

I'll bet the bulk of the records transfer began about that time," Vincent answered.

"You think the government is responsible for the Flash Storm? Isn't that time stamp about the same time you escaped from here?" asked Lexi.

Vincent shook his head, "I don't believe the government is responsible for the Flash Storm. Those greedy bastards wouldn't want to destroy themselves, but the timing is too coincidental. The clandestine experiments to create a super soldier here, the downloading of civilian records, the repeal of the 2nd Amendment... all indicate that they were preparing for something, maybe some type of takeover. I think that the events of May 7th were unexpected. It's possible that Zodiac was working within the government or had agents."

"If he had strong ties or even a high position or something, he could have easily had those flash bombs planted across the world, especially since they weren't nuclear and wouldn't have been easily detectable," Lexi pointed out.

Josh hit the "enter" key loudly shouting out, "Done! I'll run that query, although it's going to take awhile."

"Alright. Do you think the two of you can continue sifting through data on the other two terminals, see what else you can find out? I'm going to check on the others." Vincent seemed a bit distant.

Lexi and Josh looked at each other and nodded.

"Thanks. I'll be back," Vincent stated as he turned around and left the room.

Lexi and Josh looked at each other again. There was a long moment of silence as each was wondering if the other was thinking the same thing. "Alright, I'll just speak up," Josh said. He wheeled over to another terminal, the one Vincent had been using. "Look at this. Apparently, they downloaded the L.A. times and other newspapers."

"L.A. times?" Lexi inquired.

"Vincent said he had been in the L.A. area when the Flash Storm hit. He also mentioned that he had been there prior to being taken to Project Scorpion, so I decided to do a little digging," Josh answered.

Lexi had a concerned look on her face, "I don't like sneaking around like this. There are a lot of questions, I know, but this just seems wrong."

Josh turned from what he was doing and looked her in the eyes, "Don't worry Lexi, we may actually find out something that will help him. Now, look at this. I did a search for Vincent Black before; I got lots of hits, but none that matched our Vincent Black. When I did a search in the L.A. Times, I found this stuff."

Lexi's eyes almost popped out of her head when she saw what flashed on the screen. Article after article was written about a vigilante in the Los Angeles area. "Oh my God, look at this. Is this Vincent!?"

Josh clicked a button and up popped an article entitled "Night Viper Strikes Again." The content of the article described a domestic terrorist group called Rebel XCIX that had launched numerous attacks against government and public installations across the country. The article mentioned an attack on the Millstone nuclear power plant in Connecticut. Apparently, "Night Viper" was responsible for the deaths of 20 of its members.

"What is this Rebel XCIX? What does XCIX stand for?" asked Josh.

Lexi had her eyes glued to the article. "XCIX...XCIX...wait... that's the Roman Numeral for 99. The group is Rebel 99. I remember that thing at Millstone. They said that it was attacked by a domestic terrorist group. Matter of fact, I remember hearing that some bystander ran into the building and pulled out two pinned workers but then we heard nothing."

"Vincent is originally from Connecticut, right?" asked Josh.

Lexi gasped, "The Millstone thing. Holy shit! Vince said he had cancer throughout his entire system as the result of radiation exposure. It was severe too. He's the one who ran into that building. They said he should have been dead in less than 24 hours but he survived for a year, then the government picked him up and brought him here."

"My God, he's a damn hero!" Josh stated.

Lexi had tears fill her eyes. "Vincent never had any intention of making it through that alive."

"Lexi, why the hell would you say something like that?" Josh barked.

Lexi wiped the tears from her eyes, "It's something he said

when we met Crisco. We were in that trailer prison thing. He saw that Crisco and the other guy that ended up killed had a scorpion tattoo identical to his. He was angry and said something about the government not asking him if he actually wanted to be saved."

The color flushed out of Josh's face almost instantly, "Swear to me you won't ever repeat this."

"What Josh?" Lexi asked.

"You've gotta swear, dammit!" Josh demanded.

Lexi nodded her head, "Okay, Okay, I swear I won't repeat this."

Josh collected himself then said, "When Vincent and I were doing our little reconnaissance of this complex, we came across a sealed room. He had me open it. After a minute of being in there he started having all of these memory flashes. He said that he barely remembered anything about his time here because he was so disoriented, but those memories seemed to be coming back in fragments in that lab. He told me not to say anything."

"I think I know which room you're talking about. What the hell was in there?" Lexi's curiosity was getting the better of her.

"I don't know, it was pretty dark. There were shards of some type of crystalline substance everywhere though. There was some machine or something, but it was busted up pretty badly. I have no idea what it did, but I think that room was where they did whatever they did to him," Josh explained.

"Is there anything on Project Scorpion in the defense net?" asked Lexi.

"It wouldn't be in this area. This is all the stuff the feds stole from state and local databases, not the federal databases themselves. I don't know that there would be any type of record of Project Scorpion. This is crazy," Josh stated.

Lexi wiped away a few more tears that welled up. "What could have happened to Vincent that would drive him to do something like that?"

Josh shook his head. "I have no idea. Maybe he just wanted to prove that he was worth something. I kind of know how he felt, I was a reject myself. Then I got to college and things changed. College students like geeks."

Lexi laughed. "Yeah, I guess. I know what it's like to be rejected too. Everyone thought I was a freak after the cancer because I don't fear anything."

"People suck. Why the hell are we trying to save them?" asked Josh.

"Because not all people are like that. I may have been pissed at the world, but I certainly never wanted to destroy it, at any point," Lexi answered.

Josh continued to flip through articles. After the first few he managed to get to one about a year before the Flash Storm entitled, "Night Viper Dead?" Both he and Lexi read intently.

Lexi held her hand to her mouth, "Wow, this was about a year before the Flash Storm? No one had heard from Night Viper or seen him. They're presuming he died, but not before 77 deaths were positively linked to him. Rapists, gangbangers, murderers, all sorts of…well…lowlifes."

Josh was pointing to a sentence on the screen, "That 77 includes the 20 from Rebel 99. Geeze, he really wanted to go out with a bang."

At that moment the door opened and Vincent came in, "Don't bother trying to exit out of that."

"Vince, I…we…," Lexi had no idea what to say.

"Vince man, we weren't trying to do anything vicious. There's just so much that's unknown out there. You have no public record in the system but we found articles in the L.A. Times," Josh explained.

"I can't believe that this never made national news," Lexi commented.

Vincent came in and shut the door. "That's because it was suppressed. People really didn't want the story of a vigilante who was demolishing L.A.'s scumbags to get out. They were afraid more people would follow in my footsteps. As it is, there was a big to do in California about what I did. And 77 was only the number of deaths they could connect to me. I was responsible for a lot more than that."

"What is it with you and the number 7?" asked Josh nervously.

"Vince, I hope you're not mad," Lexi pleaded.

Vincent shook his head, "Nah, I should've realized that someone eventually would've tried finding out more about me. Look, after the whole thing at Millstone, I knew I was gonna die…it was just a matter of time. The mindset I had at that point - I welcomed it, but I wasn't gonna just sit idly by and wait for the inevitable. I figured I would take out as many of these bastards that hurt the innocent as I could. I declared war on L.A.'s underworld."

"Why L.A.? Why not Hartford or somewhere else?" Josh inquired.

"I couldn't put my family and friends at risk, so I left Connecticut and went to the other side of the country," Vincent explained.

Josh was fidgeting in his seat. "What did you do after this place?"

Vincent had a long look on his face. "I was severely disoriented at first. I had no idea what I had become. When I escaped from here, I did things that I shouldn't have been able to do. I remember being shot repeatedly; my body pushed the bullets out and the wounds closed within seconds. I threw armed guards around as if they were sticks in the way of a lawnmower. I sought out someone who could help me collect my thoughts and help me get myself grounded again. And like I said before, the project put this "7" tattoo on my eyelid and when I realized what the government had done and the people who had suffered the ultimate price for their indiscretions, I had the scorpion logo tattoo added to serve as a constant reminder of what had happened. This is to honor them, those who died to perfect a process that saved my life."

Lexi stood up and walked over to Vincent. She put her hand on his shoulder and said, "Those people didn't die in vain. You are a gift to all of us and I am grateful to have you on our side."

"Thanks Lexi." Vincent tried to avoid blushing so he changed the subject. "Now, what did my little query turn up?" He went over to the terminal running the query just in time for it to finish.

"What's it say?" Josh asked anxiously.

Vincent grunted. "Look at this - most of the downloading began at about the same time as Lexi's info, about the time of the Project Scorpion experiment that created me."

"They didn't download your stuff," Josh interrupted.

Vincent had a puzzled look on his face. "What?"

"I tried to do a search for all of us. There are a lot of people with the name Vincent Black. You aren't any of them. I figured maybe Project Scorpion had you removed. I could check someone else if you know any of their names," Josh explained.

Vincent began pacing. "How about Lexi's father, or Crisco?"

Josh shook his head, "Already done. They're in there, just nothing mentioned about Project Scorpion. You believe Crisco is a Sergeant?"

"Hey, speaking of Crisco, has anyone seen him?" Lexi wanted to change the subject.

Vincent and Josh looked at each other; both shook their heads. "Can you bring up the surveillance cameras in here Josh?" Vincent requested.

Josh's fingers furiously went to work once again. Both Lexi and Vincent were looking over his shoulders, watching the screen intently. "Haven't you guys heard of personal space?"

Vincent and Lexi looked at each other, then backed up a pace and said simultaneously, "Sorry."

Josh just shook his head. He brought up the live footage from the cameras which covered pretty much every square inch of the complex. Camera after camera showed no sign of Crisco. Then he brought up the footage from the outdoor cameras, which were scattered throughout the fenced area. Again, there was no sign of him. "Do you think he ran?"

"I don't know, he might have. He didn't seem too thrilled about being back here," Vincent pointed out.

Lexi stood for a moment then spoke up. "Where would he go though? Why would he leave like this?"

Josh turned around in his seat, "Maybe he had more involvement in Project Scorpion than we thought and figured we might find him out. Should we go look for him?"

Vincent shook his head. "No. Change the access codes. If he wants to come back in, he'll have to answer to why he went missing. In the meantime, we have more important things to address."

Chapter 17

Night had fallen once again. A line from a poem written by an old friend of hers kept repeating in Jade's head, "I am night, death of day." Over and over this line played. She thought about the irony that the death of day would lead to an attack that would get the assailants killed. She was unsure why people continued to stand up to the Grand Army. No one had ever been victorious.

She still had no idea where Vincent Black or Alexis Hera were, but at the moment it didn't matter. She felt a strong sensation of justice each and every time she took out those who would stand up to Zodiac's forces. She projected her anger from those who wronged her onto all those who opposed her. The small band of fools that had met in a park earlier that day was getting ready to launch their feeble attack. She admitted to herself that if she had not been expecting it, they might have done a little bit of damage, maybe set back Seeker and slave production at this particular Farm for about a few hours. If they hit the right spot, maybe some of the prisoners would have escaped. Of course, she was not only expecting this attack, she was ready for it.

The group's plan was simple. They loaded a van full of homemade explosives, mixed from supplies that they had looted from an abandoned hardware store. They were going to borrow a technique that terrorists in the Middle East had been using against foreign embassies, except they weren't going to have anyone commit suicide to do it. They would jack the wheel of the van and put a block on the gas pedal to insure that the vehicle went straight into the building. The explosives were timed so they would go off at impact or shortly thereafter. In the confusion that would erupt, they would unleash a blitz upon the Seekers.

The advantage of having a suicide driver is that he or she could make decisions and compensate when unforeseen variables arose. The person was a guaranteed casualty but the sacrifice would increase the chance of a successful hit. The discussion could go on for days about whether or not a suicidal driver would have helped in this situation. Jade watched from one of the security monitors as the van was launched. A Seeker was set up with a RPG, ready to fire on command.

"Take it out!" Jade ordered into the comm.

The Seeker fired and landed a direct hit. The van detonated harmlessly, a good distance from the Farm. Having re-tasked the satellite, Jade had been watching the grounds around the area and saw where the small, rag-tag battalion had set up. The Seekers, having orders to take no prisoners, began tossing grenades and launching mortars in the direction of the would-be liberators. Within moments, those that had not been killed or horribly maimed were making a hasty retreat.

"Pursue and destroy," Jade happily ordered into the comm.

Everything had gone horribly wrong for Carl Woods. He wanted to hit the Seekers fast and hard and retreat to fight another day. He figured guerilla style hit-and-run tactics would work well as they had in past wars like Vietnam and even the American Revolutionary War. But those wars were different. The enemy had desires, feelings, drive, and a whole slew of other emotions. This enemy felt nothing. They feared nothing. Those that believed in him feared something. They feared death. They feared further loss. They feared slavery. They feared the Seekers. The fear of the dark warriors was so intense, that there was nothing to compare it to.

Carl shouted directive after directive, but he might as well have been yelling at a brick wall. There was a greater possibility that the brick wall would have acknowledged him. Everyone was far too afraid. After the van loaded with explosives was destroyed, various ordinances were being launched at them. Several feet from where Carl was taking cover a mortar hit someone directly. He watched in horror as this person who earlier that day had trusted him, blew apart into scraps of flesh and bone. The person who was near the victim also became a victim, losing his left arm, leg and left side of his face to the blast. His body was loaded with bone fragments from his comrade that had become shrapnel in the explosion.

Within moments, their numbers had dwindled to less than half. Carl didn't need to order a retreat. Everyone was running. The Seekers were sending serious overkill. Four of the would-be heroes were making haste together when a rocket propelled grenade headed their way. They never saw what hit them. Their bodies were so broken and mangled that it was difficult to tell what piece belonged to whom.

Carl didn't want to quit. All of these people, brutally slaughtered, and it would be for nothing if he just left. He couldn't even stand up. He was so overcome with fear and anxiety that he couldn't move his legs. He quickly looked down to make sure that he still had legs. Interestingly, he was unscathed physically. He continued to take cover for a few more moments, when suddenly everything went quiet. There was no more gunfire. No more explosions. No more screams. There was only the smell of burning flesh, sweat, and blood.

Carl finally mustered the courage to look up from his cover and saw that the assault was truly over. Looking around, he was quite certain that he was probably the last survivor. Then he caught sight of the humanoids with the bright lights on their shoulders. They were Seekers. What were they? He didn't want to find out what the three were that were making their way toward him. He immediately jumped up and began to run, faster than he had ever run before in his life. The gunfire resumed.

He quickly ran down Washington Street, directly past a sign that said "2" and "32". Those old routes were quite well known in Connecticut. He continued to hear gunfire but no ordinance. A few rounds struck the pavement behind him; he felt the fragments of asphalt as the bullets struck. The sensation was like getting stung by a hundred mosquitoes simultaneously, right through his pants. Looking up ahead he saw two houses, or what was left of them. They had burned and collapsed. Carl was tired. He was in pain. The adrenaline pumping through his system would only last so long before he would collapse from exhaustion. The trees hadn't lost their leaves yet and he hoped they would cover him from view long enough to duck into the ruins of these houses.

The former Norwich police officer made a sharp turn and ran directly to the first house which was only half standing. He ran inside and started looking around. It may have been a nice house at one time but the gaping holes, the charred and sometimes absent walls had put an end to that. He took a few quick steps forward then stopped when he heard a loud creak. His body weight must have been the "straw that broke the camel's back" because the support beam that used to hold up the floor underneath him snapped and he fell into the basement. Above him, with that support now gone, more supports began letting go and what was left of the structure collapsed over the top of him.

Laying in what had been the basement of this house with a pile of rubble on top of him, Carl stayed still. He was alive. He did a quick status check and felt that he was able to wiggle his toes as well as his fingers. He tried not to make any sudden moves. Looking up through the gaps in the debris, he could see lights. The Seekers were looking around the yard. He continued to feel such intense fear that he just wanted to cry out loud, but he didn't. He stayed still. He may never know where he summoned the strength to do that but he made no noise or further movements. He even kept his breaths shallow and silent.

Bang! Bang! Bang!

Three individual shots rang out. He could hear them ripping through the debris. Carl wanted to scream more than anything. He thought his heart would stop from the sheer terror he was feeling. "Stop thinking like that you damn coward," he said to himself.

Bang! Bang! Bang!

Three more shots. This time they were further away. The Seekers didn't know where he was. He then realized why. He smelled it. A fire was starting, in the debris of this house. There must have been something flammable that didn't burn up the first time. It could have been ignited from sparks from the bullets hitting the concrete foundation. It didn't matter. Carl was buried and now the stuff that was burying him was on fire. On one hand, multiple sources of heat made it difficult to find him if the Seekers had infrared capabilities. The problem was that after surviving a slaughter, he was going to be burned alive.

Carl didn't hear any more shots and after a moment more, the lights above disappeared. He took a quick assessment now that his head was clearing. His intense fear was subsiding. For the first time since the assault began, he felt as if he might be able to get out alive. The rubble was actually only piled loosely on top of him. He managed to push it off and slither his way out from underneath to find that the rest of the debris had fallen in such a way that it created a small, almost cave around him. He took a moment to thank God with every name that the deity was known by. He noticed flickering light through the gaps in the rubble and knew instantly that the fire was coming his way.

Looking around, Carl tried as best he could to figure out what he could move and what would be too risky. He had nothing more than the flickering light of the oncoming fire and the moon-light from above. His situation reminded him of playing "Pickup Sticks" in the dark, only the penalty for everything falling was death. He did not want to lose this game. "Think Carl, think. You've got to get the hell out of here," he thought to himself.

Someone or something out there in the universe must have heard him because he had a sudden idea. He was in a concrete basement. He realized that if he could make it to one of the outer walls, all he had to do was get himself up and out of the foundation. It would be far easier than attempting to maneuver his way to the top of this pile only to try to get off it without collapsing it again. Crawling through the fragments of the house, he managed to push aside enough rubble to get to a concrete wall. Looking straight ahead, there was a gap that would allow him to squeeze himself between the wall and the debris so he did. He took in his surroundings and noticed that there was a doorway about two feet away.

"Shit, that's gotta be the cellar stairs going outside!" Carl thought to himself. There was a problem though. The door most likely opened into the basement, they usually did. He managed to slither his way over. When he was close enough, he realized that a part of the house had fallen and put a hole through the door. It wasn't big enough for him to get through, but he saw that the door was made of flimsy, hollow wood which he could easily break. He had never been so happy about shoddy workmanship until that point.

Squeezing himself into position, he managed to get a gash on his arm from an exposed nail. He cursed out loud then quickly went silent, hoping that the Seekers were truly gone. Pushing on some debris, he cleared enough room to put his arm forward then smash backward at the broken door with his elbow.

Crack! Crack!

Two good shoves and the opening had become big enough for him to climb through. He managed to worm his way out, continuing to break what was left of the door until he flopped on the stairs. He was right. They were stairs most likely going to the back yard. He looked up and saw two metal doors with a rusted latch. With some maneuvering he managed to unlock the latch and swing one of the doors out and open. He was above ground. Looking around he saw that the fire was spreading rapidly. Carl decided that now would be a good time to get away from what was left of the structure. He was cut, he was bruised, but he was alive.

Carl shot another glance around and saw that though the neighbor's house was also in ruins, the two-car freestanding garage was intact. He quickly ran over and around to the side where the door was. He tried the handle and it was thankfully unlocked…another lucky break. Inside was a brown Buick sedan. It looked to be late 90's. Despite the chaos outside, the garage held various yard care tools and equipment, even a riding lawnmower where a 2nd car would normally be parked. When he got near the car, he almost had a heart attack. Inside was a dried and decayed corpse sitting at the wheel. For a moment, he went into police officer mode and tried to establish what had happened until he realized that he would probably never be arresting someone again in his life.

This was the disgusting part. He knew he had to get out of there. The keys were in the decayed corpse's right hand. Prying the bony fingers open, he removed the keys which were slightly sticky from decaying flesh, then pulled on the corpse and removed it from the car. "Sorry about that friend, but right now I need this car more than you do," Carl whispered. He sat down, trying not to think about what kind of remnants of the previous owner were stuck to the seat. As he put the key in the ignition, he was finding it difficult to avoid total nausea. Looking at the garage door he saw that it was vinyl and lightweight. The automatic openers would no longer work without electricity, but he figured that the car should be able to bust through such a flimsy thing without a problem.

Carl turned the key and the Buick started right up. It had half a tank of gas, more than enough to get out of there. He put the vehicle in drive, and stepped on it, smashing through the garage, then turned onto Washington Street and sped away.

Chapter 18

A voice came over the comm. "Vincent, you've got to see this!" The voice belonged to John Decker and it sounded urgent. He and his wife had been analyzing the spider-like chip that they took out of the captured Seeker's head.

"I'll be right there," Vincent answered. He stood up from his terminal.

Lexi stood up immediately after, "Alright, I guess that's my queue to stop slumming it and actually get dressed."

"I'll stay here. I think I'm getting a handle on the setup of this defense network," Josh claimed.

Vincent nodded to both of them, "Sounds good. I'll be at the lab. Sounds like the Deckers had a breakthrough."

Vincent found himself once again alone in the hallways of the compound that housed Project Scorpion, the government experiment that changed the course of his life. He walked slowly, despite the urgency of John's voice. He was having trouble remembering his original visit, due to his massive disorientation. He shut his eyes as he walked, trying to remember, but he only saw repeats of the same memory flashes he had seen when they first arrived when he was with Josh in the mysterious lab-like room. He saw armed guards. They tried to stop him but they had no idea what he was capable of. At the time, he didn't either. Bullets weren't stopping him. Brute force didn't work either; he had become unstoppable.

He was gaining no new insight, despite his attempts to reach into his own mind. There was too much going on inside at the moment. He knew he would have to find time at a later point to concentrate better. He made a mental note, and then picked up the pace until he got to the doorway of his destination.

Inside, John Decker was pounding away at a computer simulation; desperately attempting to follow Eve's every instruction. In the center of the room was a holographic projector, which was showing a 3-D image of the spider-chip. "Vincent…just in time. I figured you'd want to see this," Eve stated.

Vincent shut the door and walked over to get a closer look. "That's the chip we pulled from the Seeker's brain?"

"Yeah, a 3-D rendering. This thing is incredible! It's definitely based on the design that we were working on at Berkeley, but this is way more advanced. I mean way more." Eve was getting jumpy.

John turned around in his seat. "Eve, slow it down a bit."

Eve started rubbing her pregnant belly again. Vincent was watching her. He took a few steps closer. "Eve, the baby's dropped. When's your due date?"

Eve continued to rub her belly. "A little over a month, November 10th to be exact."

"Eve, if you aren't able to continue, it's alright," Vincent comforted.

Eve shook her head, "No, I need to do this. I need to keep my mind focused. Besides, you really need to see this."

Vincent nodded. "So what am I looking at?"

"Probably the single most advanced nano-computer ever created," John interjected.

Eve smiled, then her face went suddenly serious. "Vincent, a lot of this is speculation but we do know this - there are a series of microscopic probes that resemble nerve endings. Some of them were severed when it was removed but they appear to be a mechanism to link up with the brain."

Eve was pointing to various parts of the 3-D enhanced image. Vincent was watching carefully then responded, "So basically, the Seekers are lobotomized and this thing is put in to replace the frontal lobe functions."

Eve grunted and sat down, continuing to rub her belly. "Yes, that's right. I'm no doctor but it looks like Zodiac effectively replaces the part of the brain, which allows us to think and feel for ourselves, with a computer."

"So, we know that Crisco had to practically tear open that Seeker's skull to get this out. How the hell did Zodiac get it in there without doing the same thing?" Vincent inquired.

"If you look at these spots, this thing was assembled inside of the brain. I can only assume that whatever probes are used to lobotomize the Seekers are also used to assemble these devices," Eve answered.

Vincent began pacing, "So, this is why they're not total zombies. There must be some kind of programming, something that allows them to formulate responses but not to think for themselves. It's almost like programming a combat drone or something. That doesn't answer the question of how they're controlled though."

Eve waved her hand at John, who spun around in his chair and entered commands into the computer. The rendering of the chip changed and zoomed in on a tiny wire. "This section appears to be some type of receiver. I thought maybe it was how they're programmed."

Vincent continued to pace around the 3-D image, looking it up and down as if it was an enemy that he was sizing up and getting ready to attack. "So it's the airwaves? What kind of transmissions? Radio?"

"There appears to be two receiving arrays. One of them has a small fragment of crystal attached to it," John stated.

Vincent whipped his head around. "A crystal?"

Before anyone could answer, Lexi opened the door and came in. She was back in her motorcycle attire, even though she no longer had a motorcycle. "I miss anything good?"

John and Eve looked annoyed. Vincent smirked at the frisky blonde. "The chip in that Seeker's head is some kind of nano-computer that's used to replace the frontal lobe functions. There are two receivers, one with a crystal attached to it."

Lexi walked over to the 3-D rendering. "It's a thought crystal."

John almost fell out of his chair and Eve thought she was going to have the baby right then and there. John composed himself first and said in a calm voice, "How can you be so sure?"

"What's a thought crystal?" Vincent raised his hand slightly, as if he was in a classroom.

Lexi was pacing around the image, much like Vincent. "Some new age scientists think that certain types of crystal can not only store data, but can actually capture projected thoughts."

Vincent looked intrigued as he leaned closer to the image. "So basically, operating on the assumption that Zodiac is telepathic, he could project orders or programming from his own mind and it would be received by the Seekers."

Eve went from rubbing her belly to rubbing her head. "I hate to say this, but it actually seems like the most plausible explanation. The other receiver is wired to the processor; it must be how a computer can be used to download programming into one of these guys."

John jumped out of his seat. "I think we cracked the Seeker code!"

"Don't break out the keg yet…we need to make sure that this is indeed the case. I'll ask Josh to go through the system and see if he can find some solid information. He can use what we've found as a starting point," Vincent cautioned.

"Is there a way to reverse the conversion process and give the person their mind back?" Lexi asked in a hopeful tone.

John and Eve looked at each other and shook their heads. "No, the damage to the brain by the lobotomy isn't reversible. At best, removing the chip would render them completely helpless. If done wrong, it would kill them outright. The Seekers would just be better off dead," John clarified.

Vincent was still studying the image. After a few moments of silence, he spoke up. "The more immediate question is: how do we combat the Seeker fear aura? We can amass all of the troops that we want but they'll be useless if they're pissing in their pants the entire time."

John glanced at Vincent, "We're going to amass troops?"

"We're going to need more than just the handful of us to fight back, so yes, we're going to amass troops, but not until we can have them fight with a clear head," Vincent answered without even turning his head.

"Well, Lexi's hypothesis that the crystal fragment is a thought crystal sheds some light on this assembly over here." Eve was whirling her finger around. John noticed and quickly went back to his place and reconfigured the rendering. "There's some kind of transmitter built off the crystal as well. It must emit some type of frequency. That could be what sends out the fear aura. I just didn't think something like that would be possible."

"You should see some of the new age research. Some scientists say that everything vibrates and brain waves and thought patterns can be measured by this vibration. The frequency might not be one that you would typically look for, but this may project fear and when a person hits the radius - boom," Lexi said, clapping her hands together once very loudly at the word "boom". "It's probably tuned specifically to the amygdala, which is why it doesn't affect me."

"How do you know so much about this stuff," asked Vincent.

Lexi smiled, "It's kind of a hobby of mine."

Eve looked flustered, and being pregnant decided not to hold back. "That's all unproven pseudo-science."

Lexi had her arms crossed and stood her ground. "Maybe, but unless you have a better explanation, I think we need to keep our minds open to the fact that there might be more out there than standard Western Science can prove."

"We can't go off philosophy for a real explanation," Eve argued.

"Didn't your science say that the Earth was the center of the universe and the sun revolved around it? Didn't it say that an atom couldn't be split? Those two things were proven wrong along with a lot of other stuff." Lexi wasn't backing down.

Vincent spoke up. "I don't want a debate over science and pseudo-science. If we're even willing to entertain the notion that Zodiac is telepathic, then we need to accept some of the more extreme explanations of what this device does. Until yesterday, the idea of something like this was science fiction to me anyway."

Everyone went silent.

"Alright, let's put some of this to the test. Is there any way to get power flowing through this chip again?" Vincent inquired. "If the source of the fear aura is indeed in this chip, and if we can measure the frequency, maybe we can come up with something that counteracts it."

John shook his head, "That might be a little beyond even my

brainiac wife."

Eve gave him the look of death. "Thanks for the vote of confidence, you big jock."

John hung his head in shame; he did not wish to unleash the wrath of an already irritable and pregnant Evelyn Decker. Vincent and Lexi worked miracles stifling their laughter. Vincent finally cleared the air saying, "They've got to have some kind of scientist or someone that works with this stuff, several people who have been allowed to keep their independent thought. We need to find a spot where they make the Seekers and capture one."

Everyone stopped and stared at Vincent.

"What? Any of you have a better idea?" Vincent looked around.

John shook his head and tried to make sure he heard what he thought heard. "Okay, it's not like we're ordering a pizza and deciding to get take out instead of delivery. You want to bust in on a Grand Army compound and take one of their scientists?"

Vincent nodded as if this was the most natural thing in the world. "Yeah, pretty much. While we're at it, maybe we can nab one of those commanders, see what their story is."

"I know I flipped out a little on the E, but I think I was far saner than you are right now," John pointed out.

"I'm in," Lexi volunteered. "I'm tired of running. Let's go kick some Seeker ass!"

John threw his arms in the air. "Great, you're both crazy - the guy with super powers and the girl with brain damage. This ought to go well."

Lexi waived her finger. "Well aren't we just a ray of sunshine tonight. C'mon Decker, where's your sense of adventure?"

"It washed off in the shower," John mumbled.

Eve spoke up. "How are we going to attack a Seeker stronghold?"

"We're not. I am. While their fear aura still has an effect, I don't want you guys to go near them," Vincent stated.

"It doesn't affect me, I'm coming with you," Lexi insisted.

"Of course she is." John rolled his eyes. Lexi ignored him.

"Alright, I'm going to check on Talbot and Andromeda and see what they've come up with, then we'll all have a round table and get ready to make the next move," Vincent declared. Before anyone could argue, he left the room.

John looked straight at Lexi. "You know you encourage him."

Lexi walked over to John, who was sitting in his chair and leaned in close. "I wouldn't have it any other way." She smiled and left the room before Eve could protest.

"Geeze Drom, you believe this shit!? I'd heard of this technology but I had no idea it'd been implemented!" Talbot exclaimed as he tightened the last bolt to secure the Bronco's engine back into place. Andromeda stood there silently, ready to hand him any tool that he requested. They had been working on the vehicles for hours. Their discovery was a massive fuel efficiency modification that would allow incredible gas mileage. Both of them turned their heads as they heard a door open.

Vincent held up his hands. "Hey, relax, just checking in to see how things went."

"You've got impeccable timing, Vince. This is incredible!" Despite being 52 years old, Talbot was as excited as a young child on Christmas day.

Vincent walked over to Talbot and Andromeda and raised his eyebrows. "What'd you find?"

"The Bronco and the shuttle were definitely modified by either the same person or two people with the same training and access to the same equipment. It's a good, professional job but you can tell its aftermarket, no surprise there. The Hummers were built with them. One would probably need a high clearance just to look under the hood of one of those things," Talbot explained.

"The Bronco and the shuttle? What kind of a connection do they have?" Vincent was perplexed.

"I have no idea; I just know what I see. The damn things probably get 80 or 90 miles to a gallon now. The Hummers probably get more like a hundred. It's crazy. I'd heard of this stuff. The guy who created the fuel efficiency was paid millions for the patent, then had an agreement for residual payments to continue to suppress his knowledge after the patent expired. The oil mongers didn't want this coming out," Talbot continued.

Vincent shrugged. "Can't say I blame them. These motors get 3 or 4 times the mileage that they get unmodified on the same gas? They stood to lose billions."

Talbot nodded in agreement. "Well, there's more good news. This compound has an underground tank that's still about two thirds full. Plenty to get around with since open gas stations are difficult to come by now."

"Good, glad to hear that we finally have some things going our way. Are you finished here?" Vincent asked.

"Yeah, just tightened up the last bolt actually. Why?" Talbot inquired.

Vincent put his hand on Talbot's shoulder. "I want to gather everyone in the meeting room again. We're going on the offensive."

Andromeda couldn't hide her expression. Her pupils dilated and she let out a big gulp. Talbot's heart nearly jumped into his throat. "What!? What do you mean we're going on the offensive?"

"I'll brief you in twenty minutes," Vincent responded, then turned and left the room. Andromeda and Talbot stood for a minute in complete shock.

It wasn't long before everyone except Vincent had gathered in the meeting room. They were all shooting glances at each other, wondering what the fuss was all about. Since they had nothing better to do while waiting, they decided to do what most people would do in a similar situation…speculate. Fortunately, the rumor mill did not last very long. The door opened and in walked their leader with a more determined look on his face than ever before. The room went instantly silent.

"I'm tired everyone. Real tired and I'm not talking muscle fatigue tired. I'm tired of running. I'm tired of hiding. I'm tired of standing on the sidelines while a complete lunatic decimates humanity. I don't know who else is out there. I don't know what kind of organization they may have, if any. I do know this - there's a very real possibility that we're it," Vincent explained.

"No pressure," Josh whispered.

Vincent stopped and looked at him. For a moment, Josh felt as if he was back in school and the teacher caught him talking during a lecture. His right leg started moving rapidly again and he was prepared for a scolding, but instead got a little snicker.

"There's pressure alright. Mark my words people…it's time we take the fight back to the Grand Army and in order to do that we need to be ready. Eve and John may have unlocked the secret of the chips that are implanted in Zodiac's slaves and soldiers, so Talbot, Andromeda, and Josh need to be caught up."

Vincent held his hand out toward Eve and John, so Eve spoke up. "Well, we all know that the Seekers have been lobotomized. The chip and the way it's attached is set up to replace the frontal lobe functions. It's a nano-computer that can effectively be programmed, turning the Seekers into flesh and blood automatons. There're two receivers…one that's obviously for computer based signals, and the other is attached to a crystal that's been hypothesized to be a thought crystal. Operating on the assumption that Zodiac is telepathic, he could control the Seekers with his mind as well as signal them via computer. We also think we may have identified a transmitter that sends out vibrations that trigger a fear reaction."

Talbot leaned forward, arms crossed, "So that means there may be a way to counter the fear aura. It means we could fight them."

John spoke up. "Possibly, but we need to measure the signal put out by this chip and it doesn't seem to be in the realm of our capability to do that."

"This is where the next step comes in. We need to find the location of a compound where they create the Seekers and nab one of their people. There would have to be someone who still has their free will present to oversee this process and make appropriate judgments," Vincent stated.

Josh, who had a habit of feeling like he was in school, raised his hand. Everyone looked over at him and he said, "Vince, after you and Lexi left the control room I think I found something."

"What?" Lexi asked bluntly.

Josh stirred in his seat a bit. "I know that you mentioned some kind of activity in the Southeastern part of Connecticut. I couldn't find out exactly what that was but there is something big, because heavy supply lines are being deviated there, so I dug further. William Backus Hospital in Norwich seems to be a hot spot, and they brought a substantial amount of prisoners from Danbury to that site. I don't know for sure, but I think that may be the place to start."

"Backus Hospital? Makes sense that they'd use a former hospital for the procedure," Vincent was rubbing his chin.

"You're not just going to be able to bust in though. We would need layouts, some kind of plan or something," Josh rambled.

Lexi spoke up. "They've probably hacked that place up and rebuilt it so none of the old layouts would be accurate anyway."

Vincent nodded in agreement. "We'll need to scope the place out and *then* figure out how we're going to hit it."

"What about the rest of us?" asked Eve. "And don't forget that Crisco is still missing."

"We can't worry about Crisco now; he could be anywhere at this point. We'll have to be ready if he tries to make contact or be prepared that we may never see him again. Talbot and Andromeda discovered that both the shuttle and the Bronco have fuel efficiency modifications. Actually, they were done by the same person or by people trained the same way, but they get insanely good gas mileage and we have a supply of gas here at the compound," Vincent stated.

John was shaking his head with a confused look. "That can't be. The Bronco belonged to street bandits and it was the rebel cell that I led who modified the shuttle. I know the man who did it. He died when the Seekers attacked."

Eve looked at John. "Remember, John? He had modified some of the cars that were still in the parking lot too. A couple of them went missing mysteriously."

"Don't worry about it; no one is accusing anyone of being a traitor. We have enough food, water, and supplies for a few weeks but we need to secure more. Talbot and John, I want you to take one of the Hummers, which also have the modifications, and check the surrounding area. Most towns were abandoned during the Seeker attacks, so there should be plenty of useful stuff that wasn't looted," Vincent directed. Both John and Talbot nodded.

Josh interjected, "So what do the rest of us do?"

"We can't risk the baby so Eve, I want you to continue looking at that chip and see if you can figure out anything else. Andromeda can help you. Josh, you probably figured I'd say this but you've got computer duty. There's a lot in there to sift through," Vincent stated. "Lexi and I will hit Backus."

166

Josh, held up a hand, "I want to go with you and Lexi."

Lexi looked over at Josh, "The Seeker fear aura…"

"…won't be a problem. Look, you may need someone to drive the getaway vehicle or there may be some electronic security or whatever. Just bring me along, I won't cause trouble," Josh interjected.

Vincent thought for a moment, then looked at him and said, "So be it. You're in. We'll take the Bronco. Get ready everyone, from here on out we're in this for the long haul."

Chapter 19

It was dark. Neither Jacob Post nor Kris Nelson could see anything. Their lack of sight was not because it was night time, but due to the fact that they had black bags over their heads. They had been hiding out in the small town where they had lived in, or what was left of it after a Seeker raid, when they saw the Firehawks flying overhead. They tried to run, knowing the Dark Ones had arrived, but to no avail. During the entire trip they both wondered the same thing. "Why us?" There had been many other people around who had scattered. The Firehawks only followed them though, not the rest of the civilians. Things were over quickly. One of the bladeless helicopters came overhead and a Seeker descended on a rope, grabbed Post, and then was pulled back up in seconds. Shortly after that the same Seeker descended again and grabbed Nelson. By the time Nelson had arrived in the hold, he had seen that Post already had a bag over his head. About two seconds later, he joined his companion in darkness.

Both men had known each other for a while. They had gone to High School together. They had not been close friends, but events had reunited them once again after the Flash Storm. Now all they could do was try their best not to let the intense fear they were feeling get the best of them. The two men dared not speak however, as they weren't certain what would be in store for them if they did.

The Firehawk began to descend. The surprisingly quiet engines didn't get louder as they came in for a landing; it was merely the equilibrium that was the indicator of the descent. The vehicle landed softly. Both men would have been impressed if not for the fact that they had no idea how long it had been since they had been picked up. They heard the hatch open and they were both dragged out. They couldn't fight. They couldn't run. They couldn't even scream. For both of them, their worst dream would have been fulfilling and happy compared to this nightmare.

There was activity all around, but neither man could decipher anything. The Seekers weren't being gentle, nor were they being overly forceful. Wherever they were going, they were probably supposed to be in somewhat decent shape. It was a particularly cold night, but Post and Nelson weren't dressed appropriately. Fortunately for them, they were quickly brought inside where the heated air felt a bit more comfortable.

Despite hearing movement all around, no one was speaking. If nothing else, lack of talking combined with lots of noise and the inability to see anything was quite frightening. After several moments of being carried, they were stopped. They felt a downward movement, most likely meaning that they were on an elevator. It was traveling quite fast, and they felt the sensation of their stomachs dropping from the abrupt arrival at their destination.

Both men were carried for a bit longer, until they heard automatic doors open. They heard a voice, "That will be fine. Leave them here and remove their restraints." The orders were obeyed and they had free movement of their legs and arms once again.

"Now, remove the bags and leave us," the voice came again.

Simultaneously, the bags were removed from the two men from behind. Nothing could have prepared Post and Nelson for this sight. Standing before them was someone who was easily recognizable by anyone who had been watching TV, had been on the internet, or had video feed on their cellular phones on May 7th.

"Zodiac," Post said as the Seekers who had brought them in left the room.

Zodiac stood before them, his proud and solid stance made him even more intimidating when combined with the armor and faceless helmet. "Yes, Jacob Post and Kris Nelson."

Both men looked at each other. It was Nelson that spoke. "How do you know us? Wh…what's so special about us?"

Zodiac began to slowly pace around in front of the two men, who were both still kneeling on the floor despite having had their restraints removed. "Everyone is special; didn't your mother ever teach you that? You are unique and different just like everyone else. Or are you? Are people really all that unique? It has always seemed to me that the unique ones were the ones ostracized by their peers."

"Do we know you?" asked Nelson. "There's something familiar about your voice."

Post elbowed him and said softly, "Shut the hell up, don't piss him off!"

Zodiac quickly turned and faced them. "Ah yes, Jacob…if only you had done that years ago, you might have found yourself in quite a different situation. But alas, the crime of doing nothing is just as severe if not more so than the offense itself."

Nelson stood up and attempted to put on a brave front despite wanting to throw up. "Who are you really, behind that helmet?"

If they could have seen Zodiac's face, they would have seen a smile. "I thought you would never ask." The savage dictator removed his helmet and allowed the two men to take in the sight of him for a moment. Both Post and Nelson could not hide their shock.

"Th…this is some sort of joke, that's it." Post was beginning to believe he was in hell.

Zodiac let out a small cackle and shook his head. "No, this is no joke, no deception, no lie. It amuses me that you would have never believed this face could possibly be under this helmet."

"Why? How? You…you killed so many people, destroyed cities." Nelson could barely contain himself.

Zodiac began pacing again, having absolutely no concern that the two men had no restraints. "All cities, Kris. I destroyed every major city across this world. Human civilization collapsed in less than 24 hours. I have to admit, it's my crowning achievement."

Adrenalin was probably the only explanation for Nelson being able to push his fear back and respond, "You're proud of this? What happened that turned you into a monster?"

It was this line of questioning that infuriated Zodiac, who suddenly yelled, "WHAT HAPPENED!? YOU HAPPENED! YOU AND EVERYONE ELSE! Did you think that the sins of your past wouldn't catch up to you? Did you believe that you could just do the things that you did or sit idly by and watch as a spectator and not have it come full circle later?"

It took all of Nelson's strength to not fall down and cry, but he stood his ground, knowing that this experience probably dramatically reduced the life expectancy of his heart. "You destroyed the world because of us?"

Zodiac calmed a moment then began laughing. "Because of you? Please. A pathetic little insect like you is hardly worth such a grand effort. No, the two of you are merely contributing factors to my epiphany. You see, I've realized something extremely important. Humanity is a blight on this world. The war, the profiteers, the oppression, the greed, all of it. You are all guilty of perpetrating misery and suffering on this world."

Post spoke up. "But destroying the world isn't going to undo any of that."

"As expected, you are so very nearsighted. I didn't destroy the world. I destroyed humanity. Now as we speak, my Seekers are sweeping up the debris that's left. They will not stop until every person on this planet is dead or one of my slaves," Zodiac boasted. He stopped pacing and walked a bit closer. "And I have the two of you to thank. It's because of you and the others that I was given the clarity of vision to accomplish this. There's no military. There's no resistance. There's no stopping the new world order."

Post and Nelson just looked at each other. Neither man could speak at this point. Zodiac still could. "No more witty words? Come on Post, you always had your sly comments. Same with you Nelson. You were always a funny guy. What's the matter? It's not funny anymore?"

"You're crazy. There's nothing funny about this! You were wronged. No one who knew you then could deny that, but it still doesn't give you the right…"

Zodiac raised his arm and backhanded Nelson, sending him to the floor with a bloody lip. Post had only time to take one step before the dictator's fist made contact with the center of his face, shattering his nose bone. Zodiac dragged Nelson close to Post. He put a hand on each man's forehead and said, "This is something I have waited to do for a long time. Now, feel it. A LIFETIME OF PAIN! FEEL IT YOU MISERABLE WORMS! YOU PATHETIC WASTES OF ORGANIC COMPOUNDS!"

There was nothing else Kris Nelson and Jacob Post could do except scream at the top of their lungs in shear agony as a lifetime of pain and suffering was pumped into their psyches in one short moment. The suffering was not theirs however; it was pain that had been inflicted on their tormenter, now passed to them. Zodiac felt a rush as if he had taken strong narcotics. "FEEL IT YOU BASTARDS! FEEL IT AS OTHERS HAVE AND STILL OTHERS WILL BEFORE I'M DONE! BEG ME TO KILL YOU! EXPERIENCE THE FULL WRATH OF HATRED INCARNATE!"

The two men continued to scream. It had been less than a minute but to them, they had suffered for a lifetime. Zodiac removed his hands from their foreheads and both Post and Nelson went completely limp, shaking. Their eyes were unfocused; their breathing was quick and shallow. Over humanity's history, many forms of torture had been developed. These methods had covered the gambit of both physical and psychological bombardment. Techniques such as Oxygen Deprivation, Sensory Deprivation, even brutal and constant sexual assaults had been used for generations. None of them could compare to this. A lifetime of pain and suffering experienced in one moment was something that seemed to defy nature itself.

Zodiac watched the two writhing men as they began to convulse from grand mal seizures. Nelson and Post both shook violently while foaming at the mouth. The savage dictator was amused at their reactions, but was also impressed that they had lasted this long. The last person he'd done this to had had a brain hemorrhage. Post was the first to die, his back breaking during the violent seizure and the shock causing his heart to stop. Nelson lasted about a minute longer before having a stroke that finished him off.

Zodiac stared at the two bodies for several minutes. He reminisced about times past. "They're always so surprised. That's the magic of this whole thing. No one ever suspected that I would ever be able to accomplish anything like this. Despicable creatures," he thought to himself. After savoring the moment, he donned his helmet once more. It was time to continue with his rapid progress toward the cleansing of humanity. Nothing would stand in his way. After all this time, he was finally the most powerful being on earth and no one could challenge him.

Chapter 20

J ohn and Talbot had been driving for several hours, looking for an abandoned town that hadn't already been looted. Talbot was driving the military Hummer with John Decker in the passenger seat. Both were wearing the dark army fatigues from the compound that once housed Project Scorpion. They each also wore a military grade vest for additional protection.

"I'm getting tired of this," John broke the silence. "There's nothing around here, not even anything to loot. We should try and head into the areas that used to have a heavier population."

Talbot shook his head. "I don't want to get spotted on satellite. As long as we stay in this area, under the canopy of trees, we decrease the chance of getting noticed."

John grunted. "The satellites won't spot us by simply doing random sweeps. They probably don't even know we're in New York. Let's just continue on 3 this way and we'll get to an area where we'll more likely find salvageable supplies."

Talbot thought for a few seconds then responded, "I guess. We're just going in, getting what we need, and then leaving."

John patted Talbot on the shoulder. "That's what I'm talking about...WHAT THE HELL IS THAT!?"

Looking up ahead, both John and Talbot saw what appeared to be a man in some sort of hunting gear but instead of a rifle, he was carrying a bottle of some kind and standing at the corner of a street that shot off the left side of route 3. Next to the man was a small table set up with several small glass objects that appeared to be shot glasses.

"This guy has got to be drunk. He's standing right out in the open on the side of a main road. What a damn idiot," Talbot ranted as he slowed down.

"Shiiiiiiiit. He's gonna get himself killed," John agreed. The Hummer came to a full stop. The man saw them but did not pay them any mind, as if he had zero belief that anything negative would happen to him.

Talbot opened his window and called out, "Hey! You're Seeker bait if you just stand out here in the open. The canopy of trees will only protect you so much."

The man turned his head. He hadn't shaved in a few days; his face was rough from seeing a substantial amount of the rugged outdoors. He wore a red, white, and black checkered flannel shirt, work boots, jeans, and a bright orange vest. It was not the most subtle of attire. "Howdy. You army types in for a game? Funny though, I thought the army was dead and gone."

Talbot and John looked at each other then Talbot replied, "The army *is* dead and gone, and what the hell game is this!?"

The man poured himself a shot of what John and Talbot could now see was whiskey. He downed it then said, "It's called Drunk Running boys. Definitely illegal but hey, no more cops around so why not have some fun in our world turned upside down."

"What the hell is Drunk Running?" Talbot asked. Before the man could answer he heard the roar of what sounded like a pickup truck engine and the squeal of tires. In mere moments, a pickup truck barreled out of the side road, did a 180 degree turn nearly hitting the Hummer, and pulled up to the man on the corner. They both started cheering then a hand reached out the side window. The man on the corner quickly poured a shot and handed it to the person inside who then sped away.

With a yellow-toothed smile, the man on the corner answered, "That's Drunk Running. We've got a pre-laid course with check points. Each check point has someone like me set up. The driver has to stop, down a shot and keep going through the course."

Talbot and John looked at each other again. John whispered to Talbot, "That's the stupidest thing I've ever heard of."

"What's the point of this? How does one win?" Talbot called out of his window.

"The last one who doesn't crash their vehicle wins!" the man delightfully replied.

The sound of another roaring engine rang out, soon followed by a two-door Cadillac that appeared to have been from the late 80's. The car did a 180 degree spin, this time grazing the Hummer. There was no damage to the Hummer but the Cadillac lost its rear bumper. Without missing a beat, the driver pulled up to the man on the corner and reached his hand over for his shot. "Rory, you're pretty far behind Doug, man - he's kickin' yer redneck ass!"

John looked at Talbot again. "Are you serious? And this guy has the nerve to call someone else a redneck? Talk about the pot and the damn kettle." He turned to the man handing out the shots and asked, "How the hell do you stay off radar from the Seekers?"

"Oh hell that's easy. This stuff is liquid courage so they don't scare us. And, we got us a nice supply of armor piercing ammo in case they send one of their S&D squads after us. They've left us alone thus far…probably nuthin' out here in the sticks worth comin' after. So, can we count you in for the next round?" the redneck on the corner called out.

"Maybe next time," Talbot said as he rolled up the window and headed out before another crazy drunk driver could come barreling out of nowhere.

Both Talbot and John were silent from sheer shock of what they had just witnessed. It was only after about five or ten minutes that John finally spoke up. "I just want to make sure I'm not losing it. That really just happened back there, right?" He was pointing his thumb behind him.

Talbot nodded. "Yes that did just happen. Amazing that even in a time of practically Armageddon, people still find ways to be self-destructive and extremely stupid."

John let out a little chuckle. "You think Vincent would be upset if we invited them back to the compound?"

At that, Talbot let out a laugh. "He might actually appreciate the use of them for target practice, since that's about the only function they could serve with any efficiency. Do you think they were serious about having armor piercing bullets?"

"There's no friggin' way. This bunch of drunks? I think this area is so remote that they don't even bother surveying it with satellites or S&D squads," John answered.

Talbot nodded his head. "Yeah, I guess you're right."

Continuing their journey, John and Talbot found that they could make each other laugh like drunken sailors. They were actually having fun, something neither of them had done in months. Both of them, even if only for a short time, forgot about the dire situation the entire world was in. Unfortunately, they were reminded as they approached their destination.

The sun was shining brightly for this early October morning, with only scattered clouds to interrupt it. It was a crisp fall day, topping out at 55 degrees. On a day like that, normally there would be people on the streets of this small town, visiting the shops. There was no one to be seen. There were cars still sitting in the middle of the street, abandoned by their owners or worse. Doors to various shops on the main street still had their "Open" signs displayed. Talbot slowed the Hummer to a crawl as they tried looking into the windows. Unfortunately, it was difficult to see with the reflection the sun was causing.

"I think we should get out and look around. This must have been the main stretch where everything was located in this town," Talbot suggested.

John nodded, "Sounds like a good idea. I think you're right too. I see a sign for a general store down there."

Both men armed themselves with a 9mm sidearm, a boot knife, and M16 assault rifles that had been in the Hummer at the time they left the compound. Talbot shut the engine off, they both got out, locked the doors and Talbot took the keys with him. They took a moment to assess their surroundings, but there were no sounds, save for the wind that was whipping through the area.

"It's like a bad horror movie," John said.

"Then let's not do something stupid like split up and go into dark buildings alone," Talbot chuckled a bit.

John let out a snicker. "Sounds like good advice. So, the diner might be a good place to start. Its right here and they may have stocked non-perishables in bulk." With that, he held his rifle up and led the way, Talbot following behind, shooting glances around to make sure no one was sneaking up on them. John pushed on the door, which was still unlocked and they both entered.

This was a quaint, small town diner. Along the right wall there were half a dozen booths set up running down the entire length.

On the other side were the breakfast bar and stools. Beyond that was a cooking area where the food would have been prepared in plain sight. There was a cash register at one end of the bar. At the far end of the diner was a genderless restroom and what appeared to be a back room, probably for the storage of food.

Despite the setup, they both noticed a musty, stale smell. Plates of decayed food were still sitting on the counter and tables. Various pastries that had been on display had grown moldy and attracted flies. "That's appetizing," John said wrinkling his nose. "It's like everyone just up and abandoned the place."

Talbot had worked his way to the cash register, which was so old it was completely mechanical, so it still worked. He popped open the drawer and saw it was still loaded with cash. "They did. Look up there." He pointed at a television set mounted in the corner.

John looked over at the television, and then looked back at Talbot. "TV didn't end the world."

"No, but I'll bet they saw Zodiac's announcement on that television set and everyone left in some type of actual, organized fashion," Talbot observed. "There's no sign of panic...everything is in order. Place settings are still there, nothing is broken."

John picked up a woman's purse that was sitting on the floor by a bar stool. "That's actually kind of a freaky thought. Like they had some organized retreat or something? Maybe they were expecting the Flash Storm?"

Talbot made his way toward the back room. "I have no idea John. I just know that these people either vanished, or they got up and calmly left. The people outside must have stopped their cars, gotten up and walked out. Maybe there's some kind of bomb shelter around from the Cold War era or something. They could've had some type of emergency procedure."

"Talbot, wait a sec, check this out," John called out. He had opened the purse and pulled out a folded sheet of paper that he opened up.

Talbot turned his head. "What is it?"

"It's some type of flyer. Looks like anti-government propaganda. It has the text of the 28th Amendment on it and a whole bunch of warnings of impending doom," John stated. He read the 28th Amendment to the Constitution of the United States of

177

America. "Immediately following the ratification of this article the manufacture, sale, or transportation of firearms, projectile weapons, air guns, and explosives within, the importation thereof into, or the exportation thereof from the United States and all territory subject to the jurisdiction thereof is hereby prohibited."

"Yeah, the last amendment which officially disarmed the public. I still can't believe that ever got through," Talbot stated. "Totally screwed us after the big 'Z' showed up."

John was still looking at the paper. "Neither can I. I know the amendment went on to make exceptions for active duty military and law enforcement but still. I wonder if this was some type of militia town or something."

Talbot's eyebrows raised. "Hmmm…"

John bobbed his head back and forth. "Alright, maybe I'm being a little paranoid."

Talbot shook his head. "No, I think you might actually be on to something. There were a lot of people, diehard gun advocates who believed that the passage of the 28th Amendment meant the beginning of the end."

"Yeah, the old saying, 'The first step to establish a dictatorship is to disarm the public'," John quoted.

Talbot opened the door to the supply room. "Shit. We've gotta get outta here." He held his M16 ready and started to head back toward where John was standing.

John had a puzzled look on his face. "What are you talking about? What did you see?"

"The back room is picked clean. The shelves are empty. These people are in hiding and have probably sent small groups to recover supplies. I doubt they'll appreciate visitors," Talbot warned.

John's pupils dilated at that moment and he pointed out the window in the direction of the Hummer. "They definitely won't."

"Damn," Talbot cursed as he looked where John was pointing. There were at least a dozen armed individuals, both men and women, approaching the Hummer. "I think we just alerted the natives."

Both John and Talbot ducked down, hoping that they hadn't been noticed in the diner. Unfortunately, the human eye notices movement before anything else and a petit woman carrying some type of sub-machinegun was saying something to a taller man, pointing toward the diner.

"I think they know we're here," John pointed out.

Talbot rolled his eyes, "Thanks for clarifying that."

The taller man walked in the middle of the road until he was in front of the diner while still standing on the yellow stripe. He was joined by two other men. All three carried rifles of some kind. "Come out you Seeker bastards, we're not afraid of you," the tall man shouted in a commanding voice.

"We're not Seekers - we should just tell them...," John started.

"Wait, not yet," Talbot interrupted.

"I'll count to 3 then we're throwing grenades through that window. Nice incendiary grenades that your armor won't protect you from," the tall man threatened.

Both John and Talbot sprung up, rifle straps around their shoulders with their hands in the air. They exited the diner and the moment the door was open, they saw that every person there had a gun pointed at them. "We're not Seekers! We're not Seekers!" Talbot announced.

The strange group did not stop pointing their weapons. The tall man stayed put and said, "So you're looters. Even better. Did you kill the soldiers for their Hummer? Were you going to kill us?"

John and Talbot just looked at each other, hands still in the air. Talbot spoke up, "We're not looters. We thought this town was deserted; we needed to check for supplies. We didn't kill anyone, this Hummer was abandoned. We didn't even know you all were here."

The tall man stared at them intently for a few tense moments, then finally lowered his weapon, although everyone else still had theirs pointed. "Where did you come from? Were you followed?"

"We got here via old route 3. We're in hiding in the woods to the west of here, and no, we weren't followed but we did find some Drunk Runners," Talbot answered.

"Drunk Runners? What the hell are those?" the tall man asked.

"Long story," John replied.

The tall man put his hand out to his companions, who lowered their weapons but still maintained a watchful eye. "Alright, I'm pretty sure you aren't spies."

"How did he come to that conclusion?" John grunted through his teeth to Talbot.

Talbot ignored him and continued to talk to the tall man. "Of course not. We're in a fight for our survival; we have no desire to do any harm to anyone except for Zodiac and his Seeker goons."

"Good, then get in your vehicle and get the hell out of here before you draw any more attention to us. And never come back," the tall man snapped.

"Maybe we can help each other," Talbot spoke up.

The tall man laughed. "I doubt that very much. We have a good system here. We don't need more mouths to feed."

"We're fighting back against the Seekers," John spoke up.

The tall man opened his eyes widely. His companions began mumbling to each other. He looked at John and said, "You're going to fight them? Then I definitely don't want you near me... you're as good as dead. The Seekers induce fear in all who come near them. They feel nothing, they're afraid of nothing. They're well armed and well armored. You can't fight them."

"Our allies may have found a way to stop the fear effect that they have. We know a quite a lot about them," Talbot replied.

"Oh you do, do you? Maybe you are a spy after all," said the tall man with a menacing tone in his voice, but did not raise his gun again.

"That's absurd. Hear me out. Our leader captured a Seeker. They're human like us, except they've been lobotomized," Talbot explained.

The tall man looked intrigued. "How can lobotomy patients fight then?"

"They have chips implanted in their brains. It effectively makes them living robots," Talbot continued.

The tall man gave a glance to his companions who began chattering again. "QUIET!" Everyone shut their mouths. "How did your leader capture a Seeker? How do you have the facilities to make these discoveries? Are you scientists or something?"

Talbot took a few steps forward. "Our leader is really good at taking out Seekers. He and another one of our companions aren't affected by their fear aura. We're not scientists but we have someone who has some background in nanotechnology and she analyzed it." He was careful not to reveal that Eve was John's pregnant wife.

The tall man rubbed his chin and looked down at the road for a moment, then looked up and said, "That doesn't answer my question about your facilities."

John spoke up. "We have access to some advanced facilities. There's power and everything."

One of the women standing in the group was wearing a T-Shirt that said "Ciudad De Los Angeles." That shirt caught Talbot's eye. "City of the Angels."

The tall man looked at him for a moment then noticed that Talbot was looking at his companion. "Yes, she's from Los Angeles."

"Then maybe she remembers a certain vigilante that went by the name Night Viper," Talbot inquired. The woman was obviously taken back by the utterance of that name. A bit of commotion stirred again.

The tall man asked, "What does the Night Viper have to do with anything?"

"He's our leader," John answered.

The woman shook her head and spoke up. "You're a liar. The Night Viper died."

John shook his head. "No, he didn't. He ran into some trouble, that's why he disappeared, but he's here, in New York."

The tall man turned to the woman. She was an attractive Hispanic woman with long, slightly curly hair, smooth skin, and a model-like figure. The chill in the air obviously did not bother her because the T-Shirt was short sleeved. She was wearing jeans dotted with several small holes and long, black boots. The tall man looked at her; he was just as surprised as she was. He then addressed Talbot and John. "I'll warn you that I don't like tricks. Are you aware that Night Viper was one of the most dangerous vigilantes to ever walk the streets of an American city? He took on L.A.'s underworld before eventually getting himself killed in the process. At least that's what we've always thought."

"Do you know that he's dead? For sure? Did you ever find a

body?" John inquired.

The woman shook her head. "No, they never found a body but he disappeared and never came back. Obviously some gang or the FBI or something caught up to him. They probably made sure that his body couldn't be recovered. There's no way he would've just abandoned his cause."

Talbot kept his hands up even though there were no guns pointed at him and said, "He's very much alive, young lady."

"Listen, you all obviously have done a good job staying hidden and you're obviously well-armed, but how long do you think you're going to escape the notice of Zodiac? Huh? How long? Eventually he'll catch up to you," John pointed out.

"And what do you have in mind?" the tall man asked.

John and Talbot looked at each other again. John responded, "We can combine forces. Once we figure out how to counteract the fear aura of the Seekers, we can fight them."

"You said Night Viper kills Seekers. How does he do it?" asked the woman from L.A.

John looked at her; there was something about her when she spoke about Vincent. He suspected that she and the tall man had more than just heard about him."Their fear aura doesn't affect him. We have another person with us who isn't affected either. She had some kind of brain injury and lost her ability to feel fear."

The woman from L.A. seemed to be satisfied with the answer and went silent. The tall man looked at them for a long time then finally spoke up, "My name is Alan Ryke. We're Militia 28, formed when the government passed the 28th Amendment. As a community, we had all banded together. We stocked old bomb shelters. We drilled. We armed ourselves as best we could, even if we had to go into the city and obtain arms illegally. We were one of the few communities out there that actually were prepared for something like the Flash Storm. We were tuned in on the 7th of May, just like everyone else. The moment it happened we abandoned town and went to the shelters. When the Seekers showed up, some of our people tried to fight them, but were all killed."

"Militia 28? How many are there?" asked John.

Alan snickered a bit. "No, the 28 refers to the 28th Amendment. The only reason this group exists is because of that law."

The mood seemed to be relaxing more, so John walked into

the street a bit. "How many of you are there?"

"Please don't be offended but we don't know you yet. We're good in numbers and there are other locations that are affiliated with us. We have a crude but effective communication network set up with them to relay messages and check for status updates. I don't wish to reveal any more than that at this time," Alan declared.

John looked intently at Alan. "What would it take to convince you that we're trustworthy and that we can help?"

Alan held his finger up in the form of a one and stepped back with the group. This was the first time that some of them had turned their backs, so it was obvious that they were beginning to feel more comfortable around Talbot and John. The group was whispering and debating. The woman from L.A. seemed to weigh quite heavily into this conversation. After a few minutes, the huddle broke and Alan returned, this time standing only a few feet away.

Alan eyed John and Talbot carefully. "The woman who spoke up before is Maria Esperanza. Night Viper saved her younger brother when he took down a child sex slave ring right before he disappeared. If you bring him here, show us that he's alive, that will be enough proof for her and for me and we'll open further dialog."

John and Talbot looked at each other yet again. Talbot spoke up. "He goes by Vincent nowadays. I'm sure we can arrange for him to come here, but he left on a mission. It may be a few days."

"We have no pressing appointments, we'll wait. You may bring him via the same way you came into town in the first place. We'll see you and come to you," Alan explained.

Both John and Talbot nodded. Talbot spoke up once again. "My name is Chris Talbot, and this is John Decker. We'll do as you ask. In the meantime, I think we've all been in the open long enough. Zodiac still controls all of the satellites."

Alan nodded. "Agreed. I hope that you're truthful in what you've told us. It could very well be what we've all been waiting for."

Talbot and Alan shook hands, and then Talbot began to walk toward the Hummer, keys in hand. Alan reached his hand to John who took it also but then he said, "Alan. I have a question. Do you have a doctor amongst your number?"

Alan had a slightly confused look on his face. "Yes, we do, why?"

"My wife is pregnant. Her original due date was November 10th, but the baby has already dropped. I'm deeply concerned for her." John knew he was taking a risk revealing this to someone he didn't know.

"Bring her with you when you bring Vincent," Alan stated.

John felt somewhat relieved. "Thank you." Then he walked away and got into the now running Hummer. The members of Militia 28 stood and watched.

Talbot looked at John as he put the Hummer in gear to pull a K-turn. "Think we can trust them?"

John nodded and looked in the direction of the retreating Militia 28. "Yeah. I think they're genuine. What is it with these groups and their number designations? I feel like I'm living in a math book sometimes."

Talbot just chuckled at the question, then his face got serious. "I just hope Vince, Lexi, and Josh make it back alright. We're going to need them."

John leaned his head back on the headrest. "Well, Vincent wanted a rebellion; it looks like he's going to get one. I hope he's ready for it."

As the Hummer drove away, the members of Militia 28 began to make their way back into hiding. Alan stopped Maria and pulled her aside. "So, do you think it's really him?"

Maria was looking all around and bobbing her head nervously. "I don't know. I hope so. It's just, I know he was dying. It's been over a year. It could be someone who's claiming to be Night Viper."

Alan put his hand on her shoulder. "You're not going to do this alone. I'll be here by your side; just as I swore to you I would be back in L.A. If this man is an imposter, we'll be ready."

Maria turned and watched the now empty road. "I'll pray that this really is the one who saved my brother and so many others. Of all times, we need him now more than ever."

Chapter 21

Crisco sat by an old oak tree, leaning up against its trunk. He was eating a MRE and thinking about what he had done. He knew he had to get out of the compound, that running was the appropriate choice given his situation. He knew they wouldn't pursue him. By the time they figured out he was gone, they wouldn't risk trying to come after him. He knew how to survive in the woods - he could stay put indefinitely. After his mind calmed a bit, he started wandering down memory lane, thinking back to over a year ago, the first time he met Vincent Black, the Night Viper…

It was night time in Los Angeles. Crisco was sitting in the helicopter with three other men. They were in full riot gear, but their weapons were tasers and shotguns with bean bags. The pilot and co-pilot in the front were quiet, focused on arriving at their destination. They had been briefed back at the compound in New York that they were to retrieve the latest test subject. This one was not like the others. This one was one of the most dangerous people alive. His true name was Vincent Black, but the alias he was known by was the Night Viper. He had been operating as a vigilante in the Los Angeles area for about a year at that point. Crisco did not know why this man was a candidate for Project Scorpion, but he had his orders and he would carry them out.

Sitting across from him was Captain James Hera. He was in charge of security at Project Scorpion and he was tasked to lead the expedition to extract Night Viper from Los Angeles and bring him to the secure compound. It was then that Captain Hera spoke into the comm. in his helmet, "Understood. Yes, I know, he must be brought in alive. Yes. Roger, over and out." Hera looked at his three men and addressed them. "Alright boys, it's time to get ready to lock and load. You've all been briefed; the package is a local vigilante who goes by the name of Night Viper. He's responsible for the murders of dozens, maybe even hundreds of rapists, gangbangers, drug dealers, murderers, and other scum. He's tough as they come so be careful. Under no circumstances are you to use lethal force on him."

"But sir," Crisco spoke up, "I thought he was sick."

"Night Viper's body is loaded with cancer, a result of being exposed to a massive amount of radiation at the Millstone Nuclear Power Plant in Connecticut. Despite all of that he's managed to hunt down and destroy some of the toughest and most hardened criminals in this city, including 20 members of Rebel 99. Do not underestimate him," Hera warned.

Crisco and the other two men acknowledged with a "YES SIR!"

The helicopter circled around. Crisco was not sure what building they came to a hover over, but it didn't matter. They could see a dark figure on the corner, struggling to stand up. They secured their hooks and rappelled out of the helicopter and onto the roof. As they approached the man, he looked up at them with hatred in his eyes. He was the one they were after.

"So, *cough* *cough*, about time some special squad showed up for me. I may be down, but I'm not out yet, you bastards!" Night Viper threatened. He let out a piercing yell and lunged at the four men. A moment prior, he had appeared to be ready to pass out and suddenly he was moving like a man possessed. The two other men Crisco was with grabbed his arms by the elbows. That didn't stop the vigilante, who proceeded to kick Captain Hera in the head, using the two men holding him as leverage. It was fortunate for the captain that he was wearing a riot helmet or he might have been hurt quite badly.

Hera shook his head then yelled, "Hold him down so I can sedate him!"

The two men could not contain their squirming prisoner and one of them lost his grip. Night Viper dropped down and punched the other man in the thigh, causing him to stumble. He then stood up and made a chopping motion to the throat of the man who had let go of him, knocking the wind from him and dropping him. Crisco rushed forward but was met with a boot below the sternum, also knocking the wind out of him. He looked up at the man who supposedly was dying of cancer and realized why Project Scorpion had chosen him to be the seventh subject.

Despite being taken down, the three men must have done what was needed by allowing Hera the opportunity to aim and fire a drugged dart into the side of Night Viper's neck. What he wasn't expecting was that the vigilante was still coming for him, snarling like an animal. "Jesus Christ," Hera yelled as he fired another one that struck his target's arm. Night Viper began to slow down as he pulled each dart out and threw them to the ground.

"Gonna break...your damn...NECK!" the vigilante threatened as his footing faltered. Finally, he fell over, unconscious.

Hera stood over their query, just staring. Crisco was finally catching his breath and stood up, as did the other two men. "What the hell was that!?" Crisco shouted.

Hera did not take his eyes from the black-clad vigilante, "This man should have died in the first hours of exposure to the radiation levels of Millstone. Instead, he's lived almost a full year on sheer force of will. His body is dying but his mind is ignoring it."

"But if he's dying, what good is he to the project?" asked Crisco.

"They can do amazing things to the body; it's the mind that needs to be able to survive the process. The first six subjects did not possess the willpower to make it through. Night Viper does," Hera stated. "Load him up and keep an eye on his vitals. We'll all be put through a wood chipper if we let him die now."

Following Captain Hera's orders, Crisco and the others loaded the unconscious man in black onto the helicopter, and then boarded themselves. The pilots made haste in leaving. With that, the trip down memory lane ended.

Crisco found himself back in the woods in upstate New York, miles from the compound. He had finished the MRE and drank a full bottle of water. He stood up and prepared to move again, but he needed to find shelter. He knew that if Vincent ever found out about his true role in Project Scorpion, he would probably kill him. He also knew that Lexi would not be able to accept her father's true role in the project and his level of knowledge of what truly happened.

"I don't know where I'm going to go or what I'm going to do, but I have to walk my path alone. I'm sorry Vincent and Lexi...I hope one day you'll find it in you to forgive me," Crisco said out loud. With that, he disappeared into the trees.

Chapter 22

The sun was overhead and lighting up the deserted city of Norwich as the street lamps no longer could. Vincent, Lexi, and Josh were parked on a bridge that used to be part of Route 32, a good vantage point to watch the building that was once the William W. Backus hospital while still remaining a distance away, so as not to be spotted by Seekers. Vincent was looking through high powered binoculars. There was a time when the line of sight would not have made it from the bridge to the hospital but Zodiac's troops had inadvertently cleared a path in their rampage.

"Hmmm…definitely not how I remember it," Vincent commented.

Josh twirled his finger in the air. "No huge surprise there. I'm sure they didn't lobotomize people and turn them into Seekers the last time you were here."

Vincent shook his head slightly. "The last time I was here, I visited a friend's mother after her hysterectomy."

Lexi cringed, "Ouch. That sucks."

"Yeah, it was better than dying of cancer though. At least her kids were already here and grown at that point," Vincent responded.

Josh began pacing on the side of the road. "So, you see anything worth noting?"

"Yeah, looks like someone already had the idea of attacking this place; it looks like they shot off all sorts of ordinance in the area. There's a shell of some type of vehicle, looks like it got hit by a rocket or something. The road has what looks like blood stains. I'm surprised that it isn't more heavily fortified. I can jump that fence without an issue," Vincent answered.

Lexi stood next to Vincent. "Yeah, but are we just going to land straight in Seekerville and be pumped full of holes? You may heal from that but we sure as hell won't. If this place was invaded it doesn't sound like it went very well for whoever was attacking."

Vincent moved the binoculars around a little bit then replied, "They were a larger group, but not nearly large enough. I'd say 30 or 35 give or take. Large enough to get noticed, way too small to make a difference. They probably didn't last more than a few minutes, poor bastards. This place is still crude; it looks like they threw it together out of some type of necessity."

"It might have something to do with whatever they're doing on the shore," Lexi pointed out. "They probably needed more troops as fast as possible. Maybe that's why they hit Hartford, Danbury, Bridgeport, and New Haven. They needed to collect people for conversion."

"Could very well be. The advantage for us is that the surveillance cameras leave a lot of blind spots. A large force would get noticed like I said before, but we won't, provided none of us are complete klutzes." Vincent smirked while still looking through the binoculars.

Josh was pacing more. "Alright, so we've pretty much seen this place from every angle except from straight above it. Are you still confident that you can get in there?"

Vincent put the binoculars down and bent over, picking up a rock from the side of the road, "Sure am. Here's what we're going to do. I'm going in there alone; I want you two to provide cover fire and the getaway." Vincent began drawing on the asphalt with the rock he picked up. He was making a crude sketch of the complex.

"I'm going in there too!" Lexi protested.

"No, I need you to snipe. You're going to be in closer, close enough to the Seeker fear auras so I can't have Josh do it. Josh, you're going to drive the Bronco so you'll position yourself here. Lexi, this tree over here will provide you with cover as well as a clear view to the area I'll be entering and exiting. Now this is important, when I give the signal through the radio, I want you to get out of that tree. Josh is going to come down this way, pick you up and by the time he gets to this point, I'll be there with the targets," Vincent explained, pointing to various spots on the road sketch. "Now, if we're fortunate, and I can get whoever is in charge here, it should disorient everyone else so they can't coordinate a chase."

"The commanders don't wear face plates, at least the one that I killed didn't," Lexi added.

"No, they don't, and their armor has different markings. The Seeker armor's plain," Vincent agreed.

Josh did his normal, habitual raising of his right hand while his leg was simultaneously shaking. "Question. If all of those people that were captured from the rebel cells are here, how are we going to get them out?"

"We're going to give them an opening to escape when we've disrupted their command. When I make my way out of there, it's going to be loud," Vincent answered. "Are you two ready for this?"

"Not at all, but hey, if we live it will be a hell of a story that we attacked a Seeker compound and lived to tell about it, even if I'm missing all of my damn limbs," Josh replied.

Lexi gave him a light punch to the shoulder, "Stop being such a Debbie Downer."

Josh rocked his head back and forth. "Sure, fine, be sarcastic. You're not afraid of anything, but I sure as hell am. Those Seekers would be freaky even without their fear aura."

"Josh, listen to me. We're not going to fail. We can't keep running and hiding forever. If we don't do this, we may never figure out how to beat that fear aura. We need to expose a weakness in the Seekers so we can exploit it and have a fighting chance against them," Vincent asserted.

Josh nervously nodded his head. "I know, I know. It's just that I'm tired of living in a damn nightmare, ya know? I remember being a kid and thinking that it might actually be fun to live in a post apocalyptic world where there's no government and people survived by using their brains. I was a stupid kid."

Lexi gave a light rub to Josh's shoulders. "That's why we're doing this, so that maybe we can repair the damage and make this world a better place."

"Yeah, I guess. I wonder how Talbot and John are doing." Josh tried to change the subject.

Vincent caught on quickly but just went with the subject change. "I'm sure they're doing fine. I've noticed in my travels that there's been a surprising lack of looting."

"I hope they found chocolate. I really need it. I mean REALLY need it," Lexi piped up.

Josh and Vincent looked at each other, neither willing to say what was on their minds so they let the comment drop. Josh quickly changed the subject yet again. "Eve looks like she's gonna pop."

"What's the matter, you don't feel comfortable talking about a female menstrual cycle? It's perfectly natural you know," Lexi snapped.

"Yeah, it naturally makes me feel better about being a guy." Josh snickered until he saw the look of death that Lexi gave him.

Vincent held up his hands. "Alright, alright, truce you two. We'll wait until dark and hit these bastards quick and easy, then get the hell out of here."

Josh opened the driver's side door to the Bronco "You know, in the movies, every time they say that, something goes wrong."

"Lucky for us, this isn't a movie," Vincent smirked. "Now start this thing up and get out of here."

Josh did not hesitate. He immediately started the engine and drove off to his waiting spot, leaving Lexi and Vincent alone on the bridge. Vincent took his rifle, which had a scope on it, and handed it to her. "The site is set perfectly. I have a silencer and a flash suppressor on it. Unfortunately, it kills the range, that's why I'm having you get as close as possible. If it gets too hot, get the hell out of there. If I can't make it back to the Bronco, you and Josh need to get out of here as fast as possible."

"Vince, we're not leaving without you. A couple of days ago I never expected to be a part of anything like this. It's amazing and you're the reason it's happening. Even if I could feel fear, I wouldn't feel it now," Lexi stated as she took the rifle.

Vincent nodded his head. "Good luck Lexi."

Lexi winked at him. "You too, Night Viper." With that, she took off on foot to her destination, leaving Vincent alone on the bridge. He took a moment to collect his thoughts then looked at what used to be the major hospital in the area.

"Zodiac, your time is coming. I hope you enjoyed your reign of terror because I'm kicking you off that pedestal," Vincent mumbled out loud, then headed on foot toward the fence surrounding the compound.

Within the former Backus Hospital, the man in the corner of the massive cell watched as Commander Jade entered the prison area. She came to select the next batch of people to be taken for Seeker and/or slave conversion. Where everyone else cowered and whimpered, he did not. He just watched her intently.

Jade was already enjoying the torment she was dishing out. She would stand in front of a bunch of people and watch them cower, unable to make eye contact with her. Finally, one of them would look up to see if she was still there. The first person to do it this time around was a young woman with brunette hair, brown eyes, and ragged clothes. Jade pointed to her. "Take this one."

"No, please, don't. NOOOOOOOOOOOOOOOO," she screamed in protest but the Seekers did not deviate nor feel remorse. With indifference, she was retrieved.

Jade began pacing around until she got to the cell that the onlooker was in. He caught her eye almost immediately since he was still standing and he was looking her in the eyes. "Most interesting. Everyone in here seems to be filled with fear and dread, but you are not."

The man remained silent. He felt fear; he simply did not let it show.

"What's the matter? Is your tongue paralyzed?" Jade asked.

She received no response.

"Seekers retrieve him." Jade pointed, her annoyance was reflected in her tone of voice.

Two Seekers entered and walked over to the man. There was no worry about entering a cell full of prisoners; they were far too filled with dread to even attempt a coupe. The man did not resist and came out with them. The Seekers then re-locked the door. Jade walked over and repeated, "There is much fear in this room but you do not seem to be contributing to it."

The man stayed silent.

Jade became agitated. "Speak you insolent fool!"

The man did not budge nor make a noise.

Jade reached out and grabbed him, squeezing his cheeks with her hand, and then received her answer as to the issue with the man. His tongue was not paralyzed; it was not there at all. For a moment, she hesitated. This was not expected. She regained her composure and threw him to the floor bellowing, "Take him away!"

Nightfall seemed to take forever but it finally came. Vincent stood about a hundred feet from the gate to the former William Backus Hospital. He was attempting to keep an eye on the movement of the surveillance cameras as well as the pattern of the Seeker guards' rounds. It was difficult at night; the Seekers had their extremely bright shoulder lights creating a light and dark contrast that was constantly moving around. It also rendered night vision goggles useless. Fortunately, he had spent the better part of the afternoon memorizing these patterns making it far easier to time his movement now that night had finally come. As if in an old 2-dimensional platform shooter video game, he waited for the pattern to cycle through once more before making his move. The moment the Seeker guards were facing away from his area and the camera was pointed away; he made a break for it. Moving with blurring speed, he hurdled himself over the fence, landing on the other side. He did not wait there though; he hurried forward and put his back to the wall, underneath the camera where it could not see him. He pulled out his two Berettas, which now had silencers on them and were packed with armor piercing ammunition.

Back against the wall, Vincent waited a few moments. The Seekers would be facing him soon and his destination, a service ladder leading to the roof, was several feet away. Fortunately, he moved faster than any normal person. When the camera pointed in the opposite direction of where he wanted to go, he made a break for it. Again, he moved at lightning speed. While running, he holstered his guns and then grabbed onto the ladder. He quickly climbed up and out of sight just as the dark warriors were coming back around for another rotation. He knew he could easily take them out but that would draw unneeded attention. It would eventually come to that, but it would be at the time of his choosing, after he had disrupted their command.

The roof was vast, with various air conditioners, generators, vents, and other objects that served as excellent cover. He immediately ducked behind an air conditioning compressor and waited. Seeker guards and snipers were on the roof. He made a mental note of this, as it would be necessary to return this way during the jail break and take them out to keep casualties at a minimum. It was a difficult decision to attempt liberation. He knew that some of the captured rebels would die in the process, but many would live, whereas if he did nothing, all the prisoners would face a fate worse than death, that of being a mindless zombie soldier or slave.

While waiting, he overheard voices. They were monotone voices with a creepy absence of emotion, but they were voices that were, surprisingly, coming from the Seekers. "They can talk," he thought to himself, and then realized that lobotomies did not remove a person's ability to speak; it simply destroyed their personality and identity. Since the Seekers were programmed via the spider-chip, they were given a robot-like personality; they most likely only spoke when absolutely necessary as one might picture an android of limited intelligence would do.

The Dark Ones were checking in with some type of command center. Vincent could only hear the Seekers themselves and only the ones closest to him. Despite his obvious enhancements, his hearing was no greater than a typical healthy human. They were uttering some type of code, probably their position code and indicating that things were all clear. He doubted that they were expecting any more trouble tonight; it was obvious that they'd had an adequate response to the previous incursion. After the Seekers checked in, they went about their rotations. This confirmed that he needed to avoid taking any of them out as it might put the entire place on alert.

Vincent peeked up and over the machinery he was hiding behind and observed while remaining out of sight. He knew that despite how much he wanted to get inside and complete the mission, this would require patience. He took his time and carefully observed the rotations of the Seeker guards on the roof. He also looked around for some type of access into the building. He could not see one from where he was so he took the time to map out a route to another safe spot. Once he was confident that he had found his path and waited for the guards to be in position, he made a break for it. He moved quickly and quietly, making virtually no sound and ducked behind some type of large vent. He observed that the Seeker snipers always stayed in one place with their backs to the rest of the roof. They kept watch around the complex through the scopes of their rifles. They were most likely depending on those "walking the beat" to cover their backs but Vincent also doubted the idea that those in charge would believe someone would make it to the roof. After all, the Seeker units and their commanders were used to winning.

After identifying the pattern from his current angle, Vincent spotted the access he was looking for. He would have felt a lot better if he had more information on the inside layout, but he did not and would have to make do with his own intuition. Once the guards had moved into position where he could maneuver through their blind spots, he made another break for it. He arrived at the door and felt a huge sense of relief when the handle turned and he was able to open it without any significant amount of noise. He was surprised that they would leave it unlocked, even if they were sure that no one could get in unnoticed. He could have broken the door down, but that would have made far too much noise and he wanted to avoid such attention grabbing actions. He went inside and quietly shut the door.

Inside, Vincent found himself in a stairwell and the only direction was down. He could hear the sounds of captured people screaming. He could only assume they were about to meet their fate unless he could send the place into a tizzy. He hurried down the stairs to the first landing and looked through the small window on the door. What he could see of the floor indicated that it had been hacked apart and crudely reassembled with a new layout that more befit the building's new purpose. There were exposed supports where walls had once been, wires hanging down from the ceiling and connecting to machines instead of being mounted with plates and wire molding onto the walls and supports. "This place is probably temporary, they aren't going to stay here long term…there's no way," Vincent thought to himself.

The former vigilante looked around in the stairwell for a moment to make sure he was alone. When he looked back through the window on the door, he saw quite a bit of commotion. There were several Seekers stationed throughout the now very open floor plan. There appeared to be other miscellaneous runners that were attending to mediocre tasks. Looking at them, they moved as robots and remained expressionless. "So, it is true that the Seekers aren't the only ones lobotomized and reprogrammed," Vincent thought to himself once again. "Zodiac must really have trust issues...and here I thought I was bad in that department." He continued to look and noticed that there were a few individuals who had apparently been allowed to keep their minds. He made a mental note and continued down the stairs. He was going to stop on the next landing, but then felt a tingle in the back of his head. Trusting his sixth sense, he decided to continue all the way down to the basement.

The door to the basement did not have a window on it unfortunately, so he took a moment, and listened. His head was no longer tingling, but Vincent could hear sorrowful crying and people pleading for mercy. It must be the detention area. He pulled out his Berettas again and carefully opened the door. He knew that the time was near to announce his presence.

There was a short hallway and another door; this one had an electronic lock on it. No window was present. It was at that moment that he wished Josh was there. Despite the fact that Vincent at one time had worked in Information Technology, this was beyond his expertise. That life had been gone for a while. Fortunately, since the door was not sound proof, he could hear the sound of a man speaking on the other side.

"Hurry up and open that door drone. I must get back up to the lab and I hate elevators," came the voice, with a haughty, arrogant tone.

Vincent smiled. "This couldn't be more perfect if I had planned it this way."

The door clicked open. Vincent waited on the other side as two Seekers and a man who looked to be about Talbot's age, maybe a little older with a slight hunch on his back, curly gray hair, a large nose, a lab coat that had probably been white at one time but had been stained in the blood of an unknown number of people, and glasses walked through. The door shut on its own with no one turning their backs. Vincent took that moment to fire a round through the helmet of each Seeker, instantly killing them. The arrogant man turned and looked at him, not startled at all.

"And what exactly do you think you're doing young man?" asked the scientist.

Vincent rolled his eyes. "What the hell does it look like I'm doing?"

The scientist looked at the floor where the two dead Seekers were. "Making the largest mistake of your life. I don't know how you got in here but with me dead you certainly won't get out."

Vincent glared at the man. "Who said I'm gonna kill you?" Rather than stand there and banter with the guy, he hit him with the back of his hand and knocked him out cold. "Not so tough without your Seeker buddies, are ya?"

Vincent checked the Seekers. They were both carrying a card key so he took one of them. He also grabbed one of the rifles and pulled out the clip. The ammunition was standard and worthless against the mesh armor that he would be up against. He disabled both dark warriors' weapons by bending the barrels with his bare hands. Using the cardkey, he unlocked the door again and opened it. He quickly pocketed the key and pulled out his guns again. Before anyone even realized he was there, he pointed the pistols and fired rounds into the heads of all six Seeker guards, dropping them all in just a few seconds. The last one actually had enough time to realize he was there before his brains were emptied into his helmet.

The area was large and open. The supports were still present but where walls once were, there were bars. Several large prison cells were present and filled with highly frightened people. They were all cowering at the bloodshed, even though it was the blood of their captors. Finally, one by one, they began looking up to see who their savior was. They looked at him in awe, and then the whispers came.

"It's the man in black, the one with the scorpion tattoo."

"I thought he was taller than that."

"We're saved."

"He'll call down lightning from the sky and destroy this place."

"That's absurd, he uses fireballs."

198

Vincent rolled his eyes. He hated rumors. Finally he addressed them. "Listen everyone, I'm going to open these doors, but you're not to bum rush or you'll get yourselves killed. I want you to wait until the alarms in this place go off. I'm going to disrupt their operations. I have someone outside to provide cover fire once you get out. I can't guarantee that all of you will make it out alive, but it's far better than the fate you've got here."

Everyone continued to stare at him. Vincent was feeling uncomfortable but he used the keycard and unlocked the cell doors. He left them closed only slightly so that they did not latch. "I mean it, stay here until the alarms go off...otherwise the Seekers are gonna pick you all off. Once you get out, head down Washington Street and disappear."

One person spoke up, a young man who looked to be in his late teens. "You really are our savior! We're not all that's here. There's a detention center down the road...I'm not sure where but that's where everyone else is. They bring us here in batches for processing and conversion." Everyone else remained obediently silent. The young man's words went straight to Vincent's soul. His reputation was spreading. Whether he liked it or not, he now truly had to live up to this pedestal people had put him on. The very survival of humanity depended on it. He also realized that his job in Norwich wasn't going to be finished yet. He removed the guns from the dead Seekers and sent them through the bars of the cells, along with the card keys, which the prisoners immediately concealed.

Vincent nodded and headed back the same way he came. The arrogant scientist was still unconscious, so he threw him over his shoulder as if the old man was a sweater. He re-entered the stairwell and went back to the landing where he'd had his mental tingle before. Looking through the window of the door, he saw that this floor had also been widely opened up. Just like the floor above he could see exposed supports, wires hanging from ceilings, and makeshift structures. There were Seekers everywhere but there were also people at various stations. He couldn't make out exactly what was going on, but it looked important and that meant he had to go in there and start trouble.

"Well, guess it's time to open up a can of whoop ass on these guys," Vincent said out loud. He placed the scientist on the floor and readied his weapons. He would have to move as fast as he ever had. He opened the door and busted in, immediately opening fire on the Seekers closest to him. The first shot from each Beretta landed flawlessly, one punching a hole through the dark soldier's throat; the next shot went through the chest of the one standing beside to the first. Before either hit the ground Vincent took aim and fired at two more Seekers, dropping them. Now that those directly in front of him were on their way to the ground, he pointed one gun in each direction to the side of him, spreading his arms like wings. Moving his head side to side, he charged down the center of the open area firing his armor piercing rounds, taking each Seeker out with one shot until the guns were out of ammunition. He leapt over a desk that was in his way, landed, rolled, and found cover next to a support pillar. He quickly packed new clips into his pistols. He was concerned that he was running out of the precious ammunition and with the destruction of his Mustang back in New Haven, the remainder of his supply had been lost.

The handful of non-Seekers had never been so frightened. They began to panic. Vincent had moved so quickly that they couldn't even catch sight of who had just raided them and killed several of the dark warriors. To them, Vincent Black was a force of nature, even the wrath of God himself.

The Dark Ones began to regroup and ready their weapons. At this point, Vincent had finished reloading his guns and was on the move again. The Seekers began to open fire, but his movements were quick and he was extremely difficult to hit. The enemy soldiers did manage to hit a few of the bystanders that were in the area, wiping out the few people in the complex who had not been lobotomized. Various computers and equipment were being struck by the powerful rounds from the Seeker rifles but they didn't strike their intended target.

"Don't let him near the control unit," the last person who had a functional frontal lobe said while cowering on the ground. He was actually pointing out the control unit.

Vincent smiled. "That's nice, line up to get torn apart and point out my objective." Vincent now returned fire. Since his body and mind were so in sync and he moved with such dexterity, it was like everyone else moved in slow motion around him. He began firing his pistols again, maximizing his limited ammunition by taking out each Seeker with one bullet and never missing. He charged toward the control unit, which was actually a series of blade servers in a server cabinet. He quickly holstered his side-arms and pulled out a grenade. The Seekers wouldn't dare fire at him while he was standing in front of such an important unit, so he pulled the pin and tossed it in, then hurried as far away from it as possible. Three seconds later, the grenade detonated, sending shrapnel everywhere and destroying the server cabinet along with the servers it contained. Sparks flew everywhere and suddenly the building alarms went off with flickering lights and deafeningly loud alerts.

Vincent dove behind an old metal desk and pulled out his radio. He pushed the talk button on it and simply said, "Now." Hopefully, Lexi was ready to start taking out the Seekers stationed on the outside to make room for a massive evacuation.

More Seekers began entering from the other side of the open room, probably from other areas of the floor. Vincent had only brought two grenades with him and did not particularly want to use the other one quite yet, so he decided to make another dash for it; the desk he'd been behind was not going to stop rifle fire. Sure enough, the moment he dashed he was shot at and the desk was ripped apart almost immediately. Vincent ran while return-ing fire until his guns were empty once again. He hoped no stray bullets had hit that scientist in the stairwell...he needed the guy breathing.

He did not have time to reload his guns, so he holstered them and made a break for the stairwell door. To buy himself some time, he decided that this was the moment to use his other gre-nade, which he tossed in the direction of his adversaries. They immediately stopped shooting at him and tried to get to cover. He was out the door and in the stairwell when the explosive went off and did not see what happened but he didn't waste any time wor-rying about it. He grabbed the scientist and slung him over his shoulders once again, then made his way up the stairs, loading his guns with his ever-dwindling supply of armor piercing rounds.

Lexi heard one word over her comm., "Now." That's all she needed. She had been going stir crazy, wondering what was hap-pening. She had scaled a tall tree and had positioned herself in such a way that she had a clear view of the former hospital. Fortunately for her, the tree still had its leaves which were various shades of orange, brown, and yellow. She took aim with the rifle that Vincent had given to her; the very one he had used to rescue Josh, Andromeda, and Talbot in Hartford. She could hear the alarms at the complex - they sounded like air raid sirens from back in the Cold War. The Seeker snipers on the roof were not well hidden, even though they did not have their shoulder lights on. She fired the first shot and it tore through the middle of a dark warrior's face plate, causing him to fall to the ground below. She then turned her attention to those doing the rotation on the ground and began firing. She took the time to aim but was still being as quick as she could, taking them down one at a time the way her father had taught her. The Seekers that were still alive began to fire wildly in the general direction of the tree that she was in but nothing came anywhere near her...they had no idea where she was. She kept firing, picking off Seeker after Seeker on the ground, and then the crowd came out. Pouring around the area were the rebels that had been kept as prisoners in the basement.

"Oh shit, here we go," Lexi uttered under her breath. In the lead were a few people in their tattered clothes that were armed, probably taken from downed enemies. She could see the look on everyone's faces; they were frightened beyond all belief. In this case though, the fear worked to their advantage. Adrenaline was pumping through each rebel's veins and they ran harder and faster than they ever had, making them difficult targets, especially while the Dark Ones were attempting to find the hidden sniper.

Lexi caught sight of a Seeker on the roof who fired a round through one of the armed rebel's heads. She was too late to save that one but she returned a round that went straight through the Dark One's chest, preventing him from killing any further. A Seeker attempted to fire mortar into the crowd, but instead blew a nice opening in the gate allowing them easy access to the street.

Josh was nervous. He had been nervous the entire time and sitting there waiting wasn't helping. He had been thrust into this role by either fate or poor luck. He used to be content spending hours on the computer, accomplishing feats that very few could. It had gained him recognition by the United States Government, who had hired him as a Department of Defense Consultant. His incredible skills and natural talents in Information Technology afforded him the highest security clearances that a civilian could get. It was these very skills that now had him playing a major role in what would soon turn into a full scale rebellion. That is, if they survived this psychotic mission they were on.

Josh did not like being alone with his thoughts. Just as Vincent had incredible speed and agility of the body, the young programmer had a similar scenario with his mind. It raced so fast, he pictured several different scenarios of the outcome, and worried that a rocket would be shot into the Bronco. His concentration was broken when a single word came over the comm. It was Vincent's voice. "Now." Much to his surprise, his mind cleared almost instantly and focused on the task at hand. He put the truck into gear and headed to the spot where Lexi had climbed the tree. It did not take him long to get there, although she was good at staying hidden. If he did not know where to look, he would have never found her. He pulled below the tree and shifted the truck in park.

"C'mon Lexi, get the hell down from there and let's go," Josh shouted over the sounds of gunfire at the complex.

Lexi fired a couple more shots, and then began to scale down the tree. She was quick, jumping off the last branch and landing next to the passenger door. She immediately climbed in. "Sorry, had to take out those last two Seekers."

Josh looked pale but said, "Don't worry about it, let's just get Vincent and get the hell out of here."

Vincent hurried to the roof, knowing full well that all hell had broken loose. He didn't even bother to calmly open the door... he kicked it and it busted open with a loud snap. Lexi had not wasted any time; he walked out just in time to see a Seeker drop from a shot to the head. Others had already been taken out. Vincent once again put the scientist down and began unloading on the Seekers on the roof. Snipers and guards alike fell under his barrage. His guns ran out of ammunition just as the last of the Seekers fell. He could hear the commotion of the escaped prisoners running out of the former hospital. There was still gunfire, and he hoped it was the rebels shooting at their captors, but he knew that some of them wouldn't make it. Then he received the dreaded tingle in the back of his head. He turned to see someone dressed in armor that was similar to the Seekers, but different. There was also no faceplate so he saw her face. A woman, but he didn't recognize her.

"Night Viper, I've been looking for you. Lord Zodiac would love to meet you, and your girlfriend," the woman said menacingly.

Vincent looked at her and said, "He'll meet me soon enough. You've been looking for me huh? Well now you've found me. You must be the commander for this place." He didn't even ask who was being referred to as his girlfriend.

The woman smiled. "Commander Jade. Now, make it easy on yourself and throw down your weapons."

Vincent chuckled. "Throwing down was what I had in mind, but not my weapons."

"SO BE IT," Jade shouted. She pulled out her pistol and opened fire. She moved much faster than the Seekers, but still not as fast as Vincent, who was already leaping through the air, avoiding the bullets she fired. Her sidearm only held 7 rounds, which had all been expended when Vincent's feet touched down. Jade threw a punch but Vincent ducked it, counter-punching her in the gut. If it was not for her armor, vital organs would have ruptured. As it was, the hit lifted her off of her feet and knocked her onto her back. She immediately recovered and flipped back up, then charged at him. Vincent, with one fluid motion, grabbed hold and using her momentum, threw her off the roof. To her credit, she did not even scream on the way down.

"Guess Zodiac will have to wait for now," Vincent said out loud. He immediately retrieved the scientist and went back to the mounted service ladder that he had used to climb onto the roof. While heading down, he noticed that the entire complex was in chaos. Escaped rebels were running out of the area with no one chasing them.

Vincent hurried over to where Commander Jade had fallen. He saw that, despite the fall, her armor had protected her enough to keep her alive, but she was not conscious. He picked her up and slung her over his other shoulder, then made his way to the rendezvous point for Josh and Lexi to pick him up.

Chapter 23

Carl Woods was at a loss. After he had narrowly escaped death twice in a matter of minutes, between the failed attempt at raiding the former William Backus Hospital and then the ordeal in the collapsed house, he just wanted to drive. So that's what he did. He followed Washington Street until he could pick up Route 32, and then followed that. He realized that he was heading toward New London, which was a heavily traveled area before the Flash Storm. He wasn't thinking straight though, or he would have headed in the opposite direction. He wished he had. When he arrived near the former Connecticut city on Interstate 95, what he saw defied words. As far as he could see, the area had been completely cleared and flattened. Thousands of laborers with various pieces of construction equipment and materials were covering the region like ants on an unattended chocolate cake at a picnic. There was some sort of major construction project and he had no idea what it was, but he immediately turned around and headed back.

To get away from the construction site, Carl simply went back the way he had come, so he was back near Backus Hospital. The guilt was so thick he probably could have cut it with a knife. His self-preservation instinct was screaming at him, "You idiot! Get the hell out of here! They think you're dead. If you stay here, that thought will be a reality." He couldn't though. He blamed himself for the deaths of all of those people who had looked up to him. He could not leave. He was far enough away that he was not noticed, but he was close enough to see it from a distance. As if the day hadn't been crazy enough, he saw another unexpected scene.

The entire complex had erupted into chaos. He was on foot; the car that he had taken was almost out of gas. He began jogging toward the place he had narrowly escaped from. He saw Seekers dropping like flies. He saw people, prisoners, pouring out of the complex and fleeing for their lives. He kept moving closer, not sure of what he was witnessing. There was no army. No air assault. There was nothing. He moved in closer and could see even better. He saw something happening on the roof. Someone in armor fell and landed on the ground.

Carl closed his eyes and shook his head; he couldn't believe what he was seeing. Someone was actually taking on the Seekers, and winning at that. He saw what appeared to be a man carrying someone or something over his shoulder while climbing down a metal service ladder on the side of the building. He moved in closer and saw the man hop off the ladder and hurry over to what he originally thought had been a Seeker that had fallen off the roof. The man reached down, picked the person up and it became apparent that the armored individual was female and was definitely not a Seeker. The man threw the downed woman over his free shoulder.

A vehicle, what appeared to be a Bronco from the mid 90's pulled up and the man with the two people slung over his shoulders loaded his prisoners and got in. Carl continued to move in for a closer look. He realized he was standing in the middle of the road when he saw the truck barreling straight for him. He hurried out of the way and the truck kept going as if he wasn't even there.

"Who the hell were they!?" he said out loud as he turned his head to watch the escape vehicle speeding away. Whatever they did, it completely disrupted operations, and there was no pursuit. The Seekers who were alive were aimlessly wandering the grounds of the former William W. Backus Hospital. All of the former prisoners had scattered…some had run past him. They were all over the place, raiding houses that were still standing, looking for supplies and escape vehicles. There was one person, however, that was limping in his direction.

Carl hurried to the mysterious man. He noticed that his clothes were torn; he had blood on him, and looked to be in pain.

"Hey man, c'mon, let's get you the hell out of here! What's your name?"

The man did not respond as he put his arm over Carl's shoulder and accepted the offer of help. "That's alright if you don't want to tell me," Carl stated, wondering why the man wasn't speaking until he pointed to his mouth. When Carl looked, he saw that the man had no tongue.

They made their way down the road, with no one in pursuit, despite how slowly they were going. They managed to make it to the garage he had taken the car from originally...the house that he had been trapped in had burned to cinders and was still smoldering, filling the night air with a campfire-like scent. Carl figured that the Seekers would probably not look for them there, if they even bothered to look at all. Of course, he also knew they shouldn't stay long, considering the busted vinyl door. They made their way inside, past the dried up corpse, and went into the far corner to remain out of site.

"I'm Carl Woods," Carl reported as he fumbled around some things until he found a small pad of paper and a pencil. "Can you write?"

The man, who had the darkest skin Carl had ever seen, shook his head yes and accepted the paper and pencil and began writing. "Thank you for helping me. It was truly heroic."

Carl shook his head. "Nothing heroic about me man, just trying to survive."

The man tore off the paper and flipped it over, writing, "You took a big risk helping me with my injury. That's a hero."

Carl blushed and then said, "What's your name?"

The man tossed the paper aside and wrote on the next one. "I go by Eric. I don't know the..." He turned the paper over and continued, "name my parents gave me."

It was at that moment that Carl noticed a scar on his forehead. "That scar on your head?"

Eric tossed away the previous page and began writing again. "I remember waking up in a Ugandan hospital. There was..." He turned the paper over, "an American volunteer there. She told me..." He ripped off that piece of paper and handed it to Carl, then continued on the next one, "that I had been captured by a rival tribe. They cut..." He once again flipped the paper over, "my tongue out."

"Geeze, in Uganda? That's crazy," Carl commented.

Eric nodded then ripped off the piece of paper and went to the next one. "When I tried to escape, they shot me..." He flipped the paper over, "in the head and left me for dead."

Carl was looking around for something to brace Eric's ankle with. He found a fancy first aid kit and opened it. As he sorted through the various items he asked, "So how did you get to the States?"

Eric threw away the previous paper and began writing again. "The volunteer took me back, her family took..." He once again flipped the paper over, shaking his head while Carl bandaged his ankle, "me in. They died in the Flash Storm."

Carl read the note as he finished the bandage and secured it. He stopped for a moment after he had completed his rudimentary first aid. So many people were lost when Zodiac unleashed his fury on the world. "I'm sorry, Eric. First your identity, then your family. My story isn't so tragic. I'm divorced, not even because I am...or was...a cop, but because it turns out that I'm sterile and my wife wanted to have kids. She left me for someone else and she moved to Delaware. I have no idea what ever happened to her...she had no interest in keeping in contact with me."

On a fresh piece of paper, Eric wrote, "I'm sorry, my friend. It looks as if we both..." He wiped a tear then flipped the paper over to continue, "have been left to fend for ourselves."

Carl shook his head. "Not anymore. What the hell happened in there?"

Eric held up his index finger then went to feverishly writing on the pad. After a few moments, he tore off the papers that he wrote on and handed them Carl who looked through them and read, "I was in Danbury with a rebel cell there. We were not much in the rebel department, more like survivors. We were attacked; those not killed were taken prisoner and I was one of them. They held us at a detention center, the location of which I am unaware. From there, they would bring groups of us to this place to convert us to Seekers or slaves. The person in charge here is a cruel woman. I was to be next when the compound was attacked for a second time. This time, we were freed."

"I was part of the first raid, I'm the only survivor. I don't know who it was who went in there, but he took some woman in Seeker armor with no faceplate as a prisoner and someone else. He killed lots of those Grand Army bastards. It was incredible. I wonder who he was," Carl responded.

Eric wrote two words on a piece of paper, tore it off, and handed it to Carl. It said, "Night Viper."

Carl gave a confused look at the paper and then to Eric. "Night Viper? Who the hell is that!?"

The Ugandan immigrant began writing again, hoping that he was not going to run out of paper during the conversation. He handed the papers to Carl. "I did not see him. I heard while flee-ing. People were saying that Night Viper had saved us…that he had come to deliver us from the very gates of hell. I don't know who or what he is, but he came in alone."

Carl sat back in disbelief. His whole crew was laid to waste and one man was able to enter the complex, turn it upside down, and walk out with the leader? It was difficult to grasp. "What it would take for one man to do all that. We need to find him."

Eric was shaking his hand; he was probably developing writer's cramp. He nodded his head in response. Carl then said, "C'mon. We'll take this med kit with us and find another car. I really don't want to hang around here for the reinforcements to come."

Chapter 24

Eve was lying in her bed, unable to get comfortable. Part of the reason was being almost eight months pregnant. The other part was the complications she was beginning to experience. She was developing a fever and her blood pressure was rising. Her husband was next to her, checking up on her. "How're you feeling babe?"

She had her eyes shut. She no longer cared about being comfortable; she just wanted to find a position where nothing hurt. "Like hell. John, what's happening?"

John couldn't hide his concern. Since he had gotten back from meeting the members of Militia 28, Eve had been getting worse. He placed a cool washcloth on her head and said, "You probably have a bug or something. Your fever is only slight, 100 degrees even. Your blood pressure is slightly elevated."

"I can't get comfortable. Is it supposed to be like this? Am I supposed to feel like this?" she asked.

John shook his head. "I don't know anything about this. I had thought about getting one of those guidebooks for new Dads, but then everything got blown up. Listen, I'm gonna go grab you some water…be right back."

John went out into the hallway and proceeded to the mess hall. It was definitely a lot nicer than the ones you would see in military barracks. Instead of long, rectangular shaped institutional tables, there were wooden round tables with individual chairs. There were regular salt and pepper shakers along with various sweeteners both natural and artificial, as if it was a real restaurant. When the government abandoned the compound, they didn't bother taking their condiments.

Talbot was already there, digging around for something to eat. Andromeda was sitting at a table drawing on a pad of paper that she had found. He went and grabbed a cup and filled it with water. He was fumbling a bit, his mind wandering with worry for his wife and unborn child.

"You look like you got hit by a bus," Talbot said to John.

The former soldier shut his eyes for a moment, and then looked up. "I feel worse. I'm really worried about Eve. The baby's dropped. Her blood pressure and temperature are slowly climbing. I have no idea what to do. I wish Vincent and the others would get back here. We need to strike up a deal with this Militia 28."

Talbot walked over to him. "We have to discuss it. They seemed alright but we have to make sure we can trust them."

John slammed his fist on the counter. "Dammit Chris! My wife and unborn child could be dying. If there's even a remote chance they have a doctor with them, we need to take it." His voice began to break, his legs quivered. "I can't lose them, man. I can't. I feel so damn helpless."

Talbot walked over and put his hand on John's shoulder. He felt for the guy. Prior to May 7th, Eve would have been hospitalized and would have professionals looking after her. But those days were done. They had a decent facility but it was not a hospital and none of them had the expertise that was needed in this situation. "John, getting worked up isn't going to help anything. Vincent, Lexi, and Josh will be back, don't worry. Remember, they went to Connecticut. Even with Vincent's driving, that's quite a trip."

John let out an uneasy chuckle. He guzzled the water then re-filled the cup for his wife. "I'm sorry. I'm just not good with stuff like this…when I can't do anything, I don't like it."

Talbot shook his head. "No one does, John, that's why my recent discovery is even more valuable."

"What recent discovery?" John asked with peeked curiosity.

Talbot reached into his pocket and pulled out a flask. "I found the liquor stash."

John smirked. "Let me just bring this to Eve and then I'll be back."

"Take your time…I'm gonna hang here for a little while, see what Andromeda is drawing," Talbot responded.

John began to walk away, then stopped and turned his head. "No Drunk Running though, right?"

Talbot laughed. "Hell no. I just want to take the edge off, not commit suicide."

"Alright then." John turned back around and left.

He continued through the hallways until he reached his and Eve's quarters. He walked in to find that his wife had fallen asleep. He stared at her for a moment, the love of his life carrying a new life inside of her. This new life was his child. He did not know whether they were going to have a boy or a girl, but it didn't matter. It was a miracle, which this world needed desperately. He walked over to Eve and covered her with the blanket. He placed the cup of water on the nightstand within her reach, then turned around and went back to the mess hall.

By the time he returned, he saw that Talbot was going through some of the drawings that Andromeda had made. The young girl was continuing on another sheet of paper. John went over and sat across from Talbot and the girl.

"Take a look at these," Talbot said in a serious tone as he handed a couple of drawings across the table.

John took a look at them and nearly fell out of his chair. He grabbed the flask off the table and took a big gulp. It was whiskey. With nothing more than a pencil and notebook paper, this girl, not even a teenager yet, had created an extremely detailed drawing of Vincent and Lexi killing a Seeker. It was so accurate, he would have thought that it was computer generated if it wasn't for the fact that he could see clear as day that it was done in pencil and the paper was lined notebook paper. "This is unbelievable. You drew this?"

Andromeda nodded her head. John turned to Talbot and said, "Did you know she could draw like this?"

Talbot shook his head, "No, I had no idea. This whole time she's been with me and Josh, there really weren't any pads and pencils lying around. She found this stuff here in the compound."

"Andromeda, this is amazing. You just drew this with a pencil?" John was blown away.

"I can paint too," Andromeda said without even looking up

from what she was drawing. "Maybe I could paint your baby's room."

John hadn't even thought of that, but it was actually a good idea. It was nice to have the conveniences of electricity and running water again, but their quarters still looked institutional. "That's actually a really good idea, if I can find a hardware store that hasn't been totally ransacked. This last trip to find supplies wasn't exactly fruitful in that department."

"It may have led us to something much bigger and better though," Talbot pointed out.

"True, very true," John agreed. He then turned and said, "Andromeda, why don't you ever speak?"

She did not look up from her drawing. "Silence is the cornerstone of character."

John was once again taken aback and did not respond immediately. He finally replied, "That's quite an observation."

"It's an old Native American proverb. I'll speak when there's something to say, not just to hear myself talk. I already know everything that I'm going to say, so I don't gain anything by saying random junk," Andromeda elaborated.

John hesitated…he wanted to make small talk with the girl, but he wasn't sure how. Finally, he said, "Andromeda is an interesting name."

"It's a galaxy. My dad was a professor of Astronomy. He's the one who named me. Not really an overly exciting story," Andromeda stated abruptly.

Talbot leaned back and snickered a bit. John couldn't believe that this 12 year old was effectively dismissing him. "I think it's pretty cool."

Andromeda actually looked up from what she was doing. "Then you must be really bored." She got up and left the mess hall, leaving her most recent drawing on the table.

Talbot looked at John. "It takes her a while to warm up to people."

John picked up the drawing. After looking at it, he showed it to Talbot. "Apparently, she warmed up to Eve."

Talbot grabbed the paper and saw that Andromeda had drawn a picture of Eve, sitting in a rocking chair and holding a baby. It was a stunning image. "She's a smart kid…probably too smart for us. I'll bet she's bored with idle conversation."

"Maybe she has Asperger's," John guessed.

Talbot had a confused look on his face. "What the hell is that?"

"It's a form of high-functioning Autism. My brother had it. They tend to be brilliant but socially awkward. I'm not a doctor, but talent like this is rare to find in an adult, never mind someone who hasn't even hit her teens," John explained.

"I guess it's possible," Talbot agreed. "I just figured she was a little socially awkward in light of her parents being butchered in front of her by the Seekers. That's where she got that scar from."

John went silent for a moment. "Yeah that would do it too."

"Look, I'm not saying that it ain't possible, I'm just saying that it seems like people want to give everyone a label. Sometimes people are just the way they are. Anyway, why don't you go and be with your wife. I'll come get you when Vincent and the others get back," Talbot suggested.

John nodded his head. "I hope they come back."

"They will, John. Lexi's too stubborn to die; Josh is too smart to die; and I'm not sure Vincent *can* die," Talbot assured.

Chapter 25

"We're all gonna die," Josh mumbled as he continued to speed away from the former William Backus Hospital.

Lexi gave him a light punch on the shoulder, as usual. "Stop being so paranoid...we're not being followed." She poked her head back out the window to look behind them, making sure that she wasn't about to eat her words.

Vincent was in the back with the two prisoners. "We're not being followed. Right now they probably don't even know their asses from their elbows."

Lexi was actually overcome with excitement. "I can't believe we just did that. I can't believe we attacked one of Zodiac's compounds and not only got away, but captured two of his people."

Josh gave her a similar look that Medusa would have used; only his was incapable of turning her to stone. "We haven't gotten away yet. Maybe they have a SAT on us. Ever think of that?"

"Cool it and drive Josh. We need to get to some kind of cover before these two fools wake up," Vincent commanded.

"Who the hell are they anyway?" Josh asked.

"She identified herself as Commander Jade. God knows if that's even any type of real name. It's strange though...I don't think she's military," Vincent stated.

Josh looked up at Vincent in the rear view mirror as he drove. "How do you know?"

"Someone who would end up being the head of any operation has put in some time. It gives one a certain demeanor and

215

a chiseled, tough look. This 'Jade' looks like a regular person, at least her face anyway," Vincent observed.

Lexi turned around in her seat. "Who's the guy who looks like he wore a lab coat to a butcher shop?"

Vincent admired her sass. "He's some type of scientist. Before I grabbed him, he was talking about getting back to his lab. I don't know what he does but if he was there, I figure we might be able to get something out of him about that chip."

"Look, I'm not trying to be a 'Debbie Downer'," Josh said, looking over at Lexi, "but I just want to play devil's advocate here. What happens if they're trained in anti-interrogation techniques? None of us are military. How are we going to get anything out of them?"

Vincent began fiddling with Jade's armor. "I have my ways of making people talk."

The comment sent a chill down Josh's spine, so he decided to go back to the subject of Jade's military training or lack thereof. "I'm still confused on the whole non-military leaders. How could Zodiac conquer most of the known world without having military trained people?"

Vincent looked as if he had something on his mind. "Zodiac destroyed the military. Bases were left in ruins or taken over by Seekers. He probably figured that if he decimated the armed forces during the Flash Storm, he wouldn't need trained military personnel. Hell, his commanders might have just been really good at strategy games and read 'The Art of War'."

"Well that shoots the theory that the Flash Storm was some type of military coupe or something like that," Lexi stated.

"There's no way it was a military coup. Look, everyone says that Zodiac's telepathic, right? If he is, he could have easily found his way into a high level government position with access to classified information, as well as the locations of military hardware and personnel, including Special Forces. Rather than try to stage a takeover, he may have decided to eliminate the opposition. Hell, with Amendment 28, they already disarmed the public," Vincent affirmed. "That's why there aren't all sorts of tanks and fighter jets around. Zodiac must've destroyed them all in the hopes that he would destroy any chance of a resistance."

"Jesus Christ," was all Josh could say.

Lexi sat back in her seat. "Just how powerful is he? I mean, even for a telepath, he would've had to take over the minds of a lot of people to get to a position where he would have such influence."

"Maybe the president is Zodiac," Josh suggested.

Vincent shook his head. "No, too high profile. Influencing people's minds with such severity would draw attention in a highly public figure. He would've been someone in the background. Someone that no one would know about. Someone with charisma so he would only have to use his mental abilities subtly."

"Vice President maybe?" Lexi put out there.

Vincent shook his head again. "No, even that position is too high profile. I suppose it doesn't matter anyway. We should probably just focus on the here and now."

"We're still not being followed, right?" Josh inquired.

Lexi shook her head. "No, why?"

Josh slammed on the brakes and turned into the driveway of an abandoned house. He came to a stop in front of the garage. "I figure we can stay out of sight in here and maybe find some supplies if one of you would be willing to open that garage door. Hopefully, it's not loaded with shit."

Vincent and Lexi looked at each other, then Lexi hit Josh in the arm again. "You drive like a damn maniac!"

Josh rubbed his arm. "That hurt, you know."

Lexi climbed out of the truck, turned and with a sarcastic smirk she said, "Good!"

Vincent leaned forward and put his hand on Josh's shoulder. "You were a ladies' man before the Flash Storm, weren't you?" He then cackled a bit and got out.

"Great, that's great. You're both crazy," Josh muttered under his breath.

Vincent walked over to the garage and looked around a bit. This particular house did not have an automatic opener and the owners had left in a hurry, not locking it. He easily opened it, then waived in Josh, who obliged. He and Lexi then stepped in and shut the door. "Good idea, Josh…I knew we kept you around for a reason." Vincent was enjoying being sarcastic with the computer nerd.

After a few moments, the scientist was tied up in the corner with some rope that Lexi had found. Jade was laid out on the floor. "This is some freaky shit. I don't want to wait for her to wake up," Josh declared.

Vincent was un-fazed. "I beat her before, and I'll beat her again if I have to. Strange though, she was faster than a normal human."

Josh threw his hands in the air. "Great, another genetically altered super soldier. We don't need a super powered fight."

Lexi rolled her eyes. "C'mon Josh, grow a pair."

"Easy for you to say madam fearless," Josh snapped.

"Alright children, knock it the hell off. Help me get this armor off of her," Vincent stated.

Josh scrunched his face. "Isn't that kind of…I don't know, per-verted?"

Vincent raised his eyebrows at Josh. "Give me a break. We're not making porn; we're taking a look at this armor. I doubt she's naked underneath it anyway, so get your mind out of the damn gutter."

Josh raised his hands in front of him. "Hey man, I'm just say-ing."

Lexi was observing the armor "This looks different than the Seeker armor, and I'm not talking about the markings."

The three of them began to remove Jade's armor, which came off surprisingly easily. They uncovered what appeared to be small servos and motors. "Geeze, this is more than armor. It's some kind of robotic enhancement exo-skeleton," Josh commented.

Vincent shook his head. "Where would something like this come from?"

Lexi was looking closely at one of the plates she removed. "This is like science fiction futuristic stuff."

Josh was looking at it with amazement. "No, it's not futur-istic. Don't you guys see? Science fiction has always served as a marker for humanity to attain. Everything. Hell, decades ago a guy named Jules Verne wrote about a boat that went underwater. Everyone said that was crazy talk until the submarine was devel-oped. Combat enhancement systems have been researched for a long time by every government on the planet."

"It would make sense if the commanders didn't have military expertise or combat training," Lexi pointed out.

They finished removing the armor from Jade. Underneath, she appeared to be a regular woman. She was wearing nothing more than a tank top shirt and a pair of tight fitting sweat shorts. The armor must have protected her as she only had a few bruises as a result of plummeting from the roof of the makeshift Seeker Farm. "Let's get this stuff loaded in the Bronco and secure her. We need to get these two back to the compound so we can get them talking," Vincent decided out loud.

Josh was looking at Jade. She was average height for a woman with a petite build. She had long black hair and pale skin. "She's kind of cute...too bad she's a murderer," Josh commented.

Lexi rolled her eyes and hit Josh in the shoulder yet again. "Didn't Vincent tell you to get your mind out of the gutter."

Josh rubbed his shoulder again. "You know, you'll feel really bad when you dislocate my shoulder because you hit me too damn much."

Lexi chuckled. "Stop saying and doing stuff that you deserve to be hit for and save us both the trouble!"

The scientist began to stir. He let out a groan and then picked his head up. "Where...who...I don't care. Get me a cup of coffee and Danish so I can get back to work." He hadn't even opened his eyes yet.

Lexi looked at Vincent. "Are you serious? Did he really just say that without even opening his eyes? Hey, brainiac! Ain't no Danish or coffee here."

The scientist finally opened his eyes and looked directly at Lexi. "Oh. Well, I say, it looks like I have found myself in a precarious situation."

Josh looked at him. "Yeah, that's right, you have."

The scientist ignored Josh and looked directly at Vincent. "I remember you - you're the one who got the drop on me. Tell me, how did you get into the complex and pull me away from the Seekers? You obviously don't have a wound on you."

Vincent prepared his normal speech. "I'm what happens when the government plays with forces that it shouldn't."

The scientist, oddly enough, did not ask for Vincent to elaborate; he simply replied, "Yes, that much is quite obvious. Your fame is well earned, Night Viper."

Lexi and Josh just looked at each other. Vincent was concentrating on the scientist. "And you heard that name where?"

"Why, it's in your file. Your name is Vincent Black, but you carry the alias of Night Viper. That is an interesting name by the way. How did you manage to earn it?" the man asked.

Vincent ignored the question. "My file? I have a file?"

"Oh dear, I'm afraid I've said too much. I will have to be silent now, although I am quite sure you'll torture the information out of me," the scientist stated.

Josh held his head with one hand. "What the hell is it with this guy?"

Vincent ignored Josh. "Why put yourself through something like that? Just tell me what you know."

"I'm afraid I can't do that," the scientist told him.

"Oh here we go," Josh interjected onto deaf ears.

Vincent squatted next to the restrained scientist. "And why the hell not?"

"Because I would be killed. I doubt a hero like you would kill me in cold blood. That's not what you do. No, I must remain silent," the scientist said as he crossed his arms.

"Okay, this guy is really arrogant," Lexi opined.

Vincent remained squatting and looked the scientist up and down. "Yeah. Kind of reminds me of a place I used to work. Most of those fools were pretty arrogant." Vincent did not waste any time. He reached out, grabbed the man's left hand and snapped his pinky back. Everyone could hear the bones cracking.

"AAAAAAAAAHHHHHHHHHHHHHHH! Dear Lord man, what are you doing?" the scientist asked, wailing in pain.

Vincent snapped the ring finger on the same hand and earned another loud pain scream. "You said you read my file, but I don't think you read it completely. If you saw what I did in L.A., you'd know that what I'm willing to do to you simply for the suffering and pain you've caused is unthinkable. Now, tell me about these files or this will get exponentially worse."

"It's...it's information on you. All of us who were permitted to keep our wits about us, if you know what I mean, were given access to it. You're public enemy number one, Night Viper. Lord Zodiac really wants you brought to him," the scientist spilled. "And he wants this young lady too, Alexis Hera is your name, correct?"

Lexi, Josh, and Vincent just gave each other a look. Vincent turned back and asked, "What do you know about the Seeker control chips?"

The scientist looked up at him. "Please don't go down this road with me."

Vincent's face went straight and he proceeded to break the man's middle finger on the same hand that he had broken the other two fingers, and was rewarded with yet another loud scream of pain. "No, it's you who doesn't want to go down this road with me. I don't have the time to waste on you. WHAT DO YOU KNOW!?"

"I...I...I install them," the scientist answered.

Lexi reacted this time by backhanding the man. "INSTALL THEM!? These aren't computers, they're people and you're destroying their identity, who they are, and turning them into flesh and blood robots!"

The scientist looked up at her. "That's correct. That is what I was brought on to do and as long as I do it and do it well, Lord Zodiac allows me to keep my own mind. Ironically though, it's not me who actually implants them, but the machine."

"The machine?" Josh's curiosity took a major jump.

The white-coated man had a distressed look. "Oh, there I go again. Well, I don't wish to have another finger broken so I'll tell you. The machine sends two probes underneath the eyes to lobotomize the subject. While the probes are inside, they are used to assemble the control chips."

Josh whispered into Lexi's ear, "That would confirm why the skull of that Seeker we caught wasn't torn open."

Lexi nodded but kept her eyes fixed on the conscious prisoner.

Vincent violated the man's personal space and put his own face mere inches from the scientist's. "You're coming with us. You're gonna give us all the information you have on those chips that you put in the Seekers. If you cooperate, you'll live and you may even regain use of that hand."

"That is...quite generous of you" The scientist was able to emit a bit of sarcasm.

"What's the story with this one here?" Josh asked, pointing to Jade.

221

The scientist looked over at her, then at Josh and answered, "That is Commander Jade. I know very little about her. I was told to obey her every order without question and since my superior intellect is not only important to me but important to the world, I do exactly that."

Lexi whispered to Vincent, "I want to beat this guy to death. Please, let me hit him."

Vincent whispered a response, "Not now Lexi. We need what's in his head. We'll bring him back to the compound then we'll go from there."

"I don't suppose you would stop breaking my fingers. I'm in quite a significant amount of pain right now," the scientist said as if it was perfectly normal to have broken fingers.

"Depends on my mood. Let's load him and Jade in the Bronco and get the hell out of here. We can finish questioning them at the compound," Vincent suggested.

"Compound? You have a base? Oh dear, I suppose I am about to disappear," the scientist stated.

"Don't worry old man…if you cooperate, you may live to see another full moon," Josh threatened.

Chapter 26

General Callous and Commander Triton's Firehawk touched down in the open area that used to be the parking lot for the William W. Backus Hospital in Norwich, Connecticut. They had received a SOS but could not communicate with anyone beyond that, so they left the construction site immediately. They were not prepared for what they saw.

"What the hell went through here?" asked Triton.

Callous just shook his head. "It looks as though some rebels found some momentum and stormed the place."

Looking around they saw their dark warriors lying dead and scattered everywhere. There were a handful of rebel prisoners that had been gunned down in the break-out, but almost all of them had managed to get away. With the chaos that ensued when Commander Jade was taken, no pursuit teams had been dispatched.

Triton squatted down by one of the dead Seekers, observing that he had been shot in the side of the head by a high powered rifle. "Whoever they were, they were well-equipped, which is unusual for rebels. I believe they were using some type of powerful rifle or they were able to get their hands on armor piercing rounds."

"Where is Commander Jade in all of this!?" Callous asked out loud. "Even if she were dead, her successor should have taken over immediately."

"Unless they're both dead," Triton suggested, still squatting down next to the body of the Seeker.

Callous paused for a moment and looked down at his fists. "Impossible. No ragtag group could take out two commanders - especially Jade. She was not as foolish as your predecessor."

"Agreed, but it might not have been a ragtag group at all. Maybe it was an organized gang of former military," Triton suggested as he stood up.

Callous was carefully observing the scenery before him. There were still areas smoldering from where explosives had detonated. "Are you suggesting that Lord Zodiac may have missed some? We carefully tracked all military personnel so that they could be exterminated before they could organize. We destroyed every military base that we didn't take over."

Triton put his hands up and shook his head back and forth rapidly. "I'm not saying he missed anything. I'm saying that there were a lot of military trained personnel. There were plenty of black ops teams that were off the books that we might have missed. Hell, it could have been a bunch of seasoned cops for all we know."

Callous began a slow walk toward the building. "It is possible I guess, but they should have still succumbed to the fear aura generated by the Seekers' implants."

Triton hurried and walked next to Callous. "Maybe it was Night Viper. Lord Zodiac told us that he's more dangerous than a hundred rebels."

"Despite his abilities, do you really believe that one man could've done all of this? How would he have even known about this place anyway?" Callous asked.

"I don't know, but he's managed to evade capture thus far. He's obviously resourceful and now he has help. Maybe that Alexis Hera was with him...she doesn't feel fear," Triton pointed out.

Callous waived his hand dismissively. "Pfah. That little girl couldn't have turned the tide of battle. This must have been an organized assault with large numbers."

Callous and Triton entered the complex. The directionless Seekers were now back and obedient, thanks to Callous having sent a reset signal. They stood emotionless and awaited orders. The General and Commander began their inspection of the facility in the basement. There, they saw several dead Seekers and empty cells. "No sign of force on these cells. These people were let out," Triton observed.

Callous gave him a deep, threatening look. "They are not people Commander Triton. We are. They are worms, insects, maggots, animals, cockroaches, whatever you want to call them, but they are not people. They are things to enslave or kill as we please. Keep that in mind."

"Yes sir…just a slip of the tongue was all. Old habits, you know," Triton responded.

"Yes, you are correct, they were let out. Whomever or whatever killed our warriors could have easily picked up a card key that would unlock these cells." Callous agreed with Triton's earlier statement and disregarded the latter.

Triton knelt down by one of the Seeker bodies and examined the wound quickly. "This Seeker was killed by a lower caliber bullet than the one I saw outside. This round would've definitely needed to be armor piercing. There's no way a low caliber bullet could penetrate their armor."

General Callous was still moving his head and looking around carefully. "Snipers. There were snipers set up outside."

Triton stood up. "There's really no good place out there for snipers. This facility is the largest around and then there are just neighborhoods."

"There are some tall trees near the property - they could have hidden in there," Callous suggested.

"But general, that would be in range of the fear aura from the Seekers. No sniper could make an accurate shot while experiencing such dread," Triton pointed out. He was passively trying to make his point that the assailants must have been Vincent Black and Alexis Hera acting alone.

General Callous picked up on Triton's subtlety. "I understand you still believe that it was just two people who did all of this. So be it. We will check the rest of the complex and see. I will remain open to the idea."

"That's all I ask, General," Triton stated.

Both men went up the stairs. They began looking over the first floor and saw that it had been trashed, probably in the ruckus that ensued when the attack came. There were some rebels who had been prepped for processing into Seekers or slaves that had tried to escape and were now dead when their captors opened fire. There was no sign of an attack.

Callous and Triton went through the entire complex until they came to the control area. It was in shambles. At least two small explosions had gone off, one destroying the server cabinet, the other in the center. The corpses of several dead Seekers and workers were littering the floor. This location had been the primary area where those who were not lobotomized had worked.

Ugh.

Triton looked at Callous. "What the hell was that?"

Ugh.

Callous looked in the direction of the noise and saw that one of the men who had been allowed to keep his free will was laying on the floor bleeding but slightly moving. "There, that man will provide answers."

The General and Commander hurried over and flipped the man over. "What happened here?" asked Callous.

"General. He moved like lightning. We could barely see him. He can't be human…he has to be some type of force of nature or something *cough* *cough* he ripped through the Seekers like they were insignificant flees," said the man while coughing up his own blood.

Triton knelt down, "Who? Who was it?"

"He had *cough* *cough* a tattoo of a scorpion on his eye," the man stated, barely able to keep conscious.

"Night Viper," Callous grumbled. "So he was here."

Triton was still kneeling down by the bleeding man, shaking him to keep him awake, "What about Commander Jade?"

"Don't know. I assume she's dead," the man answered, then started coughing more.

"What about her successor," Triton inquired, trying to be quick, as he realized that this man had very little time left.

In response, the man simply pointed to a body. It was the body of Jade's second in command. He was laying face up with shrapnel sticking out of his head. With that, the man went completely limp and his breathing ceased. "So, it appears that you were correct. Have the Seekers rip apart what's left of this place and look for Commander Jade or her body. We need to know if Vincent Black captured her or not," Callous ordered.

"It will be done sir. What about this place? It's in rough shape?" asked Triton.

"As soon as we're done here, we will destroy this compound. I want search teams scouring the area looking for rebels that may not have gotten far. We'll take no more chances…shoot them all on sight," Callous barked.

Triton stood up. "We still have the detention facility where we're keeping the rest of the rebels that we captured from Danbury and Bridgeport. We can choose another area and set up a new Seeker Farm."

Callous simply shook his head. "No. This act of aggression cannot be ignored. As an example we will finish here, and then we will strike true fear into them. We have plenty of slaves and Seekers. It's time to exterminate these cockroaches."

"But sir, Lord Zodiac…"

"…trusts my judgment, as should you. There will be no argument. Carry out your orders, Commander. I will contact Lord Zodiac and request that a new Commander be sent to assist us in this area," Callous stated in finality.

Triton wanted to continue, but he knew it would be foolish. He also knew that if Jade had been captured, they were facing a massive security risk if the rebels could get her to talk. "Is there something on your mind Commander?" Callous asked.

Triton shook his head. "Nothing. Your orders will be carried out to the letter."

Chapter 27

"This place has everything, even an interrogation room. That's just awesome," Josh commented. After one of the longest nights ever Josh, Lexi and Vincent arrived back at the complex with their two bound and gagged prisoners. Along with those who just arrived, Talbot and John were also in the back room looking through the one-way mirror into the interrogation room at Commander Jade. The scientist was locked up in a cell. Eve and Andromeda were asleep and no one wanted to wake them up.

Talbot rolled his eyes. "Yes Josh, now you can feel like a big bad cop. You want to go talk to her?"

Josh looked in on the prisoner. Her hands were cuffed to the metal table which was secured to the floor. She was wearing only what she had on when they removed her armor. Her knees were tucked up under her chin and she was looking down at the table, rocking back and forth. "There's something that seems just… wrong about doing this."

"We're not gonna rape her, Josh. When you remove someone's clothes, you make them more vulnerable psychologically. In a healthy atmosphere, removal of clothes for foreplay and sexual activity can allow for two people to become closer because the inhibitions go away. In the case of an extremely dangerous prisoner, making her feel vulnerable may help us get valuable information," Vincent explained.

"I'm not sure I want to know how you know that. Anyway, there's no way this girl is military, law enforcement, or anything of the type," John pointed out.

Lexi looked at Vincent then looked at John. "That's what we were thinking."

Josh did his normal hand raise. "I have an idea."

"Josh, how many times do I have to tell you that you're not in school; you don't need to raise your damn hand," Vincent stated.

Josh immediately put his hand next to his side, then nervously slipped it into his pocket. "Sorry. Anyway, I found a digital camera. I could put her through facial recognition...see what it comes up with. The problem is that it might take awhile if it's gonna search through the databases that we have access to."

Vincent nodded. "Do it - getting a background on her that's solid and confirmed may give us something to work with."

Josh pulled out a small camera that he had found and exited the back room into the hallway. Just a few feet down was the door to the interrogation room. Everyone saw him enter with the camera readied and in hand. "Smile for the camera!"

Jade looked up as the flash hit and then immediately looked back down. Josh stopped for a moment and stared at her. "What the hell is he doing?" asked Talbot.

"I have no idea," Vincent answered.

After about 30 seconds, Josh turned around and left the room. John looked at Lexi. "What was that all about?"

Lexi was looking at the door. "I don't know, but I'm going to find out." She looked at Vincent for approval.

Vincent nodded. "Yeah, check up on him. I think he's had a tough time dealing with today."

Lexi wasted no time and exited the room to follow Josh to the control room. Vincent, John, and Talbot remained. "So what are we doing now?" John inquired.

Vincent continued to watch Jade carefully through the window. "We're waiting. Watch for the subtle changes in her body language. She's alone, practically naked, and isolated with nothing more than her thoughts. Let's see if she's still human on the inside, despite the atrocities that she helped commit."

John looked at Vincent. "You've done this before?"

"Yes. Remember, I was a vigilante in Los Angeles. Even before that, it used to be my job to figure out if people were lying or hiding anything. I became really good at picking up on people's tells," Vincent explained without looking away from Jade.

"Notice anything?" John asked.

Vincent nodded. "She itches the bridge of her nose a lot when she's nervous. She's also using her free arm to hold her legs still… she's probably a twitcher. She can't take her eyes off the table. She knows we're here and can't face us, even though she can't see us."

Talbot glared at Vincent. "Wow. I guess you do know what you're doing. You gonna go in there?"

"Yes, but she needs a few moments more. She's in the middle of a thought and it's eating at her. I'm going to let her finish it," Vincent replied.

John raised his eyebrows. "You know what she's thinking?"

Vincent continued to watch Jade closely. "No, I know how she's reacting to it. For all I know, she could be replaying the death of her favorite kitten when she was five. I have no idea what it is - I just know that whatever she's thinking about now is stressing her out."

The room went silent. After a few minutes, a single tear ran down Jade's cheek. That was Vincent's queue. He immediately entered the interrogation room and sat down across from the prisoner, who did not even look up. He stared at her for a few minutes. She twitched more and more, then finally she spoke. "So, I assume you're going to torture me then kill me."

"Maybe," Vincent replied with a poker face.

Jade didn't look up. "What do you mean maybe?"

"I mean I haven't decided yet. I'll let your words and actions make the decision for me," Vincent informed her.

She sat for a moment, silent. Finally she said, "Lord Zodiac will find me. When he does, he'll kill you all."

Vincent smirked. "Brave words, but really, one who's responsible for the deaths of over two billion people isn't going to focus his efforts on you. He's more likely to assume that what you know is a threat and have you eliminated. At best, if you ever get out of here, you'll be interrogated by his people to find out what you told us. Maybe he'd just pull it out of your head himself. Face it… you've got nowhere to go now…no one to turn to…no one to help you. Be smart - work with us, it's your only chance."

Vincent then got up and left and went back into the other

room with Talbot and John. They were both watching Jade when he walked in. "Why did you stop?" asked a surprised Talbot.

"I want her to think long and hard about what I said. Silence is more likely to cause her to break than being berated by us. If you've ever been in a counseling session with someone who doesn't want to talk, just use that uncomfortable silence. It's torture. People hate it and will break it and when they do, it will be with whatever's in the forefront of their mind. I want to make sure that what she has in the front of her mind is her time serving Zodiac, not some troubled childhood that I'm not interested in," Vincent explained.

Talbot shrugged his shoulders. "Fair enough - what do we do now?"

"Wait and watch," Vincent replied.

Lexi caught up to Josh in the control room. He had already sat down and pulled the memory card from the camera. He was plugging it into the slot in the terminal when she came in. He didn't say anything. He just loaded the picture into the facial recognition system, highlighted a few options, then began running the program. "Now the boring part, waiting for it to sift through the mountains of data," he thought to himself. It was a little slower since he had another program running to hide the signal, so as not to arouse suspicion from Zodiac's people.

Lexi walked over, sat down in an office chair, and wheeled over to Josh. "Hey, I'd ask if you were alright, but I already know the answer."

Josh just stared at the screen.

"I know that this isn't pleasant, but it's necessary," Lexi pointed out.

Josh shut his eyes tightly for a moment and a few tears escaped. "I know, Lexi. I'm just…I'm not like you and Vincent. You guys are tough. John is former military…he's tough too. Hell, even Talbot, being the stubborn old coot that he is. Andromeda puts up with this stuff great. I'm just…I don't know if I'm cut out for this. I was just a computer geek. I belong in a basement on a computer."

Lexi looked around with a smirk on her face.

Josh let out a nervous chuckle. "Yeah, yeah, yeah, ha ha ha, I

get it. You know, when Vincent found me, Talbot and Andromeda, we were pinned down by Seekers in the ruins of Hartford.
He came out of nowhere and tore them apart. He was amazing.
He's saved our lives several times and I've known him for only
few days. How do I compare to a guy like that? Look at me - what
kind of man gets all teary-eyed like this?"

Lexi put her hand on his arm. "A good, sensitive man. Vincent
respects you for who you are. You've played a major role in our
progress. Combat skills aren't the only thing that's going to help
us. The things you know how to do…they're amazing. You're the
key to all of this. We wouldn't even be in this place if it wasn't for
you."

Josh looked over at her. "I just…I know she's evil but I just
can't help it. When I saw Jade just sitting there, looking like a
broken puppy, I froze. It was horrible. It just brings back memories. I just can't stand the idea of that kind of thing happening to
someone else."

"What happened to you Josh?" Lexi asked.

Josh shook his head. "It's not important."

"It is if it's bothering you," Lexi pushed.

Josh started fiddling with the mouse, moving it pointlessly
around the screen. "I didn't have an easy childhood either. Being
a geek doesn't help you until you're in college. The way those
jocks demean people who just want to do their part and move
on is horrid. I know that you and Vincent dealt with that too, but
look at you both now. You're tough. If any of those people came
back, they wouldn't even know what to do or say. I'm still the
geeky, klutzy guy I once was."

"If those people came back, they'd probably just be glad to
find someone who isn't a Seeker," Lexi pointed out.

Josh waived his hand around and nodded his head. "Alright,
point taken, but still."

"Your brain has done more than any brawn has in the last
few days. That mind of yours has more power than a whole army
of body builders. You just need to recognize it. Vincent told me
something great, 'Have faith in yourself or no one else will have
faith in you'." Lexi attempted to comfort Josh.

There was an awkward silence for a little while, and then Josh
spoke up. "What's going to happen to Jade?"

Lexi shook her head. "I don't know. I guess that's for Vincent to decide. I do notice that you're calling her by name, or at least the name that she gave us."

"She's still a person, Lexi. As screwed up as she is, she's still human. I just don't want us to be the monsters that Zodiac is," Josh told her.

Lexi nodded. "Vincent only does what's necessary."

Josh turned in his chair. "That's just it though. Vincent *is* the Night Viper. How many people did he kill because he thought it was necessary? He killed people for a lot less. Of course he's probably going to kill her."

"Calm down Josh, she's an unarmed prisoner who could prove useful. He's not going to just kill her in cold blood," Lexi pointed out.

Josh fidgeted more but did not respond. His leg was shaking at a hundred miles per hour.

Lexi leaned in toward him. "Look, I'll go back to the interrogation room and keep an eye on her. I really don't believe that Vincent is going to just kill her."

Josh nodded. "Alright, I'll be back there as soon as something comes up on this thing."

Lexi stood up, gave Josh a quick pat on the shoulder and walked toward the door. As she opened it, Josh said to her, "Lexi! Thanks."

She turned her head, gave him a smile and a nod, and then left the room.

"Instead of just sitting here waiting, why don't we go question that scientist," John suggested.

Vincent held his pointer finger to his lips while still watching Jade and said, "Quiet. We'll focus on the scientist when we're done with her. Besides, I'd rather your wife be around for that."

"I've been meaning to talk to you about that," John piped up.

Vincent did not respond. He was focused on Commander Jade. After a few moments he said, "I'm heading back in there in a few minutes. She's had enough time to stew. What's wrong?"

John looked somewhat nervous, but spoke anyway. "Eve has a fever and her blood pressure is rising. I'm afraid for her and the baby. We need a doctor."

Vincent looked over at him. "When did this start?"

"About the time Talbot and I got back. I know we haven't had the chance to talk much about our botched trip to get supplies, but we ran into that group, Militia 28. They want to meet you," John reported.

Vincent scratched his chin. "What does that have to do with Eve and why are they interested in meeting with me?"

Talbot interjected, "We told them that we were working with you to fight back against Zodiac. One of their people, some Hispanic girl, said that she knew you and you saved her brother or something."

They had Vincent's interest. "Did this girl have a name?"

John and Talbot looked at each other and started to think really hard. Finally, Talbot spoke up. "Maria. Maria Esperanza."

Vincent instantly recognized the name. "Maria? Maria's alive? She's in New York?"

"You remember her?" John asked.

Vincent nodded. "The last thing I did before I was kidnapped by Project Scorpion was to take down a child sex ring in Los Angeles. Her brother, Miguel, was one of the kids that I got out of there. They were auctioning them off, the sick bastards."

"They said that if you came back with us, they would discuss cooperation against Zodiac. They said that they're in contact with other cells too. They also said that their doctor would help Eve." John was beginning to sound desperate.

Vincent thought a moment. "If for no other reason, I'll go for the sake of Eve and to see Maria."

Vincent was dazed for a moment, his mind wandering back before the Flash Storm. Back before Project Scorpion. He was in Los Angeles, at the old meeting spot in the outskirts of the city where no one would see them…

"You don't look so good man," Detective Salaszar stated.

Night Viper glared at him, let out a hacking cough, then responded, "Yeah, yeah, yeah. You said you have something for me. Something big."

Salaszar took a folder out of his jacket and handed it to the vigilante. "There's been a child sex slave ring operating in the area for some time. We've never been able to gather enough evidence to even get warrants, but through surveillance we've been able to piece together who some of the key players are."

Night Viper looked straight at the LAPD detective, a new fire in his eyes. "Children? This is that one that's been nabbing young kids in the area?"

Salaszar nodded. "Yeah. They take them from the poorer areas, where they're less likely to be pursued. They sell them to these pedophile bastards. It's the sickest shit on the planet."

The vigilante began flipping through the paperwork. "Even with all of this, you can't get a warrant?"

Salaszar shook his head. "Nope. Look at them…they're all high profile people. They've got money, popularity, and lawyers."

"Unbelievable *cough* *cough*. Scumbags like this can just get away with anything. They can buy the justice system. You know what I'm going to do with this," Night Viper warned.

Salaszar nodded. "Yes, I was aware before I brought it to you."

The man in black was still looking at some of the profiles. "When people like this start showing up dead, we won't be able to meet like this anymore. I'll be public enemy number one. *Cough* *Cough* We're not talking about gangbangers, drug dealers, and serial rapists anymore. We're talking about some of the highest ranking people in this city."

"I know it's big. What I'm asking you to do…if you can't do it, don't worry," Salaszar commented.

Night Viper shook his head. "Of course I'm going to do it. You can see I don't have much time left anyway, so why not go out with a bang. This has been going on for awhile. What prompted you to approach me now?"

"A girl came to me, a Maria Esperanza. She lives in South Central. Something about her struck me. She wasn't like the others. She's been caring for her four year old brother since he was a baby. Now the kid, Miguel I think his name is, was added to the missing list," Salaszar explained. "Her information is in there. She might be able to help you."

Night Viper let out a coughing chuckle, "Yeah, they love me in South Central."

Salaszar shook his head. "A lot of people in that area do. The ones that just want the shit to stop appreciate you. They feel like someone is finally paying attention to them."

Both men stood quietly for a moment. "This is it then. Good luck to you, Detective. Always do the right thing," the vigilante stated.

"You too. I hope you find whatever peace you've been searching for," the detective responded.

"Hey Vincent. VINCENT! Snap out of it," a voice came and brought him out of his mental excursion. He was back in the Project Scorpion compound. A hand was on his shoulder. It was Lexi's.

Everyone in the room had a concerned look on their face. Talbot finally spoke up. "You said you were going to go in there and talk to her."

Vincent shook the cobwebs out of his head. "Yeah, I'm going." He stood up and went to the door, and stopped when he heard someone enter the interrogation room with Jade. He turned around and went back to the window to see that Josh had barged in with some type of printout.

"What's that damn fool doing in there!?" Talbot barked.

Josh sat down at the interrogation table and spread the papers out in front of Jade. "I know who you are Amanda Jade Wilson. And you're no military commander."

Jade looked up at him. She didn't respond, just stared at the computer nerd.

"Why did you do it? Why did you join him? I've got your whole life here, even your shrink's notes. Your school records are here too." Josh was pointing at various sheets of paper as he spoke.

John turned to Vincent. "Do you want me to go in there and get him?"

Vincent held up his hand. "No. For better or for worse, I think we need to let this play out."

John backed down. "You're the boss." Vincent wasn't sure if he'd ever get used to that.

Jade was glaring at Josh but still said nothing. "What's the story Amanda? Everyone used to push you around, didn't they? Did you have a crush on a popular guy only to have him play with your heart? Is that what happened?"

236

Jade clenched her hands into a fist, tears began streaming down her face, but still she said nothing. "Let me guess…he asked you out, maybe to a dance or something then made you look like a fool? Or was it worse? What could've happened to fill you with such hatred? What could've turned you to mass murder?"

Jade pounded her free fist on the table and screamed, "YOU WANT TO KNOW WHAT HAPPENED! I'LL TELL YOU, DAM-MIT! How much is one supposed to take? My whole life, I was always on the outside looking in. Even my idiot parents watched and did nothing. Hell, sometimes they blamed me, said that since I let it get to me it was my fault. I had a crush on one of the base-ball players for a long time, but I knew he would never have an interest in me." The tears were streaming down like a waterfall.

Josh leaned forward. "It was more than just making you look like a fool, wasn't it?"

Jade managed to collect herself. "He brought me to our Se-nior Prom. He brought me! I was so excited. All of the girls in the school, and he chose me. He said he wasn't worried about what people thought anymore…graduation was in a month anyway. It was the best night of my life until we went to the hotel."

Everyone watched and listened in dead silence. Jade contin-ued. "His friends were there. They were all drunk. They tied me up, stripped off my clothes and took turns raping me. Over and over and over again. After they each had a turn, they'd have a few drinks then take turns again."

Vincent turned to John. "Get her some better clothes, now."

John didn't even argue, just made haste out the door in pur-suit of clothing for Jade.

"I tried to report it. These guys, they were the stars of the school. All of them had a free ride to some stupid private school on a baseball scholarship," Jade explained.

Josh's eyes met hers. "They buried it."

Jade nodded. "They paid my parents a million dollars to keep me quiet. In the meantime I was so brutalized that I lost my abil-ity to have kids. I lost any chance of having a real life with some-one. They didn't just take my virginity that day, they took my life. Then everyone began calling me a slut. I was the baseball team slut. They all laughed and ridiculed me. The whole world. I HATE EVERYBODY! I HATE THEM ALL!" She started sobbing.

"That's when he came along," Josh said quietly.

Jade's eyes were drawn back to the table, but her mind ran through the scenario when she first met the dictator known as the Zodiac. To this day she did not know how she did it, but she managed to finish High School and graduate. Her parents had enjoyed spending the hush money a little bit too much, so they couldn't afford to send her to college.

Amanda, as she was known then, was walking home from work, the rain was coming down quite hard that night. A car drove by and purposely swerved to hit the large puddle on the side of the road and splashed muddy water all over her. "I'd love to make you beg for mercy you bastards," she yelled out, even though the car was too far away for any occupants to hear her.

It was only about 30 seconds later that another car began to pull to the side of the road. It was a limousine. Amanda had had it. She dropped her umbrella to the ground. She wasn't sure what she was going to do, but she was going to do something. This time was different though - this time the car was slowing down. It came to a complete stop next to her and no water splashed up. She could not hide the scowl on her face. The driver's window opened slightly, but she could not see a face. There was a voice though. "Get in."

"Who the hell are you and why would I just get into this car?" Amanda asked.

"Because you're tired of being bullied and pushed around. You want the power to strike back and this is your way to get it. One time offer, take it or leave it," the driver offered.

Amanda should have been frightened. After the ordeal she had gone through with the rapes, getting into a mysterious car was not on the top 10 list of good choices. But then again, it's not every day that someone gives you an offer such as this. She got in. She was the only one in the back seat of the limo. There was a small bar with one ounce shots of various liquors. She reached for one, and then hesitated since she wasn't 21. No one was there to say anything so she grabbed a couple of small bottles of whiskey and downed them. They burned like crazy, but she didn't care.

The car drove for about 20 minutes. She had a serious buzz going on and felt better than she had in a long time. "Mental note, take up drinking," Amanda thought to herself. She then looked out the window to see that they were turning into a parking garage. She had not paid attention to where they had gone and did not recognize the location. The strange thing was the structure was completely empty. They drove up to the top floor, which was open to the air. There was a lone figure standing near one side, looking off at the moon and all that was below.

The car came to a stop and the door unlocked. Amanda heard a voice, "Come out, you have nothing to fear here."

"Who said that?" she asked out loud.

"All your questions will be answered young one, just come out of the car," the voice requested.

Amanda did exactly that. She got out. It was dark. The top of this parking garage only had illumination coming from the moon. She got a better look at the figure. It was humanoid in shape but appeared to be wearing some type of dark armor. When the figure turned, she saw that the helmet had a blank face. That should have frightened her almost to the point of cardiac arrest, but it didn't. She felt no fear. She walked closer to the figure until she could see more of the detail of the helmet. It looked as if the blank face plate was on the inside of a wide open dragon mouth.

"Welcome Amanda Jade Wilson. I have been looking forward to this meeting for some time," the figure stated.

Amanda looked around quickly, then looked at the figure. "Who are you and how do you know me?"

"To answer your first question, you may call me Zodiac," the figure answered.

Amanda swished her tongue around in her mouth. "Zodiac, huh? Like the Zodiac killer?"

The imposing figure let out a sinister snicker. "There is much more in the name, but on to your second question. I know you because we are similar in many ways."

Amanda rolled her eyes. "I doubt that very much."

"You shouldn't. I know about the rapes. And if that wasn't bad enough, your own parents took blood money to silence you and selfishly spent it all on themselves with their gambling and their drinking. You were painted as a whore and ridiculed by everyone. You have paid the price while the assailants go free. Where is the justice in that?" Zodiac asked.

"There is no damn justice in this world. When you can't even depend on your own parents, who can you depend on? Everyone just wants to walk over you," Amanda ranted.

Zodiac nodded. "Yes that is quite true. But you don't have to be a victim anymore, Amanda. You can fight back, and I can give you the power to do that."

Amanda took a step closer. "Why would you do that and how?"

"I would do it to see justice finally returned to this world, for all of the wrongs that humanity has committed upon those of us that they view as…outsiders…rejects…loners. I would do this to give you what you have desired for your whole life, even before the assaults…retribution to those who have oppressed you. As for the how? Well, look over there." Zodiac pointed as another vehicle approached. It was a plain, black van with no rear windows. It pulled up near them and stopped.

Amanda immediately put her guard up. "What's that for?"

Zodiac put a hand up. "Do not be frightened. I have brought gifts for you." He motioned with his hands. Out of the driver and passenger side doors came two humanoid figures. They were armored similar to Zodiac but their helmets were simple, not the extravagant dragon head that their leader's was. They had some type of lights on their shoulders that were off at the moment. Neither spoke, but they immediately went around and opened the rear doors. There were five people in there, tied up with black bags over their heads. The two dark figures took each one and lined them up in front of Amanda, on their knees.

Amanda took a few steps closer, slowly, cautiously. "Who are they?"

Zodiac, concentrating on blocking the fear aura from affecting his new recruit, looked at her. "You know who they are." He pulled a 9mm Glock with a silencer on it and handed it to her, then looked up at the dark figures behind the hooded men and waived his hand. Obediently, the Dark Ones removed the hoods to reveal the five men who had brutally raped her.

Amanda's eyes filled with tears. Not tears of sadness but tears of rage. She could feel her hatred seething. The five men were bound and gagged but they could now see. They saw Amanda Jade Wilson, the one whom they had treated as nothing more than a piece of meat, standing before them with the power to end their lives at any moment.

"This is your chance. You may take your time, say and do whatever you wish to them. We will not be disturbed. Do not hold back...there is no reason to anymore. Show them who has the power now," Zodiac directed.

Amanda began to pace back and forth in front of them. She looked each one in the eyes and saw fear like she had never seen in another human being. They had violated her. They had decimated her. They had penetrated her. She had been powerless to stop them...that is, powerless until now. She could decide their fate and there was nothing that any of them could do about it. Now *they* were powerless.

Amanda looked at Zodiac, and already knowing what she was going to ask he answered, "Nothing you do will get you into trouble. You will not go to jail. This is your chance at justice. This is your chance at revenge. What you have fantasized about has come to pass."

She had a sudden, overwhelming feeling. It was a tingle down her spine. She had a smile on her face that she had not had in a long time. She took the butt of the gun and pistol whipped the first man, Richard Johnson. She smashed his nose and caused him to fall over backward. He writhed in pain and attempted to scream, but he couldn't - he was gagged and the most he could let out was muffled. "Not so tough anymore are you? What's the matter, don't like the feeling of having all of your power taken from you," Amanda chided. She walked over to the man she had struck. "I don't suppose I could use your guys there for some heavy lifting."

"My Seekers are yours to command." Zodiac bowed and held out his hand toward them. "Obey her orders as if they were mine."

"Take this miserable excuse for a sentient being and move him in front of the other four. I want them to watch what's being done to their friend, just as they all watched and took part in what happened to me," Amanda demanded. The Seekers did exactly that.

Zodiac watched with amusement and pride. Amanda walked over to Richard and pointed her gun between his legs. Without hesitation, she fired a round through his genitals. He began hyperventilating and squirming like a worm on a hook. The others started crying. "Crying for your friend? I cried. Do you remember me crying? Huh? DO YOU REMEMBER, YOU BASTARDS!?" She shot the next one through the throat, hitting his jugular. He fell down, squirming. She took a moment to watch as Pascal O'Brien tried desperately to free his hands, to hold the blood in his body. It didn't work.

Enrique Vazquez was the third man. Amanda glared at him, and then came in closer. He turned his head away from her. She grabbed his chin as hard as she could and turned it back around to face her. "Don't you look away from me, you disgusting creature. See what you've done? See what you've created? Look at your friends. One dead, one dying. What do I do to you? What would be appropriate?" she asked, then clocked him in the temple using the gun. He fell over, looking up at her. It did not take long for his breathing to stop and his eyes to glaze over. The damage she inflicted on Vazquez's brain was catastrophic.

Alejandro Corral was the fourth man. He watched as Richard was still writhing in pain, although he was on the verge of losing consciousness. He looked at Amanda. "So, are you sorry yet? Do you now wish you'd had more control over your own dick? It's too bad that it's too late." She pointed the gun at Richard and shot him through the head while Alejandro was watching, then shot Alejandro three times in the gut, spilling stomach acid and bile throughout his abdomen. He collapsed, fluid oozing from the holes.

Finally, Amanda turned her attention to the last of them. The one that had asked her to the prom. The one who had pretended to like her. The one who she'd had a crush on. "You were the worst one of all, Charles Chapel. There is a special place in hell for you. I want you to look at my face. I want you to die knowing that it's me who killed you. It's me who decided to take your life. No one else. The funny thing is that there is nothing you can do!" She threw the gun on the ground and kicked him in the head. He fell over and she began stomping on various parts of his body. "How does it feel to be pounded on? YOU SON OF A BITCH!" She stomped and stomped until there was nothing recognizable left to stomp.

Amanda fell to her knees, panting heavily. Zodiac walked over to her and put his hand on her shoulder. "Well done. Our work is not finished though. There are many more that are to blame for what has been done to us. I want you to join me. I want you to be a part of the new world order Amanda."

"Amanda Wilson is dead. Just call me Jade, and I swear my loyalty to you, Lord Zodiac."

The memory began to make its way to the back of Jade's mind again. She was back in the interrogation room. Josh had been watching her. She did not know how much time had gone by, but he was still there. She finally answered him. "Yes, he came at the time I was most vulnerable. He offered me everything that I had wanted. He gave me the chance to bring vengeance on those who had done this to me. He knew my every thought and desire."

"Is he telepathic?" Josh asked.

Jade looked at him with defeated eyes. "Yes."

John barged in with some clothes and put them down on the table. "They aren't anything fancy, but they should fit."

Jade looked up at him. "Thank you."

John bent over and unlocked her handcuffs. He had expected her to fight, but she did not. She merely put the clothes on, which consisted of a loose T-Shirt, a baggy pair of sweat shorts, and flip flops, then sat back in the chair and did not resist when he re-secured her to the table. He walked out and left her and Josh alone in the room again.

Jade began sobbing. "Why would you want to do that? Why would you offer me clothes? Why are you not torturing me for information?"

Josh took a risk and reached over, putting his hand on her free one. "Because you've been tortured enough for a dozen lifetimes." Amazingly, the risk paid off...she did not flinch, nor did she attempt to attack. She just sat in her chair, sobbing.

The computer nerd stood up and Jade looked up at him. "Where are you going?"

"We'll continue questioning you later. You should be put in quarters for now," Josh answered.

He walked back to the next room from where the others had been observing. They all looked at him. Vincent spoke up. "That was a serious risk you took, Josh. Fortunately, it paid off - you broke her."

"We should go back in there and get her talking while she's

vulnerable," Talbot suggested.

Josh shook his head. "She'll be vulnerable for a long time."

Vincent was staring at her through the glass again. Lexi looked at him. "What's wrong, Vince?"

"She was so sure of herself on the roof of that hospital. She was ready to take me on. Now look at her. She's falling apart at the seams," Vincent replied.

John walked over to Vincent. "She's been captured by the enemy. She probably thinks she's going to die or get raped again or something. She doesn't know anything about us."

Vincent shook his head. "No, it's more than that. After the ordeal she went through, how did she toughen up to command a legion of Seekers? I think Zodiac is more than telepathic. When he made his announcement right before the Flash Storm, I don't think people realized the truth behind his words. I think he really is hatred incarnate, and he can draw that hatred out in others."

"You've lost me," John said.

Vincent began pacing again. "Think about…who drew that?" He pointed to a pencil drawing on a piece of lined notebook paper near Talbot.

"Oh, Andromeda drew it. She's got a whole bunch of them… she's really good," Talbot answered.

Vincent looked at Lexi, his facial expression revealed that he had an idea. "Lexi, do you remember what that commander you killed looked like?"

"I'll never forget it, why?" asked Lexi.

Vincent paced faster. "We get Andromeda to be a sketch artist and Josh can load the sketch into the facial recognition software. We might be able to get an ID on that guy. I'd bet whatever's valuable nowadays that we're going to find another social reject."

Lexi gasped. "Oh my God, do you really think?"

Vincent made eye contact with her. "Yes. I think Zodiac swelled his leadership ranks with those whose hatred he was able to use to bring about their loyalty to him."

"This is the craziest stuff I've ever heard." Talbot shook his head. "Too bad it also sounds like it might be right on."

"Talbot, do me a favor and get Andromeda up here," Vincent requested.

Talbot looked at him. "She's just a kid, she needs her sleep."

Vincent made eye contact. "Whether we like it or not, she's a soldier like each of us. We need answers and we need them fast."

"What about Militia 28 and their doctor?" John reminded.

"Don't worry I haven't forgotten about that, but remember, this is an organized group and we need to show that we're every bit as organized or they may eat us for lunch," Vincent assured.

John had a disappointed look on his face and began rubbing his temples. "Vincent, my wife could be dying. We have to get there as soon as possible."

Vincent nodded. "I know. You and I will bring Eve to meet up with these guys. Lexi, I want you and Andromeda to get a sketch of that commander that you killed and have Josh run it through the system. Talbot, I want you to drill that scientist, see if you can get him to talk about those Seeker chips and how we can counteract the fear aura. I had wanted Eve to be there but you can always record it."

Lexi spoke up. "Talbot, I can help you after Andromeda and I are done. I'll go get her."

Vincent looked at John. "Go get your wife, we're heading out. We'll need to load up the ammo. We're going at night when most of the Seeker patrols are out." He then looked generally around the room. "Make sure you fit in some rest too."

After handing out orders to everyone, Vincent stopped, realizing that he hadn't asked any of them to do anything. He had directed them. Once again, they all did what he ordered. Every time it happened, he more and more realized that he was the true leader of this group, whether he liked it or not.

Chapter 28

Eric was feverishly scribbling on a piece of paper. He was sitting in the passenger seat of a small Honda Civic which he and Carl managed to find with three-quarters of a tank of gas. Carl had to hot wire it though, since they couldn't find any keys, so there were wires hanging out of the console. Eric showed the paper to his newfound partner. "Isn't Worcester along this route?"

They were heading North on I-395, which changed into I-290 and went straight through Worcester, Massachusetts. "Worcester and Boston were both destroyed in the Flash Storm. We're not going to be able to stay on this highway beyond that point. As it is, we're getting close to Thompson, Connecticut, which means we don't have a super lot of time before we hit what used to be Worcester," Carl stated.

Eric thought for a moment, and then flipped over the piece of paper he was writing on. Before he could start writing, he saw that there was some type of downed aircraft that had crashed in the trees dividing the northbound from the southbound lanes. The crash had left a gap. It was at that moment that he saw headlights from several large trucks on the other side, as well as lights from Firehawks. "Did you see that?" he wrote.

Carl had a worried look on his face. "Yeah, I saw it. I just hope they didn't see us. It looks like they were hauling flatbeds full of, I don't know, building and bridge fragments. Maybe it's stuff that was blown up in the Flash Storm or something."

It was then that Carl noticed lights shining down from the sky behind them. They had been spotted and one of the Firehawks broke off to go after them. "Oh Shit - hang on Eric!" Carl warned as he floored it. Eric grabbed onto the handle above the door and held on for dear life. The Firehawk kept up with them and began opening fire with its chain guns, tearing up the asphalt of the road. They were closing in on the exit for Thompson, so he slammed on the brakes, causing the car to skid quite a ways. The Firehawk shot past them and began making its wide turn in the sky to come back in for the kill. Carl knew he had one chance and one chance only. He slammed on the gas again and pulled off the exit. Since most exit ramps in Connecticut had sharp turns, and this one being no exception, he overestimated the cornering ability on his little, newly acquired Civic. He slid off the road and sideswiped a tree, coming to a stop in the woods.

The Firehawk began approaching overhead. They were fortunate that neither of them was injured, but the car wasn't going to be much help in its present condition. "C'mon Eric, let's get the hell out of here," Carl said. His door wouldn't open so he climbed out through the passenger side after Eric and both men ran as fast as they could into the woods. They heard an explosion behind them as the Firehawk sent a missile into the car, destroying it and setting the brush ablaze. Satisfied that the individuals were dead, the bladeless helicopter flew off to meet back up with the caravan.

Both Carl and Eric stopped to catch their breath. They sat down using trees to brace themselves and leaned their heads back. Eric was massaging his already injured ankle, the recent sprint not helping its condition. "That was a close one. Again. Shit man, I'm getting too old to constantly have brushes with death," Carl complained. "What about you man?"

Eric looked around. He had left his pencil and the rest of the pad in the car. He simply gave thumbs up.

"Damn...your pad and pencil were in the car, huh?" Carl sighed.

They were in a wooded area right by Thompson Hill Road, which ran parallel toward the northeast. Eric pointed in that direction and made a walking motion with his fingers. Carl looked at him and after a moment, it clicked. "We should stay in the woods but follow that road? Works for me, I have no other direction in mind other than wherever we need to go to stay alive," Carl stated.

Both men walked for awhile in silence, stopping quite often when they heard an animal or the wind. The paranoia was definitely building. The two men finally stopped and sat down for another moment's rest. They just looked at each other. They were hungry, thirsty, and tired. The sound of twigs snapping came from behind Carl. Eric had a frightened look on his face and pointed. Carl turned around to see a man with a shotgun pointed at him. The man was tall, with an olive complexion, and well built. He appeared to be of Mediterranean ancestry. He wore an old Hartford Whalers Jersey, cap, and a pair of blue jeans that were a little worn around the knees, as well as hiking boots.

"Hey guys, I found 'em. They're not Seekers," the Whalers fan turned his head behind him and called out.

"You do know that the Whalers left this state years ago?" Carl pointed out.

The man with the shotgun smiled a sarcastic smile. "And the people responsible should be shot dead. Since they left, now what has the state got?"

"Actually, the state doesn't really exist anymore since the United States doesn't exist anymore," Carl responded, his nervousness was bringing out his sarcasm.

The man bobbed his head. "So, a smart-ass we got here, huh? What are you two boys doing in the woods this late at night?"

Carl and Eric heard rustling. Carl looked up at the man and said, "Long story. We're just trying to stay alive and keep away from the Seekers."

A heavyset woman with her gray hair in a bun and a very thin, approximately six foot tall man with a severe case of bed head joined the first man. The woman was carrying an AR-15 rifle; the man was carrying a double barreled shotgun. "I've got time," the man replied to Carl.

"Jesse, what are you doing? Stop being rude to these boys here. Can't you see that they aren't a threat to anyone!?" the woman scolded.

Jesse instantly hung his head. "Sorry, just making sure they aren't spies or something."

"Spies? Hardly. Weren't you paying attention? One of those

bladeless helicopters shot something up back there...these guys were running away. You boys look like you could use some food and a cot," the woman welcomed.

Carl spoke up, "God, yes."

She motioned with her hands to follow. "Well come on then... we could use some recruits."

Carl and Eric looked at each other and Carl asked, "Recruits for what?"

"Militia 28, haven't you heard of us?" the woman asked as they began walking.

Carl and Eric both shook their heads. "No, can't say I have."

"Does your friend speak?" Jesse piped up.

Carl shook his head. "No, someone cut out his tongue and shot him in the head awhile back. He had a pad and a pencil but it went with the car we were driving when it got blown up by that flying Seeker contraption. What's Militia 28?"

"A group formed in relative secrecy after the 28th Amendment was passed. There are more groups in several areas. We keep in touch and keep each other updated as to what's going on. Our founders were concerned that the government was moving rapidly toward dictatorship and the destruction of our civil liberties. We constructed hidden compounds full of supplies out of old Cold War bomb shelters. When the Flash Storm hit, those of us who were part of the organization went underground," the woman explained. "Oh, how rude of me, I'm Mrs. Josee Santillo."

Carl smiled, "I'm Carl Woods, and this is Eric. He doesn't remember much because of his head injury...even his own name, so that's what he goes by."

Mrs. Santillo smiled and nodded. "Fair enough. We received a message from our people in New York. They said they may have found someone who can help us fight back against the Seekers."

"Really? Who?" asked the former police officer.

Mrs. Santillo scratched her nose and let out a loud cough. "Someone who goes by the name Night Viper. Ever heard of him?"

Carl's eyes opened wide. "Yeah. A little."

Mrs. Santillo pushed a branch out of her way; it snapped back and hit Jesse in the face. He mumbled something that sounded like a cuss. "Apparently he's supposed to meet with them sometime in the next day or two. I have my doubts that one man could change everything. After all, anytime someone lays eyes on the Seekers or gets near them, they get scared out of their minds."

Carl sighed. "Yeah, you're not kidding."

"You've been up close to Seekers before?" inquired Jesse.

"Yeah. I was with a small band who tried to free prisoners from what used to be the William Backus Hospital in Norwich. They all died and I barely escaped. Actually, the only reason I got away was that the Seekers thought I was dead when the house I retreated into collapsed. Eric here was actually a prisoner inside the place," Carl explained.

Mrs. Santillo was giving Carl an intent stare. "Backus Hospital? They converted it to a prison?"

"I had thought that until Eric got out and told me that it was more than that. Apparently, they convert people to Seekers there. It's called a Seeker Farm," Carl continued.

Mrs. Santillo shook her head in disgust. "That's twisted. How did he escape?"

Carl hesitated for a moment, as he hardly believed it himself and he saw it happen. "It was a man. He moved like lightning. He killed the Seekers like they were nothing more than ants. He turned the whole place upside down. I have no idea who he was."

Jesse interjected again, "Maybe he's Christ reborn or something."

Mrs. Santillo gave him a nasty, motherly scolding look that would send a chill straight through the soul. "Stop saying such stupid things."

"There's more," Carl stated. "There's something big going on in New London. When I first escaped the battle where all of my teammates died, I went toward the shore. I traveled down I-95 to see that they'd cleared everything as far as I could see. They had construction materials all over the place with what looked like hundreds of cranes and heavy equipment. Just before coming here we found a car and were headed northbound on I-395. Coming southbound we saw trucks carrying pieces of buildings and bridges."

Mrs. Santillo, Jesse, and the other man who had not introduced himself yet looked at each other. "We need to let the others know. We need to scope this out," Jesse suggested.

Mrs. Santillo nodded. "We're almost to the shelter. We'll get you boys fed and rested. I hope you agree to stay with us."

"It's not like we have any other place to go. I don't know about you Eric, but I'd love to stay where there's food, shelter, water and guns," Carl commented.

Eric nodded in silent agreement.

Chapter 29

Lexi joined Talbot in the room adjacent to the interrogation room where the captured scientist was now taking Jade's place. "How did it go with Andromeda?" Talbot asked.

Lexi smiled. "That kid is amazing. She drew exactly what I saw. I think she's psychic or something."

Talbot glared at her. "Seriously?"

Lexi laughed and gave him a light punch to the arm. "No, of course not. I just mean that she could give crime lab sketch artists a run for their money."

"Hey, don't even joke about this psychic stuff, especially with what we just confirmed about Zodiac," Talbot warned, but still had a slight smile on his face. "Hey, you alright? I saw the look on your face during the whole Jade thing."

"I'm fine. It's just weird. She's a social reject. I was too. I can kind of understand why she'd hate the world," Lexi admitted.

Talbot turned and faced her. "You? A reject? You're sharp witted and good looking…what's there to be rejected for?"

"Brain damage. Kids are cruel and it follows you as you advance in school. The looks never helped me…all the guys ever wanted to do was screw me. Fortunately I saw through their bullshit or I might have ended up in a similar situation to Jade. I just feel sorry for her," Lexi explained.

"With a story like that, it's hard not feel sorry for her but remember…she was one of Zodiac's commanders. We don't know the pecking order for them, but she definitely was no lackey. She's most likely responsible for the deaths of a lot of people and she's without a doubt responsible for a number of people being converted to Seekers," Talbot reminded.

Lexi nodded in agreement. "I know, it's stupid and we shouldn't feel sorry for someone who would probably have had us all killed if she could have, but I used to have a pretty low view of the world. I couldn't imagine being raped over and over by a group of guys, one of whom I'd had a long term crush on."

"Well, whatever motive she had to join Zodiac's ranks, I'm sure this guy wasn't quite as driven by commitment to anyone other than himself." Talbot pointed at the scientist who was sitting upright and looking around. His hand was bound in a cast from the broken fingers that Vincent had given him.

"Let's go in there and have a chat with him," Lexi stated as she made her way to the door with Talbot following. While in the hallway, Lexi removed her leather jacket to reveal the black tank top that she was wearing underneath. "I figured showing some cleavage may help."

Talbot opened the door and entered, then held it for Lexi. Her hunch was accurate; she could feel his eyes piercing her clothes the moment she walked in. She pulled out a chair and sat down and Talbot followed. The scientist was so focused on Lexi that he barely noticed that there was someone else in the room. "How's your hand?" Lexi asked.

"Quite painful actually. The injuries your companion inflicted upon me were barbaric and have caused me hardships performing even simple tasks," the scientist replied.

Lexi rolled her eyes. "Are you kidding me? You lobotomize people and put chips in their brains and you have the nerve to call anyone barbaric?"

The scientist looked straight at her. "Yes, actually. My work is cutting edge science and highly sophisticated. It is only a few that possess the necessary attributes for this field. The Seekers are magnificent, are they not?"

Talbot's jaw dropped. "You're serious, aren't you? You're proud of the fact that you're turning these people into living zombie slaves."

The scientist gave an enthusiastic nod. "Wouldn't you be? The Seekers are a scientific breakthrough that is virtually unprecedented. Never before have we understood the workings of the human brain as we do now."

"And you don't feel like there's something wrong with this at all?" Lexi was verifying.

The scientist shook his head. "Of course not. Those of lesser intellect must make way for those with greater intellect. No longer is brute strength or physical prowess the determining factor of survival. Humanity has evolved. The power of the mind and one's ability to think and learn and reason and plan will determine one's survivability."

Lexi and Talbot just looked at each other, then Talbot spoke up. "So, what you're saying Doctor is…"

"Dr. Albert Erinyes," the scientist interrupted.

Talbot nodded. "Dr. Erinyes, you're basically saying that if I were to beat you to death, your superior intellect would save you."

"Hardly. My survivability was severely hindered when your friend was able to penetrate the defenses of my Seeker Farm and take me as a prisoner. Beating me to death is merely a tool, and a barbaric one at that," Dr. Erinyes replied.

"Maybe, but it'll make me feel awfully good," Talbot assured.

Erinyes shot a glance at Lexi's chest, then looked back at Talbot. "Ah, yes…well, I am unsure of the point of this line of questioning. If you are going to attack me, you should do so. If you are going to torture me, you're doing it already simply by opening your mouth. If you are going to kill me, I ask that you spare me anymore of your simple minded words and get it over with."

Talbot became enraged. He jumped across the table and grabbed Dr. Erinyes by the throat and began choking him. Lexi stood up and began pulling Talbot off of the prisoner. "Chris, get off of him. CHRIS, KNOCK IT THE HELL OFF!"

Talbot let go and took a couple of deep breaths. "You're a sick individual."

"Hardly, I'm not the one who cannot control his own temper," Dr. Erinyes pointed out.

Talbot balled his fists up again, but Lexi put her hand on one of them and said, "Talbot, why don't you take a walk. I'll have a chat with Dr. Erinyes."

"Sure, fine, whatever. Didn't want to stay in here with this guy anyway," Talbot complained as he stormed out.

Lexi leaned forward, exaggerating her cleavage. "You're a hell of a talker. It didn't take you long to push his buttons."

Dr. Erinyes just laughed. "It does not take much effort to push the buttons of a simple minded barbarian. You, on the other hand though, you are not like him. Your demeanor, your control, your beauty, all point to someone of far more sophistication."

"Flattery will get you nowhere...you're still a prisoner," Lexi stated.

"I do not utilize flattery young lady, I merely remark on the truth of my observations. You are quite lovely. I hope to get to know you better." The dirty old man became giddy.

Lexi was utilizing quite a bit of concentration to avoid showing how utterly disgusted she was at the obvious advances of a man who experimented on people's brains. "Well, I'm hoping to get to know your work better. I don't suppose it's worth my while to ask questions. I'm sure your Lord Zodiac would be quite upset."

"Please, Lord Zodiac has probably already marked me for death for simply being captured. I have no reason not to tell you everything I know. After all, I do enjoy life and I do not wish for it to end. Ask away...I will tell you what you would like to know," Dr. Erinyes promised.

This was not exactly the response that Lexi expected but it did show that the good doctor was fully ego-centric, in that he would sell out everything he knew to keep his heart beating just a little longer...even if it meant being in some obscurely located prison. She was thankful for the break, however...it was relaxing to know that getting the information she was looking for was not going to be difficult to obtain.

Lexi nodded. "Okay then doctor, the chips that you put in the Seekers - how do they work?"

Dr. Erinyes smiled. "Not a surprise that you would question that first. There are two types of chips. The slave chip for the workers and then there are the Seeker chips. The slaves chips are roughly half of the size and do not induce fear. They merely allow the slaves to be programmed to perform various tasks."

"Slave chips?" Lexi questioned.

"Yes my dear," the doctor responded. "Zodiac does not trust

255

people. Most of his workers have one primary task…they are still lobotomized and programmed, only they are not soldiers and do not require as sophisticated a chip."

Lexi's curiosity was peaked. At this point she knew that Talbot was watching and listening to the entire thing. "What kinds of tasks?"

"Hmph, you are aware of less than I thought. Oh well, I will enjoy educating one as lovely as you." Dr. Erinyes did not bother to hide his flirtations. "Our main slaves right now are construction workers. They carry out various tasks like modify existing structures for the Grand Army's use. They also build the Firehawks and other weaponry for the Grand Army. They even built the BFT-5000. Before you ask what that is, it's what many have described as the Apocalypse Dozer and the Firehawks are what I've heard referred to as the bladeless helicopters."

Lexi paused for a moment. It made amazing sense. This man was a literal gold mine of knowledge. She had to be careful and make sure she kept track of where the conversation was going… she could easily get sidetracked. "Where did the design for these things come from?"

The scientist was obviously enjoying his conversation with Lexi. "They were designs that were being tested by the United States government. Lord Zodiac had them produced in secret prior to the Flash Storm. He wanted only a few weapons to remain and made sure to target military installations to destroy the rest. His logic was that he wouldn't have to worry about keeping track of the equipment if it went up in flames. He didn't want it turned against him. Then he had new equipment produced that could carefully be monitored so it would not fall into the hands of anyone who might try to rebel against his new world order."

Lexi was amazed. It seemed that every answer was finally making the events and observations of the last few months connect and make sense. She leaned forward, inadvertently showing more cleavage and getting the dirty old man to cooperate even further. "So back to these slaves. What else are they building? Does it have something to do with what's going on near the shoreline in Connecticut?"

Dr. Erinyes nodded with a large smile. "Yes. That portion of the state has much refinement of metals and materials. The cities that were destroyed are ripe with scrap metal, along with former military bases. What we can't strip down gets shipped to the shoreline, where the Millstone power plant has been converted to a plasma beam power plant."

"Zodiac recycles? How environmentally conscious of him," Lexi thought, then asked, "What is a Plasma Beam?"

"Not into the technology magazines and web sites, are we? That's okay, most people aren't. The Plasma Beam technology was experimented with in Florida. A 10,000 degree beam is fired at, well, trash. Tons and tons of garbage is more than incinerated... it is atomized, releasing no toxins into the air. Compounds are broken back down to their base elements and the release creates energy that can be harnessed for electricity. The metals fall and are separated out," the scientist explained.

Lexi was getting a little overwhelmed. She was tempted to ask the old man to write it all down but decided that he was on a roll, so she could review the recordings later on when Vincent returned. "Actually, I have to admit, that's quite amazing. What is all of this metal for?"

Dr. Erinyes shook his head in disappointment. "Of that I am not entirely sure. Something big. Lord Zodiac is modeling himself after the Pharaohs and rulers of ancient times. He wants to show that he commands the resources to surpass them. I am unsure of exactly what his intentions are though. I've heard whispers that all of New London has been flattened as a construction site. He is quite mysterious and before you ask...no, I have never seen what is under his helmet."

Lexi nodded. "Fair enough. So the slaves are building something big in the New London area. Let's get back to the Seekers...this fear aura they possess. Our people figured out that the source is from the chip in their heads, but we're unsure of how it works."

Dr. Erinyes smiled. "Are you familiar with the quantum field my dear?"

She wished he would stop calling her that, but for the moment he had all of the answers so she did not want to risk putting a stopper in this bottle of knowledge. "Yes, following New Age science is a hobby of mine."

The doctor looked impressed. "Well that is good to hear.

Many believed it to be a quack science, full of conjecture and very little viable research. Lord Zodiac felt differently, as did the United States Government. There have been experiments being conducted for quite some time now with modifying reactions from people by manipulating vibrations in the quantum field. I have to say that the Seekers are an example of a great success. The chip has a small antenna which sends out vibrations that induce fear reactions in humans. Unless you know what to look for, it is undetectable and unstoppable. The fear is so intense that most cannot fight back and they see the Seekers as much larger and far more frightening than they really are."

Lexi couldn't wait to give John and Eve a big "I told ya so." That would have to wait. Her next question was of the utmost importance and the primary reason that the doctor had been brought for questioning. "So, a man as smart as you will know what my next question is."

Dr. Erinyes let out an amused laugh. "Of course. You would like to know how we reverse the effects for those like me who still have our wits about us. It's simple really. There is an implant in our nasal cavities that, like the Seeker chips, draws on the very electricity that runs through our nervous systems. It has but one purpose…to give the opposite vibration to the fear that is sent out from the Seekers. It completely counteracts the effects, but will not prevent one from feeling fear normally, and the Seekers can still be quite an imposing presence. You are different though. You, as well as your friend Night Viper are well known for your natural immunity. Tell me…how do you do it?"

Lexi wasn't expecting a question, but she figured there was no harm in answering it. "Jury is still out on Vincent. I have no idea how he does it. I have slight brain damage from cancer."

Now it was Dr. Erinyes's turn to have a light bulb go off in his head, and it was quite obvious that the glow of understanding had indeed hit him. "I should have guessed. Your amygdala was damaged, was it not?"

Lexi nodded an affirmative.

"But that is not the case with the Night Viper. The Seekers simply have no ability to frighten him," the doctor observed.

Lexi nodded once more. "I don't think anything scares him. How did you ever figure out the fear frequency?"

"Lord Zodiac projects it naturally. We copied the vibration. He has quite the gift, his telepathy. His ability to draw memories, thoughts, and knowledge from your mind is the stuff of science fiction, but I have witnessed this ability firsthand," the scientist explained. "It is possible that Vincent possesses some natural, opposing element that allows him to counteract the effects of the fear vibrations."

"His sixth sense," Lexi thought to herself but did not speak of it. "How do we duplicate the chip that's in you?"

The doctor shook his head. "That is a trade secret, my dear. That is how I shall stay alive. I do believe that you are a woman of your word, but you can offer no guarantee of my continued life if everything I know is revealed."

"I can't offer you a guarantee of continued life if you stop helping us either," Lexi retaliated.

Dr. Erinyes applauded. "You are a good negotiator. Depending upon the facilities you have here, I may be able to construct a device that will allow you to reverse the fear vibrations from the Seekers, allowing your fear-feeling companions to stand a chance of fighting back. I would work alone though, or maybe with the assistance of a non-scientific minded person. The secret must remain with me as my continued guarantee of survival. I realize that you would have to discuss this with your leadership, which I assume is the famous Night Viper."

He was observant, Lexi knew that. He already knew enough about them to make him quite dangerous to their cause should he ever escape. His knowledge was the key to any successful retaliation against Zodiac however, so for now, they would have no choice but to go along. "You are correct about that, but I'm sure that your requests would be honored." She was glad he did not demand sexual favors from her - if that were to happen; any type of rebellion was doomed.

"Then you do what you must. Once your discussion is over, please do let me know the outcome and if I am to be allowed to continue to live," Dr. Erinyes requested.

Lexi nodded. "Of course...now I need to step out." She did not wait for a response and left the room in a hurry to go to the adjacent room. When she entered, she was surprised to see that Talbot had the company of Josh.

259

"That was quite a performance in there," Josh was slowly applauding.

Lexi sat down, leaned her head back and sighed. "We need Vincent to see this conversation. Please tell me the recorders are on."

Talbot nodded an affirmative. "Yeah. Do you think that he was lying?"

Lexi shook her head. "No. He has no loyalty but to himself. It's strange that Zodiac would allow a man like this to be in his midst without lobotomizing him first."

"That's what worries me, although I'm sure he didn't think there was any way this guy was gonna fall into our hands. The stuff he knows is better than a gold mine, especially since there isn't any money anymore," Talbot remarked.

Josh was moving back and forth in his chair. "Do we even have what he needs to make this anti-fear device he's talking about? What happens if what he makes is booby trapped or something? He doesn't want us to know how to do it, so how would we know if anything he builds would actually work?"

Lexi looked down at the floor, and then looked up again. "He wants insurance. He believes that his life is in danger if he is no longer of use to us. He would have to know that we might kill him if he creates a device that doesn't do what he says it's gonna do."

"Before Vincent left I gave him a SAT phone. I managed to rig a few so that they'll tunnel under the network sniffers, much like how I'm hacking into the defense net. We'll be able to call the other phones, but the connection will time out at 4 minutes and 55 seconds," Josh explained.

"What would happen if it didn't time out?" Talbot asked.

"The traffic would become noticeable and traceable after 5 minutes of talking. That's why I changed the programming on these phones to drop the call with a buffer. Right now, we only have three of these things but I'll set up more of them," Josh answered.

Lexi smiled and gave Josh a light punch to the shoulder. "Geeze, is there anything you can't do with electronic devices?"

Josh blushed. "Not really."

"Then let's call the boss up and see what he has to say," Talbot stated.

Josh shook his head. "Vincent told me that he'll call in. He doesn't want us to call him in case he's in a serious situation. I guess he saw too many movies where a cell phone ringing gave away someone's location, although part of the reason is the secondary timer, which won't allow another call to be initiated for 20 minutes."

"Why is that?" Talbot inquired.

"Making too many connections, even talking for 4 minutes and 55 seconds, then hanging up and calling back, will create lots of individual requests in the system. Too many of these in too short a time will also give us away. I don't want them to lock down the defense net further and prevent us from getting into it. We're extremely limited in the amount of talking we can do, but at least we can communicate anywhere in the world as long as there's a satellite that supports it in range," Josh informed them.

Lexi stood up. "Something's better than nothing. Did you get anything out of the computer on that facial drawing that Andromeda and I made?"

Josh held up some papers. "It's just as Vincent thought, take a look."

Lexi grabbed the papers and began scanning through them. The man she had killed at the Danbury mall was Richard T. Mullen. It didn't take her long to see what she needed to see. "Another one who has cause to hate the world," she thought to herself.

She looked over at Talbot and Josh. "What the hell is this? He's as bad off as Jade. Look at this. His father raped and killed his mother in front of him when he was eight years old, then proceeded to chain him up in the basement and sexually molest him over and over for a month. The kid got loose and managed to get his hands on a screwdriver, which he used to plunge through his father's neck, puncturing his jugular. He was placed with an aunt and uncle; then his cousin, who was ten years older than him, ended up getting arrested because he was beating the kid up."

"These people aren't just social rejects. They've been so badly brutalized by pretty much everyone around them with no one to turn to, that they turned to the first person who offered them a chance to strike back," Talbot commented.

Lexi had a long face. Josh looked over at her. "Are you alright?"

Lexi sat back down. "It's just that when I was escaping Danbury, I didn't give any thought to the Seekers I killed, or their commander."

Talbot put a hand on Lexi's shoulder. "Lexi, you did what you had to do to survive. No matter what happened to Jade or Mullen in their lives, it doesn't excuse turning around and performing the heinous crimes that they've committed. Remember that."

She put her hand on his and looked up. "I know. It just makes you realize that everyone has a story. Everyone has a past. Even the Seekers are more than their faceless armor with the shoulder lights. Josh, did Vince happen to give an estimate of when he'd be calling in?"

Josh shook his head. "No, but he said he would let us know as they were arriving at the rendezvous, then he would call back after the 20 minute blackout period to verify that all was well."

"Okay, then for the first time in a long time, I'm going to wait by the phone for a call from a guy." She attempted to lighten the mood with a bit of humor.

"Remember, we only get five minutes," Josh reminded.

Lexi nodded in acknowledgement. "I know. I just want to deliver the message. In the meantime, I hope Eve and the baby are alright."

Chapter 30

Eve and John Decker had been passed out asleep in the back of the Bronco for most of the trip. They were exhausted, as was everyone. Fortunately for Vincent, he was far from being exhausted physically...mentally was another story. He had not asked for the burden of leadership, but with each passing moment it seemed that this role was inevitable for him. He had a substantial amount on his mind and was wishing he could have been in multiple places at once.

Acting on a bit of foresight, he had asked John for the location of this town where he was supposed to go and meet with the leadership for Militia 28. He found himself amazed that he was looking forward to seeing Maria Esperanza again. He was relieved to hear that she and her brother had survived the Flash Storm. He pulled out his SAT phone, since he was close to his destination and made his planned call.

"Vincent, I sure as hell hope that's you," Josh's voice came through.

Vincent was relieved that this rigged phone actually worked. "Yeah, it's me. Almost to the rendezvous. Any news?"

"Yeah, Lexi wants to talk to you though," Josh replied.

Vincent could hear Josh handing Lexi the phone, then he heard her voice. "Vincent, this scientist you got was a damn gold mine."

Vincent immediately was full of anticipation. "He spilled?"

"Everything. To sum it up, we were right about the Seeker fear aura. The chip in their heads sends out vibrations that trigger

263

fear responses. He said he could build us a device to counteract the effects, but he won't share the design with us as insurance for his own life. He said he would like to have a non-scientist assistant," Lexi explained.

Vincent shook his head. "No big surprise that he'd want assurances. He just came out with all of this?"

Lexi giggled. "He was quite content to be talking to my chest, and he also has a major superiority complex."

"A non-scientist? Talbot can help him," Vincent suggested.

Lexi cleared her throat. "Yeah, that wouldn't be a good idea. I think Talbot will kill him. It can't be me because he'll be too busy trying to find a way to get into my pants and I'll probably throw up from nausea."

"Josh is out, the Deckers are out. Crisco is missing. That leaves Andromeda," Vincent thought out loud.

"She could do it. She's definitely more of an artist than a scientist," Lexi pointed out.

Vincent was careful not to tense up his left hand which was on the steering wheel as he knew he would break it off. "Not a thrilling prospect...she's a kid and we know nothing about this guy other than the fact that he helps Zodiac turn people into mindless Zombies."

"Vince, there's more. The scientist confirmed that they're also converting people into slaves with a lesser chip. They've got a whole bunch of people building something in the New London area. It's big, real big. I think we're gonna run out of time soon," Lexi explained.

Vincent was nodding with acknowledgement, even though Lexi couldn't see him. "Alright, Andromeda can help this asshole as long as he keeps his grubby paws off her and he understands that he'll be working under surveillance. I want you or Talbot ready to bust in there at all times and take him out if necessary."

"One more thing before you go...the sketch that Andromeda did came back. The commander I killed went by the name Mullen. He has a messed up history like Jade. It seems that the hypothesis was correct - Zodiac recruited people who had basically been chewed up and spit out by the world. You've really gotta see this video of the..." Lexi was cut off when the phone hung up.

"DAMMIT!" Vincent cursed loudly. It woke John up, but not

Eve.

John snorted and shook his head with a grogginess. "What? What happened?"

"Time to wake up sleeping beauty, we're almost there," Vincent responded. "How's Eve?"

John checked over his pregnant wife. "She's fine; she's got a fever though. What's happening? Why did you shout out?"

Vincent shook his head while holding the SAT phone. "This stupid thing cut me off. Seems that they had a breakthrough back at the compound. I'll tell you about it later."

"Fair enough," John replied while stretching. He looked once again at his wife to see her sleeping peacefully, then took a moment to get his bearings. He pointed and said, "You can pull over up there, by that light post. We can wait. I'm sure they already know we're here."

Vincent nodded. "They do. They had lookouts back there about 500 feet. They probably shouldn't dress in colors that clash with the background and they'd be better off if they held still. The human eye detects movement before anything else."

John looked at Vincent with amazement. "Are you sure you were never in the military?"

Vincent was looking around the area as he pulled over. "Positive. I went for the air force when I was 18 but they wouldn't take me because my eyesight wasn't correctable to 20/20. It's kind of funny that my eyesight is now 20/5. No, I had to learn to be observant because I declared war on L.A.'s underworld and they have friends in some pretty high places."

John was shifting carefully so he would not wake Eve up, but could relieve the pins and needles he was feeling in his left leg. "That would do it. I don't see anyone coming yet."

"At our 9 o'clock, there're two people conversing who think they're hidden. These guys are gonna get demolished by the Seekers if they don't start being careful," Vincent observed.

"Funny, I thought they *were* pretty careful," John thought to himself. His spoken words were different though. "Well, you can inspire them to join us. Then we can train them."

Vincent didn't reply. His attention was caught by two figures approaching from the middle of the road. He reached down and put his right hand on one of his Berettas, but then backed off when he made out who one of the individuals was. "Maria. It's Maria. C'mon John, get your wife up." Vincent quickly exited the Bronco.

John took a few moments to wake Eve, who was enjoying her escape to dreamland. She finally came to and found that they were on some type of main road in a small town. It was obviously deserted but appeared undamaged by any type of war. "John, is this it? Is this where the doctor...OW!"

"What Eve, what?" John was attempting something with his hands but he didn't know what.

"I'm fine...just a kick to the ribs by our little one," Eve assured.

They both climbed out of the Bronco. John recognized Alan Ryke and Maria Esperanza from their last visit. Maria was actually still wearing her "Ciudad de Los Angeles" T-Shirt. "That's Alan Ryke. He's their leader or spokesperson," John said.

Vincent nodded. "I know. I knew him as Lt. Detective Ryke from the LAPD. He was the one who was assigned to the task force to find me and take me down."

John had a shocked look on his face. He had no idea what to say. Vincent avoided talking about the time he spent as a vigilante in Los Angeles. He also knew that if Vincent were to say anything, chances are it would be to Lexi or Josh as they seemed to have his confidence and he theirs.

"Nice tattoo Night Viper," Ryke called out. "My job became pretty boring after you disappeared. Too bad that boredom only lasted for about a year before the Flash Storm made sure life would never be boring again."

Vincent did not respond. Instead, he and Maria were watching each other. After a strange silence, Maria ran up to Vincent and he lifted her off the ground in a bear hug. Maria was visibly crying. After he put her down, she cursed at him in Spanish.

"Maria, I didn't run. I was taken. I can explain everything later," Vincent responded as if he understood every word she said.

Ryke looked over at Eve. "So I assume you're Eve. Pleased to make your acquaintance. John, you can take her over to the shop right there...our physician is already inside and prepared to see her."

"Thank you Alan," John responded as he helped his wife walk the short distance to the indicated shop.

Ryke then looked at Vincent. "You could have knocked me over with a feather when your friends told me that you were alive. I was skeptical at first but I realized that you survived deadly radiation and a year at war with every scum bag in Los Angeles. Hell, taking on Rebel 99 should have proven to me that you can survive anything."

"No hard feelings then?" Vincent asked.

Maria looked at Ryke's hard face. He looked back at her and softened. "No. As it turns out, we all ended up here anyway. Kind of interesting, the way things work out. I was originally tasked to bring you down, now here I am asking you for help."

It was Vincent's turn to be surprised. "Help? That's why you wanted to see me?"

"At first I just wanted to see if you were alive and if you'd be willing to join us. Since your Decker and Talbot departed our company to report back to you, I've found out some interesting things from my colleagues in Connecticut. Apparently, they picked up two stragglers who were running from Seekers in one of those bladeless helicopters. Strange pair...one's a former cop from Norwich, Connecticut; the other has pretty severe memory loss, a scar on his head, and his tongue has been cut out. They said they're survivors from William Backus Hospital and they gave a description that matches you jumping around on the rooftop and blowing Seekers away as if they were tin cans lined up on a fence," Ryke explained.

"Yeah. That was me. I had help. The other two that were with me aren't here now. They were turning people into Seekers there and we put a stop to it," Vincent acknowledged. "It's funny, I've met people from three rebel cells in Connecticut, and no one's ever mentioned Militia 28."

Ryke smirked. "That's because we're not affiliated with anyone else. I'm sure you've been briefed on how we came about."

Vincent nodded.

"The problem is, we were so secretive that most people didn't know about us. There are a lot of different groups claiming to be some type of rebellion, but so far none have been affective. One of those guys I told you about claimed that he led a group in an assault on that hospital and everyone was killed but him. There's no coordination, no strategy, no nothing. Everyone is operating in a silo," Ryke pointed out.

Vincent began his pacing routine. Ryke and Maria were close enough now that they both leaned on the Bronco. Vincent looked over at them and said, "Yeah, I know. Worse yet, the Seeker fear aura renders pretty much any formal assault ineffective. John is the only military man I've met in awhile; they did a real good job eliminating them."

"Why are you looking up at the sky?" Maria asked.

"We need to get somewhere inside. We don't want to get picked up by a random SAT sweep," Vincent answered, pointing to the sky.

"Random SAT sweep?" Maria was looking for clarification.

Vincent made eye contact. "Zodiac took over all of the satellites and has the imaging ones doing random sweeps to find threats and then sends the Seeker S&D squads after them. We need to get inside of a building."

Ryke looked around then pointed to the diner. "There, let's just go in there."

The three hurried and entered the diner. Maria started waiving her hand in front of her nose. "Holy shit, does it smell bad in here. No wonder Talbot and Decker were in such a rush to come out."

Vincent went to the booth furthest from the door. "Come sit over here, keep away from the windows."

Maria and Ryke looked at each other, and then sat across from the man they always knew as Night Viper. "Look, a few months ago if someone told me I'd be saying this to you I would've told them to shove it up their ass. But obviously, things have changed and we're on the same side. We need to unite all of these various factions that are operating on their own into a fully functional response to Zodiac's insurgence into this country."

"Why me?" asked Vincent.

"Because you manage to do things against all odds. Because you're one hell of a fighter. Most importantly, because you're too damn stubborn to quit," Ryke answered.

Vincent stood up and paced again, then went to the next table and grabbed a steak knife. He turned and looked at Maria and

Ryke. "Before we go any further, you two need to know why I disappeared. I was taken after I stopped that child sex ring."

"Taken by whom?" Maria asked. "And why are you holding that knife?"

"A black ops government group called Project Scorpion. They wanted to create super soldiers. I was the seventh subject and the only one who survived. That's why I have the tattoos," Vincent stated and then suddenly stabbed himself through the hand with the knife.

Maria gasped and uttered something in Spanish that neither Ryke nor Vincent could understand. Then they watched the truly amazing part…when the former vigilante removed the knife, the wound closed up almost instantly. "What the hell did they do to you!?" Ryke asked.

"Maria, grab that tea cup and stand over there," Vincent directed. Maria did so and the two stood about 15 feet apart. "Now drop it." Maria let go and before the cup could hit the floor, Vincent was already there, holding it in his right hand.

"Jesus. How the hell did you move so fast? I ask again, what the hell did they do to you!?" Ryke was antsy.

Vincent shook his head. "I wish I knew. I know I did some crazy shit before, but I can guarantee you that when you knew me, I couldn't do that. They turned me into some type of super soldier experiment. They enhanced my strength, agility and endurance too. I don't know how they did it. My only real clue is that a birthmark I used to have is now gone and my fingerprints were changed. I don't even know what the hell that suggests… they probably wanted to eliminate identifying marks or something."

Maria, despite her Hispanic background, turned ghost white. "Do you remember anything about what happened?"

Vincent sat back down and shook his head. "Vaguely. A few flashes. I had a moment the other day, but it just gave me more questions than answers. Funny enough, we came across someone who had formerly been stationed at the compound where this all happened. He led us there, helped us set up shop inside, and then disappeared suddenly."

Ryke sat up and leaned forward. "You found a hidden government compound?"

Vincent nodded. "Yeah. It uses geo-thermal power and an underground well for water. It was deserted when we showed up, but everything still works."

Ryke and Maria looked at each other. "And you still didn't find your answers?"

"No, I found a room which I believe was the lab that they used, but it had been destroyed. There were also no records that we could find related to what they were doing there. Totally off-book. I'm sure the former president himself had no idea this place existed, which is probably why Zodiac doesn't either," Vincent explained. "Look, I don't disagree with you on uniting the various factions into a full scale and coordinated rebellion. When we raided William Backus Hospital, we were able to capture one of their scientists and one of their Seeker commanders. My people are questioning them now."

"You've been busy," Maria commented.

"I'm telling you this because I trust you both," Vincent continued. He held up his SAT phone. "This phone has software that hacks into satellite communications, so I can call back to the compound and they can call me. The problem is it cuts off after just under 5 minutes to avoid detection on the Defense Network. We can't make another call for 20 minutes after that. I was cut off from my people when they were telling me that they had a breakthrough with the scientist."

Ryke motioned with his hand. "Go on."

"Apparently, this crackpot can build us a device that'll counteract the Seeker fear aura, allowing a force that we assemble to fight back," Vincent revealed. "He won't show us how to do it though...he's using it as an insurance policy to keep himself alive - probably smart thinking."

Ryke looked almost like an excited school child. "If your guy can build that device, we can put you in touch with the other factions of Militia 28. These guys have been stockpiling equipment, weapons, and supplies for awhile. Many of them started far before our organization was formed."

Vincent nodded. "Good. We were able to hack into their computer systems undetected. Between the information we can gather and your supplies and people, we actually stand a chance."

Maria had a long face. "Not to be pessimistic, but Zodiac has an army of those Seekers. He has resources. Even if we united, could we seriously fight back? I mean, he might even flash bomb us again."

Vincent stood up. "We can do anything as long as we don't give up. Remember, I was a dying man and I took down some of the toughest scum in Los Angeles. If I can do that, think of what a large number of people fighting for their very survival could do."

Maria smiled and nodded.

"I didn't get the full story yet...someone should be calling me soon with an update; then we can talk more about this," Vincent stated.

Lexi stared straight in front of her as she put the phone down. "This five minutes is a killer. Now we have to wait 20 minutes before we can call Vince back."

Josh looked around, then stood up. "Alright, we've got all we need from the scientist for now, right?"

Talbot and Lexi nodded.

"Then I'm gonna go talk to Jade, see if she has anything other than the story of her life," Josh said in the most determined tone of his life.

Lexi stood up and grabbed his arm. "So you're just gonna walk to her cell and have a chat?"

Josh shook his head. "No, I'm going to go into her cell and have a chat with her."

Talbot rapidly shook his head and waived his hands around. "Like hell you are...she's not some damsel in distress, Josh...she's a murdering psychopath who blames the world for her problems. Let me come with you...we'll secure her and bring her up here if you're so hard up to talk to her."

"I know what I'm doing Talbot. If it makes you feel better, you can wait outside the cell and if she tries anything, end her. She wasn't faking up here...she isn't gonna do anything," Josh assured them.

"When the hell did you become a shrink!?" Talbot snapped.

Lexi put her hand on Talbot's shoulder. "Let him do it. He'll have us as backup outside the cell, but let him do it. Josh, does the phone get signal down there?"

Josh nodded. "This place has signal boosters throughout... those phones can call from anywhere and it'll put the signal through a central relay that'll broadcast it."

"So basically, yes," Lexi verified.

"Yes," Josh replied as he stood up to head to the door.

"I don't want to leave this scientist here. We'll bring him to his cell while we're at it," Talbot stated.

It didn't take them long to get to the detention area. After putting Dr. Erinyes into his cell, without a fight, Josh walked over to Jade's cell. He looked through the small, barred window on the door and saw her resting on her bed, curled up in the fetal position, but with her eyes wide open. He was nervous, but he also felt determined that what he was about to do was the correct course of action. He ran his cardkey on the reader and unlocked the door. Without looking, he handed Talbot his cardkey and entered, letting the door shut and lock behind him.

The moment he walked in, Jade sat up. He took a moment and just looked at her. He could not bring himself to see a cold hearted killer. All he saw was a confused, battered, and broken little girl. Surprisingly, Jade made eye contact with him and was the first to speak, "Josh."

"Jade. I see you're still awake." Josh found himself at a loss for words.

Jade nodded. "I don't like to sleep. When you've done what I've done, there're a lot of faces and voices that take advantage of that time to haunt you."

Josh attempted to act tough. "Don't try the hurt little girl act on me."

Jade let out a little smile. "You shouldn't try to be a tough guy, it doesn't suit you. I'm not going to try to escape. I already told you, I have nowhere to go and I deserve whatever punishment you're going to give me, which I assume is death."

Josh was taken aback by her statement. "Death? You think we're going to kill you?"

"Night Viper is your leader right? I did some research on him. He wasn't known as a prisoner taking kind of guy," Jade responded.

Josh grabbed a beat up chair that was in the room and placed it directly across from Jade, who was sitting on the bed cross-legged. "Mind if I sit down?"

Jade shook her head back and forth, so Josh planted himself in the chair. He was desperately trying to see her for a cruel and brutal killer, but it still wasn't working. "We questioned Dr. Erinyes and he fed us a whole bunch of information."

Jade let out a nervous chuckle. "Not a big surprise. He thinks he's intellectually superior to everyone. He would think nothing of revealing everything he knows to save his own skin."

"But not you," Josh stated.

Jade shook her head again. "I deserve whatever punishment you give me and I won't resist anything you do, but I have friends that I will not betray."

"Friends? Jade, I'm going to make some observations. It's obvious that you're riddled with guilt over the things that you've done to people. Is that a fair assumption?" asked Josh.

Jade found herself surprised to feel a tear run down her cheek as she nodded.

"I don't have numbers to determine how many people you've killed or had turned into Seekers or slaves, but I know it's a high number. Is this really what you set out to do? Is this world really what you wanted to create? I know you're angry..."

"YOU DON'T HAVE ANY IDEA! NONE!" Jade interrupted with a yell, the waterworks from her eyes came on again. "I told you what happened. Everyone betrayed me. They called me a whore. I was a virgin. I didn't ask to be passed around like a damn toy. Everyone I turned to just pushed me away. The entire world rejected me. Zodiac was the only one who was willing to do anything for me!"

Josh shook his head. "Zodiac wasn't helping you out of the kindness of his heart. He was using you. Your friend there, Commander Mullen? Look at this." He reached into his pocket and grabbed a few of the papers that he had printed with information on Mullen. He unfolded them and handed them to Jade. She started scanning them. It only took a minute for her to slam them down in her lap, look up at the ceiling, and continue to cry.

"I'm sure the other Commanders have backgrounds like this too. You all weren't just picked on like I was, you were brutalized. Zodiac says he's hatred incarnate...he could sense your hatred. You drew him to you. He knew that he could take that hatred, corrupt you and focus all of that energy on helping him with his plans," Josh said calmly.

Jade was shaking her head rapidly. "No."

"He may not have violated your body like those baseball players did, but he sure as hell violated your soul," Josh explained.

Jade was continuing to shake her head and said, "No" again.

"He's telepathic, you know that. He entered your mind, which was open to revenge and he began twisting it. All of this stuff that you did, it wasn't you, it was him." Josh's voice was climbing.

Jade was rocking back and forth; her "No" was slightly louder, matching Josh's elevating decibel level.

"He raped your mind just as they raped your body and you damn well know it!" Josh was almost shouting.

"NOOOOOOOOOOOOOOOOOOOOOO!" Jade screamed as she flopped herself onto the bed and buried her head in her pillow. "NO! NO! NO! NO! NO! NO! NO! NO!"

Josh stopped for a moment, not knowing if what he had done was the right thing. He was acting on pure instinct and not thinking. "Jade," he said calmly.

No response.

He looked at her for another moment. All of her strength had been completely drained from her. She truly was nothing more than a broken little girl. He felt sorry for her, even though he knew that he shouldn't. Figuring further discussion would be fruitless, he stood up and walked to the door. He heard the click as it unlocked and he grabbed the handle. He opened it only a few inches when he heard a whimpering voice. "Josh."

Still holding onto the door, he turned his head and saw that Jade had picked her head up from the pillow and was looking at him. "The prisoners I had at the Backus Hospital came from a detention center. It wasn't everyone that was taken."

Josh just looked at her.

"The detention center is what used to be Three Rivers Community College. It was modified and fenced off. Commander Triton would have taken control over the facility after I disappeared and knowing him, he'll probably close the Seeker Farm, which means they'll kill everyone at the detention center," Jade explained.

"Why are you telling me this?" Josh asked.

Jade adjusted and sat up. "Because for the first time, someone actually sees me for who I am. Despite what I've done, I can tell you're actually trying to help me. Besides, I'm already going to hell for all of the innocent people I've killed or enslaved."

Josh looked at her and said, "It is his capacity for self-im-provement and self-redemption which most distinguishes man from the mere brute."

Jade smiled. "You followed politics in Burma?"

"I know a wise person when I see one. Daw Aung San Suu Kyi was right...maybe you should keep that quote in mind," Josh replied as he walked out of the cell, the door locking behind him.

Lexi and Talbot looked at Josh. Lexi was smirking, Talbot was not.

"Don't you go getting sweet on her," Talbot warned.

"It's been about 20 minutes...we should call Vincent," Josh replied as he began walking away.

Talbot glared at Lexi. "I saw that smirk. Don't encourage him. That harpy in there will use him and then dispose of him once she has what she wants."

"He feels bad for her Talbot," Lexi stated. Josh was far enough away that he couldn't hear their conversation.

Talbot looked at the floor and sighed. "I know. The problem is that she helped bring the world down to the hell it's in now. We have no idea how far she'll go to get what she wants. If she were to escape from here or find some way to report our location back to Zodiac, we'd be screwed."

It was a sobering reality to acknowledge, but Talbot was right and Lexi knew it. She also knew that once Vincent came back, he would show this girl no mercy. She was the enemy...she was dangerous...and she had information that they needed. She looked ahead at Josh. Before he rounded the corner, he pulled out his SAT phone and began dialing. "God help you Josh Tyler. I sure hope you don't get too attached to her," Lexi thought to herself.

Ring! Ring!

Maria jumped and gasped at the sound of Vincent's SAT phone ringing. Vincent looked at her as he held the phone up. "It's just a phone."

Maria giggled and felt foolish. "Sorry, haven't heard that

sound in a few months."

Vincent put the phone to his ear. "Yeah."

"It's Josh. We have a problem," Josh stated.

Vincent began pacing as usual. "I know, the world is under the control of a savage dictator that's turning everyone into mindless slaves and there's no army to fight back."

"I'm serious, Vincent. I spoke to Jade and she told me that there's a detention center where Three Rivers Community College used to be. It's not far from the hospital. It's where they were keeping the rest of the prisoners from Danbury and Bridgeport. She thinks that Commander Triton, who I guess is another boss in the area, is probably just going to shut the Seeker Farm down and have all of those people killed," Josh explained.

Vincent's face dropped. Ryke, only able to hear what Vincent was saying spoke up. "What the hell's going on?"

Vincent put his index finger in the air. "Are you sure that we can trust what she's saying?"

"Yes. I'd be willing to bet my life on it," Josh replied.

Vincent put his hand on his forehead, faced toward the floor, and shook his head. "Even without speed limits and cops, I don't know that Decker and I can get there in time. Eve's still getting checked out by the physician."

"There's got to be a way. Vincent. She volunteered this on her own. That's got to count for something," Josh was pleading and Vincent knew it.

"Did you ever stop to think it could be a trap? Listen, don't get too attached to her…she's the enemy and we need to find out what she knows by any means possible. This isn't one of those stupid fairytales. Humanity is on its last leg here," Vincent scolded.

There was silence on the other end of the phone for a few seconds then a monotone reply, "I know."

"Then promise me right now that you're not going to do anything stupid. Stay the hell away from her. Lexi or Talbot can bring her whatever she needs," Vincent directed.

"Look, she's voluntarily giving out information to me, maybe I can…"

"I mean it," Vincent interrupted. "I can tell by the tone of your voice that you're heading down a path that you shouldn't. Stay away from her."

"Fine. Lexi's caught up to me. She wants to talk to you for the minute and a half we have left," Josh snapped then handed Lexi the phone.

"Vince, do you need me and Talbot to come out there?" asked Lexi.

"Have Josh look up this Commander Triton…see if he can find out who this guy really is. I'd like it if you could come out here. I'll call back in 20 minutes. Have Talbot stay behind to deal with the prisoners and to make sure that Josh doesn't do anything foolish," Vincent answered.

"I will," Lexi acknowledged.

"Thank you Lexi," Vincent stated, and then the phone cut off. He put the small device away.

Maria and Ryke were standing now, both looking deeply concerned.

"We have a problem," Vincent stated as he looked up at them.

"What? What's going on!?" Ryke anxiously asked.

"When we shut down Backus, we released several of the rebels who were captured at Danbury and Bridgeport. The problem is, the rest were kept at another site that we didn't know about at the time. According to the commander that we took prisoner, they'll probably shut down that whole area and kill the remainder of the prisoners," Vincent explained.

Ryke went ghost white. "How many?"

Vincent shook his head. "Hard to say, at least a few thousand, could be many more. The location is what was formerly one of the community colleges but I'm sure they heavily modified the grounds and stuffed those people in there. I'm gonna head down there as fast as I can…I just don't know if I'll get there in time."

Maria poked Ryke who responded, "I can communicate with our people down there. The problem is that Seeker fear aura."

"Yeah, and even if our other prisoner had one of his devices ready, we still wouldn't be able to get it and bring it down there in time," Vincent pointed out.

"Then they'll have to suck it the hell up!" Maria exclaimed. "Seriously, we can't just let all those people die, right? We can't. I've watched too many people die lately."

Ryke was clenching his fists. "I'm just not sure how to talk the head of the Connecticut faction of Militia 28 to agree to attack a compound when she knows that her people are going to panic."

Vincent had a sense of determination. "Let me talk to her."

"What?" Ryke wanted to verify what he'd heard.

"Let me talk to her. I'll convince her," Vincent said.

Maria and Ryke gave each other a look, and Ryke spoke up. "She's set in her ways...she's stubborn like that."

"She may be open to hearing from Night Viper," Maria claimed.

"Maria, it's just Vincent now. I haven't gone by Night Viper in awhile," Vincent interjected.

Maria looked a bit stunned. Ryke spoke up, "Look, I can take you to the radio, but I can't guarantee that she'll listen to you."

"I'll take what I can get, but we have to hurry...every moment we waste is a moment that those people don't have," Vincent warned.

John and Eve Decker had not paid attention to what the little shop that they were in had previously been. Pretty much anything that had been there had been removed and various medical supplies had been brought in. "Well, I have good news and bad news," Dr. Robert Lancaster addressed the married couple. "The good news is that the baby's vitals are stable. The bad news is that there's no way you're going to term and surviving."

Eve had tears well up under eyes. John held his wife's hand and looked at the doctor. "What do you mean?"

Dr. Lancaster placed the urine sample that he had taken from Eve on the counter and took his latex gloves off. "You have Preeclampsia, which you probably know as Toxemia."

"Oh God," Eve stated.

"What do we do, doctor?" asked John.

The doctor began pushing on Eve's pregnant belly. "Unfortunately, we don't have the equipment to do an ultrasound. I will say that your blood pressure and heart rate are not so severely high that we need to go to extremes yet. When are you due?"

"November 10th...a little more than a month away," Eve answered.

"Doctor, is there a facility nearby, maybe a clinic or something that might have what we need?" asked John.

Dr. Lancaster made eye contact with John. "Yes actually, there is. It's about a half hour drive, although it's probably quicker now since speed limits are a thing of the past. There're plenty of cars around for you to pick from. The problem is electricity…"

"Is there a generator around of some kind? Maybe a gas powered one? We can siphon gas from one of the cars outside," John suggested.

Eve was sitting up since Dr. Lancaster finished his examination. "Do you have any cars that are not out in the open?"

"Why?" asked John.

Eve looked at her husband. "If everything has remained unchanged outside and any satellites have taken pictures overhead, they may be programmed to trigger if something is different."

John sighed. "Like a car that had been there for months suddenly being gone."

"There may be a car in the garage of the shop down the road. It was a little local place that did everything from changing oil to repairing collision damage. Why not use the one you came in?" said Dr. Lancaster.

John stood up. "Can't take the Bronco. With its range, Vincent may need it. I'd rather take an unmodified car if we don't have to go far. Let me talk to the boss. In the meantime, what about that generator?"

Dr. Lancaster stood and both men helped Eve to her feet. The doctor held her steady then answered John. "We have a couple back at the shelter. I can check with Ryke."

"Stay with Eve, Doctor. Vincent and Ryke are meeting now… I'll go get both of them," John insisted.

Vincent, Maria, and Ryke were heading out of the old diner when they saw John running down the street toward them. "What the hell has gotten into him!?" asked Ryke.

Vincent was looking in John's direction shaking his head. "I'm not sure."

John stopped about ten feet from the trio and said, "Eve's in kind of rough shape. Dr. Lancaster says he needs some better facilities and says that there may be something close by."

"*May be* something?" Vincent asked.

"There's a clinic, but he hasn't been there since the Flash

279

Storm happened so he doesn't know if it's been looted or not," John elaborated.

"Fortunately, there hasn't been as much looting as one would think. Of course, most of the stuff that people would be taking is worthless now anyway. Food and guns are about the only thing carrying value," Vincent commented. "We have a dilemma too. There's a detention center that's holding the remaining people that were captured in Danbury and Bridgeport. That commander we captured thinks that her cohort is just going to pull the plug on the whole Seeker plant and kill all of those people."

John's eyes bugged out and he put his hand on his forehead. "Shit. What the hell are we going to do?"

"I'm going to their shelter to talk to the leader of Militia 28 in Connecticut," Vincent answered.

"Perfect, we need one of the generators from the shelter… that's what Dr. Lancaster said. If there's an ultrasound machine at the clinic, we'll need to run it," John stated. "I figure I can take one of the cars that are in the body shop down there."

"Alright, I'll go to the shelter with Maria and Ryke. I can pick up the generator in the Bronco and bring it back here. In the meantime, you get that car ready and stay here with your wife," Vincent directed.

John could not hide his anxiety. "Thanks Vincent…I mean it."

Vincent nodded. "I know - now get going."

John turned and hurried back toward his wife. Ryke looked at Vincent. "He looks like he hasn't slept in a week."

"He probably hasn't, at least a full night's sleep. I know that most of my people have been up for over 24 hours," Vincent commented.

Maria looked at Vincent. "What about you?"

Vincent let out a little snicker. "Ha. The government wanted me to be the perfect soldier apparently. I don't need to sleep much. My body works on a 48 hour clock, not 24 like everyone else's. I can be up for a week before I start to run into trouble."

"That's useful," Ryke said.

"It's especially useful at times like this. I don't think I've slept in 3 days. Anyway, let's get going to the shelter," Vincent suggested.

Chapter 31

Crisco was sitting in the helicopter with his teammates, including Captain James Hera. Lying unconscious on the floor was the vigilante known as the Night Viper. Despite his body being riddled with cancer, he put up a hell of a fight against four armored and armed military personnel. "He's not gonna wake up while we're airborne, is he?" one of the teammates asked.

Captain Hera shook his head. "Doubt it. I don't care how tough he is, he's still human, and he's terminally ill at that. We loaded him with enough drugs to put down a bull. He's not getting up until we decide that he is."

"Alright, but he ripped through L.A.'s toughest like they were school kids. He's already done the impossible," the same soldier suggested.

"Stop being a coward boy. I've got more darts here anyway. Besides, we're nearing the landing site. There're trucks waiting to take us and him to the compound!" Hera snapped.

Crisco stirred in his seat. He was glad that Night Viper had not seen his face. There had been six previous subjects that they had picked up for whatever it was that the scientists were doing to attempt to create super soldiers. None of them had survived the beginning stages. Logically, six healthy individuals dying in the process did not land the chances of a terminally ill vigilante at a high point. Even still, Crisco saw and felt something different about this one. "Just in case I ever meet this guy again, I don't want him to remember who I am," he thought to himself.

The chopper began its approach to the landing site. From the air they could see a van and unmarked Hummers waiting. There were soldiers dressed in the black fatigues of the Project Scorpion compound standing around with their M16 rifles ready. "Everything's gonna be fine. We're gonna land and they'll take this guy out of here and lock him down." Crisco's mind was going a mile a minute.

Captain Hera gave a light but sharp kick to Crisco's shin. "Wake up soldier, we're landing. Get ready to move out, all of you."

Crisco snapped out of his daze as the chopper touched down on the ground. The moment it touched land everyone jumped up. The hatch opened and they were already unloading the vigilante. After removing him from the vehicle, they brought him directly to the van. Crisco jumped down and headed for the Hummer that he was being motioned to go to. He got in and they immediately departed. "Hey Sergeant, I can't believe you guys actually got him," the driver stated.

Crisco was staring out the window. "Yeah, well, they told us he was dying but for a dying man, he sure put up a hell of a fight. If Hera hadn't hit him with the knockout juice, he probably would've killed us."

"I heard he took out 20 members of Rebel 99. Shiiiiiiit. Those guys are on the terrorist watch list and he just waltzed in and blew away a fifth of them. Can't wait till this guy's working for us…we'll be able to do anything," the driver commented in a tone that would befit a young child on Christmas day.

"If he survives," Crisco commented in one of the most pessimistic tones he had ever let his vocal cords produce.

"C'mon Sarge, he'll survive. He's gotten through worse," the driver assured.

The two men sitting in the back were silent. They were lower ranked than Crisco and the driver so they had the back seat. Crisco asked, "Does anyone know exactly what it is they do in that lab?"

The driver shook his head, the two men in back remained motionless. "No idea. That's so classified that not even the president of the United States knows about it. Frankly, it's probably for the best. If the oval office ever finds out about this place and puts us on the chopping block, we can honestly deny any real knowledge of what was going on in there. Besides, I've heard some of the screams…I don't want to know."

Crisco nodded and looked back out of the passenger window at the passing trees. "I guess."

Despite the fact that only minutes had gone by, Crisco felt as if he had been in that Hummer for hours. They were finally in the loading area of the complex and parked. He stepped out of vehicle and saw the van several feet away. The back doors opened and two men carrying their prisoner by the arms and legs came out. They only made it a few steps before Night Viper woke up again. The vigilante freed one of his feet and made contact with that soldier's head, dropping him to the ground. The one holding his arms panicked and released his grip. The vigilante dropped to the floor and immediately moved into a squatting position. While squatting, he spun and hit the other man in the groin, instantly dropping him.

Crisco froze in his steps. He couldn't move. He locked eyes with the man who had earned the title of the most brutal vigilante ever. He could see the anger in this man's eyes. Then he saw another dart hit. Night Viper went down again. "Jesus Christ! What the hell is it with this guy!?" Captain Hera yelled from behind Crisco. "You guys got him?"

The man who took the groin shot was still lying on the ground, writhing in excruciating pain. The man who took the head shot was unconscious. The two soldiers that had been in the front seat of the van rushed back and retrieved the prisoner. "Crisco, you go with them and make sure they actually get him to the lab," Hera ordered. Crisco's heart jumped into his throat. He did not want to be in the same compound with Night Viper, never mind in close proximity.

"And someone get those two down to the infirmary. Make sure they're not bleeding internally or some shit like that," Hera barked.

Crisco followed the two men who were carrying the prisoner. He didn't know their names. He had his rifle out and ready to go. When they finally got to their destination, there were two men in white coats standing outside. "Thank you, we'll take him from here," one of them said. Despite being brainiacs, they were

283

strong enough to lift an unconscious adult and bring him into their highly secretive lab. Crisco caught only a brief glimpse but he saw what appeared to be a giant crystal in the center of some type of machine. The door shut and sealed after that.

Crisco jumped awake, letting out a huge gasp. He was back in the woods and out of dream land, making his way as far from the Project Scorpion complex as he could. He figured he must have nodded off. He was amazed at how real his dreams felt. "I've got to keep moving. Can't slow down now. I'll just pray that I never have to meet up with Vincent Black ever again," Crisco thought to himself as he opened his bottled water, drank some, then continued on foot through the woods.

Chapter 32

"This is Josee Santillo, head of Militia 28 Connecticut," the voice came over the radio.

"Lt. Detective Alan Ryke, head of Militia 28 New York, former LAPD," Ryke responded.

"Ryke, it's good to hear from ya. I hope everything is going well up in the boonies," Josee commented.

Ryke looked at Vincent, then back at the archaic machine that they had become dependent upon. One could barely hear themselves think over the loud, gas powered generator that was supplying electricity to run the old machine. "Josee, I've got news, and you're not gonna like it."

Ryke could almost hear Josee shaking her head. "And when do you ever have good news for me?"

"Touché. Listen, that whole thing at the William Backus Hospital," Ryke started.

"Yeah, I got these two survivors here…Eric the Amnesiac and Carl Woods. They told me all about it," Josee replied.

Ryke just shook his head, and then pressed the button. "I have the guy here who busted that place up. He goes by the name of Vincent Black, but he was at one time known as the Night Viper."

There was silence for a few moments. Finally, a response… "This is the Night Viper you told me about? The one you were tasked to stop?"

"Things change, Josee. We have a situation. Apparently, Backus didn't have all of the prisoners that were captured in Con-

285

necticut. There's some kind of detention center set up at what used to be Three Rivers Community College. We have intel that they may be ready to just slaughter them," Ryke urgently spoke into his handset.

"And where would this intel be from? How can we trust it?" Josee asked.

Vincent motioned to Ryke to give him the hand unit. Ryke did so and Vincent spoke. "Mrs. Santillo, this is Vincent Black. We don't have a lot of time. When we busted that place up, we captured the commander in charge and one of their scientists. We have managed to get quite a bit of information from both of them. The commander believes that her replacement will be scrapping the Seeker Farm in Norwich and that it would be easier for them just to kill all of their prisoners than to risk transporting them to another location for conversion. For all I know, we could be too late already."

Again, there was silence for a moment. Finally, Josee's voice replied, "What are you asking us to do exactly? Bust them out? Our guys will flip out as soon as they get anywhere near those Seekers. They're just too freaky."

Vincent shook his head and picked up the handset again. "Listen. We know how the Seekers spread fear. They're nothing more than lobotomized slaves with a chip in their head to replace their frontal lobes. Zodiac's guys then issue programming via this chip. It also sends out signals that trigger a fear response in humans. It's artificial."

"Artificial or not, how am I gonna keep my people from having a heart attack the second we get near those Seekers?" Josee asked.

Vincent looked at Ryke and Maria, and then looked at the handset. "Ranged attacks are your best bet to avoid the fear aura but that may not be enough. Battle can be frightening for even the bravest person, but throughout human history, soldiers have moved past their fear and that's what we need your people to do now. We can't go on in factions Mrs. Santillo, we need to unify. Those are our people who are about to be murdered in cold blood."

"If you know that this fear aura is artificial, don't you have something to beat it back with?" inquired Josee.

286

Vincent nodded as if Josee was right there next to him. "The scientist we captured can develop such a device. The problem is, it won't be built and deployed in time to save those people. We need to attack the detention center without it. I'm going to head straight there to help you, but if you wait for me, I can guarantee we'll be too late."

"Some of my people will die," Josee replied.

Vincent knew this would come up. He'd hoped it wouldn't but logic told him that it would. "If I could bear the suffering of all of your people, I gladly would if it meant those prisoners would be free. We can't keep running. We can't keep hiding. We need to fight back and this is how it starts. If we don't stand up to Zodiac's Seekers, then we're all as good as dead anyway."

The silence came once again. It was a few seconds longer this time, but finally, "You're right, Vincent. God help us all, you're right. Head here as fast as you can. Obviously, you're the foremost authority in killing Seekers and busting up Zodiac's compounds. In the meantime, I'll assemble some of my toughest and bravest and we'll try to stop the massacre as long as we can."

Vincent felt a huge sigh of relief. "Thank you, Mrs. Santillo. You're amazing."

"You can quit with that Mrs. Santillo crap son. Call me Josee," she responded.

"Well then, Josee, I cannot ask of others what I'm not willing to do myself. I'll be there as soon as I can," Vincent assured.

"I look forward to meeting the Night Viper in person then," Josee stated then terminated the connection.

Maria and Ryke looked at Vincent. Ryke spoke up. "How the hell did you do that?"

Vincent shrugged his shoulders. "Do what?"

"Josee is the toughest old broad on the face of the planet and you softened her right up." Ryke was completely astonished.

Vincent shrugged his shoulders again. "I only speak the truth, Ryke. We need to load that spare generator into the Bronco now; we still have a pregnant woman to take care of."

Ryke stood up and began walking out. Vincent also stood, but Maria grabbed his arm and said, "So, all of this time I thought you were just a crazy vigilante with an agenda for violence. I never knew you were a leader."

Vincent looked at her and smirked. "Funny, neither did I."

"Oh my God, are you kidding me!?" Eve shouted. She was looking at the car that John had taken to drive her and Dr. Lancaster to the clinic. It had the boxy body style of the late 80's and early 90's but there was so much rust and denting that she couldn't even identify what kind of car it was.

John shrugged his shoulders. "What? It runs nice and look, it's got brand new tires!"

Eve gave him the look of death. Dr. Lancaster put his hands on her shoulders. "Keep your stress down, dear. If it drives, it will get us to where we need to go."

"I'm less worried about toxemia and more worried about getting into that damn car!" Eve growled.

"Look, I don't know as much about cars as Talbot does, but I can see this thing works," John assured her. "Now all we need is to get Vincent here with the generator and we'll be good."

"And how big is this generator? I don't know if that thing's going to hold the three of us," Eve complained. Just then, they heard the sound of the Bronco approaching.

"Thank God," Dr. Lancaster sighed.

The Bronco pulled up close to the car. Vincent, Ryke and Maria got out. Maria looked at the car and uttered something in Spanish that no one present could understand. Vincent looked it up and down. "Nice...uh...car, John. You planning on retiring in style?"

John gave him a dirty look. "Ha ha ha, you're a damn comedian. Did you get the generator?"

Vincent couldn't help but chuckle. "Yeah, it's in the back. Pop your trunk and I'll grab it." John opened the trunk. Vincent went to the back of the Bronco and pulled the generator out by himself. He walked it over to the frankencar and put it in the trunk. The back end of the vehicle dropped a few inches. The device was too big for the trunk to be able to close.

"Oh great, the trunk won't even close!" Eve tossed her hands up in the air.

"It's not like we have to worry about getting pulled over," John pointed out.

Eve didn't respond. She allowed the doctor to help her into the back seat of the beat-up vehicle. "Lay down Eve," Dr. Lancaster directed, then got into the driver's seat and motioned for John to get into the passenger seat.

"Good luck with that, John," Vincent stated. "You go and be with your wife...make sure everything is alright. I'm going back to Connecticut."

"What's happening?" asked John.

"Not too much time to explain. Militia 28 in Connecticut is gonna attempt to bust out the rest of the people who were taken at Danbury and Bridgeport. I've got to get a move on it. They'll still fall victim to the Seeker fear aura," Vincent answered.

John shook his head. "I'm coming with you."

"To hell you are!" Vincent snapped. "You need to be with your wife and your unborn child. I've seen enough life taken out of this world lately; it would be nice to have new life brought into it for once. Here." Vincent handed him a device.

"What's this," John inquired.

"It's the other SAT phone. Josh was only able to set up three of them. He's going to make more but in the meantime, he has one, I have one and now you have the third. Remember, five minutes max and it shuts you off," Vincent replied.

John nodded. "Four minutes and 55 seconds - yeah, I remember. And no matter the length of the conversation, it won't make another call for 20 minutes."

"Yeah, that means you can't call me or Josh for 20 minutes, nor can either of us call you; so if you need to use it, make sure it's important because it's blackout after that and those 20 minutes can feel like forever if you're in trouble," Vincent stated.

John nodded again. "I got it Vincent."

"I've already called Lexi...she's on her way here. Talbot and Josh are going to stay behind," Vincent explained. "Good luck."

"Thanks, we'll need it," John acknowledged.

Chapter 33

Plainville, Kansas. For the longest time, this had been a quaint little town off Route 183. The town held a secret though. Upon the passing of Amendment 28, the elimination of the right to bear arms for United States citizens, it became the home of a branch of Militia 28. They took refuge in a decommissioned underground Military bunker. The assumption had always been that the government had slated it to be filled with concrete, but they had never gotten around to it. None of the systems inside worked anymore, but it served as a good underground shelter for the members of the outlaw group to hide. That was until one of their scouts was spotted by a Seeker S&D squad. Now the base was under siege.

The Seekers who had discovered them wasted no time reporting what they had seen. Commander Stone, who was in charge of the Seeker forces in the area, immediately deployed an entire battalion to the site. He accompanied them because he had decided that this was an attack he wanted to direct personally. The militia members had dug themselves in and were fighting back, but fear made most of their shots go wild. The ones that did hit bounced off the Seeker armor as if they were gnats.

"Charge forward," ordered Commander Stone from his Firehawk. A dozen Seekers stood up and ran forward, the rebel bullets bouncing off them harmlessly.

Commander Stone shook his head. "This is too easy. Is this the best that humanity can throw at us…huh?" His boasting was cut off as one of the charging Seekers stepped on a mine and was thrown several feet in the air. "FALL BACK IDIOTS, FALL BACK!" His orders came too late for four other Seekers.

The pilot, a whimpering man who Stone simply called Igor because of the hunch he had in his back and his short stature, had not been converted to a slave or a Seeker. Stone quite enjoyed having someone with a mind to push around. In reality, he had no idea what the man's real name was, nor did he care. "Commander, a communication is coming through from Lord Zodiac," Igor stated.

Stone clenched his fist and let out a grunt. "Patch it through to my helmet."

Igor nodded. "Yes my leader."

"Lord Zodiac," Stone acknowledged.

"I see you've run into some trouble," Zodiac taunted.

Stone was annoyed but he didn't let his voice show it. "I have the situation under control. Those fools can't remain down there forever."

"No, but we don't need this siege to drag out. I am handling this personally. It's time to test the hover tanks," Zodiac announced.

"But," Stone started. He sometimes hated the fact that Zodiac watched the video feed from the various battles that transpired.

"Pull your men back Commander, or face my wrath directly," Zodiac threatened.

Stone did not hesitate. "Of course Lord Zodiac. I meant no disrespect."

The dictator ended the communication. Stone then issued a new order. "All Seekers, withdraw to the perimeter."

The former missile base had no weapons left within it. Instead, a web of various platforms and wooden huts were suspended with ropes and cables all throughout the large, open area that used to house some of the nuclear arsenal of the United States. Far more than a missile silo, many people believed that the massive weapons had been assembled at this location at some point in time. There was much commotion in the bunker at that moment. The entire surviving population of Plainville was holed up in this decommissioned military compound. Opinions were being shouted out and quickly dismissed.

"We should surrender...pray for mercy!"

"That's crazy. Zodiac has shown no mercy."

"Yeah, he bombed the cities and wiped out the army."

"We don't stand a chance against the Seekers."

"They withdrew, we won!"

"They're hanging on the sidelines. They're probably going to flash bomb us."

"We're all gonna die!"

Jack Breaker had no patience left within him. He decided to speak up. "Shut the hell up, all of you! Look at us, acting like sniveling cowards. Militia 28 was founded for this exact situation, because those who had the vision to recognize what had been going on in our country saw this reality coming and expected us to be prepared. Oh how disappointed they must be with us. Right now, the Seekers are on the border of the mine field, waiting, watching. We must do the right thing."

"And what is that!?" a voice piped up.

"One of our members must make a run for it to get word out to the other factions. The Seekers will eventually overrun us but we must take down as many as we can," Jack encouraged.

"Oh my God, I don't want to die!" one voice cried out.

"Living in this world is worse than death," another voice piped up.

"Humanity is going extinct. The book of Revelations has come back to haunt us."

"This is what our species gets for wrecking the planet!"

"ENOUGH," Jack shouted. "This isn't doing anyone any good. We need to get a message to the New York branch and the radio is being jammed by those Grand Army thugs."

"Why New York?" someone piped up.

"That's where Alan Ryke is and he's one of the founding members of Militia 28," Jack answered.

Commotion began again.

"I thought he was in Florida."

"No, he's in Montana."

"That can't be right..."

Jack was losing his patience. "He's in New York. The locations of the founding members have always been a secret in case of a military takeover or something like the Flash Storm. We don't

292

have a lot of time; the Seekers could raid us at any moment."

An older woman stepped forward. "Everyone, it's time to be brave. I say we send three people who know how to survive in tough situations. We provide as much cover as possible."

"Only three of us get to survive?" a teenage male piped up.

"None of us will survive if we stay here and argue about it and if we all run for it, none of us will survive. I do not wish to die in vain. We must get word out about what happened here, warn the others," the older woman replied.

"I know who should go," a middle aged man spoke up.

Everyone went silent and looked at him. He then said, "Shawn, Adrian, and Destiny Sundance."

"Blackfoots aren't cowards...we stay and fight," Shawn spoke up.

Jack looked at the three individuals. Shawn was only 14. His younger sister Destiny was 8 and his older sister Adrian was 18. All three of them had slightly darker skin from their heritage, despite the fact that they were only 25% Blackfoot Native American. Their last name came from their tribe, named after a Blackfoot prayer ceremony. Their parents had been quite adamant about preserving the dying history of this group, so their kids were required to learn the language and other traditions of their Native American ancestors. "Shawn, you're not cowards. We're going to lose this fight, even with the mine field out there. We're going to wait as long as possible to get as much information as possible about what we're facing and you all need to take this to New York. You can't let us be forgotten."

Destiny had tears in her eyes. "You can't all die. THERE HAS TO BE ANOTHER WAY!"

"Adrian, did your father teach you to fly a helicopter?" asked Jack.

Adrian nodded. "Yes, he did."

"Good. His old air field isn't far from here. Head in the opposite direction and take the long way around. Hopefully, there is at least one of those things that's still functioning. Make sure you fly low to stay off radar, but you'll get there a lot faster if you fly," Jack ordered.

"I will. Destiny, Shawn, come with me now," Adrian said in a stern voice. Neither sibling argued, although their body language was easy enough to read. They didn't like this idea.

After the Sundance siblings left, the older woman who had previously spoken approached Jack. "Can I talk to you for a moment?" Everyone else was conversing amongst themselves. Both of them stepped off to the side.

"We're surrounded. How are we going to get them out of here?" she asked.

"We're gonna blitz the Seekers. I don't know what it is about those things, but people freak out when they get close. We'll hit them with our heaviest stuff and create an opening for the three of them to get through. Then we'll release the smoke grenades to give them as much cover as possible," Jack stated.

The woman shook her head. "That doesn't seem like much of a plan. The three of them could get picked off before they get five feet away."

"They won't. There's going to be too many other targets," Jack stated.

"What do you mean?" the woman asked.

Jack put his hand on her shoulder. "We're going to have a squad charge. We know where the mines are so we can get by them just fine."

The woman fidgeted. "Have you forgotten the whole 'freak out' factor? The moment they start to close in, our people are going to be overwhelmed with fear."

Jack nodded. "I know. We just have to keep the Seekers busy long enough for the Sundances to get away."

"Jack, how are you going to get a squad to do this?" the woman asked.

"I'm gonna volunteer to lead them," Jack stated.

"How much longer do we have to wait out here, master?" Igor asked impatiently. "The Colorado plant is many miles away."

"Lord Zodiac was already on his way here with the hover tanks. He'll be arriving soon," Stone answered, while looking through a high powered scope on his rifle. He saw a figure climbing out of the compound and immediately fired, taking the rebel's head clean off. "God, I never get tired of that. They should learn not to poke their heads up. That's the third one."

Stone turned his head as he heard a strange noise from behind. Even though he knew what they were and that they were coming, the sight of the hover tanks was remarkable. The sleek vehicular weapons had been experimental during the reign of the United States. The vehicle had never had the chance to be adopted by the military, but Zodiac's people found the plans and decided to try it out for themselves. The tanks had a pointed, aerodynamic look in the front and widened as it went back. The main turret was in the middle and there were two small turrets in the back. Utilizing a similar anti-gravity drive that the Firehawks used, the tanks hovered three feet off of the ground making most terrain easily navigable. The magnetic drive on the tanks differed from the Firehawks...the vehicle could not fly, but it wasn't meant to.

"Well, look at that," Stone observed. Looking through his rifle's scope, he saw that the lead tank had an unusual passenger on the top. It was Zodiac. Stone looked back at the bunker to see several small objects being tossed up around the entrance pit. Moments later, they burst and released massive amounts of smoke.

The Seekers readied their weapons but did not move. Suddenly, small rockets were launched out of the smoke screen. They did not seem to be aimed directly at individual targets but they went all around, though the highest concentration of them hit to the north. Transports and Hummers were struck and flipped over into flaming wrecks. The Seekers immediately began to fire into the smoke until they were all issued a "Stop" order. It wasn't issued via the comm. in their helmets though...they felt it radiate directly into their brains. It was Zodiac. "Fools, you'll hit each other with stray bullets. We're in a circle. It's time for us to try out these tanks."

The sleek vehicles sped forward and crossed over the mine field. Small openings on the bottoms of the tanks dropped little, round, metallic balls on the ground. After a few seconds, the balls began to burst, detonating all mines nearby. The tanks came plowing through the cloud of smoke. They didn't need to fire any shots; they simply rammed the rebels to death. The maneuverability of these vehicles was uncanny. Despite hovering above the ground, they easily made twists and turns as if they were motorcycles. Above all of the screams of the dying rebels, one could hear the sinister sound of Zodiac's laughter.

Inside, the remaining members of the Kansas cell of Militia 28 readied their weapons. They were already trembling in fear from the Seekers who were directly above their heads. The rumbling of explosive ordinance was not helping to quell the mounting tensions. No one dared speak. Then the noise came. It was metal tearing; the metal of the very ceiling was being opened like cans. Soon, the Seekers began rappelling down from the openings. No one fired at them. They all just stayed under cover. The fear had built up with such a fierce intensity that no one could even move. They were like pigs being led to the slaughter as the raiding Dark Ones began to open fire and gun down everyone they saw. They cut down the suspended bridges and huts, sending them crashing to the hard metal floor of the massive bunker. Screams rang out everywhere and then were silenced by the gunfire that snuffed out their lives.

The entire last stand took about 124 seconds, with no Seeker casualties. The older woman who had conferred with Jack earlier lay on the floor, looking up at two Seekers and their M16 assault rifles. She had taken rounds in both legs and couldn't go anywhere. The Seekers pointed their weapons and were ready to end her life when they heard the sound of "STOP!" From behind them, the woman saw an image that she had not seen since television broadcasts had ended. It was Zodiac.

"I have some questions for the lady, so step back," Zodiac stated.

The woman had tears running down her cheeks but replied, "I…I…I'll never…tell you anything!"

Zodiac cackled, "Foolish woman, you stink of fear. Besides, I don't intend to ask you anything verbally." He reached and placed his hand on her forehead. She immediately went into convulsions as the savage dictator began extracting her memories and tearing her very mind apart. Images and sounds of her life jumbled and swirled all around. She couldn't cry out. She couldn't scream. She felt her very essence being ripped away from her in a violation that exceeded anything that had ever been known before.

"Yes…YES…tell me everything," Zodiac stated out loud as he saw what he was looking for. After drawing all of the information he needed, he threw her limp body to the floor. The woman continued to convulse and shake; she was foaming at the mouth and bleeding from her nose and ears. "Put this disgusting thing out of its misery."

Obediently, one of the Seekers put a bullet through the older woman's forehead. The eyes on the body were still open and looking upward toward the new hole but now the husk lay perfectly still. During the violation, Commander Stone had made his way into the bunker and stood near the dictator. "Lord Zodiac, the Seekers are finishing the sweep of the compound. As per your orders, any rebels found are being immediately executed."

Zodiac nodded. His blank faceplate hid the smile of victory. "I have discovered something most useful. Have you ever heard of Militia 28?"

Stone had a confused look on his face. He wasn't sure if this was some type of test or a genuine question.

"I take it by your silence that the answer is no. That is not a surprise...until a few moments ago, I didn't know of it either," Zodiac explained as he began to pace. "Apparently, it was formed as a result of the 28th Constitutional Amendment that we so feverishly worked to get passed. They have factions all over the country, staying in touch via low tech means, mainly short and long range radio."

"But how could they have remained hidden from us? How could they have dodged the satellites?" asked Stone.

Zodiac stopped, his faceless helmet pointed directly at the confused Commander. "I assume that you are not so young that you know nothing of the Cold War between the United States and the Soviet Union."

"Of...of course I know about it. Two nuclear powers building up a massive arsenal to take each other out. I heard there were some frightening times," Stone acknowledged.

"During the 50's and 60's many thought that nuclear war was inevitable, so they built countless bomb shelters and the government built many underground bunkers. As calm set in over the years and the eventual fall of the Berlin Wall, many shelters were used as foundations for buildings or became mere storage areas. Government compounds were abandoned, like this one. Many shelters and compounds remained functional however, whether they were forgotten about by the foolish politicians or paranoia set in and people decided that they would still be useful. That is where these rats are holed up. That is why our satellites don't spot them. That is why our S&D squads can't find them except when they do something foolish, as in this case. They're all underground," Zodiac was pointing his index finger around the air.

"So we have the locations?" Stone appeared quite anxious.

Zodiac nodded. "We have some, not all. We do however, have the most important. We have the locations of all the founding members of Militia 28, except for one."

Stone stepped forward, his fist in the air. "There may still be another of these cockroaches alive down here."

Zodiac shook his head. "No, this woman was in leadership... those left in here are lackeys and most likely annoyingly ignorant. There is an airfield near here where a dead member of this militia used to run a helicopter flight school. It's called the Sundance Academy. Apparently, this man's offspring are headed there now to get one of the helicopters and fly to the New York location."

"New York is like 1500 or 1600 miles from here. No helicopter will make that, only our Firehawks are capable of such range," Stone stated.

"Of course, but they will cover a significant amount of the distance quite quickly and I assume they will locate some other mode of transportation once they maximize the range of the helicopter that they take," Zodiac responded.

Stone was shaking his fist again. "I will have my squad destroy that airfield, and we can snuff that helicopter right out of the sky."

Zodiac shook his head again. "No. The founding member whose location is a mystery to me is the one in New York. His name is Alan Ryke, and it's quite a surprise that he would be so far from home."

"Do you know him?" inquired Stone.

"I know of him. I had hoped that his actions would free me from the prison I was in, but they did not. He is a former senior detective for the LAPD, and now he has found himself on the other side of the country," Zodiac answered. "I want you to send a small detachment to follow these Sundance siblings. Utilize a Firehawk but make sure that they do not engage the boosters as those will alert our adversaries to their presence and possibly cause them to deviate from their destination. Once the New York branch of Militia 28 is located, report it to Commander Triton in Connecticut. He will dispose of them."

"It will be done immediately," Stone promised.

As the commander left to carry out his orders, Zodiac stood for a moment and reflected. He could hear the pleas and screams of the last few rebels from the Kansas Militia 28 as they were found and subsequently murdered by the Seekers. Finally, utilizing the comm. in his helmet, the dictator demanded to be patched through to General Callous.

"Lord Zodiac," Callous acknowledged.

"What is the status on Jade and Erinyes?" Zodiac asked.

"We were unable to recover their bodies. We have reason to believe that they were both captured. We took appropriate measures and eliminated their access to the Defense Net and re-scrambled all appropriate codes," Callous reported.

Zodiac clenched his fists. "What about locating Vincent Black and Alexis Hera?"

Callous shook his head. "We haven't found them. We have search and destroy squads deployed, but there are a lot of places they could be hiding."

Zodiac began pacing. "No, they're not hiding. They're plotting. Black doesn't hide from anybody and Hera fears nothing."

"Agreed. I hope that I wasn't overstepping my authority, but I had our tech team set the satellite imaging comparison algorithm. It will compare images of areas that have been dormant and relatively unchanged to older images. We'll be able to see if something significant changed, even if it's simply a car that was parked on the street for four months suddenly being gone," Callous said, almost holding his breath.

Zodiac stopped pacing. "You did well. Have them sweep the New York area."

There was a pause on the comm. for a moment, and then the response came, "Lord Zodiac, New York is a large area."

"Focus on the more remote areas...forget the city," Zodiac clarified. "I have discovered some new information that cannot be ignored."

"Of course, it will be done immediately," Callous obeyed.

"Now, what of the world reports?" Zodiac inquired.

"It's as we thought. The middle east region is nothing more

than a radioactive wasteland," Callous answered.

Zodiac was pacing again. "The simple-minded fools destroyed themselves as I always knew they would. Too bad - that kind of hatred could have been harnessed and used for our purposes."

"The former Soviet Republics have virtually decimated themselves through war with each other. China and the southern Asian countries are in complete anarchy," Callous continued.

"Send the Seeker invasion force to Asia. It's time to solidify our hold on that area of the world. There are many valuable resources waiting for us over there," Zodiac directed.

Callous nodded with a sadistic smile. "I've been waiting to give that order. What of the other regions?"

Zodiac held up a hand. "Patience, general. We do not need to be in a rush and stretch our resources thin. I did not conceive of a flawless plan for world domination just to be overthrown by foolishness as Napoleon and Hitler."

"Agreed, Lord Zodiac. I will mobilize the troops immediately," Callous said with great enthusiasm. "In the matter of Commander Jade and Dr. Erinyes, I assume we have an elimination order."

Zodiac did not answer immediately. He had invested time and energy in his commanders. He had specifically sought them out, hand-picking each individual and utilizing their own past and hatred as a tool to win their loyalty. Jade was different though. He had given her extra attention. Her potential had been astonishing. Her past and incredible willpower made her a better candidate than anyone. She had openly and willingly submitted herself to him. She had completely released the inhibitions of her mind and Zodiac had made the extra effort to mold her into what he had hoped to be his eventual right hand and a successor to General Callous. He was not ready to give up on her yet. "For Dr. Erinyes, he is expendable. He is to be captured and questioned if possible; otherwise, dead is fine. Jade may still be useful to us, so she is to be captured and brought to me. I will cleanse her mind of whatever noise and foolishness that they've put into it."

"It shall be done," Callous answered obediently as the communication terminated.

A rustling came from a pile of debris that had been knocked down by the invading Seekers. Zodiac turned and looked to see a man crawling out from underneath the pile. He was severely battered and covered in blood. Zodiac walked closer and stood over him. "Why are you doing this? Why are you killing everyone?" the man asked.

Zodiac reached down with one hand and lifted the man by his throat. "Because I hate all of you. I hate people. I hate all of humanity and everything it stands for. I hate the cold, ignorant world that you all created. I am cleansing this Earth of you and your kind. I WILL WATCH YOU ALL DIE!" With that, Zodiac snapped the man's neck and dropped the lifeless body to the floor.

"Destiny, come on…don't slow down on me now sis," Adrian called out. Destiny was having trouble, being only eight years old, running this far for her life had taken its toll. She had tears streaming down her face, rinsing trails of dirt and grime.

"Shawn," Destiny said softly.

Adrian stopped and waited for her little sister. When the youngest of the Sundance siblings had caught up, Adrian put her hands on the child's shoulders and calmly said, "Listen Destiny. Shawn is dead. One of those bullets the Seekers fired hit him. There's nothing we can do for him now except survive."

Destiny was choked up and was having trouble speaking. "I want…to go…home, Adrian."

Adrian shed a single tear and hugged her sister. "We don't have a home left to go to. Now come on…we have to get to Pa's airfield."

They both began their jog again and Destiny called out, "Hopefully. no one stole the helicopters."

"Don't worry Destiny. Pa was a member of Militia 28. He planned for something like this. I know right where to go," Adrian assured her.

After what seemed like forever, Adrian and Destiny arrived at the abandoned airfield. It was only set up for helicopters, not for planes, so there were no runways. They both stopped for a moment to catch their breath. They could feel the burn of their over-used muscles and the shaking that comes as a package deal with massive surges of adrenalin.

Adrian looked around quickly and said, "Looks pretty much undisturbed. I don't think anyone followed us. Come on, we need to get to Pa's office over there."

Adrian began to jog again and Destiny grunted in protest, but followed. The small building was nothing more than a shack. Some of the sections of window had been replaced by Plexiglas because it was cheaper. There was an old air conditioner hanging out of a hole that had been cut for it in the side of the small structure. There were two hangers, both were closed and locked. She reached into her pocket and grabbed her set of keys. Several of the keys would probably never be used again. She'd only kept the ones to the house and the shed out back, and the ones to her car and to her Pa's car as a way to reminisce about better days. The key she was looking for was easily found. It was the one to the office which was also locked and undisturbed.

"Adrian, the bad guys might be here at any moment," Destiny warned.

Adrian smiled a half smile. "I know. We just need to get into Pa's office and get something, and then we'll be airborne soon after." She unlocked the door and both of them stepped inside.

The office was in shambles, and it had nothing to do with the Flash Storm. Adrian and Destiny's father hadn't been the most organized of people. There were numerous papers scattered on his desk that had no apparent order to them. There were also various soda cans in miscellaneous places with flies buzzing around them. Surprisingly, despite the disarray, the computer sitting on the desk had been modern at the time of the Flash Storm. Without electricity however, it was useless. None of these items were of any interest to Adrian however, only the safe that was behind the desk held anything of value at this point. She walked over and turned the dial using the numbers that her father had shown her. The combination worked the first time and Adrian opened the safe. Inside was a stack of money, which was worth less than the material it was printed on and a set of keys. Adrian ignored the money and grabbed the keys, then grabbed a flashlight out of the desk drawer and tested it. She was relieved to see that the batteries still had power.

"Say your goodbyes, Destiny. We'll probably never see this place again," Adrian stated.

Destiny had more tears running down her face, causing more grime paths. "Are we going to die Adrian? Did Shawn go to heaven?"

Adrian was not ready for this line of questioning. She remembered holding Destiny when she had been a small baby. Both she and Shawn had been excited to have a baby sister, even though the little girl had been a complete surprise to the entire family... especially since their father had had a vasectomy a few years earlier. She was a miracle child, a baby that had to have been given to the family by God. Adrian had always remembered this and decided that she needed to tread carefully. "Destiny, we're not going to die. We have a job to do, a mission from God. Shawn was part of that, however brief. His place in eternal paradise is guaranteed. We must not shed any more tears for him, as the sorrow is ours alone. Our brother is with our parents in heaven." She was impressed with herself for the explanation that she had given. She was doubly impressed that the young girl acknowledged and accepted it and let the subject drop.

Destiny followed Adrian to the hanger closest to the shack. She unlocked the side door and both of them entered. It was dark inside and the only light they had was whatever came in through the open door. Adrian pulled out the flashlight and turned it on. "Stay here, Destiny. I'm going to take a look around," Adrian stated.

Destiny started fidgeting. "Hurry, Adrian. I don't think we should be here much longer."

Adrian put her hand on her younger sister's head. "I know, baby. We'll be out of here soon." She began to walk around the hanger. Most of the helicopters at the flight school were Bell models. She walked around each helicopter quickly, shining her flashlight inside and underneath the helicopters. As she was walking to the last one, she heard a strange noise. She pulled out a small 9mm Glock pistol and had it pointed in front of her along with her flashlight.

"Great, if it's a Seeker, a lot of good this little pea shooter is gonna do," she thought to herself as she stepped closer to the last of the fleet. The human eye catches movement before it catches shapes, but Adrian wasn't thinking about biology at that moment and yelped out loud, firing her gun when she saw something quickly moving. The bullet merely hit one of the supports in the outer wall of the hanger and shattered apart. She moved

303

the flashlight in the direction that she saw the shape go, only to see that it was nothing more than a black and gray cat. She let out a huge sigh.

"Adrian, what's going on? Who's here?" Destiny shouted from the other end of the hanger.

Adrian was closing her eyes and shaking her head, having put her Glock's safety on she tucked it back into her pants. "Nothing, Destiny. I'm just jumpy. It was a cat. Can you see alright to make your way over here?"

"Yeah, my eyes adjusted," Destiny answered as she began to walk over. She did not want to jog…her legs were already sore from their recent retreat.

Adrian walked around the last Helicopter. It was a Bell 230, repainted yellow with red streaks to make it look like sunrays. Her mind wandered a bit, remembering how excited her father was to have gotten it as only a few of them had ever been built. This one had never been used for flying lessons; it had been like their 4th sibling. Because it had been off limits to any of the flyers, he had made some modifications to it. He'd added external fuel tanks to increase the range. Inside, buttons had been installed to drop the tanks in case of damage or other hazardous situations. The problem was that the tanks, when full, added a significant amount of weight to the helicopter so there wasn't much capacity to carry people or cargo. Her father had also tweaked the engines. They were somewhat better on fuel and could keep the craft up with a higher payload than normal, but the modifications were highly illegal and carried risks of overheating and stalling.

"Adrian." Destiny had made it across the hanger and tapped her older sister on the side, causing her to snap out of her trip down memory lane and let out another yelp.

"Destiny, don't sneak up on me like that!" Adrian scolded.

Destiny hung her head. "Sorry."

Adrian smiled and ruffled her younger sister's hair. "It's alright. I guess I'm just on edge, since there's an army of creepy armored soldiers trying to kill us and all."

"Are we taking Sunspot?" Destiny had an actual frightened look on her face.

Adrian chuckled. "I know, Pa always said that if he ever caught any of us in there he'd bring scalping back. I think he'd be okay with us taking it now. It's got more than twice the range of the other helicopters and we have quite a distance to go."

"New York is far away - are we going to make it?" the worried child asked.

Adrian's facial expression turned solemn and she shook her head. "Even with Pa's modifications, it won't make it all of the way. It should get us about two-thirds of the way though. Then I figure we should be able to find abandoned cars and the like around, maybe even another helicopter."

Destiny nodded then both heard a very distinct sound. *Meow!* The cat decided that it was safe to come out and ran over to the young girl, purring and rubbing up against her legs. She squatted down and pet the feline who responded by purring louder. "Adrian, he's all skinny. He's probably starving. We should take him."

Adrian rolled her eyes. "Destiny, we need to get out of here. We can't have a cat running around inside the helicopter. I'm sure there are plenty of field mice out there he can get."

Destiny looked up at her sister, her bright brown eyes giving their puppy dog stare. "But Ma always said all life is precious and we have to look out for everyone."

"Destiny, just get in the helicopter while I go and manually open the main hanger doors," Adrian snapped as she hurried across.

Destiny had a bright smile on her face as she picked the cat up and carried him into Sunspot. The entire hanger began to brighten as the massive doors slid open. It happened much slower than normal as Adrian had to use the hand crank since there was no electricity. After the doors were completely open, Adrian hurried back and climbed into the pilot's seat of the modified Bell 230. She had her helmet on and was firing up the engines by the time she noticed that they had an additional passenger on board. "You listen really well."

The cat was curled up on Destiny's lap, purring away as the young girl stroked his fur. She just looked at her sister and smirked. Adrian shook her head as she lifted off. If their father were alive he would be flipping out at even the remote idea that she was going to fly Sunspot out of the hanger, which was extremely dangerous. Of course, safety precautions were out the window in the current world situation.

Both Adrian and Destiny had a strong feeling of freedom as they took off from the hanger and climbed up to slightly above the tree line. Adrian knew she would have to keep low to avoid any radar that might be around. She kicked up the speed to gain as much ground as fast as possible.

A short distance away, an observer watched as the Yellow and Red streaked Bell 230 Helicopter flew past. It was a Fire-hawk, which engaged its anti-gravity drives and lifted off. Inside, the Seeker pilot reported, "We have them in sight Commander Stone."

"Excellent, time to put these new Firehawks to the test. Activate stealth mode and follow them. Remember, we want to find out where they're going, so do not engage them or be seen," Commander Stone ordered via the comm.

"Understood sir," the monotone Seeker acknowledged. Flipping the stealth switch to the "on" position, the Firehawk engaged a brand new type of camouflage…the light rays that were formerly striking it were now being bent around it, causing the vehicle to appear transparent.

Chapter 34

L exi arrived at her destination undisturbed. Alone in the modified military Hummer, she drove down the main street of the town that she had been given directions to. It appeared to have been completely deserted. The way it had been described, the citizens just upped and left once the Flash Storm hit. "This must be it," Lexi said out loud. She pulled the Hummer up by the small diner as she had been instructed by Vincent and waited. It did not take long to get a response.

Looking in the driver's side mirror, she saw a young, Hispanic woman making her way toward the vehicle. Lexi pulled out her pistol and had it ready. She noticed that the young woman had her hands empty and out in front of her. She stopped, several feet from the Hummer and called out, "Alexis Hera?"

Lexi put her gun back in the holster and opened the door. She exited and stood facing the young woman and responded, "You must be Maria Esperanza. Just call me Lexi."

"We shouldn't stay here," Maria said as she began walking toward Lexi. "Night...I mean Vincent...says that the Seekers use the satellites to spy on us."

Lexi motioned for Maria to get into the Hummer, and then put it in drive. Once Maria was in, Lexi immediately asked, "Where are Vincent and the Deckers?"

"The woman...Eve I think her name is, the pregnant one right?" Maria was verifying.

Lexi nodded.

"She's having trouble with her pregnancy. She and that husband of hers and our only doctor took a generator and left to go to the local clinic, hoping that it hadn't been looted," Maria explained. "Vincent went to some prisoner detention center in Connecticut."

"The place that was formerly Three Rivers Community College. Damn, I hope he's not too late," Lexi stated. "Where's this clinic?"

Maria looked at her. "Don't you want to head to the shelter?"

Lexi shook her head. "Not until I check up on my teammates. Besides, they're exposed and unsafe if they're out in the open."

Maria gave a slight nod of approval. "Good point. Head straight down this road for a few minutes and we'll be out of town. Take your first right, then go straight for a little while."

Lexi put the vehicle in gear and hit the gas. "Do you know what's wrong with Eve?"

"No, I didn't get details," Maria responded.

"So, you knew Vincent before, in Los Angeles?" Lexi brought up.

Maria fidgeted in her seat. She was not wearing her seat belt. She answered, "He saved my brother, Miguel."

"Yeah, he told me. There was some child sex ring or something," Lexi asserted.

"Yeah. My parents didn't have much money so I looked after my little brother," Maria said while looking straight ahead. "I guess I did a piss poor job because he was taken by this group of perverts. Vincent saved him, and then he disappeared."

"How did you end up out here in New York?" Lexi inquired.

"Turn here," Maria pointed. "It's kind of a long story, but the cop that was supposed to bring Vincent in is the one who helped me. I guess he realized that a vigilante who saves a bunch of kids can't be all that bad. You know, you're really pretty. Are you his girlfriend?"

Lexi blushed. "No. I don't think Vincent is one for dating."

"But you're blushing…so you want to be his girlfriend?" Maria asked.

Lexi may have lost her ability to feel fear, but she definitely could feel uncomfortable. "A little blunt aren't we?"

"Just asking. You seem like you'd be his type," Maria continued to be blunt.

Lexi bobbed her head a bit then said, "Subject change time."

Maria held up a hand. "Sorry, I was just curious is all. If it wasn't for him, I'm not sure I'd even be here right now."

Lexi smiled and nodded. "I understand...he's helped a lot of people."

"Turn here, and just head straight. It's gonna be on the right, in a plaza," Maria directed. "I don't remember the name, but it's got a blue sign with white letters and it says something about Medical Clinic or something like that."

After turning, Lexi commented, "I don't like this at all. We're out from under the cover of trees...we're exposed. If there are Seeker patrols that come through here, we might have a problem. How far down is this place?"

"It's about 15 minutes driving fast. Since there's no traffic, just gun it," Maria suggested.

"Can't go too fast. If there are bad potholes or road damage, I don't want to just plow through," Lexi cautioned.

"Good point," Maria replied.

Lexi shot a glance at the backpack Maria had put on the floor when she got in. "By the way, what's in there?"

"A radio that we can use to call the shelter with updates," she answered while adjusting it so she would not kick it with her feet.

Lexi glanced around outside. "Fair enough."

The conversation went silent. Maria's mind trailed off...

Maria Esperanza was standing on the street in downtown Los Angeles. The entire area had been cordoned off by the LAPD. She was carrying her younger brother Miguel, who had just been through a frightening ordeal, more than any 4 year old should ever have to face. The child had been kidnapped, only a week prior, from their apartment in South Central. The culprit was a crime ring that specialized in satisfying pedophiliac desires of the upper class. Maria had given up all hope that anyone would even look for her brother, being from the projects.

She had met a detective, Mike Salaszar, who promised that he had access to a way to save her brother...one that the rest of the LAPD did not. Late that same night, the vigilante Night Viper showed up. She had only heard of him, she had never seen him in person. Now, standing outside of the large building where a massive confrontation between the vigilante and the master-minds of the child sex ring had just exploded into a blood bath, she clutched her brother tightly. "Excuse me," Maria called out to a man who seemed to be in a position of authority. He was wearing plain clothes but had a badge on a chain around his neck and a 9mm Glock holstered on his hip, which was more and more becoming the standard sidearm for the LAPD.

The man motioned for her to go toward the medical personnel that had been setup to check the rescued children. "Take the kid over there. They'll check him out and determine if he needs to go to the E.R. right away."

"He's fine, that's not what I need to talk to you about," Maria replied.

The man's radio buzzed. "It's a damn blood bath up here. No bodies of any of the kids. Looks like Night Viper cleaned house and not one innocent person was injured."

"Is there any sign of the vigilante?" asked the man, who Maria identified as a Lt. Detective, or senior detective according to his badge, which she was now close enough to see.

"None. It's like he's completely disappeared," said the voice.

Maria was fidgeting while holding her brother. "DETECTIVE!"

"WHAT!?" the detective shouted back.

"My brother saw a helicopter hover over the roof," Maria began.

The detective nodded. "I know about that. We're still trying to identify it. The damn thing disappeared. Probably his getaway."

Maria shook her head. "No, he says that Night Viper collapsed on the roof. Four men got out of the helicopter. He said they were wearing some kind of weird body armor."

The detective now seemed interested. "Go on."

"There was a confrontation and they took him on the helicopter against his will. He was kidnapped!" Maria exclaimed.

"Shit," the detective cursed, then pushed the button on his radio. "Dispatch. I just talked to a witness who says that Night Viper was picked up by that mysterious helicopter, against his will. We need to find it."

"We just received word to stand down on the search for the helicopter," dispatch responded.

The detective had an angered look on his face. "Who gave that order?"

"The commissioner," was the answer that came.

The detective stopped for a moment, then pushed the button and replied, "Copy."

"Wh...what did they mean? You have to find him. He saved my brother's life! He saved a bunch of other kids. He was passed out on the roof. I think he's really sick," Maria started ranting.

The detective's look of anger now changed to a completely blank look. "He *is* sick. He has cancer all throughout his body."

The detective's cell phone subsequently rang and he picked it up. "Ryke here."

Maria could only hear one side of the conversation but the more it went on, the more strange facial expressions Ryke made. Finally, he hung up the phone and let out a sigh. "What happened, Detective?"

Ryke shook his head. "They want me to bring you and the kid in."

Maria held her now sleeping brother and moved him away from the detective. "No. You're not taking my brother. Why the hell do they want us? We're the victims!"

"There's something really weird going on for me to get a call like that, especially right after I just called in that helicopter. Listen...I want you to come with me," Detective Ryke requested.

"I'm not going to the station," Maria barked, then started cussing in Spanish.

"Listen, I'm none of those things you just said and we're not going to the station. I'm getting the two of you out of here," Ryke responded.

Maria came out of her daze of the memory of how she met Ryke by a poke to the shoulder.

"Hey, Maria, snap out of it...we're here," Lexi's voice penetrated Maria's mind cloud.

The clinic was almost like a miniature hospital. It was fortunate for the Deckers that the medical facility had not been hit by looters. Within the clinic, Eve was getting restless. "Dammit, I have to take a piss again," she barked as she struggled to stand up, no longer caring about finesse.

Dr. Lancaster switched off the ultrasound machine. "Go

ahead. We'll continue this when you get back."

"Here, Eve," John said as he reached out his arms to help her.

She pushed his hands away. "I can do it myself! I'm pregnant, not crippled."

"Fine!" John snapped.

Eve started waddling then stopped. "Sorry, John. I'm just getting more uncomfortable and the bathrooms here don't have running water."

He held his hand up. "It's fine, don't worry about it."

Eve hobbled out of the room, her discomfort apparent. Dr. Lancaster looked at John. "Her blood pressure is going up. It's significantly higher now than when we first got here."

"What are you saying doctor?" John asked.

"OH MY GOD!"

Both of their hearts almost jumped into their throats. It was Eve's voice. They ran to the bathroom. Eve was sitting on the toilet crying. "What's the matter Eve?" Dr. Lancaster asked.

Eve was beginning to realize what most pregnant women discover...you lose all privacy and modesty, especially toward the end. "I'm bleeding. You know, down there," Eve pointed down.

Dr. Lancaster looked at her. "John, we need to get Eve back to the cot, right now."

"Why, what's going on?" John inquired.

Dr. Lancaster glared at him. "Your wife's having a placental abruption. Basically, the placenta is separating from the uterus wall, which isn't supposed to happen until after the baby's born."

The two men assisted Eve for the short distance back to the room she had been in and laid her on the cot. "What blood type are you two?" asked Dr. Lancaster.

"I'm O positive, she's O negative," John answered.

Dr. Lancaster rolled his eyes. "Couldn't have been the opposite now could it?"

They heard the sound of a door opening and a familiar voice. "Eve, John, are you in here?"

"LEXI!" yelled Eve. They heard rapid footsteps. Soon after, Lexi and Maria appeared at the door. Eve had tears streaming down her cheeks.

Lexi hurried in and knelt down by the cot. "Oh my God, Eve. What's going on?"

"I'm in real trouble, Lexi. The baby's in trouble. Everything that *could* go wrong *is* going wrong. I wish I had your lack of fear right now," Eve was rambling.

Lexi put her hand on Eve's forehead. "Shhhh. Don't say that. Look at everything we've all survived just in the past few days. We're not giving up now. And trust me, you don't want brain cancer."

Maria uttered something in Spanish that no one understood, then asked in English, "What's happening?"

Dr. Lancaster wiped the sweat off of his brow and shut off the generator, which had a makeshift tube sticking out the window for the exhaust. "There are some complications. If we had power and a fully working hospital, we'd be fine. Unfortunately, we don't."

"You're the doctor. Tell me what you need and you'll have it," Lexi stated with a firmness in her voice.

Dr. Lancaster nodded his head. "Can you deliver a miracle?"

"She's burning up. She's got a fever real bad," Lexi said responded.

"I put some bottled water outside to get cold. Do me a favor and grab it, and some wash cloths," the doctor didn't actually direct what he said to any particular person.

Maria nodded her head and left. "What's your blood type... Lexi is it?" Dr. Lancaster asked.

"O negative. Why?" Lexi answered in a perplexed tone.

"I need you here...Eve needs you," Dr. Lancaster stated.

Chapter 35

The former campus of Three Rivers Community College was barely recognizable to anyone who had been a resident of the area. The enormous building that had once served as an educational facility had been sliced, diced and rebuilt into a massive, makeshift detention center. All around the once lovely grounds was barbed wire fencing. Parking lots had been replaced by rudimentary additions with the sole purpose of holding more potential slaves. The cries for help echoed for quite a distance. Josee Santillo was scared. It wasn't because of a Seeker presence... surprisingly enough, there weren't any of the Dark Ones around that could be seen. It was the inactivity of the Grand Army that was nerve-wracking. The facility was on lock-down, but there were no guards, no snipers stationed on the roof, nothing to indicate that there was a Seeker presence at all.

"There's no one here," Carl said to Josee. They were both looking through the mounted scopes on their rifles. "What the hell did they do to that place?"

Josee shook her head. "I don't know Carl. Those bastards turned it into a complete perversion, just like everything else. What scares me right now is the total lack of Seekers or anything else for that matter. Could it be a trap?"

Eric stood in silence next to them. A million thoughts raced through his head, but he did not feel like writing the jumbles down. Carl looked over at Josee. "Give us the word...we'll go in there, get those people out, and get the hell out of here."

"I don't like this. There's no way they would have just abandoned these people," Josee responded.

"Mrs. Santillo! Mrs. Santillo," a young voice yelled out. Josee, Eric, and Carl turned to see a boy, probably no older than 13 or 14 running like a champion athlete toward them.

"What's the matter son? You look like you just saw death himself." Carl commented.

The kid reached them and was panting like a puppy after chasing a stick in extreme heat and humidity. He was wearing a baseball cap that had probably at one time had some type of print or logo on it, but it was too beat up for an observer to tell. The kid had curly, jet black hair that had grown to shoulder length. He wore a torn sweatshirt and jeans with holes ripped into the knees. His sneakers may have been something fancy at one time, but now they were dirty with holes in them. "No, I saw something worse."

"What is it Joey?" Josee asked.

"Some kind of mechanical giant. It's as tall as a city building and it's ripping down everything in its way. I think it's coming here," Joey explained, still huffing.

Josee's eyes nearly bugged out of her head. "Did it have a giant, spinning set of blades in the front?"

Joey nodded his head. He was wheezing. Carl assumed the poor kid had a slight case of asthma.

"Dammit, we've got no time!" Josee stated.

Carl put his hands in the air. "What are you talking about? We've gotta get those people out."

"Have you ever heard of the Apocalypse Dozer?" Josee asked rhetorically. "It's gonna tear through here like locusts in a crop field. We've got to get out of here now or we'll be ripped to shreds."

"How far away...ERIC! WHERE THE HELL ARE YOU GO-ING!?" Carl shouted as he saw Eric take off toward the fence. He started to head after him, but Josee grabbed his arm.

"There's no sense in both of you getting killed. Let's hope he knows what he's doing," Josee stated, then patted Joey on the arm. "Tell them to get the buses ready." Joey took a deep breath and began another run.

"Are you sure going into Providence is a good idea? Wasn't it destroyed in the Flash Storm?" Carl questioned.

Josee nodded. "Yeah, but we can hide in the ruins for now, until we can regroup."

Eric was an extremely fast runner. He didn't remember if he had ever run marathons, been a sprinter, or played any type of sport for that matter, but he knew that his long legs were a huge asset to him. His original plan had been to use his jacket to cover the barbed wire at the top of the fence and climb up and over, like he had seen done in the movies, but before he touched the fence, he had a gut feeling that he shouldn't. Looking to his right, his suspicions were confirmed. The fence was electrified. He could hear the screams of the prisoners getting louder as well as the distinct sound of a large, gas powered generator which was probably supplying the power for this makeshift prison.

Eric couldn't talk, but that didn't mean he couldn't think. He reached into his pocket and took out a grenade that he had taken from the stockpile before they left the Militia 28 compound. He tossed it at the unit supplying power to the area of fence closest to him then ran. There was a three second delay on the grenade. One Mississippi...Two Mississippi...he dove and the explosive triggered, creating a large opening and rendering the closest area of the fence harmless. He readied his rifle and went in.

"Come on Carl, we need to go," Josee was tugging on his arm.

Carl shook his head. "No, I just saw Eric enter the building. We've got to give him more time."

"We'll give him as much time as we can, but the Apocalypse Dozer is on its way," Josee warned.

Carl took one last look through his scope. "Look, there are people coming out of that building. He must be freeing them. They don't appear to be Seekers."

Josee whistled and started circling her finger in the air. Members of Militia 28 popped out of hiding to meet up with and direct the freed prisoners to the entourage of buses waiting to take them away. At first, only a handful of individuals came running from the former community college and out of the fence. Then they began pouring out in droves. The massive mob was actually obeying instructions, and they made their way quickly toward the parked buses that were to take them onto I 395 North until they could get to Route 6 and follow that into Rhode Island, where they would make their way to the ruins of Providence.

Carl stood back and watched in amazement. The rumbling was getting closer and he decided to look through the scope on his rifle. In the distance he could see the metal behemoth making its way toward their location. The massive machine of rotary blades and hydraulics was ripping through buildings, trees, cars, and anything else in its path. "The weight of that thing must be more than a skyscraper. How the hell is it not sinking into the ground?" Carl asked Josee.

Josee shrugged her shoulders. "I have no idea but as far as I know, it's unstoppable. Let's go!"

As the last of the escaping prisoners boarded the former school buses, the drivers put them in gear and began to move out. The rumbling of the Apocalypse Dozer grew ever closer. People were huddled and crowded into the seats and standing in the aisle of each bus. There was silence across all buses except for the occasional wail of a young child. No one dared speak. No one dared do anything but look in front of them and pray. Fear filled their hearts, and not the fear induced by the Seekers. It was a genuine fear of impending doom. It was a fear that had most likely gripped many that were rounded up in the past for a mass genocide. Time slowed to a crawl. Some of the passengers had functioning watches and many were checking the time every few seconds believing that minutes had passed.

Josee and Carl sat in the cab of a beat up but functional pickup truck. Eric had managed to join up with them and was sitting in the back with the mounted .50 caliber machinegun. He kept his eyes fixed behind them, waiting for the bladeless helicopters to spring up at any moment. It was extremely tense. They were staying a distance away from the entourage of buses in case they needed to delay advancing S&D squads. Inside the cab Josee, who was driving, addressed Carl. "They just left all of those people in that building to die. They were gonna grind it and them up like they were wheat."

Carl shook his head. "It's like Zodiac is out to exterminate us all. Does anyone have any idea who or what this guy is?"

Josee shook her head. "No. The things that I've heard are ridiculous, like he's some kind of super alien or demon or something. I think he's a monster alright, but a monster of flesh and blood."

"He wouldn't be the first dictator to perform acts of genocide, and he wouldn't be the first to have conquered most of the known world," Carl pointed out.

"We may never know who he is...huh?" Josee was interrupted by Eric tapping on the glass on the back of the cab. Carl turned to look out the back window. Josee couldn't see anything on her rear view mirror because of the machinegun so she looked in the driver's side mirror.

"Dammit," Carl cursed as he saw that a Seeker S&D squad was approaching from behind them. There were three of the bladeless helicopters as well as several military Hummers that had been repainted black, all carrying Seekers and armed with machineguns.

"Eric, get on the gun," Josee ordered. Then she picked up her C.B. radio to communicate with the buses. "Attention all drivers...we have a Seeker Search & Destroy squad closing in fast on our position. Prepare for evasive maneuvers."

Eric stood up and grabbed onto the machinegun. He pointed it in the direction of the enemy, but they were still too far away to waste ammunition. He only had the belt that was currently loaded and a spare one in the back with him. He didn't want to waste it since this was probably the only weapon they had that could penetrate the Seeker armor with any real reliability. His palms were beginning to sweat. He could feel his heart rate kicking up. It was the normal anxiety of battle, but he knew that soon the Seeker's own fear aura was going to begin to worm its way into his psyche. He decided to close his eyes and take a moment to clear his head. He opened his eyes to see an interesting sight... the bladeless helicopter units had hidden compartments on their sides that had opened. Booster jets extended out and ignited, sending the air assault vehicles rocketing towards them.

"ERIC, SHOOT AT THE BASTARDS!" Carl screamed.

Eric didn't waste any time. He began to open fire with the machinegun. Unfortunately, it was a weapon that was made to be used against a mass of troops. Even though the bladeless helicopters were flying low, they were fast and highly maneuverable. Not a single shot hit. Then he pointed it at the approaching Hummers and began to open fire. Several shots went wild or hit the road but a few managed to strike the enemy vehicle in front. He wasn't sure if he had hit the engine or if he had simply managed to hit the driver, but the Hummer weaved out of control and was struck by one of the trucks behind it, causing it to roll over. The other Hummers in the front began to return fire in his direction. Most of the shots missed but one close call sent a round straight through the tailgate. It passed between Eric's ankles and penetrated the cab. It punched straight through the back of the cab and the back seat. Inside, Josee and Carl were startled by the bullet continuing on to tear a hole in the center console, destroying the CD player. They were fortunate that the bullet did not pass through the firewall and rip into the engine, but it was a close call.

"SHIT THAT WAS CLOSE!" Carl yelled.

Josee simply pointed up ahead. They watched as the blade-less helicopters turned off their booster jets and were prepared to take aim with their hellfire missiles. "They'll be slaughtered," was all Josee could say. Both Carl and Josee were startled again when the booster jet on one of the enemy crafts exploded, causing the thing to spin out of control.

"What the hell was that!?" Carl exclaimed.

"The cavalry." Josee actually cracked a smile.

There were many times that Vincent appreciated solitude, being alone with his thoughts. This was not one of those times. Sitting in the Bronco, barreling down the highway, his mind was drifting back, to the day that changed everything...

The buzz was all over the place. The Millstone Nuclear Power Plant had been hit by terrorists. They weren't Islamic extremists. They were domestic terrorists, American citizens. They were the mysterious and highly dangerous Rebel XCIX or Rebel 99 if you translate the Roman Numerals. This group was public in their goal to undermine and ultimately overthrow the government.

Standing outside were several bystanders, but they were no longer watching the power plant. They were gawking with great awe at a man who had run into the building to rescue two workers. He had entered without any type of protective suit. The man was Vincent Black. Now he was lying on the ground, having been hit with enough radiation to kill an elephant.

319

"My God, he's still breathing," an EMT stated. All of the emergency workers were wearing anti-radiation suits. "Hurry, help me get him into the ambulance!"

Another EMT hurried over with a stretcher. Together, the two hoisted Vincent onto it, and strapped him in to secure him for the trip. He was barely holding on to life, and at the time he was not sure he even wanted to continue. Onlookers were being pushed back by the National Guard troops that had arrived. Vincent was loaded into the ambulance and the driver immediately departed.

Inside the vehicle the emergency workers cut open Vincent's shirt. One of them asked, "What the hell happened to this guy?"

"He went into the plant and pulled out two pinned workers. The radiation leak poisoned him. He probably won't live more than an hour or two," the other responded.

Vincent could not see their faces. He was beginning to lose consciousness. He felt some light slaps on his face which were quite irritating. "Hey, stay with me pal. Stay with me."

"This guy is a damn hero," one of the workers said as he began to place sensors on Vincent's chest to monitor his heart rate, blood pressure, etc.

"Suicidal is more like it," the other worker responded.

Vincent didn't want to hold on anymore. So he didn't. In his mind, he began to let go. He closed his eyes and ignored the slaps and shakes of the EMTs that were trying desperately to keep him awake. He had done what he needed to do. He wanted to be released.

"Shit…shit…his vitals are dropping…we're losing him," Vincent could hear one of them shout, then felt himself leaving his body and floating upward. He could still hear the workers.

"He's gone into cardiac arrest. D-Fib now!"

"Charging, 200 joules. Clear!"

Vincent watched as they shocked his body, attempting to restart his heart, but it was too late. He was leaving. Floating upward he saw what appeared to be a tunnel made of pure light, so he moved toward it. When he entered, he saw the most brilliant and amazing sight. All of his friends and family members who had passed on were there to greet him, but they remained silent, staring at him with straight faces. Only one person, a person he had not known well but he had respected, stood before him as a brilliant angel, with bright white wings and a luminescence all her own.

"Sherry," Vincent said. "I'm ready. I'm ready to go."

She simply raised her finger to her lips and said, "It's not your time, Vincent. You have so much more to do." Then she placed her hand on his chest and gave him a push. He felt the sensation of a free fall. He plummeted, screaming, "NOOOOOOOOOOOOOOOOOOOOOOOOOOOO!" Within moments, he was back in the ambulance.

"Dammit," one of the EMTs said. "I think we've lost him."

Beep!

"No, look, we've got rhythm," the same one pointed out. They both stared at the vitals for a few moments, and noticed that one number was climbing quickly.

"Yeah, we've got rhythm alright. His heart rate's climbing really fast."

Vincent opened his eyes. He was back in his body and looking up at the emergency workers and their large, protective helmets. He felt a surge go through his body like none he had ever felt. It was an adrenalin rush like never before. It almost felt like he had pure energy coursing through his veins. He began to flex his might against the restraints. "GAAAAAAAAAAAAAAAAAAAA AAAAAAAAAAAAAAAAAAA," he yelled.

"Shit, he's at 250 BPM."

"Sir, you need to calm yourself."

"GAAAAAAAAAAAAAAAAAAAAAAAAAAAAAAAAAAAAA," Vincent responded, his eyes turning completely bloodshot.

"Hold him. I'm gonna sedate him."

"300 BPM…that's impossible…his heart should explode."

"Dammit, hold him still!"

"I can't. He's got so much adrenaline going through his system, and he's breaking the restraints."

Vincent felt the ambulance slowing down. He continued to fight the restraints. He could feel the metal on the stretcher bending.

"350 BPM…he's gonna have a damn aneurism!"

"I can't hold him. We need to get back. He's gonna break through and he's not listening to reason."

"RAAAAAAAAAAAAAAAAAAAAAAAAAAAAAAAAAAAAAAA,"

Vincent yelled, twisting the stretcher and breaking the restraints. Without missing a beat, he stood up and kicked the back door of the ambulance, busting the lock and causing the doors to swing open. Traffic had stopped behind the ambulance and the former dead man leapt from the emergency vehicle, landed on the hood of the car behind it, ran up to the roof, and jumped off, disappearing into the night.

With that memory, Vincent snapped back into reality, dodging around a wrecked sedan in the middle of the road. "Is this what you had in mind Sherry when you told me it wasn't my time? Did you know this was going to happen?" Vincent asked out loud. "I don't even know if I'm fit to do this. I never was a leader."

Vincent sat in silence for a moment. "Not like I expect you to send me an answer or anything. I don't know. If any of you out there are listening, just tell me what I'm supposed to do."

Vincent got his answer. The light show off in the distance was unmistakable. Vincent was heading south, but he was traveling on what had been the northbound lane on Interstate 395. He was headed right for some type of confrontation. He slammed on the gas to head into the fray.

"Alright, I guess I asked for this," Vincent said out loud. As he drew closer he saw that there was an entourage of school buses being chased by a Seeker S&D squad. Vincent looked over at the passenger seat. Part of the weapons cache that Militia 28 in New York had had was a Milkor Multiple Grenade Launcher. It was a handy weapon that they had stashed far before the Flash Storm. Currently loaded into it were 6 HEAT rounds. The device normally would have been braced on the user's shoulder and held with two hands, but there was nothing normal about Vincent. His strength alone could handle the recoil of the weapon. He reached over and grabbed it.

Pulling into the shoulder so as to avoid the oncoming buses, he continued forward. He saw that the bladeless helicopters were taking up position to aim their hellfire missiles at the buses. Vincent was surprised to also see that they had booster jets that had extended from hidden compartments. "Perfect…no matter what those things use for fuel, they've got to have something liquid and flammable in there if they have booster jets," he said out loud. He took aim. The Milkor wasn't really an anti-aircraft weapon. For

Vincent, everything moved in slow motion, so what felt like a half second to a normal person was more than enough time to take aim for the former vigilante. He fired a HEAT round at the a booster jet on one of the craft. It was a direct hit, and sure enough, there was something in there that caught fire and exploded. A burst came from the side of the bladeless helicopter, causing it to spin out of control.

Vincent did not bother watching where the crippled enemy vehicle went. The buses all began to slam on their brakes to stop. He knew that the fear aura of the Seekers was quickly draining the logic and reason from the drivers. He needed to act quickly or these people would be sitting ducks. He could hear machine-gun fire approaching and knew that these three aircraft were not alone. He took aim and fired at another of the bladeless helicopters, striking the main body and causing it to rock back and forth as both remaining craft were withdrawing their booster rockets. He fired one more time at the same craft and put another gaping hole in the main body. It unleashed a hellfire missile but as a result of the assault, the missile went wild and hit a tree on the side of the road, turning it and the trees around it into flaming splinters. He fired a third round at it, striking another spot on the body and inflicting another gaping hole. This time, the systems inside must have failed, because it dropped like a ton of bricks to the ground below with a loud *thud*.

Another hellfire missile was launched, this time from the only remaining bladeless helicopter that was aloft. The missile flew and struck one of the buses, causing it to explode and roll over onto its side. Vincent jumped out of the Bronco and fired the last two HEAT rounds in his six shooter grenade launcher. One hit the main body, the other hit the tail, causing it to break off. Sparks flew from the damaged aircraft as it began to make a wobbling retreat.

The former vigilante began to run toward the buses, motioning to the bus drivers to start moving again. One by one, despite how frightened they were, they began to put the large vehicles in gear and move out. Vincent began to load standard, high explosive rounds into the Milkor as the buses passed by him. He saw that there was a lone pickup truck that had been bringing up the rear at quite a distance and was still mobile. He also noticed that it was being fired at. There were several black painted military Hummers in pursuit. Each Hummer had a top mounted machinegun and the three in front had Seeker gunmen arming the turrets. Due to the motion of the vehicles, the bullets were horribly inaccurate, but all it would really take was one well-placed shot to end these people. Vincent stood in the path of the truck and awaited its approach.

"What the hell?" Carl cried out at the site of a man dressed in all black standing directly in their path. The man was holding a grenade launcher.

"That's got to be Vincent, the one they sent from New York. He must have taken out those Seeker aircraft," Josee pointed out. She honked the horn on the truck. "Get out of the way."

The man stood, calculating. At the precise moment that he needed to, he leapt straight into the air. When he came down, he landed in the bed of the pickup truck. Eric looked at him in horror to which he responded, "Keep firing at those bastards." Then he yelled through the open cab window, "My name is Vincent. Ryke sent me. Keep your foot on that gas pedal and don't let up."

Josee nodded, not sure what to say at the sight she just witnessed. Eric continued to fire at the oncoming Hummers. The bullets weren't really doing much in the way of damage, since most of the rounds missed, but it was keeping the Seekers from firing back as they kept taking cover. Eric was trying to conserve ammunition as much as he could, only firing a few rounds at a time, rather than massive bursts. The current belt was almost out of ammunition.

Vincent looked at Eric. "Keep laying down cover fire."

Eric silently obeyed.

Vincent took aim once again and sent a high explosive grenade round directly through the windshield of one of the Hummers. It exploded, causing the vehicle to lift slightly from the ground. The Hummer directly behind it crashed into the wreckage. Then he fired at the next one in front and the round hit near the passenger side tire, causing the entire vehicle to roll over. Then he fired a third round that struck toward the top of the only remaining Hummer that had a Seeker arming the turret. The top exploded, killing the Seeker and causing the vehicle to lose control for a moment. Vincent fired another round that destroyed the already damaged enemy truck. The two remaining Hummers broke off the attack by slowing down and pulling off to the side of the road.

Eric stopped firing…more because the current belt was empty than anything else. He was still staring behind them. Josee slowed the truck down and pulled it over to the side of the road. She put the vehicle in park and got out, as did Carl. Vincent leapt from the back of the truck and landed on the ground. "What the hell are you stopping for?"

Josee and Carl were staring at Vincent in complete awe. Carl spoke up. "What you did is impossible. You just took out an entire S&D squad in seconds. How did you move so fast? How did you jump like that?"

"No time to explain now. I've said this before and I'll say it again…I'm what happens when the government plays around with forces that it should be leaving alone." Vincent felt like changing the wording on his explanation so that he wouldn't have broken record syndrome. "Look, I don't know whose idea it was to use bright yellow buses as escape vehicles, but there's a good chance that there's satellite coverage right over our heads and they know where those people are going. Do you have any way to get in touch with the drivers?"

"Y…Yeah. R…radio in the front." Josee was actually stuttering.

"Good. Get on the horn. Tell those guys to break formation and head in as many different directions as possible. Then they can circle around and head back to the original destination," Vincent directed.

Carl looked puzzled. "Why? Isn't there safety in numbers?"

Vincent shook his head. "I'll explain later…tell them now. You need to trust me."

Josee hesitated a moment, then said, "Well, if you wanted us dead, you're obviously more than able to do that yourself, so here goes." She climbed into the cab again. Out of the corner of her eye, she saw Eric climbing out of the bed of the truck. She picked up the radio and pressed the button. "Attention everyone. Break formation, condition red." Then she got out and was face to face with Vincent again.

"Alright...we had something like this as a backup plan anyway, but why did we need to implement it?" Carl asked.

Vincent looked him in the eye. "Chances are they only had one satellite trained on the area if they had any at all. That means they can only follow one target."

Josee scowled in concern. "And how will we know which one they'll follow?"

"Because another S&D squad will go after them," Vincent answered bluntly.

Carl had a flush of anger fill his face. "You mean you've led a group to the slaughter!?"

Vincent shook his head. "The next S&D squad will be three times the size of this one and they would wipe you all out. Besides, there's a good chance that if they do have a satellite watching us, they've already made me. I'm sure they'd rather come after me than your people so they'll all be safe if I head in a different direction. I'm going to go back and get my Bronco."

"What about us?" asked Carl.

"Get back in your truck and head out of here. Follow the plan that you put together," Vincent replied as he broke into a run to hurry back to the Bronco.

Eric, Josee, and Carl just stood, staring at each other. Finally, Josee silently climbed into the truck and put it into gear. Carl hopped back into the passenger side and Eric climbed into the bed. Carl looked over at Josee. "Why aren't we going anywhere?"

Josee shook her head. "I don't know. The shifter's moving, but it's not going into gear. It's not coming out of park." She started to hit the wheel with her fists.

"DAMMIT!" Carl yelled. "Eric, take the tools and dismount that machinegun. This thing isn't going anywhere. We'll take the weapon with us since it actually might be helpful."

Carl and Josee got out and Carl climbed into the bed of the truck to help Eric, who already had the toolbox opened and was beginning to remove the high powered weapon. It only took a few minutes and as they were unloading the weapon to carry along with the last belt of ammunition, they saw a vehicle approaching. Josee pulled out her pistol, not that she expected it to be very effective. Carl continued to hold onto the gun and Eric the belt of ammunition. They were all relieved to see that the vehicle was a

Ford Bronco.

The truck pulled up alongside them and the passenger window opened. "What's the problem?"

"We took a direct hit from one of the Seeker's machineguns in the fight; it must have killed the tranny or something. We can't get it out of park," Carl answered.

Vincent motioned with his hand. "Get in, and you might as well bring that .50 caliber too. We might be able to use it."

Chapter 36

Josh sat in front of the terminal, shaking his head. "Nothing. There's no one in here by the name of Triton, and there's nothing in here about any computer code for the Seeker chips," he complained.

Talbot had entered only moments before. Andromeda was with him...she couldn't sleep. "Relax Josh. Why don't you take a break from that screen before your brain turns to shit," Talbot responded.

Josh didn't argue. He spun around in the chair, leaned back, put his hands behind his head, and stretched his neck while letting out a long sigh. "Yeah, I've only been able to catch quick naps here and there. Did you talk to that crackpot scientist?"

"Yeah, he insists he won't help unless we give him an assistant who isn't technical," Talbot replied. "I volunteered, but he doesn't trust me."

"Well, he won't take me and we need to get him working on a device to counteract the Seeker fear aura. I haven't heard from anyone in awhile and I'm getting worried," Josh commented.

"Ahem," Andromeda spoke up.

Talbot and Josh looked over at her. "What is it, Drom?" asked Talbot.

She threw her arms in the air and her eyes opened wide. "Hello...how about me? The most technical knowledge I have is downloading songs onto an iPod. I'll chill in that lab with him."

"Uh uh," Talbot insisted.

"Why not?" Josh inquired. "We need him to cooperate sooner

rather than later and we don't really have any other options."

"We'll just have to figure one out then, because I'm not leaving Drom alone with that monster...I don't care what Vincent or anyone else says!" Talbot demanded.

Josh shook his head. "Talbot, stop being a stubborn ass. Our people are out there, possibly getting in way over their heads. Andromeda is a soldier like we are. Like it or not, we can't keep hiding her because she's a kid. She's been through more than a lot of adults anyway, or have you forgotten that the Hartford rebel cell had armed her?"

"Come on, let me do this. I want to feel useful for once," Andromeda piped up.

Talbot shook his head and cursed under his breath. "Fine. Let's go talk to Dr. Erinyes. I want to be very clear about what will happen to him should there even be a suspicion of harm to Andromeda."

The girl smiled. She finally felt as if she was doing something other than drawing pictures and hiding out in an underground bunker. She jumped up and gave Talbot a hug, then exited the control room. Talbot and Josh immediately hurried after her. "Hey, wait up!" Josh called out.

The three made their way to the detention center where their guests were. As Talbot disengaged the lock on Dr. Erinyes's door, Josh stared at Jade's door. "Hey, space cadet! Let us out of here when we're done," Talbot said in a gruff voice, then entered the cell with Andromeda.

Dr. Erinyes was lying on his cot, staring at the ceiling. Talbot addressed him, "Alright, we'll give you your assistant. This is Andromeda. She's an artist, doesn't really have any technical know-how, not to mention the fact that she's a kid."

"Will she follow instructions?" Dr. Erinyes asked without even looking at them.

"Yes, I will," Andromeda answered.

Dr. Erinyes slowly sat up and faced the two rebels, "You must do everything that I ask without question."

"Within reason, Doctor. No putting her in harm's way or expecting her to help you out of here. If I so much as suspect that you're up to something or that you may do something to her, you're going to wish I killed you," Talbot threatened.

Dr. Erinyes smiled and shook his head. "Please, your barbaric threats merely show that you are a complete Neanderthal."

"You miserable bastard," Talbot shouted. "I should just kill you right now!"

Andromeda held up her hand to her angry teammate, and he calmed himself. She said nothing...she just stared at Dr. Erinyes.

"I have told you repeatedly that I have no interest in escape. I am safer here than anywhere in the world and I will not jeopardize that. As for the child, I will not harm her in any way, I can assure you," the scientist stated. "I do not see that you have any more time to waste."

"Freshen up. We'll be back in 20 minutes to get you and bring you to the lab. You'll be under constant surveillance, so keep that in mind," Talbot warned.

Ignoring him, Dr. Erinyes looked at Andromeda and smiled. "I look forward to working with you, dear. Trust me...I may be older, but I believe that you will find our work quite amazing."

Andromeda smiled back and bowed her head without saying anything. She did not feel threatened by Dr. Erinyes at all, and it wasn't just the cast on his hand from his broken fingers. They heard the door disengage and Josh opened it, letting them both out. Talbot gave the scientist a dirty look before he left.

In the hallway Josh spoke up, "Let me talk to Jade."

Talbot shook his head vigorously. "Out of the question, Josh."

"Look, she was part of Zodiac's operation. She can shed more light on things," Josh pointed out.

"Or she can screw with your head, and I do mean both of them," Talbot responded slyly.

"Real damn funny, Talbot. I'm serious," Josh insisted.

"Yeah, so am I. Look, Josh...it's for your own good. Stay away from her. Let Vincent do his thing," Talbot demanded.

Josh scoffed. "Vincent will just beat it out of her, then probably kill her."

"And does she deserve anything less?" Talbot asked.

Ring! Ring!

"Saved by the bell," Josh said as he answered the SAT phone. "I hope this is pizza delivery."

"You're a damn comedian," Vincent's voice came through.

"Vincent, ever so chipper." Josh was in a strange mood.

"What the hell has gotten into you?" Vincent asked. "Listen, Jade's tip was right...they planned on killing the rest of the prisoners. They sent the Apocalypse Dozer and flattened Norwich. Fortunately, we got everyone out in time."

"Thank God. The dozer came through though?" Josh was verifying.

"Yeah. Listen, we hit a problem. A Seeker S&D squad showed up. We knocked 'em back, but we really need that scientist to build his device," Vincent stated.

Josh was pacing around the hallway. "He's agreed to do it as long as Andromeda is his 'helper'. Talbot read him the riot act, but Drom says she's up to it."

There was silence for a moment. "I hate to say it, but if that's what it takes, we need that damn thing. These people don't stand a chance against the Seekers when they're overloaded with fear."

Josh was waiving his free arm around. "I agree. Don't worry... we'll keep a close eye."

"I know, Josh. Did you find out anything about Triton or maybe a way to crack the code on the Seeker Chips?" Vincent inquired.

Josh shook his head as if Vincent was there. "No. There's nothing. Must not be his birth name. There's nothing in there on the Seekers either."

"You think you can handle questioning Jade without getting sweet on her?" Vincent asked bluntly.

Josh had a horrified look on his face even though he wasn't in front of Vincent at the moment. "What the hell is that supposed to mean?"

"It means that she's the enemy and she needs to be treated as such. Listen, if I talk to her, she's going to feel a lot of pain. We'll probably get more out of her if you talk to her, since apparently you've formed a bit of a bond. Just don't lose sight of what's at stake here," Vincent warned.

Josh found himself excited but exerted extreme effort to mask it. "I won't, Vincent. I just think that deep down inside she wants to help us. I don't think she's evil. I think Zodiac used his mind mojo and twisted her."

"That's very possible, but she was still tainted inside so tread

331

with caution," Vincent continued with his warning. "Actually, while you're at it, see if she knows anything about any weaknesses on the Apocalypse Dozer."

"I will, Vincent," Josh assured.

"Have you heard from Lexi or the Deckers at all?" Vincent changed the subject.

Josh shook his head again, but of course body language was worthless on the phone. "No, I haven't. I was actually getting a little worried. Maybe the next call should be to them."

"Yeah, let me know if you find out anything from Jade," Vincent requested.

"Our time is about up. I'll call you as soon as I have something to report," Josh assured.

"Good. Vincent out," the former vigilante replied as he hung up the phone.

"What the hell was that about?" Talbot asked.

Josh put the phone back in his pocket. "They rescued those people at the detention center, thanks to Jade's tip. He wants me to talk to her again."

Talbot shook his head. "Great. Just remember that she's the enemy. She's not even a foot soldier, she's a damn commander."

"I know. Vincent already warned me. I'll be fine, just let me out of there when I'm done," Josh requested.

"We're not going anywhere. We've got to wait for the crackpot so have at it." Talbot waived his hand toward the cell.

Josh ran his cardkey and unlocked the door. He opened it slightly. "Jade, alright if I come in?"

"Why the hell is he asking?" Talbot whispered to Andromeda who did not answer.

"Josh? Yes, um, come in," Jade's voice echoed out through the thin opening.

Josh pushed the door open enough to squeeze in, and then let it shut behind him. He saw that Jade was lying on top of the blankets on her cot, staring at the ceiling. She was still wearing the sweat shorts and oversized T-Shirt. Without turning her head, she asked, "Were you able to stop those people from getting killed?"

Josh nodded. "Yes...thanks to your tip, they got there just in time."

"Good," Jade responded. She visibly had the beginnings of

tears welling up in her eyes.

"Alright, I just need to say this. Were you under some kind of mind control or something? I mean, you obviously have remorse for what you did," Josh asked directly, still standing by the door.

Jade sat up on the cot and looked at him. "No, there was no mind control. The things I did, I did willingly, and I deserve to die a thousand torturous deaths for them."

Josh walked closer and sat in the same old, beat up chair that he had before. It creaked when he put his weight on it. "Then why did you do it? I don't believe for a moment that you're the murdering psychopath everyone makes you out to be."

The tears began to stream down her face. "I am that murdering psychopath. I allowed my anger from the years of humiliation to get the best of me and I allowed Zodiac to use it and me, but in the end the decision to give in was mine. Josh, it felt good to have power. When I watched as people feared me, I felt indestructible. It was intoxicating."

"Look at what happened to you though...he brainwashed you," Josh insisted.

Jade shook her head. "No, he didn't brainwash me. The night I met Zodiac, he'd had his Seekers round up those guys that raped me."

Josh was visibly agitated. "This was before the Flash Storm?"

Jade nodded. "Yeah, the Seekers were around for awhile. He had them ready to go after he pulled the trigger on the world. He had kidnapped these guys and told me that I could take my revenge without fear of being caught. He told me to let go and release. I did, and it felt great. I brutally murdered all five of them. Revenge felt so right. It finally felt as though justice had come."

"Jade," was all Josh could say.

More tears came down her cheeks as she made direct eye contact with Josh. "You really are a hero, trying your best to see the good in someone like me, but please, I'm not worth it. I did these things, I deserve to be punished and I will accept whatever is dealt to me. No matter what happened, it was no excuse. I murdered innocent people. I had others turned into mindless slaves. I had a hand in nearly destroying the entire world. There is no forgiveness for that, no redemption."

Josh stood up, "Bullshit! The fact that we're even having this conversation tells me that there's someone in there worth saving. I'm going to do it whether you like it or not and if you don't want me to, well, you'd better just kill me. Otherwise, you're going to have to deal with someone having faith in you."

Jade began crying…she couldn't hold back anymore. After a minute or two, she finally spoke up. "Why are you doing this? Why are you trying to save me?"

"I already answered that, remember," Josh pointed out.

Jade nodded. "I believe you said, 'It is his capacity for self-improvement and self-redemption which most distinguishes man from the mere brute.' Be careful Josh, there are plenty of truly sadistic people out there who do not seek redemption."

"And those are the ones that will fall," Josh replied.

Jade wiped the remainder of the tears from her face. "I know you came in here to ask me questions. I know I told you that I wouldn't give up anything, but…well…just ask."

"I can't find any information on Triton," Josh stated. "You've probably figured out that I hacked into the Defense Net."

"You won't. Triton isn't his real name. His name is Nicholas Trident. He thinks he's smart. The symbol of a Trident is the planet Neptune's symbol and Triton is one of the moons, the one that orbits in the opposite direction of the planet's spin. He loved to boast about how clever he was. Josh, he's not like me or Mullen. He's a sociopath. He always has been," Jade warned.

"That's why we have Vincent. He can deal with the sociopaths. I'm just the computer geek," Josh assured. "There's something else. Norwich was flattened by that big Apocalypse Dozer. They got everyone out, but that thing has caused a lot of damage."

Jade hesitated for a moment.

"Jade, how do we take that thing out?" Josh asked point blank.

Jade looked down at the floor, then back at Josh. "It's pretty much unstoppable unless you have a flash bomb or a Nuke. It's heavily armored, has several weapon systems, and has a nuclear core for power so it can effectively continue on for years."

Josh shook his head. "Everything has a weakness. How the hell with all of its weight does it not sink into the ground?"

"You've probably figured out that the Firehawks use an anti-gravity propulsion system. I don't know too much about the physics of it. I just know they fly without using jets or anything like that. The BFT-5000 uses a similar technology. Not to fly though, but to actually make it lighter without changing its mass. Again, I don't know exactly how it works. I just know that it weighs a lot less than it looks because of that. The only weaknesses in the armor are where it opens for the various weapon turrets, which of course will rip anyone who gets close to them to shreds," Jade explained. "This thing was meant to be unstoppable."

"BFT-5000? That's the real name of it?" Josh asked.

Jade let out a nervous giggle. "Yeah, whoever named it an Apocalypse Dozer anyway? It's not even a bulldozer."

"I don't know. Vincent mentioned it when we saw it in Hartford," Josh stated.

Jade's face dropped, the tears came back. "You...you were in Hartford when..."

"What?" asked Josh.

Jade shook her head. "I'm sorry Josh. I'm so sorry."

Josh moved the chair closer and sat back down. "Listen, you're making up for what you did already by giving me answers. Because of you, Vincent was able to save hundreds, no, thousands of lives. Stop beating yourself up."

"Not so sure I can or should do that," Jade replied.

They both heard the click of the door lock disengaging. The door opened and Talbot called into the room. "Hey, Josh. Hurry the hell up in there - we've got work to do." The door then shut and re-locked.

Josh shook his head. "Listen, I've got to go. Just one more thing though...do you know anything about the Seeker implants?"

Jade shook her head again. "Other than being advanced nano-computers, not really. Dr. Erinyes knows far more than I do."

Josh shrugged his shoulders. "Alright. Well, I'm gonna get out of here now. I've been trying to figure out how to get into the satellite feeds. I think Vincent's being followed by one."

Jade looked at him, but remained silent.

Josh looked back at her and said, "What is it?"

"No, nothing, never mind," Jade was fidgeting.

"Jade, what is it?" Josh asked again.

"I can get you into the satellite feeds. I just need to be in front of the terminal," Jade stated.

Josh hesitated.

"It's alright. I know there's no reason for you to trust me and that if you let me out of here, you're taking a big risk of me running," Jade acknowledged.

Josh stood up. "It's not you running that I'm worried about. Wait here a minute, let me talk to Talbot."

Jade nodded. Josh pounded on the door and Talbot unlocked it again. In the hallway, with the door closed, Talbot, Josh and Andromeda stood. "So, you find out anything good with your flirting...I mean interrogation?" Talbot asked.

"I want to bring Jade to the control room. She can help me get into the satellite feeds," Josh said point blank.

"Oh, you want to take her to the control room. Maybe dinner and a movie afterward, a little wining and dining and then she can stick a knife in your chest? What the hell is wrong with you? I don't think you should talk to her again, never mind take her up to the control room," Talbot barked.

Josh threw his arms in the air. "She's not gonna do anything. Besides, she knows the system. She's already given us critical information. She told me how to find information on Triton and she told me how the Apocalypse Dozer works. Well, BFT-5000."

"Oh, I'm sorry. So now she's totally trustworthy. Gee, maybe we should just give her a master key to the entire place," Talbot said sarcastically.

"I think we should let her go with Josh," Andromeda spoke up.

Talbot and Josh both stopped, mouths still agape, ready to make their next argument until they were both caught off guard. Josh spoke up. "Andromeda?"

"We already locked her armor away. You two are armed and she's not. Just keep her minimally clad like she is now so we know she's not hiding anything. It's not like she'll freeze to death. Lexi walks around this place wearing less," Andromeda explained.

"That's because Lexi is crazy," Josh replied. The three of them let out a slight chuckle. Josh looked at Talbot and said, "Well?"

Talbot bit his lower lip, then rubbed his temples. "Fine, but I'm going to talk to her alone first."

"Just, go easy on her," Josh requested.

Talbot didn't answer, just ran his cardkey and entered Jade's cell, allowing the door to close behind him. He did not like this. He had to leave Dr. Erinyes alone with Andromeda and now he would need to depend upon Josh to be a proper escort for Jade. This was a dangerous situation but he knew they needed the information their two prisoners had in their heads. "Listen up, sweetheart. Josh is a good guy. The problem with guys like that is that they're bleeding hearts and they get taken advantage of real easy. I'll make sure that the violation you suffered in high school pales in comparison to what will happen to you if he is harmed in any way, physically or mentally. Are we understood?"

Jade stood up. "After everything I've done, you should probably do that anyway once you have no more use for me. I deserve it. I would like to request that you kill me because I really don't want to go through that again, but the reality is...I don't deserve any mercy."

That was not the response that Talbot was expecting. It actually made him feel better about releasing her, but far worse about what he had just said. "Well...um...come with me then," Talbot responded nervously as he pounded on the door and Josh unlocked it from the other side.

"Thank you. I know Josh is a good guy. You don't have to worry; I don't think I could harm him if I wanted to. He's the only person on this planet who doesn't see me as the monster that I am," the former Grand Army Commander stated.

Both Jade and Talbot went into the hallway. "Josh, take her with you, but keep your sidearm in reach at all times. After you're out of sight, I'll get the crackpot out. I don't want him to see that both of them are no longer in cells."

Josh nodded. He and Jade walked away. Once they were out of sight, Talbot looked at Andromeda questioningly. Her response was a nod and Talbot unlocked the other occupied cell. "Dr. Erinyes, are you ready?"

"Yes, of course," he replied and stepped into the hallway. He looked at Andromeda. "I do sincerely look forward to working with you and being in a lab again."

"Alright, let's do this. We need that device built and working," Talbot demanded.

Dr. Erinyes nodded. "You will have it."

Chapter 37

Buffalo, New York had once been a well known city in up-state New York. It hadn't been quite as massive or loaded with majestic skyscrapers as New York City, but it'd had its own qualities nonetheless. Of course, that had been prior to the Flash Storm. This city was one of the many that had had a flash bomb detonate within its borders. Adrian and Destiny Sundance had an aerial view of what remained. They were approaching in Sunspot, their modified helicopter. They had already dumped the external fuel tanks after they had emptied. Now, the primary fuel tank was almost empty. They had to land, and they had to find a place fast.

"Adrian, there's rubble everywhere…how are we going to find a place to land?" Destiny asked, observing the toppled buildings and wrecked cars that littered the entire area.

Adrian was shaking her head. "I don't know. Jesus, this is un-believable." Despite having lived in the post Flash Storm world for the past five months, Adrian had yet to see one of the devas-tated cities up close. She knew about what had happened, but witnessing it firsthand was a far different experience than just imagining it.

Destiny had a tear in her left eye. "It's horrible. All those peo-ple. They had no idea, did they?"

"No Destiny, they didn't. No one had any idea. They just lit off those bombs in everyone's face," Adrian commented as she visually scanned the area for a spot to bring the helicopter down safely. She finally found a spot, a patch of road that was not littered with debris. She turned and began piloting the helicopter toward the spot.

Destiny was looking out through the side window. "Adrian, look - there was an explosion over there!"

Adrian's eyes opened wide. "WHAT!?" When she looked over, she saw another one. The explosions were in the distance a bit but nonetheless, they knew they had a problem. It was a Seeker S&D squad. They must have found freeloaders hiding in the ruins and were flushing them out.

Destiny glanced at Adrian with an intense look of fear on her face. "What are we going to do, Adrian?"

The older sister began to descend the helicopter to the landing spot. The fuel light was flashing and an alert was sounding so she knew she was stuck with this location. They would have to stay clear of the Seekers while they searched for a vehicle of some kind. "Grab the map over there and our two packs. Once I land this thing, we're going to make a run for it."

"Fr...from them?" Destiny's face practically dropped to the floor.

"Just get that stuff now!" Adrian barked.

Destiny unclipped her safety belt and grabbed the map and supply packs. Adrian carefully set the helicopter down on the clear patch of road that she had found. She immediately unclipped her safety belt and both she and her little sister immediately jumped out of the helicopter and ran to a close by pile of rubble that was once some type of restored older building, possibly a church judging by the smashed dome with the bent cross on it. They hid themselves amongst the large chunks of debris and Adrian began to look around.

"I'm scared Adrian!" Destiny cried out.

Adrian gave the young girl a hug but was still scoping out the area. "Shhhh. It's gonna be alright. We're getting out of here. Look over there, across the street. It looks like that used to be some kind of fenced in parking lot but most of the fence blew down. Maybe there's a car that's still usable over there."

"It's so open though, the Seekers will see us," Destiny worried.

Adrian put her hands on her younger sister's face and looked into her eyes. "Listen to me, Destiny. They're still a ways off but the noises are coming closer. We have to move now or they'll find us. Be strong for me...we've had enough death in our family."

Destiny nodded. "Okay Adrian, okay."

They both stood up. Adrian took Destiny's hand in hers and they began to sprint across the street. They dodged around debris from the destroyed buildings and burnt out shells of cars. Destiny tripped over something and fell, scraping her elbow. She cried out in pain.

"Destiny!" Adrian shouted. She helped her sister up then let out a yelp when she saw what the girl had tripped over. It was a scorched human skull, probably a person who caught the blast of the flash bomb that destroyed the city. She looked around and saw the remnants of a SUV that was flipped over on its roof. There were four skeletons inside, also scorched along with the interior and exterior.

"Oh God, Adrian!" Destiny had an extreme look of shock on her face.

"Don't look at them baby," Adrian responded. She was trying not to notice all of the human remains that were scattered around. The place was a complete atrocity zone. She pulled on her little sister's arm and the two kept going. They made it into the parking lot, or what was left of it. Hurrying through, they both looked around for something that might be usable transportation.

Destiny pointed to something. "Over there!"

Adrian looked in the direction that her sister was pointing and saw a miracle. It may have been in the form of a Toyota Corolla from the late 80's with several dings and scratches and the rear windows shattered, but all it needed to do was function. They hurried over to it and Adrian did a quick inspection. The tires seemed intact and, all in all, it was a good find. Upon getting closer though, a very unpleasant odor arose. "Ugh, what's that smell?" Adrian asked.

Destiny moved closer and looked inside. In the back seat, she saw the picked clean skeletal remains of a person lying down. It had its skeletal hand on something on its chest area. Destiny couldn't speak. She opened the door and reached in. When she moved the hand, she saw what it was. A shard of glass had pierced this person's chest. Whoever it was must have wandered into the back of this car for cover and bled to death. There was dried blood all over the back seat. "I guess this is the smell," Destiny uttered.

Kaboom!

There was a mortar detonation not too far away. "Get in the front seat, Destiny. We have to get out of here," Adrian barked. She climbed into the front seat. Of course, there were no keys so she pulled out her pack and removed a flathead screwdriver. Using it, she pried the steering column open to expose the wires. When she tried to hotwire the car, there was not even a spark.

"You know how to hotwire a car?" Destiny inquired.

Adrian nodded her head. "Remember Ted, that guy that Dad hated? He taught me. There's no power in this car, the battery must be dead." To make sure, she popped the hood and got out.

"Where're you going?" Destiny asked.

"I'm gonna check under the hood so stay in the car," Adrian commanded.

Kaboom!

Another mortar exploded. They were getting closer and closer. Time was running out. Adrian looked under the hood and saw that one of the clamps had popped off the battery terminal. She slid it back on and tightened it, hoping that there was still power left. Slamming the hood shut, she hurried back to the driver's seat and began fiddling with the wires hanging out of the steering column.

Kaboom!

They both witnessed a person who had been only moments before standing on top of a pile of rubble go flying in pieces in multiple directions. "Come on dammit, come on!" Adrian ranted, sparks flying from the wires as she touched the ends together.

Destiny was grasping onto the handle on the door. She looked out of the window and saw the cat that she had picked up back in Kansas running toward the car. "Kitty!" she called out.

Adrian sparked the wires one more time and the motor lit up. "Thank God," Adrian called out.

"Wait, you have to wait for the kitty," Destiny pleaded.

Adrian put it in gear. "We can't wait! We have to get out of here!"

The cat hurried toward the shattered window of the back seat. "One more second Adrian," Destiny begged. The cat leaped into the back of the car, landing on the skeleton and causing the skull to snap off and fall to the floor in the back. Adrian hit the gas and the little Corolla peeled out.

Kaboom!

The detonations were getting closer and closer. They could see the bladeless helicopters now. The sleek aircraft were unleashing their hellfire missiles and unloading their chain guns on fleeing people below. It was a slaughter. The refugees were trying to fight back but their attacks were completely ineffective. "Look at that map. Where do we need to go?" Adrian asked.

Destiny was unfolding the map and looking at it. Her hands were shaking and she was fumbling around with it. "Are there even any roads left around here to take?"

"DESTINY, HURRY UP, I'M TRYING TO HEAD AWAY FROM THE SEEKERS!" Adrian barked.

"I'm hurrying Adrian, I'm hurrying," Destiny was almost in tears again. She found where she thought they were on the map; it was difficult since there were no visible road signs.

Adrian was dodging around various debris and obstacles in their path. It was slowing her down but she did not want to attempt to smash through any of it in the small car that they had managed to find. "I know, just hurry, find me a route out of here," Adrian stated.

After a few moments, Destiny had a look on her face as if a light bulb had gone off. "Go straight then turn up there. Follow it and you should be able to get onto the highway. We can follow it for awhile then split off about half way."

Adrian smiled. "Not bad for a kid. Are there any major cities on that route?"

Destiny followed the road on the map with her finger. "We'll go through Sy…Sy…ra."

"Syracuse?" Adrian filled in.

Destiny nodded. "Yeah, what you said. Was it destroyed?"

Adrian shook her head. "I have no idea, but it was a major city. Hopefully the highway is clear enough that we can cross through it."

"It says we'll be going through Adirondack Park Preserve," Destiny stated.

"Good, should be a lot of trees that can give us some additional cover. How many miles? Use the key at the bottom of the map." Adrian stated as she swerved to avoid hitting the smashed up remains of a car.

Destiny used her thumb and index finger to match the distance on the scale, then ran it in sections along the roadway. "I don't know. Maybe 400 miles."

"Shit. We've got about three quarters of a tank but we're gonna have to pick up another car or find a spot to fill this one. There's no way we're going 400 miles with what we have," Adrian complained.

"It's okay, Adrian. We'll figure it out." Destiny was newly optimistic.

Adrian turned onto the interstate. The sign had fallen onto its side and had a giant hole in it where the highway number had once been, but it didn't matter. It was completely clear. Looking in the rear view mirrors, she didn't notice anyone following them. "Yes we will. I think the danger's passed for now. Let's just sit back and relax for a bit."

"Sir, we're still in pursuit of the targets," the Seeker pilot reported.

"I assume that you have remained out of sight," Commander Stone stated.

"Yes sir, and we have visual," the monotone soldier replied. "Subjects are in an ash colored Toyota Corolla, late 80's model."

"Keep following them and continue to update me with your progress," Stone ordered.

"Yes sir," the Seeker acknowledged.

The stealth capability of the experimental Firehawk aircraft was working as planned. With the craft's ability to bend light, it was almost impossible to see, especially while it and the observers were moving. It silently continued to follow the Sundance sisters on the way to their destination.

Chapter 38

Vincent was engulfed in his own memories once again. The silence in the Bronco was stirring up his highly active mind. He was remembering more about his escape from Project Scorpion...

Night Viper was on foot, hurrying through the vast wooded area around the compound that he had only recently escaped from. With the havoc he had wrought, he was unsure if he would be pursued. It seemed surreal. He took bullets from their guns, yet he had no injuries. He had felt the shots land...he had blood on him...but there were no wounds. What had they done to him? It occurred to him that either he was moving extremely fast, or everything else was moving extremely slow. It didn't matter. He didn't even know where he was.

After a period of time that could have been seconds, minutes, or even hours (he had no idea), he came across a road. It was out in the open, but he wasn't thinking clearly. He just needed to get his bearings. He wasn't going to get that chance. A military Hummer was headed straight toward him, so he ducked back into the woods. The vehicle pulled over and four men got out. They were wearing black military fatigues, were armed with rifles and were shouting to each other, but he couldn't figure out what they were saying. He looked around then looked up. There were some thick branches above him. He squatted down then put power behind a leap. He jumped higher than he should have been able to, far higher than any person should ever have been able to. It was high enough to grab onto the thick branch and climb up further. Night

344

Viper watched the men coming down the embankment from the road.

"He went this way!" one of them called out to the others.

"Remember, shoot on sight. This guy took out a lot of our people," another one said.

"I heard that they shot him repeatedly and he just healed up from it. His body just spit the bullets out," the third one said.

"Let's see him do that with a grenade up his ass," the first one threatened.

Night Viper still had no idea what was going on, but he figured that he might get some answers from one of his pursuers. If nothing else, their words revealed their hostility and he wasn't about to take chances. When they were just beneath his position, he jumped from the tree and landed on one, feet first. The collision snapped the soldier's neck, killing him instantly. Before any of the other three even realized what had happened, the vigilante turned super soldier had them all on the ground and hurting. He grabbed their weapons and tossed them aside, keeping one rifle for himself. "Get over there, all three of you," Night Viper ordered.

The three looked at him with intense fear written on their faces. They struggled to their feet, never taking their eyes off him, but they still kept their hands up. It took longer than he wanted, but the three soldiers did as he asked. "I want answers. Who the hell are you and what did you do to me?" Night Viper asked.

The three men remained silent. The vigilante shot the first man through the head, dropping his corpse by the feet of the other two. "Oh shit!" one of them cried out.

Night Viper continued to point the commandeered firearm at them. "This has been a real shitty day for me. I'm not in the mood to screw around. If you won't give me the answers that I want, I'll just kill you and get them somewhere else."

"We don't know anything, they don't tell us sh…"

Night Viper ended him with a bullet through the mouth which tore out the back of his head. "Are you gonna waste my damn time or are you gonna be smart and survive this ordeal?"

"Oh God, don't kill me. I'll tell you what I know!" the soldier pleaded.

The vigilante continued to point his weapon at the man and

nodded. "Smart. Now talk or I send you to join your friends."

"You were part of a super soldier experiment, trying to en-hance people to make better soldiers. I don't know what they did or how they did it. I know that there's been this kind of experi-mentation done for awhile," the soldier stated.

"Keep going," Night Viper demanded while motioning with the gun.

"Look, the place you just busted out of is Project Scorpion. There were six others that they did the same procedure on, all of them died. You're the only survivor, and you're the only success," the soldier continued.

"Why me?" Night Viper asked.

The soldier shook his head. "I don't know the details. I'm not a damn scientist!"

Night Viper shot his left hand off with the rifle, causing the man to cry out. "I'm not in the mood to play games!"

"Ugh...son of a bitch...they picked you, specifically. One of my friends...was on the team that retrieved you from Los Ange-les," the soldier stated.

"Where am I now?" the vigilante asked.

"You're...in upstate New York," the soldier answered.

Night Viper took a step closer. "Why me? I had cancer all throughout my body. I was dying. How did that make me a can-didate?"

The soldier shook his head again. "I don't know. My buddy said something about them being more interested in your will-power, said your body would recover fine. Maybe it has to do with this healing power that you have. Please, I don't know any-thing else."

Night Viper looked at him, and then looked around. "How do I get out of here?"

"If you follow that road there, it will lead you to Interstate 87. You can follow that to wherever you want," the soldier said.

"Good, you're coming too. We're taking that Hummer of yours. You're going to disable the tracking device that I'm sure is in there, and then I'll let you out a few miles down the road," the vigilante stated. "I might even let you patch up that stump of yours."

"Vincent, snap out of it," Josee was nudging him.

Vincent was back in the here and now, behind the wheel of the Bronco. "Sorry about that," Vincent stated. "Guess I drifted a bit."

"When was the last time you slept," asked Josee.

Vincent was watching the road. "A few days ago. Don't worry; I can go a long time without sleep."

"A few days is a long time," Carl replied.

"Damn these roads, takes forever to get anywhere," Vincent thought out loud.

"Huh?" Josee inquired.

Vincent shook his head. "Nothing. I'm just impatient. That scientist we nabbed. . . he said that there was something big going on in New London, but he didn't say what."

Carl had a horrified look on his face. "I know what it is."

"You do?" Vincent was verifying.

Carl nodded. "Yeah. Listen, I'm the one who led the assault on the Backus hospital before you got there, the one that failed. When I got away, I followed I-95. I can't even begin to describe to you what I saw when I reached the New London area. Miles and miles of property had been cleared and flattened. It looked as if it was the largest construction site in the history of this world."

"Any idea what they were building?" Vincent was still watching the road.

Carl shook his head. "Not a damn clue. After I saw that I turned and hid out for awhile. When I came back toward Backus, that's when you assaulted it. I met up with Eric and we grabbed a car. When we got to Thompson, we saw a whole bunch of trucks transporting what appeared to be junk and pieces of buildings and wrecked cars and stuff. We got chased by one of those bladeless helicopters...we barely escaped. That's when we met up with Militia 28."

Vincent scratched his chin. "395 and 95 must be major supply routes for them. What you saw was fuel for the plasma beam power plant that they built. It heats garbage and things up to 10,000 degrees, causing them to break down to their base elements. The metals fall away and can be recycled. The energy released is used to generate electricity. It's based on an experimental design that was being tested in Florida before the Flash Storm."

"Maybe they have more than one of these places," Josee

pointed out.

"It would make sense," Vincent replied. "They would need processing plants for the metals so they could turn them into usable alloys and materials to build whatever it is they're building. Do your people know what they're doing?"

Josee batted her eyebrows. "What do you mean?"

"Are they going to be able to take care of themselves?" Vincent clarified.

Josee nodded. "Yeah, of course. They're gonna hide out in the ruins of Providence and the Rhode Island branch of Militia 28 is going to get them organized."

"Good, then the three of you are coming with me to New York, to the underground compound we commandeered. It's time we get Militia 28 fully involved in what we're planning," Vincent stated.

"And what are you planning?" asked Carl.

Vincent made eye contact with him in the rear view mirror. "A rebellion."

Ring! Ring!

Vincent grabbed the SAT phone and answered, "Vincent here."

"Vince, its Lexi," the reply came. "We have a problem."

"Of course, that's how every single one of these conversations starts," Vincent thought, then asked out loud, "What's going on?"

There was a pause for a moment. "Its Eve. She's having a lot of complications. Dr. Lancaster thinks the baby might need to come early."

Vincent fidgeted in his seat. "A C-Section?"

"Yeah, probably. He's got her on a pitocin drip He's trying to induce natural labor but he also has to keep her on magnesium sulfate because she has preeclampsia and deathly high blood pressure. I guess a side effect of magnesium sulfate is that it stops labor," Lexi explained.

"Where the hell did you guys get this stuff? Did you find an abandoned hospital or something?" Vincent had a confused look on his face.

"Something like that...it's a clinic, but they have the stuff to do this. It was abandoned and hadn't been looted, thank God,"

Lexi replied.

Vincent sighed. "If she needs a C-Section, she may need a blood transfusion right? It's not like the blood bank is still open."

"John isn't a match to her blood type, but I am. We're set up for a transfusion if she needs it. Maria came with me to help out," Lexi clarified.

Vincent couldn't hide his concern. "How are John and Eve doing?"

"They're both passed out right now. Dr. Lancaster is resting up too, so I'm watching Eve. I'm glad I don't feel fear right now, because I'd probably be as scared as Maria looks," Lexi commented.

"Alright, listen. I'm with three people from the Connecticut Militia 28. We were able to save the people who were in that detention center near Backus. They're regrouping, but it's time we bring them in on what we're doing. I'm bringing them to the compound," Vincent explained.

"We're really going through with this, aren't we?" Lexi inquired.

Vincent nodded, not that Lexi could see him. "Yes, we are. Zodiac's goons are running rampant and now we've learned that they're building something massive in what used to be New London. We can't sit around and wait anymore. Hang in there, Lexi."

"I will, Vince. Oh, and thanks," Lexi responded.

"Thanks for what," Vincent said while dodging a pothole in the road.

"Thanks for taking me with you when we escaped from Southern. It seems like it was so long ago but it's only been a few days." Lexi was getting sentimental.

"Yeah, it shows how much can happen in just a short amount of time. I'm glad you showed up on that motorcycle. In the meantime watch over the Deckers and Maria..." The phone cut off as it reached the time limit.

"What happened?" Josee had a look of concern. "And where did you get that phone?"

"One of my people hacked into the Defense Net. He was able to create a few SAT phones but they have a talk limit of 4 minutes and 55 seconds before they cut you off. It takes 20 minutes to reset the algorithm to continue to keep the communication hidden," Vincent explained. "That was a report on one of our people. She's pregnant and is having complications; she's still a month from her due date."

"Oh man," Carl said. "Do you have a doctor or something?"

"The New York branch does. He's looking after her now," Vincent replied.

"Hey, how about you tell me where we're going and let me drive for awhile. You really should at least try to sleep a little," Josee suggested.

Vincent shook his head. "I'm fine."

"If you're looking to start a ruckus with Zodiac, you need to make sure you're 100%. Now you saved our lives so at least let me do this for you," Josee demanded. "Not like we're gonna take advantage of someone who can stand up to the Seekers like you do."

Vincent thought about it for a moment. He was not getting any danger vibes so he said, "Look, I don't know exactly what they did to me when they took me, but I'm fine. I've gone for over a week without sleep before."

Josee looked straight at Vincent. "Who did this to you?"

Vincent continued to watch the road and dodged another pothole. "As far as I can tell, the U.S. government in some clandestine experiment. The compound which they used is the one that we took over. It was abandoned. The lab that they used to do whatever they did was destroyed, but the rest of the place is fully operational. That's where we're heading now."

Josee leaned back in her seat and tipped her head back. "Oh God. Their corruption knows no bounds."

Vincent shook his head. "No, it doesn't. But that doesn't matter now. They're all dead and the U.S. government is gone. Judging by the information we've gathered, the military was targeted during the Flash Storm also. As far as we know, other than a few scattered personnel, every vestige of the federal government was wiped out by Zodiac. He knew exactly where and how to hit the country, the world even."

"Jesus," was all Josee could utter.

"Do your people have access to the satellite feeds, since they hacked into the defense net?" Carl inquired.

Vincent shook his head. "Not the last I knew, but they're figuring more stuff out all the time. We're getting an avalanche of information since we nabbed one of their scientists and one of their commanders."

Eric started feverishly motioning with his hands. Carl looked at him. "Eric, you really need to learn sign language. Of course, in order for that to be effective, we would need to also."

"Josee, check the glove compartment...see if there's any paper," Vincent directed.

Josee opened it and pulled out a memo pad. It was beat up and missing half of its pages but it was a pad. There was also a pen from some strip club in the city that was probably blown to bits at that point. She handed it back to Eric who scribbled so fast, his words were barely legible. Carl read the note. "Is it the commander from the Backus Hospital?"

Vincent nodded. "Yeah, why?"

Eric scribbled some more, "Just wondering."

"Seems a little more important than just wondering. Yeah, she's in our detention center. Don't worry, it's not like she can get out or anything. The complex is underground and we took her armor," Vincent assured.

Eric nodded and then put his head back. Vincent continued full speed ahead to the compound that at one time housed Project Scorpion.

Chapter 39

Jade sat at her terminal, pounding away at the keyboard in the control center of Project Scorpion. She looked over at Josh who had succumbed to his fatigue and fallen asleep at his own terminal only ten minutes before. She stared at him for a few moments. Despite the fact that she was hardly dressed appropriately for the season, she felt warmth for the first time in years from the dedication he had shown her. She could do what they feared. She could alert Zodiac with the equipment she now had access to. She could take Josh out; make sure that he couldn't stop her. Something strange had happened to Commander Jade, however. The only thought she gave this choice was the thought of not wanting to do it. Josh Tyler, computer geek, had given her something that she never thought she would receive: the chance at redemption. She would not give that up, no matter what. She wheeled her chair over to him and stroked his hair. "Sleep Josh, sleep. I will take care of everything. You have given me a gift that is beyond human means to place a value on, I will not squander it."

Josh stirred a bit but continued to snooze. He even had a bit of drool coming out, but Jade thought it was kind of cute. "Zodiac, you turned me into a monster and for that, I will be an instrument of your downfall. You used me like you use everyone and everything else and you will pay dearly," Jade mumbled out loud. She heard the door open behind her. It was Talbot.

"Before you accuse me of anything, Josh is fine. He's not a soldier, he's a computer nerd. Computer nerds can only stay up ridiculous hours as long as they have a steady supply of caffeine.

The next time you try to find supplies, I suggest you find him some or he won't be able to function," Jade commented.

Talbot held up his hands. "I didn't come here to fight with you, Jade. I came here to apologize. I marginalized what happened to you and I was out of line. You helped us save lives, and that's evidence enough that for whatever reason, you're on our side."

Jade continued to look at the screen. "You don't need to apologize to me. The atrocities I have committed are unforgivable and I will be judged accordingly, as I should."

Talbot shook his head. "No. That young man asleep there has the utmost faith that you're not the enemy anymore. He and I have been through a lot and that should have been good enough for me."

Jade spun around in her chair. "I will never hurt Josh, especially after he reached out to me as no one has ever done. In time, you'll realize that. In the meantime, you're at war and I am an enemy combatant. I will do what I told Josh I would do and help out with this computer system. Maybe one day I'll earn your leader's trust."

"I don't know if you'd ever earn his trust. Hell, he'd probably beat me within an inch of my life if he knew you were in here, accessing the computer with no observation and no shackles. He's a good man, Vincent. He…well…he went through a lot and it hardened him more than any man should ever have to be hardened," Talbot explained.

Jade looked at the floor, and then looked back at Talbot. "Then he and I may have more in common than either of us thought. Listen Talbot, I patched us through to the satellite feeds. There are a lot more of those things in space than anyone ever thought, but I know the ones they task on this area. I'm going to set up a program to monitor them. I just need to know what I'm looking for."

Talbot sighed "Alright, Jade. Chances are the site of the detention center was monitored by satellite. Knowing Vincent, he would have had the prisoners divide up and head in different directions and re-converge on their rendezvous. Are there any satellites in the Norwich area?"

"Yes, they were watching the area and you were also right about them dividing up. Vincent is a wanted man by Zodiac. He gave him and Alexis Hera priority for capture," Jade revealed.

Talbot shook his head rapidly and looked at her. "Lexi? Why Lexi?"

"He's intrigued by her inability to feel fear, even the fear generated by the Seekers. He realizes that she poses a particular danger because of that fact. I figure he wants Vincent because of him being a super soldier and having those enhancements," Jade explained.

Talbot walked over to the terminal and looked over Jade's shoulder. "Vincent barely knows anything about why he is the way he is. He was a diehard vigilante in Los Angeles whose body was riddled with cancer prior to being taken and experimented on. He doesn't remember much about what the government did to him."

Jade was furiously pounding away at the computer. "It looks like he's found a way to dodge the satellites. They've lost him. They're probably scrambling to figure out how to find him as we speak."

"Listen, Jade. I don't know how Vincent is going to react when he sees you here," Talbot admitted.

"You want to put me in shackles again?" Jade asked.

Talbot shook his head. "No, you do too much good here. I'm just saying that I'm not sure how he's going to handle seeing you walking around free like this."

Jade scratched her nose nervously. "So, you no longer see me as the threat you once did?"

Talbot had a half smile. "No. After thinking about our last conversation I realized that for whatever reason, you really do regret what you did. I can't say that I'll ever trust you completely or that I would ever vote you as citizen of the year, but I think you've proven that you're at least attempting to redeem yourself. Besides, Josh is sound asleep and doesn't have his throat cut... that should count for something."

Jade nodded. "That's fair enough, although I'm not sure there is redemption for someone like me. Josh seems to believe that no one is beyond redemption."

"Josh sometimes has his head in the clouds, but maybe he's right," Talbot acknowledged.

Jade went silent for a moment, then spun around and began

typing on the terminal again. "There's something else. Josh told me that he managed to set up a few SAT phones. He said that after 5 minutes, the network sniffers would pick up the trail and the Grand Army would realize what was happening."

"Yeah, he set the calls to automatically terminate after 4 minutes and 55 seconds. He said something about it taking 20 minutes to reset the algorithm or something like that. I don't know what the hell he's saying half the time," Talbot replied.

"Basically, the program he wrote uses a special method to hide the signal. When a call is ended, the program has to reset itself and load all sorts of variables and encryptions. Now since the Flash Storm, there are very few places left with power that Zodiac doesn't control, so the cell towers that survived are sitting there dormant, but the old Satellites are still working fine. When we wanted to re-establish world communication for deployment of the Seekers, we started using those satellites in conjunction with the defense network. I should be able to set it so that you guys can have longer conversations and not have to wait 20 minutes after each call," Jade explained.

Talbot looked impressed. "Geeze, no wonder you two get along. You both speak the same language and confuse the shit out of me. If you can do it, go for it. Maybe we can get some more phones programmed. In the meantime, I'm going to check on Dr. Erinyes and make sure he's not doing anything to Andromeda."

"You have nothing to worry about. That man cares about self-preservation. He won't do anything to risk that," Jade said as she continued on the computer. "He's kind of a weasel but he's probably one of the most knowledgeable people in the world."

"Fair enough, but I'm still gonna check," Talbot said as he left the room.

Jade looked over at Josh again. She thought he might want to see what she had done, but decided that he needed to sleep. "Hopefully your boss doesn't put a bullet in me when he gets back," she uttered out loud. She went back to looking at the screen. That's all she did was look. She was tired, actually exhausted was more like it. Everything was beginning to blur and soon her mind lost focus on the here and now and began to drift back to the time before the Flash Storm...

The location was deep in the New Mexico desert. It was remote, extremely hot, and flat enough to see someone coming from miles away. Similar to other installations that were to be kept a secret, this one was mostly underground. The surface buildings were typically hangers and other structures that looked shabby from the outside. As a matter of fact, to the casual observer, it looked like an old, abandoned air field. It was far from abandoned, however. This base was being funded by the United States Government, without their knowledge. Such occurrences were not unheard of in the time before the Flash Storm. They tended to be located in remote places that were difficult to get to and were typically the sites of clandestine experiments like the Project Scorpion complex or sites of prototype testing. This particular site was called "The Farm". It housed the original location for the creation of the Seekers, as well as the manufacture of top secret military hardware that had been nothing but prototypes previously.

Jade stood and watched in what she would later find out was called the War Room. She was alone and filled with curiosity. She walked over to the far wall where there was a map of the world displayed on the large LCD screen. Across the map were various symbols that she did not recognize. She ran her fingers across one and discovered that the screen was touch sensitive. An image popped up with Andrews Air Force Base. She hesitated for a moment, then heard the sound of the door to the room opening.

"Magnificent, is it not?" Zodiac boasted as he entered the room.

Jade whipped her head around as if she was a child who had been caught by her parents raiding the cookie jar. "I hope I didn't mess anything up."

Zodiac merely chuckled with amusement. "No child, you did not." He began to walk toward the screen.

Jade stepped aside and said, "What does all of this mean?"

The armored man stepped up to the screen and opened his arms to it as if he were going to give it a hug. "This is my master plan. This is the ultimate layout for the foundation of the new world order, Jade. It's what I want you to be a part of."

Jade was confused and did not bother to hide it. "All I see is a bunch of symbols on a map."

Zodiac crossed his arms, still looking at the screen. "Of course, let me enlighten you. All of these symbols are major cities across the globe. Capital cities, both state and federal, famous metropolises, tourist sites, etc, all outlined here."

Jade merely nodded. "Okay, there's a lot of them."

"Yes there are." Zodiac lifted his finger and pointed to another symbol "...and these are military installations, some on the books, some off."

"What's the purpose of this map and this place for that matter?" Jade asked.

Zodiac turned and faced his new recruit. "We call this facility 'The Farm'. Here we prepare for the implementation of my plan."

Jade moved her hand around in a circular pattern. "And that would be?"

"To cleanse this world in the fires of the Apocalypse and rebuild it in my image," Zodiac answered.

"Fires of the Apocalypse? Are you starting a Nuclear War?" the new recruit inquired.

Zodiac shook his head. "No, although I'm sure there will be a certain level of nuclear exchange. This place is here for the creation of my new army, the Grand Army. We will use technologies that this world has never seen. We will strike a blow that will shatter the very fabric of modern world civilization in one moment."

Jade gasped as the sudden realization came to her. "You're going to destroy all of the major cities and military bases at once!"

"Bravo," Zodiac said as he slowly clapped his hands.

"But how? If you nuke that much, the whole world will be poisoned with deadly radiation," Jade warned.

"That is the magic of this whole operation. Nuclear devices would be picked up by satellite. We wouldn't be able to even have a fraction of them in place before we would be discovered. Come, walk with me." Zodiac motioned with his hands.

The two left the room and began to walk down the hallway. Jade continued the conversation. "If it isn't a bunch of nukes, then what are you using?"

"There is a new type of device, one which can cause the level of destruction that nuclear weapons do; only there is no fallout. They're called flash bombs. We are able to manufacture them here," Zodiac explained as they approached the elevator doors.

The armored man pushed a button and the doors opened.

"Then who's planting these things? How many people are working with you?" Jade interrogated as they entered the elevator and Zodiac pressed an unlabelled button.

The future dictator was amused. "You ask many questions. Here are your answers."

The elevator doors opened and Jade stepped out, followed by Zodiac. Nothing could have prepared her for what she saw. It was a giant factory, only it wasn't processing pre-packaged foods or assembling vehicles. It was processing people. Thousands were in various stages of whatever process was happening. The young woman was in complete awe. "What is all of this? Who are these people?"

"These are the soldiers of the future! They are called the Seekers. We take our subjects and lobotomize them. We then insert a chip into their brains to replace their frontal lobe functions with our own programming. They are our agents. They are the ones who will do as we command without question or hesitation," Zodiac proudly enlightened her.

Jade whipped her head around and looked at her reflection in Zodiac's face plate. "We?"

"Yes Jade, WE," he responded. "I want you to join me as one of my commanders. You will have a legion of Seekers to follow your every command. They will never betray you. They will never fail you."

Jade snapped out of her drifting and found herself back in the Project Scorpion complex. The tears began to run down her cheeks at the unpleasant reminder of what she had helped plan and implement. She wondered again if there was truly redemption for her.

Dr. Erinyes and Andromeda were in the lab where the Deckers had analyzed the Seeker chip. "I do have to say my dear, that I am quite glad to be in a lab that wasn't built makeshift into what used to be a hospital," the scientist stated.

Andromeda remained quiet and awaited her next instruction. Dr. Erinyes had the image of the Seeker chip displayed on the 3-D projector. "Yes, this shouldn't be a problem to create an opposing vibration that will cancel out the fear reaction. The problem is getting enough power to counteract the chips of a full battalion of Seekers. We simply do not have the supplies to create implants for an army of rebels. They will need to broadcast it somehow," Dr. Erinyes was thinking out loud as he did quite constantly. "What would we have access to that would vibrate at a high decibel?"

Andromeda grew tired of the only sound being the scientist's voice so she walked over to a radio that had been set up in the lab and turned it on. The unit had a 5 CD changer, 4 speakers, a center channel, and a subwoofer. It was obviously capable of much more powerful sound than needed. Before she could hit play on the CD controls, Dr. Erinyes spoke up, "Oh my dear, you are a genius!"

Andromeda turned and looked at him. She didn't think it took a genius to operate a sound system.

"The sub-woofer on that system is what we need. Okay, maybe not that particular one as we could use some music down here, but we could find a powerful subwoofer that I could modify." Dr. Erinyes became quite excited. "The problem is finding an appropriate delivery apparatus."

"A car," Andromeda responded.

The scientist looked at the young girl with pride. "I truly have chosen an excellent partner. Yes, young people used to have contests on who could hit the highest decibel rating on a car stereo. The systems were so powerful that they would shatter glass and move solid objects. We could modify a vehicle with a powerful system that will counteract an army of Seekers. My dear, have you had your IQ tested?"

Andromeda just shook her head.

"You do not speak much, probably why you are so intelligent. After all, many people just talk to hear themselves speak, although I have been accused of that myself on occasion," Dr. Erinyes snickered.

The door to the lab opened and Talbot walked in. He saw Andromeda sitting on a stool by the counter where the radio was, fiddling with the temperamental play button. Dr. Erinyes was already scratching notes onto a pad of legal sized lined paper, which was amusing since there were sophisticated computers in the room. "So, any progress?" Talbot asked.

"Our little friend here is amazing. She has completely solved the dilemma of delivery of the anti-fear signal," the scientist stated without looking up from his notes.

"Okay, what's the solution?" Talbot questioned.

Dr. Erinyes looked up and held the pad up for Talbot to see. "We need a vehicle. It needs to be rugged, maybe even military grade. The windows need to be superior to commercial or they'll shatter. As is, we may need to brace them."

Talbot smiled. "Would a military Hummer with bulletproof glass be good enough?"

"That would be perfect my good man, that would be perfect. Do you have one handy?" the scientist asked.

Talbot nodded. "Yeah. It's already armored so it'll protect whatever it is you're building into it."

"I would very much like to see it and take some measurements. Then I can determine power needs, wattage for amplifiers, amount of wire, things of that nature," Dr. Erinyes explained.

"Of course you can see it, but I'm not sure where we're going to find all of that stuff you want...it's not like we can just hop online and order it," Talbot pointed out.

"We should look in a store that carried car stereo stuff. I doubt anyone raided it since anyone with a functioning car probably doesn't want to draw attention to themselves with a loud stereo system," Andromeda suggested.

Dr. Erinyes had a cheery look on his face. "As I said before, this young one is an absolute genius."

"I can raise Vincent on the SAT phone. He's on his way back here, maybe he can find something on his way up. We just need to give him a 'shopping list'," Talbot said making quotation marks with his fingers. "That guy is resourceful as anything and has a way of finding whatever it is that we need."

"Then we should waste no time. Once I have the measurements and the materials, I can assemble your device," Dr. Erinyes assured.

Talbot nodded. "Then let's get moving."

Chapter 40

"Lexi, why don't you get some sleep?" Maria suggested. "You've been awake for hours." They were still at the clinic and Lexi was keeping a careful watch for any Seeker S&D squads. The Dark Ones weren't all that inconspicuous with their bright lights.

Lexi looked over at the Deckers. John was sleeping like a rock; Eve was stirring and moving more in her sleep than she did while awake. Dr. Lancaster was getting some rest; he wanted to make sure he was in top shape in case he had to perform a C-Section in less than optimal conditions. "It's okay Maria, you guys should rest up."

"Lexi, we've all rested…you're the only one that hasn't. You need to be on top of your game too, especially if Dr. Lancaster needs you to give blood," Maria commented.

Lexi didn't need much convincing. She felt as if she could sleep for a whole week, nonstop. "Alright, I assume you've been lookout before?"

Maria nodded. "Ever since this whole ordeal happened."

"That thing in L.A.…the pedophiles, what did Vincent do to them?" Lexi inquired as she made herself comfortable.

Maria stood up, moved the shade, and peeked out the window. The wind was blowing the extremely overgrown grass. "He killed them. The ring was run by some highly connected people. That's why the cops weren't able to do anything. That's why Detective Salaszar used to go to him. There was so much corruption. Vincent used to get things done when no one else was willing to do it."

"Good. If there was ever someone who should lead us it's someone who's willing to do what it takes to get the job done," Lexi pointed out.

"The corrupt commissioner wanted my brother and I brought in but Ryke hid us away and we made our way out here," Maria explained. "He's a good man too. I'm glad he and Vincent are on good terms now."

Lexi leaned back and her eyelids became extremely heavy. "I wonder why he stopped going by the name Night Viper."

Maria shook her head, moved the shade back into place, and backed away from the window. "I don't know. It really seems as though whatever was done to him by the government really screwed with him. I asked him why he didn't come back after he escaped. He said he couldn't but he was really cryptic. I guess it didn't matter. I left L.A. too and didn't look back. It's kind of ironic that he wasn't far from here and I had no idea."

Lexi had passed out from sheer exhaustion. Maria stood and looked around at everyone. The only person she really knew was Dr. Lancaster. These others had only recently come into her life but if they were okay by Vincent Black, they were okay by her. She wondered how things were going with the rest of the members of the New York branch of Militia 28. She stepped out of the room and pulled the radio out of her bag. She hoped that it had enough range to reach the shelter.

"Hey, it's Maria…you guys hear me?" she spoke into the device.

It was a bit crackly but understandable. "Yeah, it's Ryke. Do you have an update?"

"Not much here. Everyone is beat so I'm taking watch. Eve is stable for now, but Dr. Lancaster thinks the kid is coming early," Maria explained. "I feel helpless. I really hope Vincent knows what he's doing."

"Me too, kid…me too," Ryke agreed. "Anyway, I appreciate the updates you've been giving, but we should cut this short in case anyone out there is listening."

"Fair enough. Maria out," she said as she checked the front door and made sure it was locked. It didn't matter much; the door was made of glass and the Seekers could smash right through it if they wanted to. They were keeping the place dark to make sure that activity couldn't be seen from the outside. She hoped that the random satellite sweeps didn't include infrared imaging or they might be screwed.

Chapter 41

Vincent could see the large electronics store from the highway, but he didn't like what he saw. It was under siege by a Seeker S&D squad. "Dammit, what the hell is this!?" Vincent cursed.

"Alright, next one then," Carl suggested.

Josee shook her head. "No, look. There're people there. They must have holed up in the store."

Carl looked at Eric, then into the front rear view mirror so he could see Vincent's eyes and the menacing scorpion tattoo. "You're not seriously thinking…"

Vincent interrupted him by slamming on the gas and jerking the wheel to the side to make the exit ramp which thankfully was still intact. "Yes, I am."

Carl could already feel himself getting nervous but he wasn't sure if that was the Seekers or just the idea of risking his life for the umpteenth time in the last couple of days. "We just got away from them…what the hell are we doing?"

"Saving lives. I'm not just going to ignore these bastards while they continue their damn genocide. When we get there, I want you guys to take that machinegun and the last belt and secure it, then give me some cover fire," Vincent ordered as he rounded the corner, almost putting the Bronco up on 2 wheels.

"What are you gonna do?" Josee asked.

Vincent continued to watch in front of the vehicle. "I've still got two grenades left in this launcher. I'd hate to the let them go to waste."

"G...good, use them to take out that bladeless helicopter. It looks like there's only one," Carl offered.

Vincent shook his head. "Nah, I've got a better idea."

As they approached, they could see the aircraft launch a hellfire missile at the corner of the building, knocking out some of the supports and collapsing a section. They heard and saw the flashes of significant amounts of gunfire as the place was lit up like a warzone. "I hope they didn't just destroy the stuff that we came to get." Carl was holding his temples with both hands.

"They have two troop transports...I've got two grenades. I'm gonna take them both out. You guys need to get that machinegun set up and start firing at that aircraft. The .50 caliber bullets should be able to punch through its armor," Vincent directed.

He pulled into the parking lot. With all the commotion, they were unnoticed. He hurried out of the Bronco then ran in the direction of the transports, each capable of holding 12 Seekers. He moved as a blur and closed in before anyone could notice. He took careful aim, which took only a fraction of a second with his reflexes, and fired the first round. It landed flawlessly, destroying the vehicle. Before anyone's brain could even register the destruction, he launched the second and last grenade, destroying the second transport.

Of the 24 Seekers that had arrived, 23 were still standing. The people inside had only managed to take down one. The survivors turned and faced Vincent, their blank faceplates reflecting the light from the flaming wrecks. Vincent just smiled. "How about picking on someone your own size?"

The Seekers raised their weapons and fired directly at the spot Vincent had been standing in only a moment before. He had already leaped into the air. Doing an aerial cartwheel, he drew his pistols and fired a round into the head of two of the Seekers, dropping them instantly. He landed on the other side and fired two more shots, dropping two more of the dark soldiers.

From across the parking lot, Josee witnessed the spectacle. "If that isn't the damndest thing I've ever seen. What the hell is he?"

Carl and Eric were busy securing the machinegun to the back of a pickup truck that had been abandoned in the lot. Carl looked up and said, "I think he's the wrath of God himself."

Vincent did what he could to stay as close to the Seekers as possible. He was hoping that the Firehawk would not shoot when he was in such close proximity to the soldiers. Out of the corner of his eye, he could see people inside the store looking out at the spectacle. The Seekers were no longer interested in them. They were interested in him. He ran straight into one of the emotionless warriors, knocking him to the ground. Then he grabbed the Seeker next to him and threw him into two others as if they were a group of rag dolls.

The Firehawk hovered about forty feet above, waiting for the opportune moment to strike. One of the Seekers had the opportunity to take a shot so he did, but Vincent had felt the tingle of his sixth sense in his head and ducked before the round could hit. He returned fire, putting a bullet through the chest of the enemy that had fired at him and the one standing next to him. Vincent felt another warning, but it wasn't from the Seekers. Apparently, the aircraft was no longer interested in being a spectator. It opened fire with its chain guns. Vincent dove out of the way before he could be hit and two more Seekers were downed by the massive rounds, each of them blown in half.

At this point, the Seekers were in a jumble. Their programming had obviously not prepared them for an adversary such as Vincent. Unable to coordinate their attack, Vincent used his speed to get in close. He grabbed the first Seeker's head and twisted it, snapping his neck. He then punched the next one directly in the center of the face plate, crushing it and the dark warrior's skull. He grabbed a third one and held him in front, using him as a human shield. He could see his own hand healing from the torn skin of punching an armored face plate. Then he drew one of his pistols and emptied it, killing five of the remaining Seekers as the bladeless helicopter aligned itself for another burst. Feeling the telltale tingle again, he pushed his prisoner down in front of him, squatted, and jumped off to the side just as the air assault vehicle unloaded its chain gun, killing the last of the Seekers in the S&D squad. Vincent drew his other pistol while still in the air. He landed, turned, and fired the armor piercing bullets through the dark tinted front window. He completely emptied the weapon. He wasn't sure who he hit inside or how bad it was, but the aircraft turned, opened its booster jets, and blasted away.

Vincent stood for a moment to observe the area. He took in

a couple of deep breaths. More people were visible in the store now. No one spoke, they just stared at him. He turned and saw that Eric and Carl had finally finished setting up the machinegun. Carl was staring at him with his arms in the air in frustration. Then he looked at the people he had just saved. "All of you listen up because this is important."

They apparently were listening because no one moved, they just watched him. "As you can see, the Seekers are not invincible. They can be defeated."

"You move like lightning. You are some kind of Prophet," a voice with an Arabic accent came from the store.

Vincent shook his head. "No, I'm what happens when the government plays around with things that it shouldn't. I'm flesh and blood as you are. The fear that you feel when the Seekers are close is a false fear. It's the result of a chip implanted in their heads. We've discovered a way to beat that fear and we'll be using it. We're going to stand up to them and I invite you to join us."

People began stepping out of the store. "What, like a rebellion or something?" a man asked.

Vincent nodded. "Yes, something like that."

The same man then said, "Well...join you here? Now?"

"No," Vincent answered. "Any of you who would join us, make your way to the ruins of Providence, Rhode Island. The group you're looking for is Militia 28. You shouldn't have a difficult time finding them."

"But, we have no weapons," a woman spoke up.

"We'll equip you. In the meantime, all of you need to get away from here. This is now a hot spot," Vincent stated.

They wasted no time. The people began to vacate the store and disperse. Vincent made his way to the pickup truck. "Do you even need us?" asked Carl.

"Yup," Vincent responded.

"Why is that? You seem to take these guys out without a problem," Carl replied.

Vincent shrugged his shoulders. "Well, the problem is, I'm out of ammunition and the Seekers don't normally carry armor piercing rounds. Their mesh armor can stop a bullet from an assault rifle."

"Okay, but we just went through the trouble of mounting this thing only for you to kill all of the bad guys. Really, why do you need us?" Carl asked again.

Vincent pointed to the highway. "Because reinforcements are on their way and I have no damn bullets left."

Carl looked behind him. "Oh shit."

"What the hell do we do now!?" Josee cried out.

"Get the Bronco and bring it up to the store. That missile hit on the front. I saw signs that the car stereo installation bay was around the other side, so the stuff we're looking for should be fine. We'll load what we need and you guys are going to get the hell out of here," Vincent stated.

Josee shot a glance at him. "What're you gonna do?"

"I'm gonna draw them off. They're most likely after me anyway. They have no idea what we're going to build. Now, get the damn Bronco," Vincent demanded as he hurried on foot toward the store. He ran through the debris that used to be the front of the store and hurried to the car stereo installation area. The irony did not escape him that, as he ran through the store, there were large, flat panel TVs, Blu-Ray players, and all sorts of other goodies that were still sitting there. He made it to the back but the door was locked.

"No time to screw around," he barked as he kicked the door and broke it apart as if it was made of glass instead of metal. He hurried in and ran to the garage door. Using the chain, he opened it manually. The Bronco sped up to the bay and stopped in front of it. Josee and Carl got out.

"Where the hell is Eric!?" Vincent asked.

"He's got the machinegun. He's gonna hold them off as long as he can," Josee stated.

Vincent ran to the shelves and began pulling sub-woofers, amplifiers, wire, and everything else that Dr. Erinyes had requested and handed it to Carl and Josee. They loaded the Bronco. Then Vincent pulled out his SAT phone and dialed.

"Night Viper, is that you?" a female voice sounded.

Vincent had a strange look on his face. "Who the hell is this?"

"It's Jade," the voice responded.

Vincent was concerned. "Why do you have the SAT phone? I don't have a lot of time on this thing."

"Look, it's a long story but I'm helping Josh with his hacking.

I've managed to tweak the hack program so that you no longer have to limit the time of your calls. Did you get the stuff that Dr. Erinyes needs?" Jade asked.

Vincent was not getting any danger twitch, so he replied, "We're getting it now, but we ran into a hitch. A Seeker S&D squad had chased a bunch of civilians into the store that we're grabbing the stuff from. I took them out but they've got backup coming. Since we don't have time limits on the calls anymore, I'm going to give the phone to one of the people I'm with and I need you to direct them to the compound."

The sound of buttons being pushed on a keyboard came through the phone. "I have your location on satellite, and it's the one that the Seekers are using to watch you. Apparently, they tasked this one to the area when they hit those people, but now that they've found you, they want you bad."

"Look, just get them back there...prove Josh right," Vincent stated.

"I will, I swear to you," Jade's voice quivered.

Vincent heard the sound of machinegun fire. He handed Carl the phone. "Here, take it. The person on the other end will help you get to the compound. I'll go draw their attention." Without waiting for a response, Vincent hurried from the room. He made his way to where the dead Seekers were. He took a M16 Assault Rifle and two .45 automatics. He pocketed as many magazines and hand grenades as he could. He checked the weapons but just as he thought, the bullets weren't armor piercing. Despite that, they were still better than nothing.

Vincent watched as the Bronco sped toward the disabled pickup truck with the machinegun mounted on it. Eric managed to load the first troop transport with gunfire, tearing it up. He jumped off the truck and got into the Bronco, which sped off just before a Hellfire missile was fired from an oncoming Firehawk, destroying the truck and the machinegun with a fiery vengeance. Vincent watched as his allies retreated and the troops did not increase their speed to follow. Instead, they turned their attention to the last man standing.

The man who had once gone by the name Night Viper walked toward the oncoming Seekers and simply said, "Come get me, you bastards."

Josee felt as if her head was going to burst. She realized that her blood pressure must have been dangerously high, but she couldn't deal with that now. She did everything she could not to look in her rear view mirrors. She needed to look forward and get as far away from the Seeker reinforcements as possible.

Carl held the phone to his ear. "You said you have us on satellite coverage?"

"You're almost out of range; I'm hacking into their signal so I can see what they see. It's not following you so you'll be out of sight momentarily. Once you are, you'll have to tell me verbally where you are. For now, you need to get back onto route 87 and head north. Be careful, there are some potholes from explosives that can be pretty nasty," Jade explained.

Carl turned to Josee. "Get onto the 87 and head north." Josee nodded nervously. Then he looked forward again and spoke into the phone, "Where exactly is this place and what is it?"

"It's a U.S. government underground compound that was top secret and off the books that they used to fund clandestine experiments, including the one that made Vincent Black what he is now," Jade answered. "I'm sure you've seen what he can do."

"Yeah, and it's a scary thought that the U.S. government was able to do *that* to him," Carl commented.

"The first six they tried it on all died. Vincent is the only one that survived, but the equipment they used was hopelessly destroyed so it doesn't look like the process could be duplicated even if we wanted to," Jade told him. "As for where it is...you ever heard of Lake Placid or Saranac Lake in the Adirondack Park Preserve?"

Carl leaned back in his seat. "Yeah, I've heard of them. They're in the middle of nowhere."

The noise Jade made pounding away on the keyboard continued to come through the phone, then her voice, "Good, this place is just north of them. It's in the woods and you'd miss it if you didn't know what to look for. Okay, now I've lost you on the satellite feed, which is good news for you. The Seekers are going after Vincent."

"Alright, thank God. By the way, who are you?" Carl inquired.

Jade paused for a moment, and then answered, "Amanda. Amanda Wilson."

"Well, thanks for helping us out. I really hope Vincent makes it out of that mess," Carl stated.

The sound of another person in the room came over the phone. Carl could hear Jade talking to the person. "Finally awake?"

Carl could make out a male voice. "Yeah, who are you talking to?"

Jade didn't answer him, at least not verbally; instead she answered Carl. "I've seen Vincent in action. The Seekers have more to be concerned about than he does. I'm sure he's not confronting them anyway; he's probably going to draw them off. He moves so fast he's hard to hit and if you hit him he just heals anyway."

Carl was looking straight ahead at the length of highway in front of them. "Alright, so it's gonna be awhile. I assume there's signs and stuff?"

"Yeah, once you see them, call me back," Jade warned.

"What the hell is your phone number?" Carl asked, realizing that the phone system of old was no longer in existence.

"Push and hold the 1 on the keypad. It's pre-programmed to dial this phone," Jade answered.

Josee motioned with her hand to Carl who turned to her and said, "What is it?"

"Ask her if this thing is gonna make it. It says we only have a little less than half a tank of gas," Josee said with great anxiety.

"The driver says we have less than half a tank of gas. Are we gonna be able to make it?" Carl inquired.

"Yes. That truck has been modified. It gets about 80 miles to a gallon, so you won't have a problem," Jade eased his mind. "You should be able to get here within two hours. There's not very much Seeker activity in this area because there's not much in the way of settlements."

Carl rolled his eyes. "Well, that's a relief. Alright, I'll call you when we see the signs." He hung up the phone.

Josee gave Carl a quick look. "Who was that?"

Carl shrugged his shoulders. "She said her name is Amanda Wilson. I don't know. I don't really care. As long as she can get us out of the line of fire, she could be a one-legged hooker."

Eric sat in the back seat in silence. He was not looking to write anything on the pad. He just sank himself into deep thought.

Chapter 42

Adrian and Destiny had been driving for what seemed to be forever on route 8 in New York. It was heavily wooded and they couldn't see anything on the sides of the road except for trees with leaves that had changed to various shades of orange, yellow, brown, and red. The branches on the trees hadn't been pruned so they were stretching above the road, blocking out much of the view of the sky. "By this time next year, there's gonna be a whole canopy of those damned branches over this road that never ends," Adrian said out loud.

Destiny was petting the cat that was asleep on her lap. "What are we gonna do for gas?"

Adrian was glancing around but everything looked the same in the area. "The next turn I see for a side street, we're going to find another car. If it won't start, we'll see if we can at least siphon the gas out of it and fill this thing up. It just needs to get us to where we're going."

Destiny went silent. She had not done much talking in the past few hours. Adrian was concerned for her. The young girl had found herself in the middle of a war for survival. It was wrong in Adrian's eyes. The whole world was completely wrong. She turned down the next street she came upon, as she had promised, and pulled into a driveway. It was long and went slightly uphill, twisting and turning. "Who the hell would want something like this in upstate New York? This driveway's really gotta be bad in the winter!" Adrian commented, attempting to lighten the mood.

Destiny did not respond. She was just staring straight ahead. She apparently had plenty of time to think about their predicament and how everyone they knew had been killed by the Seekers and some new hovering tanks that they had never seen. Now they were on an important mission to get to the New York branch of Militia 28 and both sisters constantly felt as if they were being watched.

They pulled up to the house at the end of the driveway. It was a quaint, contemporary style house with cherry stained wooden siding. It had a two car garage and quite a bit of land, although most of it was treed. The windows appeared to have black-out shades drawn so little or no light from the outside would get in. There was nothing in the driveway, so Adrian opened her door and got out of the car. "I'm gonna go inside and check it out. Maybe they have a car parked in the garage or something. How about you stay here," Adrian suggested.

Destiny looked into the back seat at the skeleton they hadn't had a chance to remove then looked at Adrian and shook her head rapidly. "I'm coming with you. Kitty can stay here and watch the car."

"Fair enough," Adrian said. She had hoped they would find a better car that would actually start. The little Corolla was nice but without the back windows, she had to keep the heat on full blast to avoid freezing to death in the October weather. It would have been unbearable if the front windows were missing.

Destiny closed the cat in the car. "Stay here kitty and behave."

The sisters walked up a small set of stone stairs to the front door of the house. The bushes outside must have looked good at one point, but were now growing out of control and in desperate need of a trim. Adrian drew her gun and tried the door handle. It was unlocked. She slowly turned the handle and opened the door, which creaked like a door in a haunted mansion. The smell of air fresheners filled their nostrils the moment the door was open.

Destiny had a nervous look on her face. Adrian held her free hand up indicating silence, then faced forward with her gun pointing in the same direction and stepped into the house. The little sister followed directly behind her. Inside the front door was an entryway with a half flight of stairs leading down to what appeared to be a finished basement, the other half led upstairs. "Destiny, pull out that flashlight."

Destiny obliged and flicked her heavy-duty flashlight on. "Which way are we going first?" she whispered.

Adrian motioned her head toward the downstairs, so the young girl shined the light in that direction. They went down and saw that the basement was indeed fully finished. It had a mostly open floor plan with the exception of one room that had the door ajar, which revealed a bathroom. Next to that door was another one which Adrian assumed led to the garage. Someone had built in a customized bar which was still stocked with a nice variety of liquor. There were some older looking couches set up with a giant wire spool as a coffee table and a flat screen projection TV on an entertainment center. The center included all state of the art equipment including game systems and surround sound. There was also a wood stove with brown tile around it. Adrian walked over to the bar and grabbed a bottle of whiskey and a bottle of blackberry brandy and handed them to Destiny. "Put these in your bag."

Destiny gave her a distressed look. "Why are we taking these?"

"Because I'm stressed and this should help to relieve it," Adrian admitted. "Just pack them away."

Destiny did as she was told. "Okay, Adrian."

Adrian shot another quick glance around then said to her sister, "There's nothing down here...let's go upstairs. Just stay behind me...I don't know if we'll meet anyone or anything hostile in this house and I don't want to take chances."

Destiny shined the light toward the stairwell and they both went up, Adrian continuing to point her gun in the direction of her eyes. They ascended to the landing by the front door then continued up. At the top of the stairs, Adrian saw that they could go left down a hallway to what were probably the bedrooms and maybe another bathroom. Straight and slightly to the right was the way to the kitchen and the dining area which was illuminated in its entirety when Destiny shined the flashlight. Adrian looked to the sharp right. "Destiny, shine the light this way."

Destiny shined the light into the living room then gasped and dropped the illuminating object on the floor. Tears streamed down her cheeks. Adrian lowered her gun at the horrid sight they were witnessing. On the floor were the remains of four people. The bodies had decomposed, but judging by the number of air fresheners hanging from the ceiling, it wasn't a huge surprise that they couldn't pick up the smell of death. Judging by the attire on what was left of the corpses, there were the parents and two teenage children. Both children were males, close in age and possibly twins as they were about the same size. The body that Adrian assumed was the father was holding a gun. "Murder suicide," Adrian stated as she bit her upper lip and shook her head. "Must have thought it was Armageddon and decided to end it."

Destiny dropped to her knees and broke down crying. "When is this going to end, Adrian? All we ever see is death and destruction! I want our old lives back. I miss TV and running water and the internet. I miss Mom and Dad. I miss sleeping a full night without worrying that Seekers are gonna come and get me."

Adrian holstered her weapon and knelt on the ground, hugging her sister. Both of them cried hard. "Destiny, all this means is that we need to stay strong and find Alan Ryke as we were directed. If we stop now, all we're doing is surrendering to the enemy and we face certain death. We need to be strong," Adrian encouraged.

Destiny shook her head. "I'm tired of being strong. I can't keep doing this. Our parents are dead. Our brother is dead. Everyone is dead! Maybe we should just be dead too!"

Adrian held both of Destiny's shoulders and shouted, "Don't talk like that. Don't you give up on me right now little sister! I need you. I can't do this without you."

Destiny was shaking like a refrigerator with a bad compressor. "I can't watch this anymore. I should have died with Mom and Dad! At least they're in Heaven and don't need to see all of these dead people!"

Adrian still had tears running down her face. "Destiny, I know it's hard but we're still here and we can still help change things. Please, don't give up."

Destiny stared at her sister for a moment. Adrian let go of her shoulders and she hugged her sister again. Both cried hard yet again and Destiny said, "Let's just get to this place that we're going. Maybe they can kick Zodiac's ass."

Adrian couldn't help but snicker. "You've got a hell of a mouth on you."

Destiny crossed her arms and smiled. "I learned it from you."

Adrian stood up and took her sister's hand. "C'mon, let's go to the garage and leave this family to rest in peace, in the house that they lived their lives together in. We won't defile this place any more than we need to."

Destiny nodded as they walked down the stairs to the garage. Once they entered, they saw that this particular family had two brand new Hybrid cars, one was a small SUV. She saw that there were keys hanging on a cork board in the garage and easily matched them to the appropriate vehicle. She and her sister used the manual override on the garage door openers to see the outside once again. Adrian tried the sedan first but had no luck. Then she tried the SUV and also no luck. She punched the steering wheel. "DAMMIT!"

Destiny was standing outside, staring at a work bench. "Look at that Adrian!"

"What is it?" Adrian asked. "Wait a minute, it's a jump pack."

She popped the hood of the SUV and hopped out. She hurried over to the workbench and grabbed the jump pack. Connecting it to the battery, she got back into the vehicle and turned the key. It took a couple of tries but the vehicle started right up. "Thank God," Adrian commented. "I can't believe this thing held a charge for 5 months."

"How much gas does it have?" Destiny asked.

Adrian looked at the gas gauge. "A little more than half a tank."

Destiny walked to the other side of the garage and grabbed a 5 gallon gas can and some hose, "This should solve that problem." Working together, they siphoned the gas out of the sedan. There was enough to fill the SUV and the gas can completely.

"We should have no problem getting there now," Adrian exclaimed. "Grab that cat and get in."

Destiny hurried over to the Corolla and opened the door. The cat jumped out and began rubbing against her legs. It occurred to her at that point that the cat could have easily just jumped out of one of the rear broken windows but hadn't. She picked it up and hurried back to the SUV. She jumped into the passenger seat and looked at her sister. "This is much more comfortable and smells a lot better than that other car did!"

Adrian cackled a bit. "Yeah, I have to agree." She put it in gear and drove around the car that had gotten them this far.

Destiny was petting the cat again. "It shouldn't be too much longer, right?"

Adrian shook her head. "A couple of hours I think, according to that map."

Destiny unraveled the map again and looked. "Yeah, that should be all it takes."

Adrian reached her right hand over and grabbed her sister's hand. "Destiny, thank you."

"For what?" the girl asked.

"For being here. I meant what I said before…I don't think I could do this without you," Adrian stated.

Destiny shook her head. "I'm your sister, and it's my job to look out for you."

They both laughed. Adrian stopped the car at the end of the driveway for a moment and looked back. "Thank you, whoever you were. We'll make sure that you didn't die in vain." Adrian pulled out the bottle of whiskey and took a swig of it. Destiny gave her a glance. Adrian, without a word, handed the young girl the bottle of blackberry brandy. She took a swig out of it too, then both of them put the bottles down. Destiny and Adrian looked at each other, smiled, and then faced forward. It was a difficult road but they were determined to make it, no matter what.

Chapter 43

Josh was pacing in the control room. Occasionally he would stand still, but then his right leg would shake and he would continue to pace again. Jade was in her chair facing him, fiddling with her hair. She finally spoke up. "Josh, they'll be here soon."

Josh nodded. "I know…it just feels like it's been forever. We haven't heard anything about Vincent either. I don't know if we can do this whole rebellion thing without him."

Jade did not know what compelled her but she stood up and walked over to the pacing man. She put a hand on his shoulder and the other gently on his arm. He stopped and looked at her and she made eye contact. "Vincent is a one man army. We've both seen him in action and I've borne the brunt of his strength. He'll be coming back. In the meantime, once the others get here, we can at least get everything prepared for Dr. Erinyes to make the machine that will beat the Seeker fear aura."

Josh turned so that he was completely facing her. "I'm glad you decided to help us. It's good having you here."

Jade broke eye contact and looked at the floor. "You don't need to flatter me. It doesn't change what I did. I'm still a murderer and I don't deserve your kindness."

Josh lightly pushed up on her chin to direct her to look at him again. "Jade, we're going to make a new rule. You're not allowed to talk down about yourself anymore. I wouldn't let someone else do it in my presence…I'm certainly not going to let you do it."

There was silence. Jade began tearing up. "I don't know what to say."

"Well, another rule too. When Carl last called in I heard you refer to yourself as Amanda. How about you start going by that name again and drop this whole Jade thing. That's not who you are anymore. That's from when you were a puppet of Zodiac," Josh suggested.

Amanda nodded. "Okay. I probably shouldn't meet up with them when they get here though. One of their people is a survivor from Backus. He may recognize me."

"I don't want you to feel that you need to hide here," Josh stated.

"I'm still a prisoner, remember that. I'm hardly on equal grounds. You may be convinced that I'm renouncing my former self, but I doubt I'll be able to convince the others...at least not for awhile," Amanda replied.

"You convinced Talbot and he's a stubborn old man," Josh pointed out.

Amanda let out a light chuckle. "I guess. Listen, I wasn't out to show you up when I modified the SAT phone hack program you created or any of the other stuff."

Josh shook his head. "Are you kidding me? I've been sorting through this system since we got here. I had no idea where to begin. I need the help. Vincent knows a bit about I.T. but he's too busy in the field being a super soldier and all. The rest of them are end users. Lexi was a little helpful, but she doesn't know any advanced stuff. You're totally saving us here."

Amanda began fidgeting. She had trouble with taking compliments so she decided to change the subject. "Speaking of Lexi... maybe we should call her and see how Eve is doing."

Josh realized what Amanda was doing but decided to let it go. "Sure."

Amanda turned and walked over to the SAT phone and picked it up. Before dialing though, she addressed Josh. "Isn't there a medical bay here? Why send Eve away?"

"There is one but there are no doctors here and most of the equipment and supplies have already been removed from here. The only reason the lab that Dr. Erinyes and Andromeda are in is usable is because the equipment is attached to walls, counters, and tables," Josh answered.

"Got ya," Amanda replied as she dialed the phone. She waited but there was no answer and the look on her face dropped.

"What's the matter?" Josh inquired.

Amanda hung up the phone. "There's no answer."

Josh briskly walked over to Amanda and she handed him the phone. He held it for a moment then dialed again. The phone rang several times with no response. "That's not good."

Amanda sat down at her terminal. "How about this - you run some diagnostics to make sure that I didn't screw up the programming when I changed your hack tool. I'll see if there are any satellites converging on the area."

Ring! Ring!

No one was paying attention to the phone. Only moments before, Eve had awakened coughing loud enough to wake the dead. She looked down and saw she was bleeding again and began to freak out. Dr. Lancaster was checking her vitals. "Eve, I need you to calm down."

Eve was on the verge of becoming hysterical. "My baby… what about my baby?"

The doctor placed his stethoscope on her pregnant belly. "Hold still…let me see…I hear the heartbeat. The baby is in there but is under duress. I'll need to perform a C-Section."

John looked at him in horror. "Have you ever done one before?"

Dr. Lancaster made eye contact as he put on gloves. "Do you want an answer to that or do you want me to save your wife and baby's lives?"

John put both of his hands in the air and backed off. "Fair enough."

"What do you need us to do?" Lexi asked.

"I need you to lie down on that cot over there," Dr. Lancaster directed. "Maria, I need you to get a pint of blood from Lexi. We're going to need it. John, you stay right where your wife can see you."

He had prepared for this. Well, he had the instruments and supplies necessary, but he was not mentally prepared. Everyone was doing as they were directed so he began setting up to do abdominal surgery in less than optimal conditions. As far as post-apocalyptic scenarios went though, they were quite fortunate to have access to the supplies and tools that they needed. There wasn't any power however, and they were saving what power the generator could provide for a heat lamp, should they need it for the baby.

Lexi was lying on the cot. Maria had taped the tubes and set up the blood packet. She had the needle in her hand, ready to insert it into a vein in Lexi's arm that she had marked with a dot. She penetrated the skin and blood began to extract into the bag. Lexi looked up at her and whispered, "You did good...you've done this before?"

Maria shook her head. "No, and I was a nervous wreck. I wish I didn't feel fear like you."

Lexi smiled. "No you don't. I had to re-learn so many things that used to be instinctive. You know, after everything happened, I couldn't even recognize the look of fear on someone's face? I had to learn that. I know it anecdotally now, but not naturally."

"At least you're immune to the Seekers' fear aura. It's unnatural when they're around. It defies all logic. I can't describe it," Maria tried to explain but was at a lack for words.

"Listen Maria, we'll find a way to beat the Seekers," Lexi said and then motioned with her free hand for Maria to come in closer and when she did, Lexi whispered, "You take as much blood as Eve needs. Don't worry about me."

Maria did not want to hear that. "She'll be fine. She won't need much...it's just a little blood."

Lexi shook her head. "Maria, promise me. No matter what, that kid does not need to grow up without a mother. You take whatever you need and don't hesitate. Promise me, dammit."

"I promise that I won't need to take more than you can safely give," was all that Maria was willing to say at the moment.

Ring! Ring!
Amanda immediately picked up the phone while watching the surveillance footage. She saw that the Bronco had pulled up to the entrance to the underground garage. "I see you on the surveillance cameras. I'll open it up for you."

"Thanks," Carl replied and hung up.

Josh got on comm. and addressed Talbot. "Hey Talbot, the Bronco's here."

"Good, I'll help them unload the stuff. I've already built some housings for the subs so we should be good to go pretty quickly," Talbot responded. Josh had forgotten that he had been a carpenter at some point prior to the Flash Storm.

"JOSH!" Amanda yelled.

Josh almost had a heart attack. "What!? What is it?"

"I've got good news and bad news," Amanda stated. "The good news is that I intercepted a flash message on the system saying that they completely lost track of Vincent...they have no idea where he is. The bad news is now they have satellites converging on the Militia 28 stronghold here in New York."

Josh sat down and wheeled his chair over next to Amanda. "Oh shit."

"We've got to warn them...what's their SAT phone number?" Amanda asked.

Josh sat back, put his hands on the sides of his head and shook. "They don't have one. Dammit! So stupid and slow!"

Amanda turned toward him. "Josh, what's wrong?"

Josh took his hands from the sides of his head and looked at her. "I only had a chance to program three phones. We have one; Vincent had taken one which he gave to Carl there; and the last one Lexi has at that clinic. We have no way of getting in touch with them."

Amanda pointed at the screen. "Look, they're just converging now but it doesn't look like the enemy forces are going to be there for a little while. They may not know exactly where it is. We have time."

Josh sat forward, his face suddenly lit up. "Wait, I have an idea. This girl Maria is with Lexi and the Deckers. Lexi told me she has a radio that she's been using to keep in touch with Ryke, their leader. We can just call Lexi and warn them."

"If they answer. You said the diagnostics were fine, right?" Amanda was checking.

Josh nodded. "Yeah, and we know the program works since we just talked to Carl."

"Alright, go ahead and call...I'll monitor the satellites," Amanda stated.

Josh dialed. As it rang, he said out loud, "C'mon dammit, answer it!"

"Hello," a shuttering male voice came over the phone.

"John, is that you?" Josh asked.

"Yeah," he acknowledged.

"You sound like you got hit by a train. Why didn't you guys answer before?" Josh was clearly nervous and a little annoyed. The reception on the phone was loud enough that Amanda could hear the entire conversation.

"Listen Josh...we have a problem. Dr. Lancaster is...preparing to do a C-Section to get the baby out. Eve's...in rough shape," he reported.

Amanda was fiddling with her hair again. "It's my fault that they're suffering like this," she thought to herself.

Josh took a deep breath. "Look, I'm sorry to be the bearer of bad news, but there's another problem. Satellite coverage is converging on the area around the Militia 28 stronghold, but we have no way of warning them."

There was silence for a moment, then a response. "I'm about a 20 or 25 minute drive away but...hold on...Maria can get in touch with them."

Josh could hear the conversation going on in the background...

"What's wrong?" Maria's voice came.

"Josh says that Satellites are converging on the area where your stronghold is," John's voice responded.

"It's underground, how do they know it's there?" Maria asked.

"I don't know, just get on that radio thing of yours and give them a heads up," John commanded.

Josh could hear rustling. After a few seconds he heard some banging and cursing in Spanish, then he heard Maria's voice again. "It's not working, there's just static."

"Shit!" Josh cursed out loud.

"Josh, we'll find a way to warn them, don't worry," John assured.

Josh stood up and began pacing again, a habit he had definitely picked up from Vincent. "Alright, listen. We've almost finished the device to counter the Seeker fear aura. It looks like the hostiles aren't advancing yet. That may mean they don't know quite where the stronghold is yet, so that gives us some time.

We'll get down there with the device as soon as it's done."

"I hope it works, Josh," John said.

Josh nodded. "Me too."

John was staring at the phone after he hung up. "What are we gonna do?" asked Maria.

John looked over at her. "One of us needs to take the car and go warn everyone that the Seekers are coming. Josh says that they're almost done with a device that they hope will counter the Seeker fear aura. Looks like they'll have to field test it."

"I can go." Maria stated.

John shook his head. "No. You need to watch over Lexi. I have to go."

Eve grabbed his arm, shook her head, and mouthed the word "No". She was mildly sedated and was emotionally drained. Dr. Lancaster was starting the preparations to open her up.

"Look, I've done some pretty cowardly things. I'm not backing out of this one. Lexi is a match to your blood type so she needs to stay. Ever since I did that E, my hands aren't great with precision stuff so I can't take Maria's place and I sure can't perform a C-Section. A lot of lives are on the line...I've got to go," John stated.

Eve couldn't even respond, she just looked away and began to cry. "Take care of her everybody, and the baby. I'll be back in a little while to hold my new bundle of joy," John assured. He grabbed his pack and began to head out the door.

Dr. Lancaster jumped up and stopped him in the hallway. "John, are you sure you want to do this? People who face Seekers tend to die."

John was still looking forward. "I have to do this. Swear to me that you'll take care of my wife and kid."

"Your wife and son," Dr. Lancaster corrected.

John turned around, a single tear in his eye. "Son?"

"Yes. When I did the ultrasound, it was pretty easy to tell the gender...he's not exactly shy. I didn't say anything because I know you two wanted to wait until he was born, but I figured I'd give you the extra incentive to get back here in one piece," Dr. Lancaster explained. "And I will do everything in my power to make sure that both of them are fine when you return."

John did a slight nod. "Thank you, doctor." He then turned and walked out of the clinic.

Chapter 44

One thing there had never been much argument about was that Vincent Black was highly resourceful. Having been able to cross the North American continent undetected after the Flash Storm, he had become quite adept at remaining out of sight. In those rare circumstances that he actually had been discovered, he'd managed to evade the pursuing forces with relative ease. The pursuit he recently experienced was no different. While riding on the Harley he managed to find and get started, he made a silent chuckle to himself at the frustration Zodiac's commander must have experienced when he realized that his Seekers had lost track of their prize.

Vincent's original plan had been to return to the Project Scorpion compound to reunite with Carl, Josee and Eric, but as he was riding, he remembered a conversation he'd had with his comrades. John had mentioned the Drunk Runners that he had come across in Redford. Vincent wasn't about to visit for a drink, but it was the rest of what John had told him that struck him. The drunken fools had armor piercing bullets...so they claimed. He had no idea how they would have gotten these rounds, where they might have found them, or why they would even have them, but he didn't really care. All he cared about was whether or not the statement was true and if he could get his hands on some.

As he entered Redford via Route 3, it wasn't long before he saw the people he was looking for. A well lit area up ahead illuminated three vehicles in the middle of the road, facing toward a side street. One was a beat up pickup truck, one was a two-door Cadillac that was missing a bumper, and the third was a bright yellow Volkswagen Bug. There was one man standing outside of each of the vehicles, as well as a man across the street wearing hunting gear. There was a small table placed next to him with what appeared to be a few bottles of whiskey and several shot glasses. As they heard the roar of the Harley motor, they all turned to see who was coming. Vincent approached and stopped the bike several feet away.

"Well lookee here…we got us a biker guy," the man next to the pickup truck called out.

Vincent got off the bike and started walking toward the strange sight. He was quite sure he had found the right guys. "Hey, who's in charge here?"

They all looked at each other for a few moments then all four of them erupted into a loud, boisterous laugh. After they calmed down a bit, the man by the table said, "I'm in charge of the game here, my friend. Ya interested in getting in on this?"

Vincent decided to play dumb. "And what game are you playing, other than the get-your-ass-killed-by-Seekers game?"

"This guy reminds me of those other guys that came here in that Hummer the other day. We ain't afraid of no damn Seekers. They're just a bunch of brainless fools who go runnin' around lookin' fer folk to use as target practice. The targets you see here shoot back at them, so they don't have much fun comin' here," the 'leader' said. "The game is called Drunk Running. It's pretty simple. You get into or onto your vehicle. We have a course setup in the back streets here with some obstacles. The area's marked by all them lights you see over yonder. Your job is to dodge 'em and make it to each check point. If ya crash or go offa' the road, yer out!"

"Sounds easy enough," Vincent responded.

"It usually is, except you have to stop at each check point and take a shot o' the drink o' the night. Tonight, its good ol' fashioned Tennessee whiskey," the hunting man clarified.

Vincent realized that he had an opening so he took it. "Well, I didn't really come to play games. I heard tell of some guys in Redford who had access to armor piercing bullets."

The Drunk Runners all glanced at each other and laughed again. The one by the Cadillac spoke up. "And why would you want something like that, boy? You lookin' to get yerself into a fight?"

Vincent nodded. "Actually, that's exactly what I'm looking to do. The last Seeker squad I killed used up the last of my armor piercing bullets. I need more."

The man by the truck was scratching his unshaven face. "You killed a Seeker squad, huh? That's funny."

Vincent was beginning to lose patience. "Do you really have them or am I wasting my time?"

"Oh, we got 'em. Matter of fact, we even know how to make 'em," the man by the VW bug called out.

The one standing by the pickup truck raised his hand in the air and said to the VW man, "Shut the hell up. We don't know who this guy is!"

Vincent put his hands out in front of him. "Relax, I'm not here to start a fight with you. It's the Seekers who are everyone's problem and it's them I want to take out. Do you have the stuff to make more armor piercing bullets? For any gun?"

The leader spoke up. "Listen, I'm gettin' way too sober fer conversation, so either you're in or you're out, but we got us a run to get on with!" The others cheered.

"Well then, I have a proposition for you." Vincent had now crossed his arms in front of him.

The leader squinted one eye intriguingly. "A proposition, huh? Go on."

"I'll join you for a drunk run, but I'll do 10 shots first, then I'll ride this Harley. If I win, I want armor piercing ammo," Vincent stated. He hadn't had alcohol since the process at Project Scorpion had changed him, but he knew that with an immune system that could fight off nerve gas and cyanide, he could probably stomach quite a bit of alcohol as well.

They all started mumbling comments about Vincent being crazy. Then the leader looked back at him and said, "Boy, you must really want those bullets. You tryin' to start a rebellion or something?"

Vincent nodded slightly and replied, "You could say that."

The Drunk Runners all looked at each other and one by one shrugged their shoulders. Finally, the leader spoke up again. "Alright boy, you're in. Pull yer bike over by them and come over here to take yer 10 shots."

Vincent obliged and parked his new found bike next to the VW Bug. Then he walked over to the table where the leader was pouring the last few shots into various shot glasses that had images of naked women on them. These guys were definitely high class. One by one, Vincent downed each of them, his arms moving quickly in a blur. The Drunk Runners were quite taken aback. "Man, you really like your whiskey," the leader said.

Vincent wiped his face with his fingertips that were protruding out of the fingerless leather gloves. "You could say that. Ready when you are." He walked back to the bike and mounted. He turned it on and revved the throttle, making a substantial amount of noise.

"Alright men, take your opening shots," the leader called out. He took a shot himself while the others each took one. They then got into their cars. The leader held a revolver in the air and fired.

The process seemed relatively simple. Starting from right to left, they would enter the course one at a time. It wasn't a race per se, but Vincent had the feeling that if he fell behind he might have some trouble. The first to go was the beat up pickup truck. Once he'd entered the side street, the Cadillac went next, then the VW, then finally, him.

The roads here were short and the speeds were high. He hit the throttle and had no trouble keeping up with the VW. They stopped at the check point only a few hundred feet away and each took a shot. Then they turned left and dodged a series of potholes. Next they took a sharp right and dodged a concrete wall that was built into the center of the road. On the other side they turned right and stopped at the next checkpoint to take another shot. Vincent did a mental status check...the alcohol did not seem to be affecting him. They continued onward. There was a patch of road that had been removed and replaced with mud. The truck passed over it without a problem, then the Cadillac. The VW driver must have been pre-gaming on his own because he completely lost control and spun out onto the side of the road. Each checkpoint had a person to hand out shots and every obstacle had a "judge". This particular judge was a lovely looking young redhead who had a beer in one hand and a cigar in the other. She waived her arms around at the VW as Vincent sped by and easily passed over the mud. Next, they took a right turn and passed through an intersection.

On the other side of the intersection was a checkpoint and they all took another drink. They then had to speed up and go around a sharp bend in the road. Immediately upon exiting the bend was another completely graveled patch. Vincent maintained excellent control and they headed around another sharp bend. At the end of that bend was another checkpoint and everyone had their drink. They all went slightly forward and turned right, where there were a few hundred empty beer cans scattered over the road. They sped through it and then each had another drink at the checkpoint. They headed to a left turn where they came across a series of Jersey barriers to dodge. At the end of the stretch, they took another left and stopped to have yet another drink. The roadway stretched the entire length of the course... every few hundred feet they had to stop to have a drink. Finally, they came to a left turn that put them back on the road where they had started. They sped down to the starting point. The pickup truck skidded as it tried to stop and ran off the road into a bunch of overgrown brush. Vincent could hear the leader say, "Nice goin' Doug. Yer out, ya stupid redneck!"

Vincent did not bother to listen to the response, but he could hear a string of cursing as he turned around and headed back down the course. He did another status check but still felt fine, other than an extreme need to urinate. The first obstacle, the concrete wall, was narrowly avoided by the driver of the Cadillac. Vincent was concerned as the other driver was weaving back and forth. They made the turn and Vincent actually had to pull ahead of the Cadillac to avoid a collision. Passing wasn't illegal in the game...it just wasn't all that necessary. They headed toward the mud patch and Vincent had a tingle in the back of his head. He went over the mud and slowed down. Looking in his rear view mirrors, he saw that the Cadillac was out of control and was spinning toward the drunken red-head judge. He stood on the seat of the Harley, carefully balancing it while it was still moving and jumped off, flipping through the air and landing next to the judge. He pushed her out of the way and took the hit from the car himself, which sent him flying several feet through the air and he landed on his back.

The driver of the Cadillac stumbled out and walked over to the girl who kicked him in the shin and yelled, "Stupid drunkin' redneck! Ya almost killed me! Ya just killed our guest!"

Vincent was quite happy that the onlookers were intoxicated. They might not respond with fear or anxiety as people normally would at the sight of him sitting up after such an ordeal. He could feel his body mending; bones that were broken were fusing back together. It was painful, but over in a few moments. He shook his head and stood up. The Cadillac driver and the red-head were staring at him. "Hey, this run's over, everyone," the red-head yelled out, then started cursing that she had dropped her beer and cigar.

Vincent walked over to the red-head and Cadillac driver. "You two alright?"

"You must be a ghost or something. How did you survive that? What the hell are you?" the red-head asked.

Vincent always loved answering this question. "I'm what happens when the government plays around with things that they shouldn't."

The red-head stood up and walked over to Vincent. She threw her arms around him and said, "My hero!" She smelled like a brewery. She was definitely quite attractive, although he was not sure how long that would last with her drinking and smoking habits. She leaned in to kiss him and something strange happened. He immediately thought of Lexi and as a knee-jerk reaction pulled back.

"What's the matter ace, you like boys?" she asked.

Vincent gave her a dirty look. She pulled back and said, "Oh my, I'm sorry…you've got a girl. My, my, I'd sure love to meet the woman who roped a guy who's this loyal to her in this day and age…especially one that's able to resist my charms."

Vincent didn't debate it. He wasn't with Lexi. He hadn't realized until that moment that his attachment to her was more than friendship. In the last few years Vincent had done many things that most people would find unthinkable. He'd run into a nuclear power plant that had a radiation leak to save two workers pinned down inside. He'd dared the streets of Los Angeles as one of the most brutal vigilantes in recorded history. He had been captured by the United States government and experimented on. He'd fought Seekers when the odds were significantly stacked against him and walked away. In all of these cases, he had shown no fear. Now, the thought of having any type of romantic attachment to someone else frightened him beyond words…and he didn't like the feeling. "It's alright, ma'am. I appreciate the gesture," Vincent said trying to smooth things over.

The man who Vincent had labeled the leader of the Drunk Runners was coming from around the corner along with several of the others who had been scattered throughout the course. When he got close enough he yelled, "What the hell happened? Who won?"

The Cadillac driver proudly proclaimed, "I did. I was the last to crash. This guy here crashed first."

Vincent was not impressed. The red-head elbowed the man in the gut. The alcohol was really settling in at this point, as he fell over laughing and moaning about being in pain at the same time. The red-head turned to the leader and said, "This idiot almost hit me. If it wasn't for our guest, I'd be road pizza right now."

"Rory, you dumb son-of-a-bitch…ya nearly killed my daughter! I should have you horse whipped," the leader said as he walked over to Rory and kicked him in the gut, causing him to stop laughing and just simply moan in pain.

The red-head hurried over to her father and gave him a hug. "It was amazing, Daddy! He stood up on his motorcycle and jumped off, landing right next to me. He pushed me out of the way and took the hit. Then he got up! You believe that? He's like, invincible or something."

The girl's father looked at Vincent, eyes filled with scrutiny. "That true boy? You invincible or something?"

Vincent shook his head. "No, I just heal fast."

The leader said to him, "What's your name, boy?"

"Vincent Black," he replied.

"Well Vincent Black, my name is Todd McKinley and this is my daughter, Lauren," Todd stated. "The dumbass you see on the ground is Rory. Doug was the one driving the pickup and Shep was the one driving the VW that spun out in the beginning."

"So, did I prove myself enough to warrant some of that armor piercing ammo?" Vincent asked.

Todd laughed. "Just the fact that you drank enough to knock

out a full grown elephant and you don't even seem buzzed is enough for you to get in on that. C'mon, pick that bike up. We'll get these heaps back on the road and you can follow us back to our campsite."

For a moment, Vincent was annoyed at the fact that all he probably had to do was drink these guys under the table and they would have given him what he wanted, but it wasn't like the Drunk Run took very long. It barely had gone into the second lap when it ended, almost in tragedy. He wondered what had caused this group to engage in such extreme self-destructive behavior.

Todd McKinley was true to his word. He drove the Cadillac with amazing control, considering he had been drinking the entire time the Drunk Run was taking place. Vincent was surprised the dilapidated car was still running after the beating it had taken. Todd's daughter was sitting in the passenger seat while Shep and Rory sat in the back. Shep had banged up the VW pretty badly, so it wasn't drivable. Vincent had expected the "campsite" to be similar to the street bandit camp where he rescued Crisco from. It wasn't. It wasn't anything like it. He recognized it instantly for what it was. It was a former U.S. military ammunition dump.

The entourage pulled into the gate that probably had never been closed since the Drunk Runners had set up shop. Vincent parked the bike as the others were getting out of their cars. "Home shweet home!" Todd yelled, with a slight slurring of his words.

Vincent wasn't sure how he felt about these guys having access to some of the stuff that was kept in the area. "You guys actually live here?"

Rory whipped his head around. "Yeah! There a problem with that?"

"Other than there being live ammunition and explosives stored here that could go off if someone isn't careful and you all like to drink? No, not a problem at all," Vincent said sarcastically.

Everyone began laughing hysterically. "You're all right, Vincent Black," Rory said as he was cracking up.

Vincent rolled his eyes. He couldn't believe the irony of actually depending on a bunch of raging alcoholics to provide him with weapons for a strike back against the Grand Army. He took a minute to look around the lot outside the ammo dump and saw that several vehicles of various varieties and condition were present. One in particular caught his eye. It was an armored vehicle that one would have seen picking up bags of cash from a bank for transport. This one had been modified with gun ports all around and a heavy machinegun on top. There were small missile launchers mounted on either side. These guys were busy. There were also several commercial solar panels around. The depot itself was located in a clearing.

Todd walked over to Vincent and put his hand on his shoulder. "That there is Sally. She's a beauty. We figure if those damn Seekers ever show up here, she'll give 'em what for." He was indicating the modified armored car.

"C'mon Daddy, let's show Vincent all the cool stuff that we've collected." Lauren was rapidly motioning with her right hand as she headed toward the depot in a drunken stumble.

The group headed inside. It was illuminated via LEDs that were connected to various batteries. "Wouldn't have been surprised if they were using oil lamps in here with the way they've been going," Vincent thought to himself.

The grand tour included the liquor room, which was loaded with whiskey, rum, vodka, and beer. He saw a small refrigeration unit that could hold a few cans or bottles of beer at a time but did not plug in. He assumed they would charge it with the solar panels outside then bring it back inside to cool the beer. The rest of the stuff was fine warm, especially since they drank it straight up.

The remainder of the tour included sleeping quarters and the ammunition storage. The sleeping quarters were just a bunch of cots, but the ammunition and explosive storage was interesting. It looked like the inside of a ship transporting illegal arms. There were guns, rocket launchers, grenades, rockets, various bombs and explosives, and of course the prize…armor piercing rounds. There were 9mm, .45, and 5.56x45mm NATO rounds that were armor piercing. In addition, belts of .50 caliber rounds meant for a machinegun as well as standard rounds were stored there. Vincent had difficulty believing his eyes. "This was all here when you found it?" he asked.

Todd nodded his head. "Yup. Everything 'cept for what we already took out. I reckon there's some stuff here for your winner fee."

"There's enough here to take over a small country, Todd," Vincent pointed out. "Let me ask you something, and I don't want you to take it the wrong way. Aren't you tired of just hanging around drinking and running through an obstacle course?"

"Shit, I ain't never gettin' tired of drinking," Todd laughed.

Vincent shook his head. "No, I mean don't you want to be doing more? You're effectively waiting around to die if you don't kill yourselves first. Is that the existence that you want?"

Todd actually seemed to have a sober moment. "Damn man, you're gettin' deep on me here. Look, we're all gonna die. Eventually, those Seekers are gonna figure out we got this whole stockpile and they're gonna come to blow it up and take us all with it. The world sucks, but it sucks a lot less when you got booze running through your veins and Drunk Running."

"Why don't you come with me?" Vincent asked. "Look at Sally out there. Look at your arsenal. I think deep down you've been thinking about fighting back, but you weren't sure how."

"What the hell do you know? You just came stumbling through here." Todd snapped.

Vincent stood his ground. "I know what your body language and your actions tell me, and it's a different story than your words. Look, the Seekers are systematically killing or enslaving everyone they find. You know they're actually lobotomized people? Zodiac has chips put inside their heads to control them. They're basically living zombies."

Todd thumped himself down on a crate of grenades. "Is that so? And you're planning on fighting back before they kill everyone?"

"Yup," Vincent said proudly. "I'd rather go down fighting than wait for them to come and get me. I think you'd prefer that too."

Todd sat for a moment, then stood up quickly with a large grin on his face. "Oh, what the hell. I'm in!"

Vincent was relieved, "Glad to hear it."

Todd turned and yelled out, "Rory, get Sally running. Doug, Shep, you guys help our friend here load up some of this ammo." Then he turned to Vincent and said, "We'll take some now, and then we can bring your people and come back for the rest."

Vincent nodded. He began to think about the idea of getting into a firefight with a bunch of drunks on his side, then decided to stop thinking about it since there was really no other option. "What about everyone else here?"

"They'll stay here and watch the stockpile until we get back here for more stuff. I assume you got a base or something," Todd stated.

"I sure do," Vincent said.

"Good. Now I got me a nice long-ranged radio in Sally so's we can check in with our buddies back here. In the meantime, let's move out," Todd exclaimed.

Chapter 45

"Is this it?" Destiny asked Adrian as they approached the area that they had been instructed to get to.

"I don't know," the older sister answered.

They had driven down a makeshift dirt road just outside of town. The trees provided a dense canopy overhead that would make the area difficult to see from the sky, including a satellite that wasn't using thermal imaging. There was some type of mortar and steel structure that was built into the network of trees. It was an expansive shelter that still allowed for tall trees to provide cover. Soon Destiny's question was answered...two men carrying AK-47 Assault Rifles approached.

"Step out of the car!" one of them commanded as they both pointed their weapons. The cat hissed.

Destiny pet her feline companion and said, "Shhhh kitty, don't make them mad."

Adrian showed her hands and slowly opened her door. "Destiny, c'mon, let's get out."

"Move it, now!" the armed man shouted again.

Adrian and Destiny exited the car. The cat remained inside, still hissing. Adrian spoke up, "We were sent by Jack Breaker from Plainville, Kansas. We're here to see Alan Ryke."

The two men looked at each other, then looked back and spoke up. "That car doesn't have a Kansas license plate."

Adrian rolled her eyes. "What are you, the Department of Motor Vehicles? We flew a modified Bell helicopter to Buffalo where we happened to land right outside a war zone and almost got killed. We managed to salvage a car and drove until we were almost out of gas, then we picked up this car and came here."

The two men looked at each other again and mouthed words to each other. They then lowered their weapons. "Come with us." Destiny looked up at Adrian who nodded with approval.

"Stay here, kitty," Destiny called out to the cat who was now closed in the car.

They followed the two men closer to the massive structure that almost looked like it was a patch of old Mayan ruins. They walked down a set of stone stairs where there were two large blast doors. One of the men pulled out a two-way radio. "We have a young woman and her kid who're here to see Ryke. They claim they were sent from Plainville, Kansas by Jack Breaker."

"She's my sister," Adrian corrected. "Seriously, do I look old enough for her to be my daughter?"

The man with the radio ignored her. He listened for the response. "Bring them in." There was the sound of metal sliding on metal and the massive blast doors were opened from the inside.

Destiny grabbed Adrian's hand and squeezed. The older sister looked at her and said, "It's gonna be all right, baby."

Destiny and Adrian followed the two men into the shelter. The area that might be considered the foyer was large and open. There were members of Militia 28 everywhere. They could see side hallways that reminded them of old documentaries on the discovery of Ancient Egyptian tombs. They didn't leave the entry area. A man in army fatigues approached them. "So, you two are the ones who came all the way out here from Kansas. I'm Alan Ryke...I hear you're looking for me."

"I'm Adrian Sundance, this is my sister Destiny," Adrian introduced. "We were sent here by Jack Breaker."

"How is Jack? Kansas is outside of our comm. range so I haven't spoken to him in quite awhile," said Ryke, making small talk.

Adrian paused for a moment, remembering the horrible ordeal of the Seeker invasion that was less than 24 hours prior. "He's dead. We're the only two survivors of Kansas Militia 28."

Ryke had a serious look on his face. "What happened, Adrian? How did they find you? Last I'd heard, you had that former military bunker that was pretty much completely underground. It was huge. You could have built an entire town under there."

Adrian nodded. "We think that some of our scouts were picked up by satellite or something and were followed. The Grand Army came at us with a vengeance."

Ryke wiped his brow, more as a nervous habit because it wasn't all that warm. "How did you escape?"

Destiny was still holding onto Adrian's hand as she responded, "The others chose the two of us and our brother Shawn to get word to you about what happened. They gave us cover but Shawn was killed on our way out. Our father had had a Helicopter training school nearby. Being a member of Militia 28, he had modified an old Bell with additional fuel and some other stuff to give it better range and speed. We flew it as far as we could and then nabbed cars to get us the rest of the way here."

"I'm sorry for your loss," Ryke stated. "The destruction of the entire Kansas Militia 28 is truly a tragedy."

"Listen, the Seekers brought hardware at us that we've never seen before. Some type of futuristic looking tanks that hover above the ground. We had the shelter surrounded by a mine field but these things went right over them, dropping these little metal ball things, and all of the mines detonated. I still can't believe we weren't followed out of there," Adrian explained.

Ryke shook his head. "New weaponry? It would make sense. All the information that we've been able to put together indicates that Zodiac annihilated the armed forces during the Flash Storm, including any known military bases and bunkers, complete with their weapons. Those bladeless helicopters and now hover tanks are things that were never seen before. He must have taken experimental equipment and started producing it, knowing any resistance would have no knowledge of such weaponry. But why is he just unveiling these hover tanks now?"

"I don't know," Adrian replied.

Ryke looked Adrian in the eye. "Are you two sure you weren't followed? Those bladeless helicopters can be ultra silent when they want to and they're far more maneuverable than a regular helicopter."

Adrian shook her head. "No, we couldn't have been. We would have seen them long before we got here and we wouldn't have come until we shook them."

Ryke nodded in approval. "Okay, good."

John decided to take the beat up old junker that he had used to get to the clinic in the first place. He wanted to leave the far superior Hummer with the others in case they needed to make a getaway. "I hope I'm not too late," he said out loud. He had left the SAT phone with Maria, so he was truly on his own.

He headed down the dirt road and made his way to the Militia 28 shelter. When he pulled up, he saw a brand new SUV that had probably rolled off the factory floor within the last few weeks before the Flash Storm. He immediately exited the poor excuse for a vehicle he was driving in time to be greeted by two guards with AK-47 Assault Rifles. They immediately recognized him and one said, "Decker, you're back?"

"No time to explain, I need to see Ryke...what the hell!?" John trailed off as he saw a strange sight in the small gaps of the canopy of trees above them. It appeared to be a slight distortion as one would see when looking above something hot. The only reason he was even able to make it out was due to the complete clarity of the sky and the moon being directly behind it.

The two guards looked in the same direction. "What? What are you looking at?" one of them asked.

John was still looking up. "There's something up there, above the tree line. I can't make out what it is, but there's some kind of visual distortion. I doubt there's a source of intense heat up there."

One of the guards started frantically pointing with his hand. "Holy shit! I see it!" He fiddled with his rifle and managed to point it up, then opened fire.

John grabbed the weapon from him. "What the hell are you doing? Now they know that we know they're here. Get me inside that shelter, now!"

The trigger happy guard lowered his head in shame. The other one picked up his radio as they all hurried toward the entrance. "Hey, Decker's back, alone. Open the door, we've got trouble."

The doors opened from the inside and John hurried in. He immediately saw Ryke standing with two newcomers that he didn't recognize. "John, what's wrong?" Ryke asked.

"This place is about to get pounced by a battalion of Seekers.

399

They're closing in as we speak," John warned.

Ryke looked as though the news had caught him completely off guard. The young girl standing near him gasped. Ryke turned to face the two newcomers then faced John and said, "By the way, this is Destiny and her older sister Adrian. How do you know the Seekers are coming? We're quite well hidden."

John put up his index finger. "Wait a minute. Did these two just come here in that shiny new SUV outside?"

"Yeah, we did. Why?" Adrian inquired. "We came from Kansas to warn everyone here about new technology that the Seekers have that we haven't seen before."

John fidgeted. "There's new technology alright. Look, before I left the clinic, my allies saw the satellite feed that the Seekers are using. It was moving in this direction. I figure someone was following that SUV."

Adrian shook her head angrily. "No, there's no damn way we were followed. I don't know who you think you are, but we're not stupid."

John was losing his patience. "I never said you were, but you were followed by something none of us has seen before because you can't see it. I saw a visual disturbance hovering over the tree line outside. I think they have some type of new stealth craft. We've got to get everyone out of here before they overrun you."

Adrian spoke up. "This is paranoia. You saw some kind of 'visual disturbance'? Something that turns invisible? That's crazy. And how are you looking at their satellite feeds anyway?"

John scratched the back of his head. "Look, Ryke. There's no time to argue. One of your guys saw it too. I left my pregnant wife to come here and warn you. I hesitated at Southern when Lexi and Vincent warned me to evacuate. I had convinced myself that my people were safe, and because I didn't give the order, they're all dead and it's my fault. You don't want that on your conscience."

Ryke stared at him for a minute then called out, "Everyone on full alert. The Seekers are on their way."

"Commander Stone. We've located them sir, but they saw us," the Seeker pilot reported.

"They 'saw' you? How did they see you? You're invisible for

Chrissake!" Stone was skeptical.

"They pointed and shot some type of rifle at us," the emotionless Seeker responded.

"Very well. I will notify Commander Triton. In the meantime, get out of there," Stone ordered.

"Yes sir," the Seeker responded as he turned the stealth Firehawk and headed away from the site of the Militia 28 compound.

Commander Stone initiated contact with Commander Triton, who appeared on his view screen. "Commander Triton, I recommend an immediate strike on the New York Militia 28. One of their more savvy members seems to have spotted the stealth unit."

Triton rolled his eyes in disgust. "Stupid, brainless Seekers. Sometimes I question the wisdom of having mindless slaves as soldiers…Well, whatever. My troops are in position. I will give the order to attack, but no air strike. I don't want to end this quickly. We're going to take our time as we drain their hopes and dreams of freedom from the very core of their souls."

Stone actually felt a chill go down his spine. Triton was a sadistic sociopath that he didn't trust at all, but the newly activated commander had the ear of General Callous so he played along. "Very good, Commander. I look forward to the extermination of these pathetic pockets of resistance."

Triton smiled. "And if these rebels live long enough, they'll be able to see the prize I have in store for them." He followed the comment with a sadistic laugh.

"What're we gonna do? How are we gonna fight them? I don't want to die!" Destiny cried amongst the hustle and bustle of the members of Militia 28 gathering weapons and preparing to enter battle.

"We have to avoid panic. The fear aura that those Seekers put out is an illusion. We need to get past it," John commented.

Ryke looked him in the eyes. "They're already panicking, and the Seekers aren't even in range." He sighed then continued, "We need to evacuate. That's what we need to do."

John nodded. "Agreed. I have an idea. I'll lead a guerilla assault team to use hit and run tactics. The running shouldn't be too difficult once we get anywhere near those Seekers. The woods should help us out. In the meantime, you gather everyone and any supplies that you can and hightail it as far from here as you can possibly get."

Ryke wiped his completely dry brow. "That sounds like a suicide mission."

John shook his head. "All we need to do is hold them off long enough for you to get everyone out of here, then we'll disappear into the woods ourselves. Think your guys could rig this place to explode? Once those bastards get in here, they'll be blown to bits. At least we can give a final 'screw you' to Zodiac."

"It's already rigged," Ryke admitted. "The whole place, plus an entire chamber packed with fertilizer. Nothing would survive the blast once it came in here, not even wearing full body armor."

John smirked. "Good. Then let's get ready. You have any heavy artillery or anti-tank weaponry?"

"A little. A couple of anti-aircraft missile launching tubes and a few anti-tank rockets. As long as our guys don't miss we should be able to do some serious damage," Ryke answered.

"Alright, then let's get ready to move out," John stated.

Chapter 46

Josh and Amanda were hard at work at their terminals in the control room of the Project Scorpion complex. Talbot accompanied Josee to field test the new anti-fear device against the advancing Seeker battalion headed toward the Militia 28 stronghold. Carl was asked to wait in the lab with Andromeda and Dr. Erinyes. Eric had gone to an empty dormitory room. He had an excruciating headache which he was prone to since his head wound.

Andromeda was assisting Dr. Erinyes with plans for a new device that could be implanted into a rebel's nose and work off their own body's electrical charge to counteract the Seeker fear aura. The scientist already had a similar implant, but he was not one of the people who originally worked on it, so he had decided to try to reverse engineer it.

"Andromeda, my dear, I will need your help for what I must do next," the scientist stated.

She dutifully walked over to him and nodded. "I must have you utilize this device and enter through my right nostril, that is the one to my right so to you it would be the left, and remove the implant. I cannot reverse-engineer it while it's still in my head," he continued.

Andromeda had a look of horror on her face when she looked at the device. It looked like a thin metal snake-like device that had a laser eye and a set of retractable clasping pinchers. It reminded her of something that she would see in a scary science fiction movie.

"Now, now, don't worry. You simply use that screen and the controls. It's like playing a video game, only if you miss with the laser you will probably kill me or cause permanent brain damage," Dr. Erinyes explained as if he was the subject of risky procedures frequently.

Andromeda gasped.

Carl rolled his eyes. "Oh, so now that you've joined us you're ready to play the martyr?"

The scientist glared at Carl. "Now young man, I am simply giving the girl a warning. She is quite capable and I have no doubt that she will perform exceptionally well. After all, I value my life and my mind. I would not allow someone of inferior intellect to even attempt such a procedure on me."

"Yeah, whatever," Carl answered.

Dr. Erinyes laid down on the table and Andromeda set the machine up as she had been instructed. Her back side was facing Carl, who began to stare at her. He couldn't take his eyes off her. He watched her the entire time as she prepared the unit. As she began to move from her spot, he immediately looked away before he could be discovered. He needed a drink. He needed it bad. "Hey, do either of you know if there's anything to drink in that mess hall area?" he asked.

The scientist responded, "This complex draws its water from an abundant well, there is plenty to drink."

Andromeda said, "Bar's in the back of the mess hall."

Dr. Erinyes cleared his throat. "Oh yes, I see. Truly remarkable my dear."

Andromeda smiled at him. Carl stood up and headed toward the door, shooting one more quick glance at Andromeda then said, "Thanks kid. It's been a long couple of days." He quickly exited the room.

Dr. Erinyes looked up at Andromeda. "He's a strange fellow, that Carl Woods. I know that I am not one to talk about strange, but he is definitely a different breed altogether."

Andromeda snickered and prepared to utilize the device. She activated it and the "metal snake" entered through the scientist's nose. She saw a display on her screen and, using the controls, she was able to guide it carefully and gently through the doctor's nasal cavity.

"Oh man!" Josh blurted out.

"What's the matter?" Amanda responded.

Josh pointed to his screen. "Look at this!"

Amanda looked at the screen and saw that it was picking up a large, heavy object heading toward the rebel camp. She gasped. "Triton is sending the BFT-5000 up to New York, right where the Militia 28 stronghold is!"

"BFT-5000?" Josh said, squinting his face in question.

Amanda looked at him. "Remember? It's what you guys call the Apocalypse Dozer. Triton isn't taking any chances. He's going to crush that place to dust. To make matters worse, it's pretty close to here. They might find this place."

Josh slammed his hand on the counter. "Dammit, that Seeker squad that was holding a perimeter is moving in. They must have figured out where the base is. I hope John got there."

"We've got to warn them about the BFT-5000. If they hole up in that stronghold, the Seekers will just pin them there until that thing can come through and steamroll them," Amanda warned.

Josh nodded. He picked up his SAT phone and dialed. He didn't wait for a response. When he heard the sound of it being answered he immediately said, "Who is this?"

"It's Maria, Josh," Maria responded, annoyed. It had always been a pet peeve of hers for someone to call and ask the person on the other end who they were instead of first introducing themselves.

"Maria, listen, are you in the room with Eve?" Josh asked.

"Yeah," she responded.

Josh fidgeted in his chair and started talking with his free hand. "I need you to excuse yourself for a moment."

"Okay," Maria said. He heard her mumble something to everyone, then footsteps and the opening and closing of a door. "Alright, what's going on?"

Josh took a deep breath. "The Apocalypse Dozer is headed toward the Militia 28 stronghold. A whole load of Seekers is about to descend on that place. Have you been able to re-establish radio contact with them?"

"No, it's just static and John already left. He's probably there by now. I'm sure they're already working on an escape route," Maria replied.

Josh felt a tap on his shoulder. "Hold on a second, Maria."

Amanda had a desperate look on her face. "Josh, the satellite they have over the area has thermo-imaging. The whole compound is surrounded. They're anticipating that our people are going to run for it. They'll be slaughtered."

Josh could hear Maria gasp on the other end of the line. "So you heard that?"

"Yeah, I heard that!" Maria confirmed and then let out a string of expletives in Spanish.

"Maria, calm down a second," Josh urged.

"You don't get it, man. Dr. Lancaster is cutting into Eve right now to get the baby out. I'm already pulling a second pint of blood from Lexi so she'll be of no help, and we only have one vehicle here." Maria was completely stressed.

"Two pints? From Lexi? She's not all that big, what the hell are you doing?" Josh asked urgently.

"She told me to take it all if I have to," Maria replied.

Josh pushed off the side of the counter with his feet while sitting in the chair and it wheeled across the room. "Well I sure as hell hope you're not going to."

"Of course I'm not going to," Maria whispered in a harsh tone. "But the point is that things aren't great here either. You guys don't have any way to send a radio signal or some kind of burst transmission to them?"

Josh leaned back in the chair. "No. And if they're jamming the signal it wouldn't do us any good anyway. God, I hope John knows what the hell he's doing. I wish Vincent was there."

Maria silently agreed, and then said, "Look, I gotta go check on Lexi and prepare to give this blood to Eve so she can live to see her baby."

"Alright Maria," Josh said and hung up.

"What happened?" Amanda curiously asked.

Josh shook his head. "We need a friggin' miracle."

"Alright, so here's what we're going to do," John directed. "The heavy stuff can only come in through the south, from where the roadway is since the tree coverage is far too dense here. We send the big guns there to take out as many of their tanks and aircraft as possible. That should stifle their ability to reasonably pursue us when we retreat. In the meantime, the charges at the shelter are set and ready to detonate when they go in to search it. We have cover of night, people, and they're shining their lights nice and bright."

It seemed straightforward. John was ducking into the foliage along with several members of the forward group of Militia 28. The rest of the members were already heading North, East, and West to get away. John's group had the wonderful task of holding off the enemy. The problem was that even though the task was straightforward, it did not eliminate the fear that was beginning to overwhelm the rebels as the Seekers got closer and closer. John managed to muster the courage to head forward first. He motioned for the others to join him. They slowly prowled toward their adversaries when one of the tanks fired in their general direction. The shot penetrated trees and vegetation but did not hit anyone. It didn't need to. Roughly one-fourth of the forward group instantly broke into a run, their fear getting the better of them. John knew there was no time to waste. Using his RPG, he fired at another tank and landed a direct hit. The others followed his lead and soon another tank joined the first as a pile of smoldering metal while its anti-gravity drive shorted out and it crashed to the ground. All three Firehawk units had been successfully shot down, not expecting the rapid outpouring of high explosive fire from the rebels. The two remaining tanks opened fire in their general direction along with the Seekers on foot.

"Fall back," John called out as everyone began to turn tail and run. Shots followed each and every one of them. All around him, John could see members of his forward team falling. A man running only a few feet from him was caught in the head by a round from one of the Seekers' M16s, blasting off the upper third of his skull. Another man took a round to the elbow, losing his arm from that point down and then took another shot through the back that came out through his stomach, opening a large hole with pieces of organ falling out. Screams and cries of fear, panic, and pain filled the air.

The situation was bad, but it would still be difficult for the Seekers to pursue them through the thick forestation as they went deeper and deeper into the woods. The problem was, as they made their way back toward the shelter, they saw that they were not being pursued from behind. Instead, their comrades who had retreated in the other directions were also headed back. They, however, were being pursued. John stopped. "Oh no, they've completely surrounded us."

Ryke approached. "Yeah, making us completely screwed. Those bastards are everywhere. They really knew right where to hit us."

John shook his head. "No, I won't give in to this fear. We're gonna take these pricks down, now."

"Does your team have any rockets or anything left?" Ryke asked.

"No, but we took down their air support and two of their tanks. There didn't seem to be a whole lot of foot patrol there. They definitely weren't expecting us to hit fast and hard like that. Come on, we just need to charge them," John demanded.

Several people heard him and he received a number of responses...

"We're all gonna die!"

"We're no match for them!"

"We need to surrender...maybe they'll show us mercy."

He looked over and saw that Adrian was kneeling on the ground, cradling her younger sister. Both were terrified that this was the end. "Don't you all see? This is why people who've rebelled haven't won. The Seekers aren't better strategists. They don't even have free thought. We're letting the fear they instill control us. It needs to end here. If we all just give up, then we're all going to die. If we keep fighting, then some of us have a chance. Down there is the weakest point of their assault. We just wasted a number of them. Now come on, before their cavalry catches up!"

Though uneasy, the other rebels listened and they began to charge back toward the road. As the Seekers there began to open fire, the rebels returned fire, forcing the enemy to take cover. Most of the shots went wild from the combination of intense fear and the fast movement but the return fire was helpful in reducing their likeness to ducks in a shooting gallery.

"Woo hoo," Todd yelled, still completely drunk as he drove Sally toward the battle in front of them. "Looks like the fireworks started without us! Ain't you glad you followed your gut?"

Vincent rolled his eyes. "Yeah, and judging by the look of things, our guys blitzed the Seekers. They have assault vehicles that are smoking piles of junk." What he didn't say was that his sixth sense was once again extending out and sensing danger to others, not just himself.

Todd pointed in front. "Except for those two funny lookin' tank like things. Now we're gonna blitz 'em from behind!" He flipped the trigger and fired a volley of rockets at each of the hover tanks. The attack emptied all of the small rockets, but both remaining hover tanks were blown to scrap metal. The Seekers on foot began to turn toward the oncoming assault vehicle.

Vincent grabbed Todd's shoulder. "Run 'em over and get me up close. I'll give them a dose of hurt they'll never forget, even with lobotomies."

Vincent turned and headed up the hatchway in the ceiling. "Hey, where are you going boy," Todd called out. He shrugged his shoulders and yelled, "ALRIGHT! TIME TO KILL SOME O' THESE SEEKER BASTARDS!"

Vincent climbed to the machinegun turret on the roof, then stood up. Using the machinegun as leverage, he watched as Seeker after Seeker was plowed through by Sally. He realized that ironically, it was actually useful to have a drunk driver in this situation. The remainder of the Seekers began to return fire, the bullets harmlessly bouncing off the armored hide of the custom assault vehicle. Out of seemingly nowhere, one of the troop transports slammed into the side of Sally. Vincent let go of the machinegun and allowed the force of the sudden stop to throw him into the air. While in mid-air, he pulled his pistols out, now loaded with fresh armor piercing rounds, and began firing at the Seekers on the ground. Shot after shot penetrated vital organs of his adversaries as Vincent once again showed that he was a one man army.

He landed on his own two feet and fired two rounds at the Seekers in the cab of the troop transport that had rammed into Sally, killing them both. He dropped the empty magazines from his pistols and reloaded. Glancing around, he noticed a young woman with a girl who couldn't have been older than nine or ten. They were staring at him. He had a massive tingle in his head, but it was different. Once again, for reasons unknown to him, his sixth sense was now extending to people around him. He saw a Seeker coming out of the woods with his rifle raised, ready to fire at the two. Vincent instantly went into a sprint toward the dark warrior. As fast as he was, he could not get there in time. The Seeker fired, but the two females were no longer standing there. John had dove and pushed them out of the way, taking the rounds himself and falling, critically injured to the ground.

The former vigilante reached the Seeker and snapped his neck before the dark soldier could even react. Then he rushed to John's side, bullets still flying around. The two females knelt down next to him. Both had tears streaming from their eyes. "John man, stay with me, okay? Stay with me," Vincent demanded. "I'm gonna move you out of the line of fire." Vincent picked John up and brought him to cover behind the flaming wreck of a hover tank.

"MARIA, GET THOSE BLOOD UNITS READY! SHE'S HEM-MORHAGING!" Dr. Lancaster called out. They had taken two full pints of blood from Lexi who was now barely able to stay awake enough to drink the bottled water they had given her.

Maria quickly obliged. Eve was crying. "Oh my God, my baby!" Dr. Lancaster wished he had been an anesthesiologist so he could have put her completely under instead of just localized numbing.

"Eve, we're not going to let anything happen to the baby. Stay calm and don't move," the Doctor ordered.

"Ready," Maria stated. She had learned a decent amount of medical skills over the previous few months patching up wounded members of Militia 28.

Lexi reached her hand toward Maria and said weakly, "You take...the rest of it. You take...it all. Save baby...and Mama."

"They're gonna be fine, now keep quiet," Maria barked as the first pint of blood was being emptied from the bag into Eve's bloodstream.

Dr. Lancaster wasted no time. He reached into the opened uterus and removed the little baby boy. He motioned to Maria, who came over with a blanket and he placed the baby in her arms and cut the umbilical cord. The baby was not breathing. The doctor gave the child a small whack on the foot but there was nothing. "C'mon, C'mon," he mumbled. "I hope Eve didn't have too much magnesium sulfate."

Maria had tears coming. "What do we do?"

"Oh my God, what's wrong with my baby!?" Eve cried out.

Maria looked at the baby. "That's a bad boy for not breathing." She gave him a solid slap on the behind.

WAAAAAAAAAAAAAAAAAAAAAAAAAAAAAAAAAAAAAH!

Dr. Lancaster breathed a huge sigh of relief. "That's the sound that we want to hear."

"Oh no, I think I slapped him too hard, he's really mad," Maria said as the baby squirmed in her arms, his little face beet red.

Dr. Lancaster shook his head. "You did fine, Maria. I just need to get this placenta out and then I'll patch Mom up. In the meantime, there are some wipes and things over there. How about we clean Junior off a bit so we can put a clean baby in Eve's arms."

Lexi looked over at Eve. She took a drink of water and said quietly, "Congrats...Mom!"

Eve smiled at her and leaned back. She was extremely lightheaded from the C-Section and the loss of blood, but she felt a huge weight had been lifted from her shoulders when she heard her newborn son cry. The brief amount of time that he wasn't breathing felt as if it had stretched on for days. Never had she been more frightened than in that moment. It was over now. The baby was fine. She was being patched up. Soon, John would be back and they would be a family.

It seemed as though everything was falling apart. The initial blitz of the rebels was more of a knee-jerk reaction to being cornered, just like a wild animal. Their fear, both natural and artificial was overwhelming them. The Seekers in the woods were pushing the rebels out into the open. Vincent looked up from his dying friend and saw rebel after rebel get gunned down as they tried to flee from the relentless Dark Ones.

"John, hang in there, we'll get you out," Vincent assured. He looked at the two females that John had saved. "Stay with him and stay down behind this wreck."

"What are you going to do?" the older one asked.

"What I do best...cause damage," Vincent responded. With fresh clips in his pistols he stood up and charged into the fray. He made every shot count as much as he could. Firing quickly but carefully, he took down Seekers that were closest to fleeing rebels. There were just too many of them. They began firing back and he had all he could do to dodge the oncoming barrage. It was then that he felt strong vibrations. It was almost a rumbling sensation.

Across the battlefield, Alan Ryke was having trouble keeping it together. He was running in the woods, trying to get his bearings on the incoming Seekers but was overwhelmed with a fear sensation as well as concern for those he led. Not long before the attack, Destiny and Adrian Sundance had arrived from Kansas to inform him that the Militia 28 branch in that area had been completely decimated. Now, even though his people put up quite a fight, it looked as if the same thing was going to happen in New York. It was then that he saw a military Hummer smash through the foliage. He looked at it and said out loud, "What the hell?"

The driver and passenger doors opened and out stepped Chris Talbot and Josee Santillo. Ryke had never been as relieved as he was at that moment. "My God, you guys are a sight for sore eyes," Ryke called out to them.

Josee shot the Seeker that was chasing after Ryke. "Take that you blank faced bastard!"

Talbot had some type of remote device in his hands. Ryke looked at him and asked, "What's that?"

Talbot looked down at it and then back at Ryke. "Our salvation, I hope. Or it's a very fancy car stereo system." He pushed the button. Inside, the modified subwoofers began thumping out vibrations. They were barely audible but everyone could feel them. They were directed toward the battlefield.

Ryke was the first to notice a change. He turned to face the war zone. His fear was gone. At that moment, all he could say was, "Anyone want a Seeker sandwich?" He loaded a fresh clip into his weapon and immediately went running toward the advancing Grand Army. Then it began to happen everywhere. Rebels who were running for their lives now turned and fought back against their enemies. The shots they fired had deadly accuracy. Groups of rebels who were close enough simply grabbed the dark soldiers and beat on them worse than a football team sacking a quarterback.

Vincent watched as the rebels who had been pouring out of the woods were turning around and going back in to face the Seekers head to head. "It worked," he said out loud.

Todd had exited Sally and was running toward him. "Hey, what happened? First everyone was runnin' away...then there was that loud thumpin' and now everyone is chargin'!"

Vincent had a half smile on his face. "My people did it. They found a way to beat the Seeker fear aura. The mindless pricks weren't expecting it so they're being demolished. Look, they're retreating!"

"We did it? We didn't even need to use all of the stuff that was inside o' Sally?" Todd checked.

Vincent shook his head. "It's not over yet, Todd. My friend is badly hurt. We gotta get him into the shelter." Vincent jogged over to where John was laying. The two females that he had saved were still there attempting to stop the bleeding.

"How is he?" Vincent asked.

The older one shook her head. "Not good. By the way, I'm Adrian...this is my younger sister, Destiny."

"Vince." John reached for him weakly.

Vincent grabbed his hand. "Hang in there pal, we're gonna bring you into the shelter."

John shook his head slowly. "Don't bother...look down there...the blood is black...the bullet hit my liver...I don't have much time."

"Hey guys, I'm picking up a signal," Shep yelled as he ran toward Vincent and Todd carrying the C.B.

"bzzzz...Maria...need to talk...you," was coming through the radio.

Vincent motioned for him to come over. "Maria, it's Vincent... go ahead."

"The baby...born...doing fine. Lexi...2 pints of blood...," Maria said. They could hear the cry of a baby in the background. John had a tear in his eye.

"Vincent...let me talk to...Eve." John reached his hand out.

Vincent pushed the button, "Do me a favor, and put Eve on."

"...kay," was the response. Vincent handed John the radio. The victorious Militia 28 began to pour out of the woods, having chased off the remaining Seekers. They gathered around but kept their distance from the mortally wounded John Decker. Ryke pushed to the front with Josee and Talbot.

"Eve...baby," John said weakly.

"John! He's...beautiful baby boy...got your eyes," she replied.

"Eve, I know I said...I'd make it back...but I won't be," John stated. "I just...wanted to hear...your voice again, and hear my son."

"John...no...," came Eve's voice, knowing what the news was without having been told any details.

"I love...you both...," John replied weakly.

Everyone could hear Eve's hysterical crying. Talbot had hurried in close and was standing behind Vincent. He took the radio and walked a few feet away. John reached for Vincent.

"John, I'm sorry," Vincent said. "I should have been faster."

John laughed a bit, and some blood came out of his mouth. "Don't be...guess I'm not...a coward after all."

Vincent shook his head. "You aren't a coward. You'll be remembered as the hero you are."

"Vincent." John grabbed his hand. "Promise me...promise me you'll become Night Viper again. That you'll lead this rebellion to victory...promise me you'll make this world a better...place for my son."

Vincent hesitated a moment. He did not expect the dying wish of his friend to be this. "John..."

"PROMISE ME!" John called out then hacked up more blood.

Vincent had a sudden chill go up his spine. Everything that had happened in his life had led him to this point. He knew what he had to do. He held John's hand and said, "I swear to you John, I will not stop until we've taken our country and our world back."

"Th...thank you...Night Viper," John said his final words as his eyes shut and he took his last breath. There were many casualties in that battle, but none more tragic than the man who would never see his newborn son face to face.

Vincent stood up and looked around. The faces of men, women, and children were all looking at him. They weren't just staring, they were waiting for direction. Whether he liked it or not, he was now the leader of Militia 28 and the rebellion against

Zodiac.

"Vincent," Talbot called out. "We have a problem."

"What now?" Vincent replied.

"The Apocalypse Dozer is headed this way," Talbot revealed.

Vincent took another look around at all of the faces looking up to him. He jumped to the top of a wrecked Firehawk and addressed everyone. "Today has been filled with a lot of tragedy. We now have the dreaded task of burying friends and family. But today has also shown us that we are not helpless. I see these hover tanks for the first time and that tells me something. Zodiac rushed into this. His army, his power, is not yet complete. We've proven that we can beat the Seeker fear aura, which means we can beat them."

Everyone began to look back and forth at each other.

"Look, this not only has been a rough day, it's been a rough few months. But let's be clear about something…Zodiac isn't going to stop until he's enslaved or exterminated every human being on this planet. We cannot continue to run and hide. We cannot continue to hope that he'll go away. He may have his army of Seekers…he may have his hover tanks and bladeless helicopters and whatever else, but remember this: *we have our will*. That's right…the very thing he stripped from his soldiers is our greatest weapon. We're not just fighting for territory; we're fighting to keep our lives. The human spirit is the strongest there is and HE'S NOT GONNA TAKE THAT FROM ANY OF US!"

A series of cheers rang out from the crowd. Vincent was inspiring them. He didn't know how he was doing it. He had spent his life as a loner and now fate had thrown him into a leadership role. It wasn't just any leadership role either…he was leading the fight to save humanity.

"What are we going to do?" a voice called out.

Vincent had the most serious look on his face when he said, "We're gonna take down the Apocalypse Dozer."

The commotion began. Vincent hopped off the wrecked vehicle on which he had been standing. Ready to greet him was Talbot. "Vincent, are you sure you know what you're doing?" he asked.

"Yes, I do Talbot. I'm going to keep my promise to John," Vincent answered.

Chapter 47

General Callous's image appeared on the view screens of Commander Stone and Commander Triton. He did not look pleased. "So, the rebels have defeated you fools."

"General..." Commander Stone began to talk but was cut off.

"They have done no such thing!" Commander Triton snapped.

Callous was visibly taken aback by the comment. "Mind your tone, Commander, and do not forget who you're talking to. It seems that the rebels have somehow found a way to counteract the Seeker fear aura. Not to mention that Night Viper continues to slaughter every squad you send after him and is right now leading this Militia 28. I am not pleased. Lord Zodiac is not pleased. This should have been dealt with already."

"It doesn't matter what those rebels think they've done. All they've accomplished is to delay the inevitable," Triton pointed out.

Stone spoke up. "I think we need to be honest with ourselves. They know things that they couldn't know. I think they're accessing our satellites. Even now we see them mobilizing..."

"That's impossible!" Triton demanded. "Even if Commander Jade has betrayed us, we've locked her out of the Defense Net. There's no way those fools could get into it. They'd have to find a computer first and then hack into the satellite data grid."

"Triton, you are far too overconfident for your own good. I will have the Defense Net swept again for hackers. In the meantime, finish them off...Night Viper with them," Callous ordered.

"Am I to understand that the capture order on Night Viper and Alexis Hera is revoked?" Triton sought confirmation.

Callous showed obvious impatience. "Just get rid of that annoying bunch of whelps by whatever means necessary, Triton. Commander Stone, you will relinquish command of the stealth unit to Commander Triton."

"Yes sir," Stone replied.

"I trust that this will be the last conversation we need to have about those damn rebels," Callous threatened.

Triton nodded. "I am handling this personally. They will feel the full wrath of the BFT-5000. According to satellite imaging, the fools think they've won and are remaining stationary."

"Lord Zodiac has returned to NORAD and is awaiting word of the destruction of the rebels. Do not disappoint either of us, Triton," Callous warned.

Before Triton could respond, the communication ended. Staring at the blank screen, he said out loud, "One day, Callous, I'll be General. All you manage to do is hold us back. Why Lord Zodiac trusted you as part of his inner circle I will never know."

Speaking into his comm., he alerted his entire squad. "Attention. We're moving forward with the attack on the Militia 28 stronghold in New York. ETA, 5 hours and 30 minutes. All Seekers prepare yourselves. You will not have the benefit of your fear auras in this battle. We are to annihilate the enemy and leave no survivors. Commander Triton, out." His comm. lit up from the stealth Firehawk so he pushed the button.

"Sir, we await your orders," the Seeker pilot stated.

"Join up with my battalion. You will be my contingency plan," Triton directed.

"Very well sir," the emotionless drone responded and ended the communication.

"By the time the sun rises, Night Viper and his little rebellion will be no more. So much for the famous Los Angeles vigilante," Triton said out loud to the blank screen.

Chapter 48

The members of Militia 28 were busy stripping the armor, weapons, and equipment from the dead Seekers. For most of them, the armor was still quite intact. They knew that the Seekers did not typically use armor piercing rounds as a way to make sure they didn't kill each other from "friendly fire", if there is such a thing. They were also removing the bodies of the dead Militia members as well as tending to the injured.

Night Viper stood off to the side with Ryke, Talbot, Josee, Adrian, Destiny, and Todd. "Alright, we have about five-and-a-half hours before the Apocalypse Dozer gets here along with a whole mess of Seekers. We need to be prepared."

"That thing is huge...how are we going to take it down?" asked Ryke.

Night Viper pointed in the direction of the shelter. "The world's largest land mine. The information we have is that the hunk of junk uses the same anti-gravity drive that those bladeless helicopters use. That's how it manages to ride all around and not sink into the ground. Since the anti-gravs lower the thing's weight but not its mass, if we have enough explosives, we should be able to knock it on its side."

Josee visibly got excited. "Then we can blast it with everything we've got!"

Todd took a drink from a bottle of whiskey since he was beginning to feel a little sober. "We got lots o' armor piercin' ammo. Dig in. I can go back to my bunker and get the rest of the stuff that goes boom. We got all sorts of fun toys, thanks to the army dumpin' and forgettin'."

Night Viper nodded his head. "Good. Talbot, I want you to go with him...see if they can rig up some extra protection for the Hummer. We can't risk anything happening to it. That thing is the key to this fight."

Talbot put his thumb up. "Will do."

"Adrian, Destiny, we need to know everything you remember from the battle with the Seekers in Kansas," Night Viper requested.

Adrian spoke up. "I didn't see much...there was so much dirt and debris in the air. We had a mine field all around the shelter, but those hover tanks just floated over them and dropped these little metal ball things. They all exploded and took out every mine in the area. That's when the rest of the group swarmed us. Destiny and I escaped...our brother and the rest of our people didn't."

"All right. Destiny, I need you to go with the kids and help them load all of the magazines with armor piercing ammunition. We want to be able to unload on those Seekers the moment they come into sight. Adrian, I'd like you to go with your sister and help her make sure all of those kids know what they're doing," the former vigilante directed.

Adrian and Destiny both nodded. Neither of them knew Vincent Black, but what they had seen of his actions and the unconditional loyalty that so many others were showing him led them to the conclusion that it was in their best interest to follow his instructions to the letter.

"What about Josee and me?" Ryke asked.

"You know most of these people better than anyone and they know you. We need a forward infantry line. They'll be the ones who will be equipped with the armor we took from the downed Seekers. Try having them put some kind of design or something on it to set themselves apart. The unarmored people are going to serve as snipers and distance combatants. We have no assault vehicles outside of Sally, so a direct confrontation would be suicide. We need to strike at them from a distance, from hiding, and from all over the place and dwindle their numbers. The most important thing is once we topple that Apocalypse Dozer, we need to make sure it never stands up again," Night Viper answered. "Ryke, you know this area better than anyone. They most likely have satellite coverage on it using thermo readings instead of direct imaging since the trees are in the way."

"We have hundreds of magnesium flares. We can light them up, create additional heat sources in clusters and make it difficult for them to make out what we're doing. By the time the enemy gets here, the sun will be coming up so we won't have cover of darkness anymore anyway," Ryke pointed out.

Night Viper nodded. "Good. Let's do it. Without the darkness, the contrast created by their lights will be ineffective as well."

Everyone hurried to their assigned tasks except for Talbot, who motioned to Todd that he would be a minute. He walked over to the man who had helped make it possible to stand up to Zodiac, "Vince. You realize if this works it will be the first time that any type of rebel group stood up to the Seekers in a full scale battle and won."

"Yes, I do," Night Viper answered.

"Things will never be the same again. We'll truly be engaged in full scale warfare with the man who managed to annihilate every military and their technology across the globe in the span of one day," Talbot reminded him.

Night Viper put his hand on his friend's shoulder. "Talbot, Zodiac did what he did through manipulation and subterfuge. He is consumed by hatred and that blinds him. I know he'll close the weaknesses that we expose in his forces today, but we'll do what lawyers and accountants did when they closed loopholes in the law...we'll find new ones. I'm not quitting. I did that once before, and I made a promise that I wouldn't do it again."

Talbot grabbed his leader's hand and gave a firm shake. "I know you won't quit. I knew that about you back in Hartford in the sewer tunnels when you wouldn't allow anything to be your barrier from getting me, Josh, and Drom out of there. I think I knew you wouldn't quit before you did. Funny, it seems like it's been a lifetime since you saved us from that place but it's been less than a week."

"Here comes the other Hummer. I'll go over there and meet up with them," the rebel leader stated.

Talbot nodded and hurried off to get the modified Hummer and follow Todd to the ammunition dump. Night Viper walked toward the oncoming Hummer, which stopped several feet before him. Dr. Lancaster and Lexi got out of the front seat. Maria, Eve, and the baby remained inside. "We're here, Vince," Lexi stated. "Tell us what you need to take these bastards down."

"He needs you to get back inside the car. You've lost two pints of blood and you weigh less than my leg," Dr. Lancaster stated.

Lexi gave him a dirty look. "I'm fine. I can fight."

The doctor shook his head in annoyance. "She's stubborn. Real stubborn. She's a damn hellfire."

Night Viper chuckled. "Yup, that's Lexi. Don't bother fighting with her, it won't work."

Lexi ran up and gave the rebel leader a hug. "I can't believe that John…"

"I know. He gave his life to save a girl and her little sister. He's a damn hero," Night Viper stated. He looked over at the Doctor. "How's Eve's health?"

"We shouldn't be moving her, but in light of a full scale assault coming this way, I don't see another choice. She isn't talking much and someone should definitely keep an eye on her. In the meantime, I'll stay here and see what I can do for the wounded. Maria will keep an eye on her," Dr. Lancaster explained.

"Alright, Doc," the man with the scorpion tattoo acknowledged. "There's more than enough wounded back there."

Dr. Lancaster wasted no time. He grabbed a large bag of supplies out of the back of the Hummer and hurried off. Night Viper walked over to the driver's side window, which was open. Maria was sitting in the driver's seat and Eve was in the back seat with the baby, who was sleeping peacefully in her arms. She just sat silently, watching her son who she had yet to name.

"Lexi told me how to get to the compound and I have one of the SAT phones," Maria stated.

"Alright, good. Take care of them both. Once you get there, make sure that you keep an eye on her," Night Viper requested.

Maria gave a quick glance to the back seat then back at Night Viper. "I will."

"Eve, I'm sorry. I want you to know that your husband is a hero and will be remembered that way," he attempted to comfort the widow. "Take care of yourself and that little miracle you're holding."

Eve looked up and said, "Just make sure you all come back

alive. I don't have anyone else. And if you could, John wanted to be cremated."

"Of course Eve," Night Viper acknowledged. He tapped the side of the Hummer and Maria sped off. Then he picked up the SAT phone and dialed.

"Josh here," the voice on the other end came.

"Josh, what's the status of what's coming at us?" Night Viper asked.

The sound of a keyboard getting pounded on came through and Josh answered, "Looks like the Apocalypse Dozer and a whole armada of Seekers coming in from the south. It looks like they're just planning on steamrolling you."

"Good. They're predictable, the damn idiots," Night Viper stated. "Look, Maria is headed back there with Eve and the baby. Keep an eye on Eve."

"I can't believe he's gone," Josh replied.

Night Viper clenched his eyelids then re-opened them. "I know. A lot of people have died today, but we're going to take that damn thing down. Did you find anything out on this Triton guy?"

"Nothing. I looked him up by his real name but what I found showed that his records had been deleted some time ago. He definitely didn't want anyone finding out anything about him," Josh explained.

"Alright, have Jade...I mean Amanda, monitor the incoming goons. In the meantime, we're about to lose a major source of cover when we detonate it like a giant mine. We need to find out if there are any more bases or compounds that were off the books," Night Viper said with a sigh.

"I looked but this stuff was highly secretive so there's no record of any of it in the system," Josh complained.

Night Viper looked around at all the hustle and preparations. "There may not be formal records of those places, but I know that there were a lot of unsanctioned installations for the United States government. The best way to find them is by using a similar mentality that astronomers use to find black holes. Find the ripples that they cause. Find the effect that their existence has on other areas and you can trace it back to them."

Josh let out a huge gasp. "That's perfect! This stuff had to have cost money so the drain had to be somewhere, as well as the stationing of personnel and things like that. I can whip up some good queries that should help us uncover those places. Hell, I'll go and talk to Dr. Erinyes…maybe he might know something. He strikes me as the type who would keep secrets from Zodiac."

Night Viper began walking toward the activity. "Good, Josh… and thanks. Night Viper out."

Josh put the SAT phone down. It occurred to him briefly that Vincent had referred to himself as "Night Viper". He looked over at Amanda and said, "Hey, listen, could you do me a favor? Could you monitor the incoming dead-headers and let Vincent know if there's anything weird?"

Amanda smiled at him. "Sure, even though I know Night Viper asked you to have me do it. So, is the new nickname for Seekers dead-headers?"

Josh chuckled. "Sounds good to me. I'm gonna go ask Dr. Erinyes something…I'll be right back." He stood up and started to walk toward the door, then went back and grabbed his gun from the table.

"Are you going to kill him or something?" Amanda asked.

Josh shook his head. "No. It's just that Vincent has been pounding into all of our heads to keep our side arms on us at all times. He'd probably be pissed if he found out that I left it out in front of you all of this time."

"Your secret is safe with me. He already threw me off a rooftop with no effort…it's not like I want to piss him off," Amanda acknowledged.

Josh nodded and left the room.

Dr. Erinyes sat up from the "procedure" where Andromeda had extracted the chip that allowed him immunity to the Seeker fear aura. He rubbed his nose for a few seconds then turned to her and said, "Absolutely amazing, my dear. You missed your calling as a surgeon."

Andromeda blushed. She removed the chip from the robotic "snake" using a pair of tweezers and placed it on a small glass dish. She brought it over to the apparatus that was used to analyze the Seeker chip. She actually found working with the scientist to be fascinating. He was constantly complimenting her. Neither of them was yet aware that John Decker had died. Josh and Amanda had thought it better to keep it from them for the time being so that they could concentrate. "No dizziness?" Andromeda asked.

Dr. Erinyes shook his head. "None whatsoever."

The door to the lab opened and Carl came stumbling in, visibly intoxicated. He sat back down on the stool he had been sitting on previously and began to stare at Andromeda. It didn't take long for the young girl to feel uneasy. Dr. Erinyes spoke up. "Young man, now is not the time to become intoxicated. We have serious work to do."

Carl looked at him with seething anger. "No, you have work to do…I'm here to babysit you, murderer."

"Now, now, there's no need for that. Whatever I have done, I'm helping you now," Dr. Erinyes pointed out.

Carl clenched his teeth and then stood up. "You know, I don't know how I feel about Night Viper's decision to include you and this Jade chick in what we're doing. I don't think this young girl here is safe with you. Andromeda, come over here and I'll look after you."

Andromeda walked over to Dr. Erinyes and stood by him. The doctor looked at Carl with contempt. "Do not think I didn't notice you watching her earlier. You obviously weren't concerned how safe she was with me when you decided to feed your addiction. I suspect though, that the drink is but one addiction. Maybe that's why you don't wear a wedding ring."

Carl stood up and flipped the stool to the floor. "Oh really? So are you a mind reader like your master?"

"Andromeda, I think it would be best if you left this room and went immediately to the control room," Dr. Erinyes suggested.

Carl slammed his fist on the counter. "Andromeda, you have no need to go anywhere. I am in charge here and you will stay."

Dr. Erinyes held his casted hand in front of Andromeda. "I will not allow you to do this."

Carl threw his arms in the air. "Oh really! So now we'll change your name from Dr. Erinyes to Dr. Morals! You turned God knows how many people into mindless slaves and you have the nerve to judge me? Ha!"

"She is a young girl. There are women your own age out

there," the scientist said, obviously deeply concerned.

Carl kept approaching slowly. "Don't worry, Andromeda. You'll like it. Girls your age always do. Once we get going you'll find it to be quite enjoyable."

Andromeda was shaking her head rapidly and began to blink back tears from her eyes. Carl stepped forward and Dr. Erinyes immediately pushed the young girl back and lunged at Carl. The former police officer, despite his intoxicated state, easily grabbed the out of shape scientist and slammed his head on a close by countertop, knocking him unconscious. Andromeda was backed up against a wall and held her hand up, still shaking her head and mouthing the word "No."

Carl reached his hand out. "Relax Andromeda, just relax. This is a perfectly natural and beautiful thing. You have no need to worry."

Andromeda, in desperation, grabbed the advancing former police officer's hand and bit it as hard as she could, tearing into the flesh as if it was a hamburger. Carl screamed out in pain and backhanded her, knocking her to the floor. "You little bitch! Now you'll pay for that!"

Just then, the door to the lab opened and Josh was standing there with his gun drawn. "Carl, what the hell are you doing?" Josh took a quick glance and saw Dr. Erinyes unconscious and Carl holding a bleeding hand. Andromeda was on the floor, wiping blood from her lower lip.

"I…um…just helping Andromeda up. Dr. Erinyes…"

"HE WAS TRYING TO RAPE ME!" Andromeda cried out.

Carl turned toward her and reached for the gun he had stuffed in the back of his pants. Josh quickly fired three rounds. The first struck Carl in the neck, the next in the chest, and the third went through his mouth. Blood splattered on the wall behind the would-be rapist and his lifeless body fell to the floor. Josh stood for a moment, his weapon still pointing where the assailant had been standing only seconds before. His arm started shaking. "Oh God," he said out loud.

Andromeda immediately crawled her way over to the downed scientist. Josh regained his wits and holstered his gun. He rushed over also. Immediately, he checked the doctor's pulse. "He's alive. I think he's just knocked out."

Andromeda began crying and Josh cradled her in his arms. "Shhhhhh…it's okay Drom…you're safe now."

After a full minute, Andromeda looked over at Dr. Erinyes who was beginning to stir and groan in discomfort. "He tried to help me. He tried to stop him."

Josh nodded. "I know. C'mon, let's help him up."

The lab door opened again…this time it was Amanda, still wearing the sweat shorts and baggy T-Shirt. "I happened to glance at the security camera. What happened?"

"Carl apparently was a pedophile and he tried to get Andromeda. He knocked Dr. Erinyes out after he tried to stop him. I think I'd rather work with mass murderers," Josh explained.

Amanda rushed in and assisted Josh with the now conscious scientist. They managed to get him into a chair where he sat, leaning forward slightly and clutching his head. Amanda addressed him. "Dr. Erinyes, are you all right?"

The door to the lab opened yet again and Eric came in, having heard the gunshots. Still a little delirious the scientist said, "Yes Commander Jade, I think I just hit my head."

Amanda looked up at Eric who made direct eye contact with her. In that moment, she remembered him. She remembered him from the prison cells in the lower level of the William Backus Hospital. He had stood in the back of the cell and watched her cruelty to the prisoners. His eyes instantly filled with rage.

Amanda looked at Dr. Erinyes and made sure to say loud enough for Eric to hear, "Dr. Erinyes, it's just Amanda now. I don't go by Jade anymore."

The doctor rubbed his forehead. "Yes, yes, I am sorry about that. Old habits I guess."

Eric rushed toward Amanda. Josh saw him coming and stood up. "Eric, back o…" Eric shoved him out of the way and grabbed Amanda's throat with both hands and began to choke her. She brought her knee up to his groin as hard as she could. Despite Eric being in obvious pain, he did not release his grip. She tried to peel his fingers back but it was as if they were vice grips. She was losing strength fast.

Josh stood up and pointed his gun at Eric. "Let go of her now. I don't want to shoot you. I had to shoot Carl because he tried to assault Andromeda."

Eric wasn't listening. He kept choking Amanda, who was struggling desperately to get out of his grip.

"ERIC! LET GO OF HER!" Josh yelled.

Eric looked over at the skinny computer nerd, then looked back at Amanda. He released his grip and let her drop, panting like a tired dog. It finally occurred to him that the blow he took to the groin was extremely painful. He sat back, breathing heavily while staring at Amanda with a look of death in his eyes. "What the hell was that Eric? Why don't you type it onto that computer terminal right there so we can all read it," Josh barked.

Amanda shook her head. "No. He has reason to hate me. Really good reason."

"And what the hell would that be?" Josh asked.

Amanda slowly stood up, rubbing her neck. "He watched me murder some of his fellow prisoners and have others carted off to become Seekers. He was imprisoned at Backus."

Josh was speechless. Andromeda was standing by Dr. Erinyes who was also speechless. Amanda looked over at Eric. "There isn't a reason in the world for you to believe me when I tell you that I'm renouncing my old ways. I was consumed by anger over things that were done to me by some very bad people. It's not an excuse, but it is a fact."

Eric had a single tear run down his cheek. He was still looking at her angrily but he did not dare attempt to walk…he was in far too much pain. Josh walked over to Amanda. "Are you alright?"

"I'll be fine. You should probably check on him," she answered, pointing at Eric. "I'll head back to the control room and monitor the 'dead-headers'." Then she left the room.

Josh looked over at Dr. Erinyes and Andromeda. "You two should just take a break. I don't think this could have happened at a worse time."

Dr. Erinyes spoke up. "I don't believe there is ever a good time for madness such as this."

"Vincent and Militia 28 drove off the attack Dr. Erinyes, thanks to your device," Josh reported.

Dr. Erinyes was invigorated with a sense of pride. "Yes, well it was a crude model and I am capable of much higher quality, I assure you."

Josh dropped himself onto a chair, staring at Eric. "Well, it's not over yet. There were a lot of casualties. John Decker was killed, along with a large number of Militia 28 members."

Andromeda began to get choked up. Eric leaned forward and put his face in his hands. "The good news is that Maria Esperanza is heading back here with Eve and the newborn baby. They're both fine...well, as fine as can be expected."

"Are they pulling out of there?" Dr. Erinyes asked.

Josh shook his head. "No. They're planning on taking down the Apocalypse Dozer."

"The BFT-5000!?" the scientist exclaimed.

"Yeah, that thing," Josh confirmed.

"How do they plan on doing that, it's unstoppable. It has no week points in the armor that I've ever heard of, there are no un-explained openings that one can fire something into and blow it up like in the movies," Dr. Erinyes warned.

Josh smiled a twisted smile. "They're gonna knock it over."

The scientist rubbed his nose a bit, then said, "Yes...I can't believe I never thought of that. The anti-gravity drives reduce its weight so that it doesn't sink into the ground. If one set off an explosion...that's genius!"

"Yeah, Vincent thought of it. As much as I hate to say it, we should get this body out of here...maybe take it down to the in-cinerator," Josh stated.

Andromeda was breathing rapidly. "When is this all going to end Josh?"

He rubbed his chin and responded, "That's just it, Drom. If Militia 28 succeeds, this is the beginning."

Chapter 49

Night Viper walked the line of infantry soldiers that had taken the armor from the dead Seekers and did what they could to patch it. They had put various designs on the armor, some of them quite unique. One in particular, who had taken the armor from a Seeker that had been shot through the head, had drawn blood dripping down the side. On his chest he had written, "Die the rest of the way Seekers." Another man had drawn a cartoonish picture of Zodiac's helmet with blood coming out of the bottom. There were various phrases that had been written on some of the armor including, "Militia 28 Forever", "Rebels Rule, Seekers Drool", "America, Land of the Free, Home of Militia 28", and a personal favorite, "Night Viper = God".

"Just finished unloading and setting up all of the explosives," Talbot called out from the entrance to the shelter.

Night Viper hurried over and went inside. They had not exaggerated. The place probably had enough explosives to level an entire town. In the center of the large entry area, laid the body of John Decker. His hands were crossed on his chest and various candles and trinkets had been placed around him. Names of various fallen members of Militia 28 from the previous battle as well as over the past few months were written on several crates and packages of explosives. He walked over to the body and gazed upon his friend one last time. "Rest in peace, my friend. I won't forget my promise to you." Then he walked away and exited the shelter.

Ring! Ring!

"Go ahead," Night Viper answered his SAT phone.

"Vincent, its Amanda," the voice sounded shaky. "It looks like the dead-headers are following the Apocalypse Dozer."

"Dead-headers?" he asked.

"Sorry, a nickname Josh made up for the Seekers," Amanda's voice was still shaky.

The rebel leader responded, "I like it. It's catchy. What's going on over there?"

"There was an incident. I'll let Josh tell you about it in a minute. You won't have a lot of time to topple the BFT-5000 before the rest of the troops get there. You're outnumbered," Amanda reported.

"I figured we would be. We've passed the point of no return though, so just let me know if anything else develops," Night Viper directed.

"Okay," Amanda acknowledged with her voice still shaky. "Here's Josh. He just walked in."

The sound of the phone being handed over to someone came through the speaker. "Vince, it's Josh."

"You guys okay over there? Jade...I mean Amanda, didn't sound so good," the former vigilante observed.

"Listen, that guy Carl Woods went a little nuts. Decided to get drunk and knocked out Dr. Erinyes. He tried to assault Andromeda," Josh was explaining but hesitated.

Night Viper made circle motions with his free hand. "And?"

"I had to kill him. He tried to pull a gun on me when I interrupted his pedophile ways," Josh admitted.

The rebel leader had a special hatred of pedophiles but he still shook his head and sighed, "Shit. This isn't good. How's Drom, and how's that scientist?"

"They're both shaken up but they'll be alright. Listen, Eric came in too. It was like a damn hub in that lab. He remembered some not so great things from when Amanda was Commander Jade," Josh told him. "He tried to kill her with his bare hands. I got him to calm down but he's pretty pissed. I know he was friends with Carl."

"Dammit. Listen...just keep one thing in mind...until a couple of days ago, 'Amanda' was Commander Jade. Don't forget that. I know you want to play the hero with her and that's commendable, but Eric is justified in the way he feels. That being said, he needs to put those feelings aside because we need her and Erinyes both and we need them intact and loyal to us. Make sure she's alright and make sure he keeps a cool head," Night Viper insisted.

There was a pause for a moment, and then Josh replied, "I know, Vincent. Amanda is going to continue to monitor the enemy forces. Meanwhile, I'm going to try what you suggested and find any hidden government compounds that we might be able to use."

"Good," Night Viper responded. "And Josh? You did the right thing. The guy was a pedophile and wouldn't have stopped. It's not easy to take a life, but you saved Andromeda from something pretty terrible."

"Thanks," Josh answered. They hung up their SAT phones. Ryke, Josee, and Talbot came rushing up.

"Vince, everyone is ready. We just need to know where to set up for the assault," Talbot reported.

Night Viper looked around and said, "They're watching us from above. They're gonna know that we're set up and ready for a fight, so they're probably going to attempt to plow the Apocalypse Dozer right through us. That means we need to have everyone move to the opposite side of the shelter from where that big hunk of junk is coming. Once it blows and topples over, we only have a few minutes to make sure that it's disabled before the rest of the dead-headers get here."

Everyone nodded. Josee was shaking a bit. "I can't believe this is real. I mean, we're actually going to fight back."

Night Viper looked her in the eyes and stated, "And we're gonna win."

"How are we going to know what direction the Apocalypse Dozer is coming from?" Ryke asked.

"We're gonna continue to use their satellite footage against them. The beast is currently coming from the south. It's possible that it'll circle around and come at us from the side or the back, but it's not like that thing can make a hairpin turn. We should have plenty of warning if it changes direction," Night Viper assured.

"Then let's get everyone into position," Talbot suggested. "I'm ready to kick those bastards across the damn Atlantic!"

Zodiac sat in his control room at NORAD watching the satellite feed of the BFT-5000's approach toward the New York Militia 28 compound. On additional screens were video feeds from the massive doomsday machine as well as various other vehicles in the arsenal that were also on their way. He viewed in silent contemplation. Underneath his helmet was a sadistic smile, for he had the knowledge that if Militia 28 failed, the resistance was over. If they won, however, it still fell into his plans. Either way, he couldn't lose.

Commander Triton watched the view screens in anxious anticipation of his great victory. He turned to the Seeker next to him and spoke, "The rebels think they're smart, loading their bunker with bombs. If they believe those little firecrackers are going to do anything, they're sadly mistaken."

The Seeker stood in silence.

"I hope one of our cameras catches the look on their miserable faces when we plow right over them, unharmed. Apparently, Jade didn't tell them how heavily armored the underside of this thing is," Triton babbled.

The Seeker remained silent.

"Do you know why my name suits me so well?" Triton asked the Seeker.

The dark warrior continued to remain silent.

"Of course not...you no longer possess the ability to think for yourself. Triton is a moon that orbits the planet Neptune. The unique characteristic is that it orbits in the opposite direction of the spin of its host planet, yet remains bonded to its gravity. It's actually the only thing in the solar system that does that," Triton explained. "Of course, you probably can't make the connection but nonetheless, I had that on my mind and needed to say it. Now, let's plow through them!"

The rebels of Militia 28 could hear it. There was the sound of snapping of full grown trees, the crushing of distant structures, and the rumble of the massive motors and hydraulics that operated the gargantuan harbinger of destruction. The BFT-5000, aka the Apocalypse Dozer, had no need of a fear aura - the fright it

432

instilled was completely natural.

Standing in the woods just north of the shelter, the forward line of Militia 28 clad in Seeker armor waited. Standing in front of them was their new leader, the former vigilante, Night Viper. Next to their leader was Alan Ryke, the former leader of the New York Militia 28. There hadn't been a formal acknowledgement or transfer of this leadership. It had been a natural and accepted transition that neither man had planned and neither man could undo. On the opposite side of the vigilante stood Alexis Hera, one of the few survivors of the assault on Danbury.

"Alright, we've confirmed the dead-headers are making their way from the south. Everyone hold your positions. As soon as that thing gets to the shelter, I'm gonna trigger the explosion. We'll move in on my command," Night Viper ordered.

Everyone waited in anticipation. Talbot had already started the anti-fear aura signal. The emotions everyone felt were natural ones. The crashing was getting closer. They still couldn't see the monster, but they knew it was coming in the guise of impending doom. The seconds felt like hours. Night Viper watched the red light on the trigger remote, which would indicate that the BFT-5000 had tripped the sensor at the shelter and it was time to fire off the explosion.

Crash!

It was getting even louder. Ryke looked at Night Viper and said, "Maybe the sensor isn't working."

"It's working fine, calm down," the rebel leader assured.

After a few more seconds, Ryke spoke up again. "Listen, it sounds like it's right on top of us, and we're quite a distance from the shelter. It may already be too late."

"Ryke, knock it off. We can't even see the damn thing yet. It hasn't crossed the sensor," Night Viper snapped. "We're the ones that everyone's looking up to. Don't lose it on me now."

Lexi looked at Night Viper then grabbed and held his free hand. "He's anxious...we all are."

"I know, Lexi. Are you sure you're up to this? You lost a lot of blood," the vigilante asked.

Lexi nodded. "If I wasn't it would be too late now. I drank lots of water and an unopened energy drink that someone left at the clinic. If this is it, I want to be on the front line next to the man who made this all possible. I'm glad you found me in New Haven."

Night Viper smiled and nodded. "You really are a hellfire Lexi." She smiled back. Roughly three seconds later, the indicator light came on. "FIRE IN THE HOLE!" he yelled then pressed the button.

KABOOM!

The sound wasn't as loud as everyone had expected, but the shockwave that traveled along the ground was a lot more powerful than anyone had anticipated. Several of the rebels fell over as the ground shook and rippled. Trees began to fall in a domino effect, but the most incredible sound was that of twisting metal. The canopy ahead had cleared...they could see the beast. The explosion shot like a geyser from beneath the massive Apocalypse Dozer, toward the front right side. The arm on that side that held the massive grinding blades in the front snapped and the body of the beast toppled onto its side. The remaining arm on the left side did not have the strength to support the blades in the fall and the entire section snapped off and crashed into the ground. The plan had worked. The behemoth had fallen. The rebels stood up and composed themselves just in time for Night Viper to yell the order, "CHARGE!"

With that one word, Militia 28 let out a massive battle cry and started running toward the downed BFT-5000. With Night Viper, Lexi and Ryke in front they passed through what was left of the foliage between them and their quarry and made it to the now massive clearing. The scene before them was one that would remain in everyone's minds for a very long time. The once frightening metal giant now lay on its side, its massive grinding blades severed from the main body. Smoke was pouring out of holes and cracks in the armor. Several Seekers were climbing out of the husk in time to be met with the armor piercing bullets of the rebels.

Night Viper charged ahead of everyone and jumped onto the husk of the Apocalypse Dozer. He rapidly began climbing to the highest point. During his ascension, he came to a hatch that opened. When the Seeker who opened it stuck his head out, the vigilante grabbed it and snapped his neck. Then he hopped into the chamber where there were two more Seekers regaining their composure. He clenched his fist and threw a punch straight into the faceplate of one of them, caving in the Seeker's skull and helmet between the metal wall and his own knuckles. When he pulled his hand away, the cuts and scrapes on his knuckles quickly closed and healed. The next Seeker pulled his gun out too late as Night Viper grabbed his arm and slammed him head first into the wall. Despite the helmet, the Seeker's spine snapped under the rebel leader's incredible strength.

With his adversaries downed, the former vigilante took in his surroundings. He noticed that emergency lighting was on which most likely meant the metal behemoth had lost primary power. There was a door underneath his feet. Since the BFT-5000 was on its side, he would need to drop into the next room. He was sure that Commander Triton was inside somewhere and the rebel leader was determined to find him.

Giving two pints of blood to Eve only hours prior had not affected Lexi's ability as a sharp shooter. Taking careful time to aim and fire with her trusted sidearm that had been gifted to her by her father; she made well aimed shot after well aimed shot, taking down Seekers with two or three shots at the most. "Lay down and die, you dead-header bastards!" she yelled.

Despite their dwindled numbers from the previous assault, Militia 28 held its own. Their blitz on the dark soldiers in the smoldering BFT-5000 gave them a distinct advantage as they cut down their enemies almost as quickly as they ascended from the various hatchways and openings. There appeared to be assorted turrets and weapon systems on the massive metal monster, but none appeared to be functioning. Within only a couple of minutes, the Seekers had been completely overrun.

Ryke and Talbot began to scale the Apocalypse Dozer. Once they reached a decent landing, they stopped. With the other rebels scouring the husk, looking for more Seekers, Talbot pulled out his pair of binoculars and looked south. He slowly brought them down after only a few seconds.

"What's wrong?" Ryke asked.

"We're screwed," Talbot said. He handed Ryke the binoculars, who peered through them to see a massive invasion force with bladeless helicopters, hover tanks, and transports. He couldn't even get an estimated count.

Amanda was shaking her head quickly. "No, no, no."

Josh sprang off the side of the counter where his terminal was with his feet, causing his chair with him in it to roll over next to the former Grand Army commander. He looked at the screen and instantly figured out what the problem was. "Oh no."

"They're hopelessly outnumbered, Josh. They took down the Apocalypse Dozer but they've taken too many casualties. Even with Night Viper there, they don't stand a chance against such a large force with the hardware that they're packing," Amanda announced.

The door opened and Eve came stumbling in with Maria behind her carrying the infant boy.

"Christ, Eve. You should be in bed! You just had massive abdominal surgery like five or six hours ago," Josh scolded as he hurried over and helped her into a chair.

"I know...I just want to be here. I need...to see what's happening," Eve responded as she held out her arms for Maria to give her the baby.

Maria placed the still unnamed little boy in his mother's arms then said, "Yeah, I can't sit down in one of those dank rooms. I need to be here, which is the closest thing to the action that we're going to get."

"Well, we are underground. This is actually a dank room too," Josh pointed out.

Maria flipped him the bird and cursed at him in Spanish.

The door opened again. Dr. Erinyes and Andromeda walked in. "I realize that I am a prisoner, but I do hope that it is appropriate for this young lady to escort me here," the scientist commented.

"The good news is I'm a prisoner too and I'm here, so hopefully you'll have permission also," Amanda stated while still watching her screen.

"As long as you two aren't staging a coupe, gather 'round," Josh said as he waived his hand in a circular motion.

"Hey, what are all of those dots on the screen? The ones coming in behind these which I assume are the dead-headers?" Josh pointed.

Amanda shook her head. "I have no idea."

436

Commander Triton lay in the corner of the control room, which was where the gravity was since the BFT-5000 was on its side. On top of him was the Seeker whom he had been talking at prior to the start of the battle. "GET OFF OF ME!" he barked as he pushed the Seeker away, the commander suit enhancing his strength.

"Sure, pick on 'em when they're down. You're real tough," a voice came from above. Triton looked up to see a sight that he and his fellow Grand Army officers were quickly learning to fear, just as the lowliest of the Los Angeles underworld had learned to fear him only a couple of years before.

"Night Viper!" Triton grumbled.

"So you're Commander Triton," the vigilante stated as he jumped down and landed several feet from the commander. Does Zodiac give all of you those ugly suits?"

"This ugly suit will spell the death of you vigilante. You're not in L.A. anymore," Triton taunted. "And I will not fall as the weak Commander Jade did."

Night Viper nodded. "Good, I actually want to have a little sport."

The two warriors rushed at each other and collided, tumbling to what had once been a wall but had now become the floor. Triton was faster and stronger than Jade. Night Viper figured it was either due to further enhancements that had been made to the armor in an effort to combat him or, knowing what he now knew about Jade, Triton's far more fierce dedication to his cause and the rule of Zodiac.

As they tumbled onto the floor, Night Viper maneuvered his foot between the two of them and pushed, utilizing momentum as well as strength to send Triton flying through the air, the journey ending with abrupt contact on the far wall. The vigilante sprung to his feet just as he received a tingle in the back of his head. With a smile, Triton raised his arm in front of him and a pistol extended from a hidden compartment. The commander opened fire.

The rebel leader jumped and twirled in the air, bullets speeding past him. One round managed to strike his right thigh, off to the side. With a grunt, Night Viper landed in front of Triton and grabbed the gun. The commander grabbed onto the vigilante's hand with his free hand and slammed him against the wall. Then he backed up a few steps so as to avoid a direct retaliation. Both combatants faced each other. The Grand Army Commander witnessed the bullet wound and scraped face on his adversary heal within a few seconds. "Remarkable...you really do have an extraordinary ability to regenerate."

Night Viper spit blood at Triton's feet. "Yeah, I'm pretty sure you don't have that."

The two began to circle each other, each sizing up their opponent's timing. Night Viper jumped through the air and landed on the other side of Triton, then unleashed a back kick onto the commander, sending him toppling several feet. Wasting no time, the rebel grabbed his enemy and threw him into a wall.

Triton stood up and audibly said into his comm., "Pickup, my location." He waived to Night Viper, then jumped up through the entrance to the room. The vigilante chased after him but as they got outside, he saw a ladder hanging down from a transparent distortion in the air. The distortion appeared to be a shape much like the bladeless helicopters that they had so regularly encountered. The commander had already grabbed onto it and was beginning to head away. The rebel leader reached down and grabbed several bent shards of metal and threw them as hard as he could at his enemy's head. Since the commander helmets left the face exposed, several of the shards hit their mark, tearing flesh and embedding themselves in his face. The wail of pain was almost inhuman. The stealth Firehawk sped away with Triton grasping as hard as he could to avoid being dropped. His armor's enhanced strength was the only reason that he still had a grip.

Watching as his enemy retreated, horribly disfigured, the rebel leader had a newfound sense of victory which lasted only moments before he heard Talbot's voice, "VINCENT!"

Night Viper turned and saw Talbot and Ryke standing on a landing that had been created by twisting, severed metal. He hurried over to his allies through a series of well placed jumps. He landed next to them and said, "What's wrong?"

Talbot pointed. "That."

The enemy force had come into view. "We're severely outnumbered; it's like a damn Roman Phalanx. They're just going to come through here and flatten us. We need to pull back. We did good here today. Let's live to fight another day," Talbot urged.

Night Viper couldn't believe what he was hearing. They had come this far only to sound a retreat? He didn't want to. He grabbed the binoculars and looked with his own two eyes and he saw that the concerns were well founded. He thought back to the ordeal at Southern Connecticut State University when John had not given the order to fall back and the entire rebel cell had been butchered. He couldn't let that happen again. Talbot was right; they had struck a major blow. They could regroup and fight another day.

It was then that the explosion was heard. Ryke and Talbot both looked at Night Viper, who immediately looked through the binoculars again. One of the bladeless helicopters had gone down in a smoking pile of rubble. The forward march of the Grand Army began to slow as the units began to engage an enemy behind them. The rebel leader put the binoculars down. "The cavalry just arrived. Come on, we're gonna sandwich these bastards!" He immediately hurried down the side of the Apocalypse Dozer. Ryke and Talbot just gawked at each other.

"He's crazy!" Ryke said.

Talbot cracked a smile. "Yeah and you've known him longer than I have." They both started the climb down to the ground.

"Forward line, we're moving in on the enemy. We have allies hitting them from the back. Let's give 'em some support. Artillery and snipers, make your way to the top of the Apocalypse Dozer and give us as much cover fire as you can. Let's take those deadheaders down!" Night Viper commanded.

Lexi stood several feet away and looked at the rebel leader. He made eye contact with her and said, "Lexi, you're the best sharp shooter I've ever seen. Can you get to the top of this thing?"

Lexi nodded, "Of course."

"Good, I trust no one in this world more to have my back," Night Viper assured. She nodded and began to climb. The former vigilante waived his hand to his troops and charged toward the oncoming enemy.

"What's happening?" Maria asked.

Amanda was messing around with control settings. "The Seekers are engaging whomever or whatever came up behind them.

They're not reinforcements for them; they're reinforcements for Militia 28."

"Guys, you're not gonna believe this," Josh called out.

All of the heads in the room turned and looked at him.

"Vincent gave me an idea to find possible hidden stashes and compounds that were kept off the records. I ran a query and I found a bunch of possible locations. If even half of this stuff pans out, we'll be able to load up with arms and facilities, courtesy of the over-spending and completely dishonest United States government," Josh reported.

The baby was awake and cooing. Eve held her son close. Maria looked at her, then glanced around the room. "Has anyone seen Eric?"

"He's in his quarters," Amanda reported.

Josh wheeled over to Eve and the baby. "Wow, he has his father's eyes. So, you think of a name yet?"

"I think so. It's my original idea. John was against it though," Eve replied.

"What?" Josh was confused.

"He believed that naming a child after someone who is currently alive is taboo. That's no longer an issue…meet John Decker Jr.," Eve announced.

Josh smiled and put his finger in the baby's hand, who responded by grasping it. "Little Johnny."

Eve gave him a dirty look. "We're not going to call him that."

Josh gave her the confused look again. "What? What did I say?"

Eve shook her head. "I'm just remembering those stupid Little Johnny emails that used to go around all of the time about that perverted kid."

Josh broke out laughing like a madman.

The charge was on. Night Viper ran straight into the fray. All around him, bullets whizzed by and took out Seekers who were close to him. He knew Lexi was acting as his guardian angel. The anti-tank and anti-aircraft rockets in the arsenals on both sides were being unleashed, destroying vehicle after vehicle. Despite most of the cavalry not being equipped with armor piercing rounds, they seemed to be holding their own with various explosive ordinances.

The rebel leader began stomping through the enemy ranks, taking out the dark soldiers with his guns, and at times with his bare hands. The remaining infantry collided with the Seekers on foot. Like many battlefields, this one was stained in blood; but this time, the Grand Army was not fighting a bunch of helpless, frightened refugees but people who regarded themselves as freedom fighters. These were people who had the inspiration and the spirit to defend their lives. The mindless ranks of Zodiac's lackeys could not compete with that, and they had paid the price in severe losses. Coupled with the severe injuries to their commander, they began to withdraw.

Chapter 50

In the aftermath of the battle, the two groups of rebels met face to face. Night Viper, with Lexi standing by his side, looked at those who had joined the battle and helped secure victory. He recognized some of the people as having been at the electronics store where they had taken the sub-woofers. They had joined up with Militia 28 at Providence and had made their way as a legion to New York. The Apocalypse Dozer had compressed the area that it tore through so much that it had created a wide, flat roadway for the rebels to follow.

Several prominent members of the cavalry stepped forward to shake Night Viper's hand. One in particular, who had been at the electronics store, was of obvious Middle-Eastern descent. "I have been waiting to meet you in person. My name is Kalim Mohamed Assard. I was born in Saudi Arabia. Never before have I witnessed one such as you. You have done a great service here."

They shook hands and Night Viper replied, "I know what Zodiac did to your homeland...it's unforgiveable."

Kalim shook his head. "No, Night Viper. Zodiac did this to the world. We are all a part of it, which makes us all responsible for working together to set things right."

The crowd of rebels stood around with Night Viper and Lexi standing in the center. She looked at the vigilante and said, "You should probably say something to everybody. You are their leader, after all."

"I didn't ask for that," the rebel leader responded.

She smiled. "Well, like it or not, you've got it." She used one of the SAT phones to dial up Project Scorpion. When the phone was answered, all she said was, "Just listen."

Night Viper addressed the group. "Everyone…today we've won a great victory for our cause. As far as we know, this is the first time anyone has stood up to the Grand Army of Zodiac and emerged victorious. We have all done a great thing here, but let us not forget those who made the ultimate sacrifice. People like John Decker, a friend of mine who never got to meet his baby boy. We will not let their sacrifice be in vain."

Many in the crowd began nodding. Back at the Project Scorpion compound, they could hear everything. The talk of John Decker brought tears to Eve's eyes as she gazed upon the bright face of her newborn child.

Night Viper continued his speech. "I've heard people tell me that standing up to Zodiac would paint a target on our backs but I say this - the targets were there anyway because of our mere existence. As Kalim told me moments ago, we are all responsible for working together to set things right, and that's what we're gonna do. It won't be easy, but I tell you that we've already done the impossible, so why stop now?"

Ryke elbowed Talbot. "I never knew he could give such an inspirational speech."

Talbot nodded. "He surprises me every day."

The rebel leader continued, "There are dates that are said to now be etched in history. On May 7th, the Flash Storm came. September 6th was the day of the fall. Well now we can mark another day on the calendar…today, October 10th, we will forever remember as the day…THAT THE REBELLION BEGAN!"

Cheers rang out amongst all the ranks as they looked to their new leader and the beginning of a full, unified rebellion. Lexi took Vincent's hand again as they both looked up into the sky to watch the sun rise, bringing a new day of hope for the future of humanity.

Breinigsville, PA USA
10 December 2010
250946BV00003B/4/P